"RESISTANCE IS FUTILE," SEVEN SAID.

The words, a standard greeting when she had been Borg, rarely sprang to mind anymore, but were deliciously appropriate under the circumstances.

She felt him relax beneath her and move his left arm down his chest. Sensing his target, she removed her right hand from his throat, plucked the combadge from his uniform and tossed it well out of reach. The motion destabilized her long enough for him to roll forward. The side of her head impacted the nearest stasis chamber, causing her to release his neck.

He didn't have the strength to scurry too far. He made it only to his hands and knees, gasping for air before Seven lunged at him again, throwing him facedown to the floor. She climbed over him and used the chamber to pull herself to her feet. She stood before him, winded but still flushed with adrenaline, as he pushed himself back on his knees and peered up at her.

"What . . ." he croaked, then cleared his throat and tried again. "What can you possibly hope to accomplish here?" he asked through ragged breaths. "Kill me and you'll spend the rest of your life in a Federation penitentiary for murder."

STAR TREK VOYAGER®

ATONEMENT

KIRSTEN BEYER

Based on *Star Trek*®
created by Gene Roddenberry
and
Star Trek: Voyager
created by
Rick Berman & Michael Piller & Jeri Taylor

POCKET BOOKS
New York London Toronto Sydney New Delhi

Pocket Books
An Imprint of Simon & Schuster, Inc.
1230 Avenue of the Americas
New York, NY 10020

This book is a work of fiction. Any references to historical events, real people, or real places are used fictitiously. Other names, characters, places, and events are products of the author's imagination, and any resemblance to actual events or places or persons, living or dead, is entirely coincidental.

First Pocket Books paperback edition September 2015

POCKET and colophon are registered trademarks of Simon & Schuster, Inc.

For information about special discounts for bulk purchases, please contact Simon & Schuster Special Sales at 1-866-506-1949 or business@simonandschuster.com.

The Simon & Schuster Speakers Bureau can bring authors to your live event. For more information or to book an event, contact the Simon & Schuster Speakers Bureau at 1-866-248-3049 or visit our website at www.simonspeakers.com.

Manufactured in the United States of America

10 9 8 7 6 5 4 3 2

ISBN 978-1-4767-9081-7
ISBN 978-1-4767-9083-1 (ebook)

For Catherine "Cady" Coleman

"*From books and words come fantasy, and sometimes, from fantasy comes union.*"

—*Rumi*

HISTORIAN'S NOTE

The Borg Invasion has left billions dead, worlds shattered, and Starfleet in tatters (*Star Trek: Destiny*).

Now, Starfleet Medical believes a catomic plague is spreading on the worlds that managed to survive the Invasion. Doctor Sharak and Lieutenant Samantha Wildman have learned that a rogue Starfleet commander has artificially magnified the plague. Meanwhile, Seven—who is just beginning to understand the true nature of her catoms—has become a captive of the Commander. Axum, a former drone, may be working in concert with the Commander, while seeking to forward his own agenda: forcing a new Collective on all who possess the advanced Caeliar technology.

Admiral Kathryn Janeway has risked the Full Circle Fleet's safety, and ultimately, her life, in an attempt to help the Confederacy of the Worlds of the First Quadrant make peace (*Star Trek Voyager: Acts of Contrition*).

This narrative begins in early March and continues through May 2382.

Prologue

SCION

Form was insignificant. It was a shell, a garment, a means to an end. *But it was real.* Flesh, muscles, organs, bones were composed of cells built from molecules containing atoms expressing subatomic interactions.

The dun scutes that covered the surface of this form looked and felt solid. Large obsidian pupils tinged with golden irises stared coldly beneath impressive cranial ridges. Claws filed to fine points extended from the three digits of each hand and were quite lethal, as the original inhabitant of this form, Voth Minister Odala, had felt keenly in the last few moments of her life.

But were they real?

A thought, faint as a whisper, and the image reflected in the smoky glass surface before her shifted.

A human woman.

Barely.

Little more than a girl stared at her now. The black uniform with blue trim made this form look even smaller than it was. The face was pale, dominated by large, pleading eyes. Weak hands were meant to comfort, to administer care. Her only power lay in a small piece of technology that both created and was suspended within her photonic matrix.

What consciousness had once belonged to this "Meegan" had dissipated like the morning mist as soon as she had chosen the hologram for her vessel. The device meant to hold Meegan's program was now hers to command. Over the last several months, necessity had required her to assume dozens of new forms, each essential to gathering allies. She tried to think of her new existence as a gift.

But it did not *feel* real. She missed the beating of a heart. Inhalation. Exhalation. Hunger pangs. Pain that burned, ached, stabbed. The pleasure of a cool breeze or the gentle graze of fingertips. She would never have come so far so quickly had it not been for this hologram's manipulative properties. But the thought of spending eternity encased in a shell of light, incapable of experiencing all that made eternity worth attaining, was unimaginable.

"Soon," she said softly to her reflection.

Soon, she could shed this form. Soon, subterfuge would no longer be required. Soon, she and the others who had been forced into agonizing solitude would be reunited. Soon, the short-lived species infecting this quadrant would rise as one under the patient tutelage and loving care of their betters to a new understanding of the true nature of existence and all of its wondrous possibilities.

Soon, she and her companions would finish the work that had begun so many millennia ago.

Soon.

A series of short tones sounded, alerting her to an incoming communication.

"It is time."

Emem.

Devore Inspector Kashyk, she reminded herself.

The form she had chosen for him resembled the ancient Seriareen more closely than any of the others. His smooth flesh was paler than the last he'd worn, but his features were strong and pleasantly arranged apart from slight cranial crests above each eye. Emem had chosen to keep Kashyk's thick, dark hair cut short in the Seriareen fashion for males, out of vanity as much as utility.

Kashyk was too short, of course. No matter how he struggled to maximize the potentials of a Devore body, Emem would never attain the physical strength, agility, or heightened senses of the Seriareen. But the Devore had been easy to rally to her cause because of these limitations. Their fear of the mental acuity of others had led them to dull their own, rather than develop them.

Still, their technology was formidable and their aggressive natures well suited to her purposes. At least Emem could eat again. At least his flesh could rise in anticipation of her touch. At least he could *feel* satisfaction in all they had achieved. At least he could love her again.

She could not do the same.

Much as she wished to give herself again to him mind, body, and soul, without said body, it was impossible. The fierceness of his passion for her had not been dimmed by the millennia they had spent confined. But there were other changes that troubled her. Not that it mattered. Her new form was capable of wonders, all of which satisfied Emem's needs while leaving her unable to achieve any sense of real connection.

Dispirited, she broke a promise she had made to herself when she had first learned of her ability to assume any form she wished.

Another fleeting thought, and the last Seriareen body she had known prior to her confinement appeared before her.

She stood half a meter taller than Meegan, with skin the color of burnt umber, merciless moss-colored eyes, and a mane of pitch-black hair that tumbled in loose waves down her back. Wide strips of soft, well-worn rouge hide rode the curves of her body like a second skin. A delicately carved tusk circle cinched the black belt around her slim waist, the garment's only ornament.

The memories of that life caused significant mental distress, but without the accompanying churning of the stomach, pounding of a pulse, or tensing of muscles, the distress was a distant echo.

"Release me."

The sound of Obih's voice returned unbidden. It had been her constant companion during the centuries of insensate darkness. It could not keep her warm, but it had breathed continuous life into the faint sparks of defiance that had remained when this body had been lost.

She no longer stood in the dimly lit quarters of the Voth minister's personal ship, the *Scion*. Instead, the deck plates of the *Solitas* shook beneath her feet.

A series of loud concussive blasts pummeled what remained of the ship's shields, and acrid smoke burned her lungs with every breath. Emem worked furiously at the weapons terminal, determined to send as many of their enemies as possible into oblivion. Xolani was attempting to seal multiple hull breaches, shouting status updates over the chaos that engulfed the ship's central control station. She worked desperately to keep their course steady as the next swarm of aggressors assumed attack formation.

Only Obih seemed calm.

"Seriareen vessel, stand down," a harsh voice demanded.

"Release me," Obih said again, turning to her, the ornate hilt of his ceremonial dagger mere inches from the hands she pretended were preoccupied with flight control.

"Our reinforcements are on their way, Obih," Emem assured their leader.

"They are already too late," Obih reminded them. "The hax must survive."

"The other ships," she began.

"They are all Nayseriareen now," Obih reminded her. "Release me," he said again.

To what? she wondered. To release him now was to all but admit defeat, and that was impossible.

Xolani had seen the truth before she grasped Obih's intention. To release Obih was to ensure ultimate victory. Xolani's was the hand that accepted the hilt she had refused. His was the arm that reared back and struck with all its might, burying the dagger in Obih's heart.

The cry that escaped Obih's lips in response reverberated through the Solitas; absolute refusal to yield.

Obih fell to the deck just as another ear-splitting roar obliterated all other ambient sounds, including further calls for their surrender. She had no choice but to begin searching the heavens for a new body.

"Lsia?"

Emem had entered her quarters soundlessly and stared at her now in suspicious pity.

"Did you not hear my summons?"

"Since when do you summon me anywhere?" she asked.

"It is time," he said again. "The others are already aboard the *Manticle*."

"They can wait."

"We have all waited much too long," he reminded her.

"This is a mistake," Lsia said for the tenth time since Emem had hastily assembled the officers selected to determine the fate of their prisoner, Admiral Kathryn Janeway.

Lsia had argued from the first that a formal trial be convened, an advocate assigned to the prisoner, and testimony be elicited through open questioning of the available witnesses by expert counsel. While more time consuming, the process would have demonstrated to the Confederacy that the *Kinara* were a fair and civilized alliance, intent on the pursuit of justice rather than revenge.

Emem had favored making a decisive example of the admiral through a military tribunal, and Janeway had obliged him by insisting that she would represent herself during the proceedings.

The first consul of the Confederacy, Lant Dreeg, had initiated contact with the *Kinara* several days prior to their armed confrontation and agreed that Admiral Janeway should be turned over to their custody prior to continuing negotiations. A swift resolution to the "Janeway issue" would please him and push the Confederacy and the Federation further apart.

To Lsia's consternation, Emem had easily swayed Tirrit and Adaeze. Rigger Meeml, the sole representative of the Skeen, Karlon, Muk, and Emleath forces and the only *Kinara* leader present not currently hosting one of her Seriareen companions, had seemed inclined to agree with Lsia, but ultimately they had been voted down. Emem had called this "democracy at its finest" despite the fact that he had nothing but contempt for representative forms of government.

Emem shook his head in warning. "It has been agreed."

"She could still be of use to us."

"The Confederacy must not be permitted to embrace the

Federation as allies. Revealing her treachery will end any doubts Dreeg's superiors may still nurture. If we allow her to live, she will counter us at every turn. And with each moment that passes, those she commands repair the damage we inflicted and plan her rescue. That cannot be allowed. The Federation must see our determination. They must know our power. They must fear us."

"You sound more like Kashyk every day," she chided him. "This will not make them fear us. It will make them hate us more."

"Are there degrees of hate? Surely they hate us already."

Lsia did not agree. But she had already lost this argument.

Reluctantly, she returned to the form of the saurian female, Odala.

Soon, she thought again as she followed Emem from her quarters.

1

Captain Chakotay had asked Captain Regina Farkas, of the *Vesta*, and Commander Glenn, of the *Galen*, to join him as he brought his acting first officer, Lieutenant Harry Kim, and Commander B'Elanna Torres into the small circle he intended to utilize in managing the current crisis. Lieutenant Kenth Lasren, his Betazoid ops officer, Counselor Hugh Cambridge, and Admiral Janeway's personal aide, Decan, were also present. Both were already well aware of how complicated their mission had become in the last few hours.

Torres and Kim appeared stunned and sickened by their captain's revelations. The shock had already passed for everyone else and been replaced by mingled trepidation and determination.

Commander Torres was the first to speak. "I just want to make sure I've got this straight."

"Please," Chakotay said.

"The *Kinara* are about to put Admiral Janeway on trial for crimes she supposedly committed during *Voyager*'s maiden trek in the Delta Quadrant. Once that trial ends—"

"Presumably with the admiral's execution," Counselor Cambridge interjected.

"Almost certainly," Captain Farkas corrected him.

"*Once that trial ends,*" Torres repeated, refusing to acknowledge or accept their pessimism, "the *Kinara* intend to open negotiations with the Confederacy for passage through their local network of subspace corridors for the purpose of acquiring some unknown resources that lie beyond Confederacy space but can only be readily accessed by utilizing their corridors."

"Which we cannot allow to happen," Captain Farkas noted.

"Because *we now know* that whatever the *Kinara*'s objectives might once have been, in the last few months they have come under the influence of at least four of the original eight Neyser essences," Torres continued.

"Individuals believed to be so dangerous that their own people intentionally disembodied them and kept them incarcerated for thousands of years," Cambridge reminded her.

"And who have used their first taste of freedom to convince or coerce some of the most powerful Delta Quadrant species already predisposed to mistrust the Federation, including the Turei, the Vaadwaur, the Devore, and the Voth, to ally themselves against us," Kim added.

"Is our potential alliance with the Confederacy off the table?" Torres asked.

"Admiral Janeway indicated prior to her departure that she did not believe the Federation and the Confederacy could ever form an alliance," Farkas replied.

"And that was without hearing my report on *Voyager*'s joint mission with the *Twelfth Lamont*, the results of which, in my opinion, would make any such alliance unconscionable," Chakotay noted.

"It doesn't matter anymore," Torres argued.

"Excuse me?" Chakotay said.

"*Vesta* isn't in bad shape, but *Voyager* lost her main deflector in the last battle and is, conservatively, *days* away from being completely repaired. *Galen* is no match for the *Kinara*'s firepower. That gives us *one* starship against the *Kinara*'s ten, including that Voth monstrosity that almost destroyed us. We're going to need help rescuing Admiral Janeway and the Confederacy is our only option right now."

"After what Inspector Kashyk—*or whoever he really is*—said, I'm not sure how inclined the Confederacy will be to offer assistance," Farkas suggested.

"There is no question that the first consul, Lant Dreeg, arranged for the admiral's capture in order to force us to offer the Market Consortium the technology they requested— technology with which we cannot responsibly part at the moment—in return for aiding us in recovering our admiral," Cambridge asserted.

"Be that as it may," Chakotay said, "General Mattings has indicated that he intends to assist us, and nothing I've heard has convinced me that Presider Cin entirely approved of her first consul's actions."

"We need to find out where the Confederacy stands right now," Farkas said.

"Among other things," Chakotay agreed.

"Meanwhile, the Doctor has suffered some catastrophic damage?" Torres asked.

"Barclay has transferred his program back to the *Galen* and is working on it as we speak," Chakotay reported. "The Doctor made some alarming discoveries about the catomic plague before I had to deactivate him. He asked that we try to get that data back to Seven as soon as possible."

"If not sooner," Cambridge insisted.

"*Demeter* has yet to report in?" Farkas asked.

"*Demeter* should have returned to Confederacy space more than twelve hours ago. If she's not back soon, someone is going to have to go after her," Chakotay replied.

Farkas nodded. After a few moments of tense silence she said, "This is a mess, but our first priority is rescuing the admiral."

"She has no desire to be rescued, and indeed left explicit orders that we should do nothing to risk the current cease-fire," Decan said, speaking for the first time since the briefing had begun.

"That's absurd," Torres said. "They're going to kill her. We can't just sit here and let them do it."

"We must not allow our fear for her safety to force us to act precipitously," Decan insisted. "There is no question that Admiral Janeway intends for us to keep the lines of communication open between ourselves and Presider Cin. She sacrificed herself, *in part*, to ensure that the *Kinara* did not succeed in allying themselves with the Confederacy and turning them against us. But she also intends to discover 'Meegan's' true intentions toward this region of space."

"That's going to be a little hard to do while she's fighting for her life," Cambridge said.

"Not necessarily," Decan said.

"I realize that Admiral Janeway is accustomed to multi-tasking, Lieutenant, but that's a tall order," Cambridge observed.

"In addition to requesting a personal security detachment, the admiral's only other nonnegotiable demand prior to her surrender was that the *Kinara* transmit her trial in real time to the fleet and the Confederacy," Decan said placidly. "I suggest that our first duty is ensuring that all parties assembled here enjoy unrestricted access to the upcoming trial."

"How are we supposed to do that?" Lieutenant Lasren asked. "The trial is set to take place aboard the *Manticle*. They are the ones who will control any transmissions. They can shut it down whenever they like."

"No, they can't," Torres corrected him.

"Once they open the transmission," Kim continued for her, "we can capture the frequency and send our own control virus through their carrier wave. Our open channel will replace theirs and stay open as long as we want."

"Or until they shut down their entire communications array and perform a hard reset," Torres noted.

Chakotay stared at Decan's implacable face. Although *Voyager*'s captain had known Kathryn longer and much better than her aide, Decan had been by her side constantly throughout her negotiations with the Confederacy. His observation struck Chakotay as significant, and he was frustrated that he could not yet make the connection it seemed Decan already had. "Why did Admiral Janeway insist on this?" Chakotay finally asked.

"It is my belief that the admiral intends to resolve this situation long before her trial can conclude," Decan said.

For the first time since Kathryn's capture, a faint spark of hope lit Chakotay's eyes as the significance of Kathryn's nonnegotiable demand suddenly became clear to him. That spark faded just as quickly as the many possible flaws in her plan began to take horrific shape in his mind's eye. Setting them aside, he smiled grimly, saying, "That's how she intends to beat them."

MANTICLE

Admiral Kathryn Janeway should have spent the last several hours reviewing her memories of *Voyager*'s first encounters with the Turei, the Vaadwaur, the Devore, and the Voth.

Instead, she could not stop thinking about a kiss.

When Decan had told her of his telepathic sense that Devore Inspector Kashyk was literally of "two minds," internally divided between ancient rage and a desire to see Kathryn safe, the final piece of the puzzle she had tried to solve for weeks—ever since she had learned of the alliance between the Devore, the Vaadwaur, and the Turei, and the actions of the Voth against her fleet's communications relays—had finally locked into place.

Lieutenant Barclay had been obsessed for months with locating their rogue hologram, "Meegan." Janeway had added this concern to her lengthy to-do list upon assuming command of the Full Circle Fleet, and it had rested in the back of her mind until it was forced out of the shadows by Decan's revelation. The only plausible explanation for the recent alliance between these four familiar, hostile, and xenophobic species was some powerful outside influence, and an ancient species with access to all of *Voyager*'s databases that could possess high-level individuals at will was an incredibly likely candidate.

Janeway had asked Lieutenant Lasren to accompany her to the *Manticle*, and his subtle nod before he departed had confirmed what the kiss with which she had greeted Inspector Kashyk had already told her.

She had kissed him once before. It had been a spontaneous gesture, born of the closeness that had developed between them over several days and nights when they had seemed to share a common goal and purpose. But it had also been a test. Hers might not have been the most experienced lips in the galaxy, but they had assured her of Kashyk's genuine response. The heat and desire in that kiss had been unmistakable.

His heart, of course, had never been hers.

The truth of the second kiss had been more painful than the first. The moment their lips had touched in the *Manticle*'s shuttlebay, Janeway had felt Kashyk's desire once again, but this time there had been urgency, *desperation* to it. The sensation had vanished too soon as his lips had hardened and rough hands had pushed her away.

Decan had been right. Kashyk was still there, but he was no longer controlling his mind or body.

Her thoughts unwillingly returned to what little she remembered of her time as a Borg Queen. Some small shred of Kathryn Janeway had existed, secured in a cell within a mind that was no longer hers. From that cell she had witnessed atrocities. She had *felt* the Queen's ecstasy. She had fought desperately to regain control, but it had been impossible.

Despite the fact that Kashyk had been her enemy, she wondered if *that* was now his reality. If it was, he did not deserve it. No sentient being did.

That the entity that now possessed Kashyk clearly wanted her dead was neither surprising nor relevant. Janeway could not hate Kashyk. She couldn't even fear him. All she could do was pity him.

The door to her "quarters" slid open and a Devore security officer flanked by two armed guards entered holding a set of heavy silver manacles. Lieutenants Psilakis and Cheng, her personal security team, rose and moved to stand between her and the Devore officer.

"You will remain here," he advised them.

"No. That was not our understanding," Psilakis said firmly.

"It's all right, Lieutenant," Janeway said, placing a hand on his arm and gently pressing him back. She then lifted her eyes to meet the Devore officer and extended her hands to him, her palms upward.

Her life might be over within a matter of hours. But until it was, a number of battles remained that must be won.

FIFTH SHUDKA

"There was no good answer, Presider," Captain Chakotay insisted. "We settled for the *least* bad one, which was often the case during our first journey through this quadrant."

Most of Chakotay's interactions with the peoples of the Confederacy had been with Leodts like General Mattings: dark-skinned humanoids with black eyes, flattened noses, and mouths composed of a ring of sharp protruding teeth. Presider Isorla Cin was Djinari. The golden, diamond-shaped scales that covered her scalp did not seem to allow for a variety of facial expressions that might betray subtle reactions to his words. The long, thin tendrils that extended from the base of her neck were more fluid. They tensed and relaxed conspicuously, but Chakotay had yet to assign meaning to their movements.

Cin had sat placidly behind an ornate, gilt desk in her receiving room aboard the *Shudka* and listened patiently while Chakotay had provided some much-needed context to the charges "Devore Inspector Kashyk" had made against Admiral Janeway and the Federation before the battle that had cost the Confederacy thirty-five of their ships and the Full Circle Fleet their admiral. The captain had not yet advised Cin that he believed Kashyk, and several of the other *Kinara* leaders, to be possessed by Neyser essences. The truth of *Voyager's* first contact with the Voth, the Turei, the Vaadwaur, and the Devore Imperium should have been more than enough to convince Cin whose side she should take.

The presider had seemed relieved by Chakotay's recounting of *Voyager's* encounters with the Delta Quadrant powers. She clearly *wanted* to believe that Admiral Janeway had been on the right side of these conflicts. She had cooled visibly, however, when Chakotay began to recount their introduction to the Devore, rising from her desk and pacing the room fitfully.

"But you knew the Devore could not countenance the presence of telepaths in their territory," Cin argued. "As your crew included telepathic species even before you encountered the

Brenari refugees, surely you would have been better served by simply charting a course around their space."

"We understood, as the Devore did not, that the telepaths who were part of our crew posed no threat to them," Chakotay insisted. "I agree that assisting the Brenari might be construed as crossing the line, but we were not aiding individuals who had come to make war on the Devore. Had their ship not been damaged, they would never have found themselves in Devore space. They were civilians, some of them young children. Their only goal was to get safely out of the Devore's territory as soon as possible. We shared that goal. *Voyager* possessed technology we believed would allow us to protect the Brenari the same way we were already protecting our telepathic crewmen. It seemed unconscionable to refuse to aid them."

Cin shook her head. Clearly frustrated, she said, "Often when I spoke with Admiral Janeway in the last several weeks, I was struck by your Federation's seeming contradictions. You possess powerful advanced technology, but do not use that technology to conquer new territory. You hold your member worlds to basic shared standards but allow them to engage in species and cultural-specific practices that are completely alien to those of your Federation's founding members. You embrace diversity as one of your highest values even when that diversity leads to conflict between your member worlds. How have you not learned in more than two hundred years of existence how complicated your predilection for acceptance and tolerance makes your lives, or how much security would be gained by limiting either your exploratory efforts or the freedoms you permit your member worlds?" she demanded. "Your willingness to seek out the potential good in every species you encounter seems to constantly embroil you in avoidable conflicts."

Chakotay considered her words carefully before responding. "They do," he finally agreed. "But there is no way to add to our understanding of the universe, of the very nature of existence, and accept the limits you suggest. It is not necessary that every species we encounter share our views. We would likely have grown bored with exploration long ago if they did. It is our differences that make our efforts worthwhile. Our determination is to honor the views of others, even when we do not embrace them. Defending ourselves and those unable to defend themselves from simple misunderstandings is not an idealistic fantasy. We have seen firsthand how different civilizations can evolve from deep-seated hatred to mutual acceptance and understanding. The Djinari and Leodt are a prime example of such an evolution. To adhere to a rigid and antiquated set of standards is to limit not only the potential progress of others, but our own possible development as well."

"Pardon the interruption, Presider Cin," a voice came over the *Shudka*'s comm system. *"General Mattings is reporting in as requested."*

"Put him through," Cin ordered, raising a hand to pause Chakotay's remarks. "General Mattings, are your advance preparations complete?"

"All has been done according to your orders, Presider," Mattings reported. His voice was low and rough. It sounded to Chakotay as if the general was exhausted but refusing to admit it. The last time they'd spoken, Mattings had clearly been injured. But he had sworn to protect Chakotay's people as his own. The captain had no reason to believe the general was not living up to that promise.

"Very good, General," Cin said. As soon as the words had left her lips, the doors to her suite opened and her Leodt first consul, Lant Dreeg, entered quickly and moved to stand directly in Cin's line of sight.

"Forgive me, Presider, but I have received the CIF's latest report, and I cannot allow you to risk destroying the accord that was purchased with so much Confederacy blood less than one day ago. The *Kinara* have what they want. They are prepared to continue negotiating with us in good faith. You must not allow any personal concerns you might have for Admiral Janeway to cloud your judgment at this critical juncture."

The presider squared her shoulders. Her tendrils stiffened behind her and remained taut as she said, "General Mattings, have you assumed command of the *Third Calvert?*"

"Yes, Presider."

"Stand by," Cin ordered. Locking her bright green eyes on the black stones set below Dreeg's brow ridge, she said, "I appreciate your concerns, First Consul. As always, I will bear them in mind before I reach my final decision regarding the *Kinara*. For the moment, I do not require anything further of you."

"Presider," Dreeg said.

"Lant," Cin said sharply, taking him aback. "Before my mission to open *negotiations* with the *Kinara* had begun, you worked behind my back to secure an agreement favorable to the Market Consortium but on terms you knew would be unacceptable to your presider. You did so because you did not trust me to act in our people's best interests. You betrayed me. You betrayed Admiral Janeway. You have grossly overstepped your authority. That ends now. Your counsel is noted. Leave my presence and do not presume to access it again until I request that you do so."

"The people of the Confederacy—" Dreeg began.

"Elected me to lead them," Cin finished. "And I will continue to do so until another is chosen to take my place."

Undeterred, Dreeg said, "You realize, of course, that the Consortium may call for a vote of no-confidence at our discretion."

"I do," Cin acknowledged. "You might best use the rest of the current cease-fire to return safely to the First World and begin collecting the necessary votes. In the meantime, I will do what I can to mitigate the damage you have caused."

Dreeg nodded warily and departed. As Chakotay watched him go, a newfound respect for Presider Cin took root. He had wondered up until now what might have caused Kathryn to risk so much on the Confederacy's behalf. Finally, he was beginning to understand.

"Presider," he said softly, "is it your intention to order the CIF to rescue Admiral Janeway, or merely to end the *Kinara*'s hold on this region of space?"

"That determination has yet to be made," she replied. "The *Kinara* indicated that they wish to place the admiral on trial for her past transgressions against them, and she willingly agreed to participate in that trial."

"Only because she feared that her refusal would result in the loss of every CIF vessel in the area," Chakotay noted. "Do you honestly believe they intend to give her a fair hearing?"

"That remains to be seen," Cin said.

"Presider Cin, we are receiving a transmission from the Manticle,*"* the communication officer's voice reported.

"Put it through to my suite," Cin ordered.

Chakotay turned to face the large viewscreen that sat opposite the presider's desk. It took every ounce of self-control he possessed to remain where he stood rather than returning to *Voyager. Or better yet, arm myself with two phaser rifles and transport directly to the* Manticle.

This was the only location from which he could take the Confederacy's temperature moment by moment. Once the trial began, their responses would be critical. His experiences with General Mattings had destroyed any confidence he'd once felt in his ability to predict Confederacy choices. He hoped that Kathryn had been wiser in her assessment of the presider.

Her life depended on it.

VOYAGER

The doors to engineering were open as Lieutenant Harry Kim approached them, weaving through the constant flow of foot traffic with some difficulty. Officers and crewmen double-timed their way in and out, their hands heavy with freshly replicated replacement parts and tools. No one spoke in conversational tones. Orders, requests, and reports were shouted over the constant din and commotion. Despite the sense of chaos, their focus was singular: get *Voyager* moving again as soon as possible.

Fleet Chief Engineer B'Elanna Torres stood in the eye of the storm, her face and uniform covered with grime, her hands flying over the main console stationed just beneath the combined warp/slipstream core that was the heart of *Voyager.* The ship's chief engineer, Lieutenant Nancy Conlon, stood on the catwalk that circled the room's second level just outside the doors of her private office, deep in conversation with two of her subordinates who had the good sense to simply nod quickly as she tersely issued their orders.

Kim caught Conlon's eyes as he headed toward the central console without distracting her from her current duties. A smile so faint he might have imagined it crossed her lips. Kim felt his own face soften a bit and nodded in response without missing a step.

On any other day, the speed, precision, concentration, and devotion Kim saw before him would have buoyed his confidence in his ship.

Today, they merely reinforced the fragility of *Voyager*'s current predicament and reminded him how close they had just come to annihilation.

"B'Elanna," he said softly, certain she was already aware of his presence.

"What is it, Harry?" she demanded without lifting her eyes from her console.

"It's time," he replied.

She turned sharply to face him.

"The *Manticle* just established an open channel. They're going to start in a few minutes."

"Have we sent *our* transmission?" Torres asked.

Kim nodded. "*Vesta* is handling it. Their comm systems are fully operational."

Torres's face hardened. Kim wondered why she wasn't already moving to join him in the briefing room. What other possible response was there?

We are currently hanging dead in space surrounded by hostile alien vessels. Until I can get our shields restored, we are too vulnerable for me to leave my post, Kim could hear her protest.

Instead, she said softly, "I can't watch it, Harry."

Her words set his stomach churning. Kim squared his shoulders. "You heard Chakotay. The admiral's going to be fine."

"Maybe," Torres agreed. "But if she isn't . . ." Her words trailed off.

"Hey," Kim said, placing a hand on her shoulder.

"My first duty is to the fleet, to this ship," Torres said. "I'm needed here."

"Okay," Kim said. His feet were noticeably heavier as they carried him back to deck one.

Counselor Cambridge was the only senior officer waiting in the briefing room when Kim arrived. He had not taken any of the available chairs, but stood with his back resting against the bulkhead, his arms crossed over his chest, and his eyes glued to the large viewscreen embedded in the wall.

Five individuals were seated on a raised platform behind a long table. Kim recognized three of them, the Voth Minister Odala, Devore Inspector Kashyk, and the Skeen commander, Rigger Meeml. The others were Turei and Vaadwaur officers who looked familiar, but Kim could not place them.

Cambridge's back stiffened as Admiral Janeway was led into the room. Kim's stomach soured again as Cambridge said softly, "I tried to tell her."

2

STARFLEET MEDICAL, CLASSIFIED DIVISION

Hello, Seven of Nine."

Seven risked an educated guess. "Commander."

The large bay located somewhere in the bowels of Starfleet Medical and containing almost fifty stasis chambers was nearly pitch black. Seven stood only a few meters from the man who had orchestrated her capture and placed her in one of those chambers without her consent. Worse, he had spent weeks using the catoms he had extracted from her when she arrived to perform reckless, painful, and deadly experiments on individuals who, as best as Seven could tell, were not victims of the catomic plague. Seven had been led to believe when she was asked to return to the Alpha Quadrant that her assistance was vital to the efforts of the medical staff here. The implication was that her skills as a scientist and the insights unique to her as a former Borg would be critical to stemming the devastation of the plague. They had played on her personal concerns for the well-being of another former drone, Axum, who had been found at a starbase in the Beta Quadrant and who she had believed was undergoing medical tests inside this lab that could be classified as torture.

Everything she had been led to believe was a lie. The last thing she was prepared to do was to confront the party responsible for those lies in a dark room.

"Computer, increase ambient illumination," Seven ordered.

The computer did not even beep in response to her verbal request.

"Apologies, Seven of Nine," the Commander began. "Our central processor only accepts vocal commands from authorized officers of this division. You are not one of them."

"Maintain your current position," Seven said. She tried to keep the fear that set her heart racing from creeping into her voice. "Order the computer to turn on the lights."

The silence that followed her request lasted long enough for Seven to begin considering the few tactical advantages she had. She was strong, though not necessarily stronger than some Federation species, and she had no idea what the Commander's planet of origin might be. She was fast and could use the stasis pods to conceal her position.

But the muscles of her body had lain useless for weeks. Intense physical therapy would restore them in a matter of days, but she didn't think the Commander would call a truce long enough to allow her to return to fighting condition.

Suddenly a voice sounded so clearly that it took her a moment to realize it only existed in her mind. *Enhance your sensory processors,* the voice suggested.

Axum. Even here, in the real world, their catomic connection remained unbroken. He could only see *through her*, but that did not make his observations less valuable. In the gestalt—created by their catoms while both of them were held in stasis—they'd had access to a shared reality. It would undoubtedly take some time for her catoms to adjust now that she was conscious. But in time, she might be able to return to that gestalt at will.

Useful information, but not as helpful to her as Axum's simple suggestion.

Seven did not trust her catoms as completely as Axum did. She would have preferred to explore their capabilities in a quiet, safe place. But this was no time for doubts.

Closing her eyes briefly, Seven ordered her catoms to show her what she could not see. The moment her eyes were open, it no longer mattered that the room was lit only by the faint illumination of the stasis chamber's controls. It may as well have been high noon. In addition, the almost silent footfalls of the Commander as he approached her echoed in her mind like thunder. The click of the hypospray he held in his hand was a sharp crack.

Immediately, she lifted her right arm to bat away the Commander's hand. Throwing her weight to the opposite side, with her left hand Seven pushed the surprised man to the floor. Straddling him to pin him down, she grasped him around the throat with both her hands, limiting, but not completely extinguishing, his air supply. The hypospray had been thrown clear.

Now that she could see him, Seven wondered that she could ever have feared such a small man. He was human. Sweat was pouring profusely down his clean-shaven scalp. His dark eyes were small, bulging in their sockets. His bulbous nose and thin lips were his face's most prominent features. His arms flailed uselessly at hers for a moment until he gave up and concentrated on prying her hands from his neck.

"Resistance is futile," Seven said. The words, a standard greeting when she had been Borg, rarely sprang to mind anymore, but were deliciously appropriate under the circumstances.

She felt him relax beneath her and move his left arm down his chest. Sensing his target, she removed her right hand from his throat, plucked the combadge from his uniform, and tossed it well out of reach. The motion destabilized her long enough for him to roll forward. The side of her head impacted the nearest stasis chamber, causing her to release his neck.

He didn't have the strength to scurry too far. He made it only to his hands and knees, gasping for air, before Seven lunged at him again, throwing him facedown to the floor. She climbed over him and used the chamber to pull herself to her feet. She stood before him, winded but still flushed with adrenaline, as he pushed himself back on his knees and peered up at her.

"What . . ." he croaked, then cleared his throat and tried again. "What can you possibly hope to accomplish here?" he asked through ragged breaths. "Kill me and you'll spend the rest of your life in a Federation penitentiary for murder. Stand down, return to stasis, and once the catomic crisis has passed, you will be released."

"After you have killed how many using the catoms I allowed you to extract and study?" Seven asked. "Perhaps I should take my chances with a Federation court."

"I have killed no one," he said so sincerely, she found it hard not to believe him. Ample evidence to the contrary existed in her memories of the past few weeks, but she was not yet able to discern to an absolute certainty which of those memories were real and which were products of catomic nightmares.

"I've seen your experiments, Commander," Seven said. "I've felt the pain of your victims as their bodies rejected the catoms you injected into them, as the atomic bonds holding their molecules intact disintegrated. I've seen you irradiate their remains. I'm not even sure anymore that you're actually trying to cure the catomic plague."

He blanched at this. "How?" he demanded.

"You have been studying Caeliar catoms for how long?" Seven asked. He did not reply, but she hazarded a guess, given his reluctance. "Since the moment of the transformation of the Borg?"

His breath had almost returned to normal now, and his eyes held both suspicion and desperation.

"You are attempting to unlock the programming portals contained within each catom, but their complexity is beyond your current capabilities," Seven continued. "You are making minute alterations and testing them on live patients. None of them have succeeded. There are more than a trillion nodes on each catom, Commander, and you haven't even begun to map their locations and interactions. You're not going to be able to kill that many people without someone questioning your methods and you know it. You are correct that properly reprogrammed catoms could easily destroy any malfunctioning catom, even one that has bonded with another viral or bacterial life-form. But without my help, you will never achieve that goal."

The Commander's face had turned to stone as she spoke. Without requesting her consent, he placed a hand on the nearest stasis chamber and used it to pull himself to his feet.

"Then help me," he said.

Never, Seven thought, but remained silent. He'd already reached for the bait.

"That was always my intention," she said instead.

"I had no idea that you had even begun to dissect your catoms," the Commander said. "Nothing in your files or the holographic doctor's research indicated that your understanding had so far surpassed my own."

Seven could not truthfully take credit for this. Neither she nor the Doctor had dared delve this deeply into the mystery of the particles that had sustained her existence since the Caeliar transformation of the Borg. Their work had occurred in fits and starts as circumstances had required. But Axum had not felt any reluctance to explore his catomic nature. He had shared briefly with her the truths he had already made his own, the realities she was only beginning to grasp.

"Both the Doctor and I feared that any dissemination of our work would result in circumstances like those in which I currently find myself. To you, I am not an individual with rights,

I am an object of inquiry. I never wished to find myself at the mercy of men such as you."

"Forgive me," the Commander said. "So many have died. So many more will die unless I can complete my work. You and the others are essential to my ongoing research."

"Is that why you placed us in stasis when we arrived?" Seven demanded.

"I required continuous access to your catoms," the Commander replied. "I assumed that beyond that, you would be unwilling or unable to assist me."

"I suggest that next time, *you ask*," Seven retorted.

The Commander dropped his head and shook it back and forth slowly. When he raised it again, he was nodding and clearly already revising his priorities. "I'll have quarters and a lab prepared for you."

"First, you will comply with my demands," Seven said.

"Demands?"

"I came here willingly. I volunteered my catoms willingly. Axum's status is in dispute and will likely remain so until you decide to release him. Riley Frazier also agreed, though under duress, to assist Starfleet Medical. But the rest of her people, and their children, are another matter. Riley was promised that they would be relocated to a safe place here on Earth until she was released from this facility. You have not honored that promise. That will be corrected immediately."

"How could you possibly know that?"

"Is the fact that I do enough to convince you to stop wasting time?"

"I require as large a sampling of catomic material as is possible for my work," the Commander countered.

"Not anymore," Seven corrected him. "You will cease immediately any experiments involving the catoms you extracted from the inhabitants of Arehaz. You may continue to work with mine, Axum's, and Riley's until I return."

"Where are you going?"

"You will release Riley's people from these pods and prepare them for transport. I will depart this facility immediately and make arrangements for their care until our work is concluded. You will transfer them to my custody, and once they are secured beyond your reach, I will return and provide you with all of the information you require to cure the catomic plague."

The Commander considered the request. "How long will this take?"

"Ten days," Seven estimated.

"And if I refuse?"

"You can put me in stasis again," she replied. "But you can't keep me there. You will not live long enough to discover on your own how to program a single catom. Agree to my demands, which are no more than you have already promised, and I will return without advising your superiors of my suspicions of the illegality of your actions. I will submit to any tests you require. I will share all of the information I currently possess. Axum and Riley will remain to secure my compliance. Once I return, we will solve this problem in a matter of days."

"When you leave this facility, you will be tracked. All of your interactions will be monitored," he insisted.

You can try, Seven thought.

"There aren't many on Earth I can trust to assist me," she said. "I will only contact—"

"Commander Paris and Doctor Sharak," the Commander finished for her.

Seven nodded. "Yes."

"Where will you take these people?"

"That is not your concern."

"And if you don't return in ten days?"

"I have given you my word, Commander. To me, that actually means something."

The Commander stepped forward. Seven retreated automatically as he extended his right hand. Only when she understood his intention did she take it, unsurprised by its cold, clammy feel.

"One more thing, Commander," Seven said as she shook his hand quickly and pulled away.

"Yes?"

"To whom am I speaking?"

"My family calls me Jefferson. My associates call me Doctor Briggs. Those who work here call me Commander."

Seven nodded. "Very well, Commander. You may address me as Seven. The rest of my designation is no longer accurate."

MONTECITO, NORTH AMERICA

"Mom?" Tom Paris called again.

He stood on the porch of her home, a large ranch-style house that had been in the Paris family for several generations and that his mother, Julia, had redesigned to her own specifications almost half a century earlier. She had envisioned a vast space where multiple generations of Parises would create happy memories during holidays and extended visits. Those dreams had been frustrated by the realities of her husband's death during the Borg Invasion and the failure of her daughters to provide her with grandchildren.

Paris might have finally won a few stingy points from his mother over her favorites, Kathleen and Moira, by giving Julia Paris a granddaughter, Miral. That his wife, B'Elanna, was currently carrying Julia's grandson would normally have been announced to the entire Federation, and his birth would have required a gathering of at least a thousand people to celebrate the momentous event. But those hopes had evaporated when Julia had learned that her son had lied to her about the deaths of his wife and daughter; deaths that had been fabricated to stop an ancient fanatic Klingon sect from murdering Miral out of fear that she was some sort of Klingon savior. Julia's disappointment had been so savage she had actually attempted to gain custody of Miral through the Federation Family Court.

The mediator had ruled in Tom's favor, ending his current troubles. But the look on his mother's face when the judgment was rendered had filled Paris with fear on his mother's behalf. As soon as he and his attorney had completed the required paperwork, Paris had transported to Montecito to assure himself that Julia Paris was not going to make any other inexplicably stupid decisions.

"Mom, I know you're in there," Paris said, pressing the doorbell with one hand while simultaneously putting the large brass knocker through its paces with the other.

Finally, the door opened a crack. His mother's face did not fill it. All he could see was a solid metal guard that secured the door while open. It would take several hundred pounds of pressure to break the door open. *Or a phaser,* Paris thought.

"Mom," Paris said again.

"Go away, Tom."

"I'm not going to do that."

"I have nothing more to say to you."

"I have plenty to say to you. Let me in."

"No."

Paris turned his back to the door and leaned against it. "We're not going to leave things like this, Mom. I'm worried about you. I know you thought you were doing the right thing by going to the Family Court. It's going to take some time but I'll make B'Elanna understand. I promise you'll see Miral and the new baby when the fleet returns from the Delta Quadrant. But I'm not going to be able to do what I have to do when I get back out there if I don't know you're okay, and right now, I don't. Right now, you're scaring the hell out of me."

"I'll be fine."

"Mom."

"Just go, Tom."

"What are you going to do?"

"What do you mean?"

"What are you going to do when I leave?"

"Finish my tea."

"And then what?"

"There's some reading I've been meaning to catch up on."

"And tomorrow?"

A long pause followed. Finally, Julia said, "I don't know."

"This is what I'm saying, Mom. You've still got a lot of years ahead of you, and if they're not going to be filled with baby-sitting or looking after Dad, find something else."

"Don't be ridiculous."

"I'm not. You are one of the most driven human beings I have ever met. You're like me. You can't stay still. You need a constructive place to throw all of your time and energy. You can't just sit in this big old house drinking tea and watching the news feeds. You need—"

"Thomas Eugene Paris," she cut him off. The vehemence of her tone forced him to snap to attention.

"What?"

"You need not trouble yourself on my behalf. Now, just go. Please."

Paris turned back to the door. As he lifted both hands to touch it, to come as close as he could to touching her, the door rushed forward and clicked shut in his face.

Paris shook his head. Several times as a teenager he'd managed to climb to the roof via one of the large mesquite trees that edged the north side of the house. He could break his old bedroom window if he pocketed a large enough rock before he ascended. He had stepped off the porch and was searching the base of the low hedge that bordered the porch when his combadge chirped.

"Starfleet Transporter Control to Commander Paris."

"Go ahead," Paris acknowledged.

"We have received a request to transport you to San Francisco, grid four-nine-seven, immediately."

Where is that? Paris thought. "From whom?" he asked.

"Constance Goodheart."

"I'm sorry, can you repeat that?"

"Constance Goodheart," the officer replied.

Paris knew the name well enough. Constance Goodheart was the long-suffering assistant to Captain Proton. But both she and the captain were fictional characters, part of one of Tom's favorite holodeck programs. During the years he'd served on *Voyager,* wasting countless hours with Harry Kim running that program, a number of women had played Constance. But none of them would be contacting him now.

Unless . . .

"I'm ready for transport," Paris said quickly. "Go ahead."

He and his mother weren't done, but there was one other person on Earth who might need him more than Julia.

Once the transporter had released him, he found himself in a vast park. He knew it instantly. He'd spent more time there in the years between *Voyager*'s trips to the Delta Quadrant than he liked to think about. *But where would she be?*

As he searched among the monuments of Federation Park, a large luminescent sphere caught his eye. It was the memorial that had been erected to ships of the Full Circle Fleet lost to the Omega Continuum. Even in the fading light of day, it burned bright as a baby star.

He found her seated at its base, wrapped in a large, deep-plum wool shawl that looked hand-knit. She came to her feet unsteadily as he said, "Seven?"

Despite the heavy wrap, she trembled. Seven was a dear friend and one of the strongest people he had ever known. It was chilly, barely spring on the western coast of North America, but he didn't think that was the cause of her shaking.

"What happened?" he asked. "Where have you been?"

The last he'd heard, Seven had been exposed to a deadly virus while working inside a classified lab at Starfleet Medical and placed in stasis. He'd hoped to soon hear that she had been released. Nothing about meeting her here like this made any sense.

"I apologize, Commander. The last several days have been somewhat disorienting."

"It's okay," he assured her. "Sit down," he suggested, motioning toward the stone base that held the fleet's monument.

She did as he had bidden, and he joined her there. "Your hands are like ice," he noted, taking them between his and doing his best to share some of his warmth with her. When she didn't begin immediately, he said, "Where'd you get the shawl?"

"It was my aunt's," Seven replied. "It always travels with me now, but I never think to wear it. After the last several weeks, I needed something that was real, that was mine. I needed . . ." She trailed off as her eyes began to glisten.

"Is your work done? Is the plague cured?"

Seven shook her head.

"Seven, talk to me."

She took a deep breath to calm herself. "Where is Doctor Sharak?"

"He took a shuttle with Sam Wildman to Coridan more than a week ago. They should have been back by now. I haven't heard from either of them since they left."

Seven blinked rapidly as this new information was added to whatever mental puzzle she was now trying to solve. "Then he cannot assist us."

"Us?" Paris asked. "What are we, I mean, why do we need help?"

Slowly, she began to explain. As the story fell from her lips, Paris moved through disbelief and shock before settling on mind-numbing fury.

"You never even met Commander Briggs until this morning?" he finally asked.

"He had no intention of seeking my assistance. He only wanted my catoms, *our* catoms."

"He kept you in stasis for weeks?"

"Yes."

"And these experiments, you're sure they aren't intended to cure the plague?"

"That might be part of his agenda, but what I saw suggested his intentions go well beyond that mandate."

Paris nodded. "So, our first meeting is with the chief of Starfleet Medical."

"No," Seven insisted.

"Briggs is making a mockery of both his Starfleet and Hippocratic oaths. He has to be shut down. Today."

"What makes you think Starfleet Medical is not already

aware of his actions? There are dozens of officers working with him and their experiments must be reviewed and approved by their superior officers."

"Starfleet would never condone experiments like the ones you've described."

Seven looked away, searching the horizon. The sun had dipped beneath it, bathing the sky in scarlet, blue, and orange ribbons. "Starfleet is a powerful force for good. I know this to be true. But the Federation has stared annihilation in the face too often. In the last days of the Borg Invasion, mine was not the only voice that pleaded with President Bacco to deploy every weapon in our arsenal to defeat the Borg, even those classified as genocidal. Neither you nor I are in any position to assume that those in the upper echelons of Starfleet would not authorize any research necessary to ensure their survival."

"The Borg are gone, Seven. Who's coming after us now?"

"The Caeliar."

"Nothing our fleet has discovered since we returned to the Delta Quadrant has even hinted at the possibility that the Caeliar did not do exactly what they said they were going to do after they transformed the Borg. If they'd wanted to destroy us, they could have done it then. They didn't. The Caeliar are gone."

"People don't trust what they don't understand," Seven said. "The sleep of those leading Starfleet now is broken by nightmarish visions of staggering death tolls. Their waking hours are devoted to ensuring that those nightmares can never be made real." Turning back to Paris she said, "Until we know exactly what Briggs is doing and who above him condones his work, we cannot risk trying to expose him. We need more information. But first, we have to find a place to secure Riley's people."

Paris sighed. "Okay. Any ideas?"

"Nowhere on Earth is safe. Nowhere in the Federation is safe."

"No unaligned world would be terribly safe either," Paris noted. "There are millions of refugees out there and even our allies aren't rushing to help us relocate them. Everybody's got their own problems, not the least of which is the Typhon Pact. We're talking about families with young children and infants. We can't send them out there and hope for the best, and we can't go with them to protect them."

"We can't protect them as long as they are on Federation soil," Seven insisted.

Paris paused. "Federation soil," he said softly.

"Tom?"

A smile cracked his face. "That would work."

"What?"

"Do you have any idea how much land on Earth does not actually belong to the Federation?"

"No."

"I do. Come on, Constance."

GOLDENBIRD

Lieutenant Samantha Wildman made a slight course adjustment before activating the automatic navigational controls. Turning to her companion of the last several days, *Voyager*'s CMO, Doctor Sharak, she found him studying a map of the capital city on Aldebaran, their intended destination.

When this mission had begun, a brief trip to Coridan to facilitate the gathering of data regarding a classified medical project, Wildman's involvement had been limited. She was simply taking a few days off at the request of an old friend, Tom Paris, to ferry a fellow officer to a distant world.

As soon as they had left orbit of Coridan, Doctor Sharak had briefed her thoroughly on the nature of the classified project. The many odd things they had discovered together on Coridan finally made sense. They also painted a damning picture of several officers at Starfleet Medical, and for all she knew, Starfleet Command.

The first thing Sharak requested was that she file an official flight plan indicating their destination as Ardana, one of three Federation worlds currently suffering massive casualties from some sort of new catomic plague that had arisen in the last year. His second request was that she set course for Aldebaran. After hearing his full report, she concurred wholeheartedly with his plan.

"If you are right that Ria was an agent of Commander Briggs, and he ordered her to terminate her work on Coridan, it is highly likely that he would have made similar requests of any other agents he had on Ardana and Aldebaran," Wildman suggested.

"That is my fear as well," Sharak acknowledged. "At the very least we can assume that he will have terminated operations on Ardana, as he believes that to be our next destination."

"If Doctor Frist told him," Wildman said.

"She did," Sharak said, turning to face her. "When I made my report to her, I intentionally included our supposition that Ria was, in fact, a Planarian, which everyone, including Doctor Frist, knows to be impossible. Planarians have been extinct for thousands of years."

"Until Commander Briggs reconstituted their genome," Wildman interjected.

"A theory I indicated that we intended to explore on Ardana," Sharak continued. "Doctor Frist holds Commander Briggs in the highest possible regard. He is the savior upon whom Frist and her fellow officers have pinned every hope of eradicating this plague. Until now, his results might have convinced her to turn a blind eye to his methods. Few dare question living geniuses. But she knows her ethical duty. She would have briefed Briggs on my report, and he would have taken any actions necessary to cover his tracks, should they exist."

"We're two days out from Aldebaran at high warp," Wildman noted. "Are we going to start at the central hospital? Doctor Frist ordered you to cease your investigations. She might have contacted them and ordered them not to even talk with you."

"We should begin our investigation in an unofficial capacity," Sharak suggested. "Our status as medical officers will permit us to bypass some quarantine restrictions. But we will not assault the hospital directly."

Wildman smiled. She'd learned more in the last few days about the Children of Tama, Sharak's people, than any report she'd ever read. The Tamarians were not members of the Federation. Their language was one of the few that universal translators could not accurately parse. The words were clear enough, but their meanings had been a complete mystery, as had the fact that their communication was based upon metaphors unique to their civilization, until an amazing contact had been made years earlier by the Federation flagship, the *U.S.S. Enterprise.*

Formal diplomatic relations now existed and a handful of Tamarians had begun to work directly with Starfleet. Sharak was the first to sufficiently master Federation Standard to earn a post aboard an exploratory vessel. But he still struggled at times with simple words.

"You and I will not be 'assaulting' anything," she teased.

"Do not underestimate us," Sharak advised, smiling. *"Samantha and Sharak. Seeking the truth."*

"Samantha and Sharak. At Aldebaran."

"I will see to it that our story is remembered by the Children of Tama," Sharak said.

This brought a smile to her lips as well. Sharak's missteps with Standard were nothing compared to her butchery of Tamarian, but he was a patient teacher, and she had become an avid pupil.

A shrill tone from the *Goldenbird*'s computer indicated an incoming transmission. "It's Gres," she said simply.

Sharak nodded and rose from his seat beside her. "I will replicate a light dinner for us. You should speak privately to your husband."

"Thank you."

Once Sharak had made his way to the rear of the ship, she opened the channel and was warmed, as ever, by the sight of Gres's face staring back at her.

"Hi, honey," she greeted him.

"Sam."

The Ktarian face held a certain savage beauty Wildman had always found appealing. But Greskrendtregk's normally soft eyes held hers now with abnormal intensity.

"Naomi?" she asked immediately.

"Is fine," he hurried to assure her. *"She is not happy and still trying to hide it from me. But, otherwise, she is well enough."*

"What's wrong?"

"I have received another request from Commander Paris."

Wildman's heart stilled in her chest. "The hearing?"

"Concluded in his favor."

As her heart resumed a normal rhythm, she sighed. "Then what?"

"He wishes me to pilot a runabout for the next few weeks. I am free to do so and happy to be of assistance to him, but I worry about both of us being too far from home given Naomi's current state."

Wildman shook her head. "I have no idea how soon I can get back. Can it wait?"

"Apparently not."

Wildman knew her husband and Tom Paris well enough to understand that a great deal was going unspoken right now and most of her questions should *not* be asked. If Tom had become involved in any way with Sharak or Seven's current project, that could easily account for Gres's circumspection. But she and her husband had carefully planned their lives after *Voyager* returned home from the Delta Quadrant in order to prioritize accessibility to their daughter, Naomi, who was struggling in her first year at Starfleet Academy.

A new thought occurred to her. "Take Naomi with you."

"She is not scheduled to be done for several weeks, and her liberty is only four days long."

"Call it a family emergency," Wildman suggested. *Come to think of it, that wasn't even a lie.*

Gres's eyes softened. *"I'd love having her all to myself for a few weeks."*

"Do it," Wildman insisted. "It will be good for both of you. Will you be able to stay in contact?"

"I doubt it."

Wildman's jaw tensed. But the stakes were too high to allow fear a foothold. "Take care of her. And yourself."

"Always, my love."

Wildman nodded.

"One more thing?"

"Yes?"

"Does Doctor Sharak have any friends on Earth right now?"

"I'll—" she began.

"Ratham," Sharak's voice said clearly over her shoulder. Turning, she saw him standing behind her, a tray heavy with two bowls and glasses in hand.

"I apologize for dropping eves," he said.

"Teema at . . . where was it?"

"Gayara," Sharak replied.

"Teema. At Gayara," Wildman repeated. Turning back to Gres, she asked, "Did you get that?"

Gres was chuckling at both of them. *"Ratham, was it?"*

"Yes," Sharak confirmed. "She is a fellow at the Federation Language Institute."

"Sam told me you were teaching her Tamarian."

"Your wife is a very quick study."

"That's not how I remember her," Gres teased.

"Hey," Wildman interjected.

"Safe travels, you two," Gres said.

"Samantha and Sharak on the ocean. The winds fair." Sharak nodded.

"For all of us, I hope," Gres said.

3

STARSHIP VESTA

Captain Regina Farkas stood before her bridge's center seat giving half her attention to the report of her chief engineer, Lieutenant Phinnegan Bryce.

". . . are estimated to be complete within the next three hours," Bryce finished.

"You're telling me that the majority of our systems are fully operational but you wouldn't call us 'battle-ready' just yet?" Farkas asked.

"I don't believe our temporary repairs to the secondary shield generators would be sufficient to meet the demands you would place on them should we again face that Voth ship," Bryce said.

Farkas smiled faintly as she glanced toward the earnest young man who'd earned her respect and confidence in only a few months.

"I don't believe ten more years of tinkering would be sufficient for that, Bryce. Your concern is noted. I'll do all I can to keep us out of harm's way."

"Thank you, Captain," Bryce said.

Returning her eyes to the main viewscreen where most of the major players could be seen taking their places for the admiral's trial, she asked of her operations officer, "Jepel, do we have control of the transmission frequency?"

"Aye, Captain. Our *modifications* are stable."

"Can the *Kinara* detect them?"

"A really good communications officer might notice the errant compressed wave," Jepel admitted.

"Then let's hope they don't have one of those," Farkas said. "Sienna?"

Her tactical officer, Kar Sienna, replied, "Status unchanged. The Voth vessel is holding position near the *Manticle*."

"Do we have a name for her yet?"

"The *Scion*."

"Lovely. And the rest?"

"Two Turei, one Vaadwaur, and one Devore vessel have stationed themselves just outside the Gateway. The Skeen *Lightcarrier* and the Karlon *Denizen* are continuing their perimeter sweeps. The other three *Kinara* vessels we still can't identify, but they are positioned to protect the *Manticle*'s flank."

"What about our ships?"

"*Galen* is holding position to port. We are standing by to extend our shields around *Voyager* on your order."

"Then we are as ready as we could possibly be," Farkas noted. "Ensign Jepel, route the *Manticle*'s transmission to my ready room."

"Aye, Captain."

A familiar face was seated at her desk, already watching the show when Farkas entered her sanctuary.

"Hello, El'nor."

"Regina."

"Can I get you anything? A *borst* ale? Maybe some pretzels?"

"This is the first chance I've had to sit in thirty-six hours," Doctor El'nor Sal replied. "And *this*," she added, gesturing to the small desktop screen, "isn't my fault."

"It isn't mine, either."

The captain's oldest friend favored her with a withering glare.

Farkas perched on the front edge of her desk for the second-best view in the room of the transmission. "I realize I didn't give you enough time to yell at me before I ordered you over to *Voyager*. I'm sorry about that, El'nor."

"I know Admiral Janeway gave the relevant orders, but as far as I'm concerned, if we're under fire, you failed to do your job, Captain."

"I agreed with you the first time you made that pithy observation. Thirty-five years later, I still do."

"Good," Sal began, then paused as on-screen Admiral Janeway was ushered into the room. The admiral's hands were shackled by heavy metal circlets connected by a short bar. Her shoulders were pulled forward by their weight, making it difficult for her to walk in her normal poised and steady gait.

More alarming, her personal security detachment, Lieutenants Psilakis and Cheng, were not present.

Farkas heard her breath catch. Wordlessly, Sal placed a comforting hand over hers and patted it gently.

A lump was forming in the captain's throat when a face Farkas had grown to dislike intensely, Devore Inspector Kashyk's, appeared, taking up most of the screen. Compassion was replaced by fear. Anyone who could lie that easily and convincingly scared the living daylights out of her.

"*Greetings to our friends of the Confederacy of the Worlds of the First Quadrant and our former acquaintances of the Federation. Prior to turning herself over to the custody of the* Kinara, *Admiral Janeway requested that her appearance before the tribunal established to weigh the charges presented against her be transmitted in real time, and we have agreed that it is only appropriate that you bear witness to it.*

"*The tribunal empaneled to hear evidence of the admiral's illegal, immoral, and unjustifiable acts of aggression against current* Kinara *members consists of myself, First Minister Odala of the Voth, Magnate Veelo of the Turei, Commandant Dhina of the Vaadwaur, and Rigger Meeml, representing the Skeen, Karlon, Muk, and Emleath. Once the charges have been read and answered, a swift verdict will be rendered.*

"*Our goal is not revenge, but justice. As you will all realize once you have heard the charges, Admiral Kathryn Janeway, formerly captain of the Federation Starship* Voyager, *has personally transgressed against us. The time has come for her to answer for her past actions. Once this matter has been resolved, we look forward to continuing our peaceful negotiations with the Confederacy.*"

Everything about the scene before her, particularly Kashyk's obvious relishing of his position as arbiter of Admiral Janeway's fate, suggested that what was about to unfold was worse than Farkas had yet dared imagine.

MANTICLE

Lsia tried to focus on Emem.

Kashyk, she reminded herself again.

She tried to keep her face neutral, her affect professional. But her eyes betrayed her, continuing to stray toward the face of Kathryn Janeway. Despite Emem's insistence that she be shackled—a needless humiliation that served no security purpose—the admiral still managed to carry herself like royalty. The pride, determination, and utter fearlessness of the woman might have been galling had these not been traits common among and held in high regard by the Seriareen.

Of course, the admiral probably believed that no fair tribunal would find her guilty when her side of the story was set beside the one Emem would tell. Had there been anything "fair" about the tribunal, she might have been right.

Lsia watched Janeway study the face of each panel member as they introduced themselves. The admiral's gaze was curious, penetrating, as if she were sizing them up. For the few moments her eyes locked with Janeway's, Lsia experienced the momentary certainty that the admiral could see *through* her, but quickly dismissed the notion.

Finally, Emem addressed Janeway directly and from that moment forward, her eyes remained glued to his.

"Admiral Kathryn Janeway, a list of charges has been prepared and submitted to this panel by individuals with firsthand knowledge of your previous interactions with their species. As each charge is read, you will be permitted to answer it with direct testimony either substantiating or refuting the charge. Once you have addressed all of the charges, panel members may ask follow-up questions. When that process concludes, the panel will render its verdict on the charges and issue your sentence.

"Please bear in mind that while many lesser violations were submitted for the panel's consideration, they were too numerous to add to the present list of charges and have been waived. Only the most serious issues have been brought to this tribunal for consideration and, in most cases, the proscribed penalty is death."

"I understand," Admiral Janeway acknowledged.

"Do you have any questions before we begin?" Emem asked.

"No."

"Very well." Emem smiled cheerily at her, then turned to include the panel. "Admiral Kathryn Janeway, you stand accused of the following crimes.

"You did knowingly and willfully bring prohibited telepathic individuals into the territory controlled by the Devore

Imperium, in breach of the agreement you accepted in return for safe passage through Devore space.

"You did not turn those individuals over to Devore custody, as was required by your agreement. Instead, you harbored them aboard the vessel you commanded, the Federation *Starship Voyager*, to hide them from Devore inspection teams and violated your course restrictions on at least two occasions in order to access an unstable wormhole that allowed the telepaths in question to escape Devore territory without facing charges for their illegal trespassing."

Emem studied Janeway's face for a moment before asking, "Can you offer any evidence to refute or mitigate this charge?"

Janeway's chin dipped ever so slightly, though her eyes continued to hold Emem's steadily.

"No," Janeway replied.

FIFTH SHUDKA

Captain Chakotay's heart had stilled the moment Kathryn was brought in to face the panel. He had forced his breath to remain steady, reminding himself that he was going to enjoy watching Kathryn frustrate the designs of those she now confronted.

But one word from Kathryn set Chakotay's pulse pounding furiously.

"*No.*"

He was risking everything on his certainty that he *knew* Kathryn's mind as well as his own.

But did he?

"I do not understand," Presider Cin said softly.

Chakotay didn't either, which severely limited the range of responses he could offer her.

MANTICLE

Cautious jubilance rose in Emem's eyes at Janeway's response.

Lsia should have been relieved at such an auspicious beginning. Instead, soft internal alarms began to sound insistently.

"Moving on, then," Emem continued. "You, Admiral Kathryn Janeway, did knowingly and willfully refuse a direct and reasonable request by Turei Magnate Veelo to allow his officers to board your vessel in order to delete the information your ship's sensors had gathered while traveling through the 'underspace' the Turei claimed as part of their sovereign territory. You fired illegally upon the Turei as you attempted to flee and in doing so, caused the deaths of thirty-nine individuals and the loss of two Turei vessels."

Janeway's eyes found Tirrit's, dark holes embedded in a face so ghastly, even by alien standards, that Lsia had hesitated on principle to consider the Turei acceptable Seriareen hosts. The Turei visage was roughly humanoid, but composed of several small, pasty-white overlapping flaps of flesh that gave it an unformed appearance, like something half-melted. It occurred to Lsia that the admiral might never have known exactly how many Turei had perished during that encounter. The death toll seemed to trouble her deeply.

"You did knowingly and willfully bring six hundred nineteen Vaadwaur officers out of self-imposed stasis. That act was in direct violation of Turei law. Under their code of justice, any Vaadwaur individuals discovered in their space were to be immediately transferred to Turei authority. You further assisted the Vaadwaur in activating several of their grounded vessels in preparation for assisting them in fleeing their former homeworld. This, too, is considered treason under Turei law.

"In the battle that ensued between the Turei and the Vaadwaur, another seventy-three Turei officers were killed, forty-seven were injured, and four vessels were destroyed.

"Do you wish to dispute these facts, Admiral?" Emem asked.

Returning her gaze to the man she believed to be Inspector Kashyk, Janeway replied, "No."

"You agreed to protect the Vaadwaur you had brought out of stasis from harm while seeing them safely to an uninhabited world beyond Turei space. You refused to arm them appropriately to enable them to defend themselves, in fact insisting that several disarm themselves completely for the transit, and then knowingly and willfully abandoned those ships to battle the Turei. You are also responsible for the deaths of two hundred ninety-one Vaadwaur officers and the destruction of sixteen of their vessels.

"Do you—" Emem began to ask again.

"No," the admiral cut him off.

"You did knowingly and willfully violate Voth space, capturing two of their scientists and offering them fabricated evidence of a genetic link between ancient inhabitants of your homeworld and the Voth species. You suborned heresy from both scientists, also considered treason by the Voth."

Finally Janeway spoke up. "The Voth scientists you speak of boarded my ship using cloaking technology to study my crew. When we discovered them, the lead scientist, Gegen, took my first officer prisoner. We only entered their territory to retrieve him."

"So your search for a genetic link to further what is known as the 'Distant Origin Heresy' was simply a means to pass the time while you trespassed?" Emem asked congenially. "And your intention to corrupt as many Voth as possible through the wider dissemination of that heresy should fall under the heading: *the peaceful exchange of information between species?*"

At this, the panel members on either side of Lsia chuckled lightly.

"No charges were brought against us by the Voth at the time of that encounter," Janeway noted.

"A fact that will be taken into account during the panel's final deliberations, I assure you," Emem said.

"Thank you."

Emem paused for a moment.

"You have offered almost nothing in response to the charges presented. Have you no wish to speak in your own defense?"

A ghost of a smile passed over Janeway's lips. Turning her head, she addressed the entire panel.

"Each of the charges brought against me by the individual species concerned is valid, *from their point of view.* To argue the merits of each would be a waste of time. Your judgment of me, your ultimate verdict, and the sentence you pronounce is not important here. What's really on trial today is the United Federation of Planets, whom I represent. With your permission, I *would* speak briefly about the Federation's presence here, our beliefs, and our intentions toward this region of space."

Lsia could feel waves of pleasure rolling off Emem. He had hoped that the admiral would open herself up to the most damning evidence that could possibly be presented against her and her Federation, but had known this was not a foregone conclusion.

Until now.

"An excellent suggestion, Admiral," Emem said, his dimples carving deep crevices in the sides of his face. "Before you speak, however, I would like to present a single witness to offer direct testimony on the issue you have now raised: the character, the nature, and the core values of your Federation."

Janeway appeared taken aback, as Emem had intended.

"Please escort Mister Prilch into the chamber," Emem ordered the single Devore guard standing just inside the doorway.

Moments later, a humanoid male, his species indeterminate, walked with considerable difficulty into the room and was immediately offered a chair opposite the panel. His face had been pathetically mangled. His left eye and ear were missing and overlapping scars covered what remained of that side of his face. His right arm had been amputated below the elbow.

Emem continued, "Let the record show that Mister Prilch is a former Devore officer whose ship was lost nine years ago when it came upon an uncharted wormhole. Mister Prilch and all thirteen of his fellow officers were subsequently found and assimilated by the Borg."

Janeway stared dubiously at Prilch's face as he began to speak.

"I was Borg," Prilch began. "I was freed from the control of the Collective when our small scout ship was damaged and its crew was killed. I wandered alone for some time before finding another abandoned vessel I could use to make my way back to Yshandi, my homeworld in the Devore Imperium. Although conscious of myself as an individual for many years, I retained a one-sided connection to the Borg. I continued to hear them in my mind, until a little over a year ago, when they were slaughtered by the Federation."

"Go on," Emem suggested gently.

"*Voyager* first encountered the Borg while I was still part of the hive mind. An alliance was offered and accepted to assist the Borg in defeating an aggressive alien force we identified as Species 8472. That alliance failed after only a few days, when *Voyager*'s crew abandoned several of our cubes to destruction. From that point forward, the Collective chose to cease trying to assimilate Federation citizens, as their unworthiness for perfection had been clearly demonstrated.

"*Voyager*'s unprovoked attacks continued, however. The last was the most devastating, destroying a transwarp hub along with millions of Borg stranded there and on nearby vessels.

"Unsated by that victory, the Federation developed a weapon designed to destroy the Borg completely. They called it the *Caeliar*. Before my connection to the Borg was severed, I experienced the deaths of trillions in a single moment of blinding, excruciating pain."

"But surely, Mister Prilch," Emem interjected, "the actions of the Borg, their aggressive and destructive behavior toward all species of this quadrant, must be taken into account. Can you blame the Federation for seeking to destroy an enemy as implacable as the Borg?"

"I was relieved to be severed from the Collective," Prilch replied. "I was one of many victims they claimed. But I still find it difficult to accept that genocide was the only option at the Federation's disposal. The Borg's territory was far from the Alpha Quadrant. The Borg had ceased assimilating Federation targets found in our territory. A détente of sorts existed, or so the Borg believed. Despite the well-known atrocities committed by the Borg, I do not fear the Federation any less. They could not halt the Borg's progress, so they destroyed every last one of them. Any civilization capable of such an act is not worthy of the trust of any other advanced species."

"Thank you, Mister Prilch," Emem said. Prilch was helped from his seat and escorted out of the room.

"As I indicated, Admiral," Emem went on, "this testimony was elicited in order to present the most accurate picture possible of you and your Federation for the panel. Obviously, you are not personally being charged with genocide, but it is most telling that the Federation you have presented as altruistic, devoted to study and exploration, and dedicated to peace could conscience the actions Mister Prilch described."

Lsia had watched several emotions pass across Janeway's face as Prilch spoke; sadness, anger, regret, and frustration had been the most obvious. But the alarms that had been sounding internally since the tribunal had begun started to blare when Lsia now beheld the absolute defiance etched on Janeaway's face.

"Inspector Kashyk, Magnate Veelo, Commandant Dhina, Minister Odala, and Rigger Meeml," Janeway said, "with your permission, I would very much like to set this portion of the record straight."

Emem faltered briefly. Prilch was one of Kashyk's officers. He had never been assimilated. His injuries were sustained in another recent Devore military action, and his testimony had been dictated verbatim by Emem prior to his appearance. It was based on material readily available in the logs Lsia had taken from *Voyager* before she departed. Given some obvious errors in those logs—*for instance, the fact that Admiral Kathryn Janeway was alive*—and the paucity of intelligence on the Caeliar but for a few references to classified data, Lsia had cautioned Emem about calling Prilch to testify.

As usual, Emem had refused to heed her, confident that this issue would drive a decisive wedge between the Federation and the Confederacy.

Janeway's face assured Lsia that finally, Emem had overreached.

Rigger Meeml spoke for the first time since the proceedings had begun. His flesh was jet black and arranged in generous folds covering his large body. His eyes were silver and his voice low and rich. Lsia had actually grown rather fond of the sound of it.

"I don't know what your experiences of the Borg might have been," Meeml said, "but ours was terrifying. If this Federation really put an end to them, I want to know how. I also want to know how certain they are that the Borg are truly gone."

"Thank you, Rigger Meeml," Janeway said, focusing her attention upon him. "I am more than willing to share all relevant data with you and the Confederacy. Where trust does not exist, the sharing of intelligence is difficult. But I see now exactly how the mistrust that was at the heart of our past interactions with the Devore, the Turei, the Vaadwaur, and even the Voth led to senseless conflict and loss. And I wonder how it might have been avoided had our interactions been guided by a better understanding of one another.

"In the interest of facilitating that understanding, I hereby order all of the Federation Fleet's classified logs on the Borg and Caeliar transmitted to the *Kinara* and the Confederacy. This may be the last order I give," she added, a faint smile traipsing across her lips. "It may also be the most important one I have ever given. From this point forward, there will be no more secrets between our people. If we are to find any way to move beyond this moment without further unnecessary loss of life and property, it will only be in the light of mutual understanding."

"Admiral, if it is your intention to delay these proceedings in order to give your forces adequate time to attempt to thwart the justice being rendered on this day," Kashyk began, warning clear in his tone.

"It is not," Janeway said. "I left standing orders with my crew not to take any action that would jeopardize the ceasefire. My only goal, before a verdict is rendered, is to shed as much light as I can upon events that are as relevant to you as to the Federation."

Looking again at Rigger Meeml, Janeway continued, "My experience of the Borg was also terrifying. When my ship, *Voyager*, was first lost in the Delta Quadrant several years ago, we encountered them many times and each of those times, we barely escaped with our lives.

"The alliance Mister Prilch referenced occurred the first time we came face-to-face with them. I was desperate to avoid assimilation, and the Borg were desperate to turn the tides against Species 8472. What I learned as our alliance progressed was that the Borg had initiated that conflict. Species 8472 are native to a realm we call 'fluidic space' and only entered our space/time continuum when theirs was invaded by the Borg. We developed a nanoprobe-based weapon that leveled the playing field. We were able to assist the Borg in bringing an end to their war with Species 8472, but only after heavy losses were sustained on both sides.

"It is also worth noting that we eventually encountered Species 8472 again and were able to come to a more lasting, peaceful understanding. It is my sincere hope that history might repeat itself now with the Voth, the Devore, the Turei, and the Vaadwaur. Our first encounters were disasters. Regardless of the final results of this tribunal, I expect every officer under my command to leave the past behind and do whatever they must to lay the foundations for better future relations between our peoples.

"*Voyager* destroyed the Borg's transwarp hub as stated. Like you, Rigger Meeml, we feared the Borg. We risked our lives and our ship in an effort to limit their ability to expand their network of transwarp tunnels and to continue assimilating innocent people throughout the entire galaxy. We were never, however, as Mister Prilch suggested, in a state of détente. Every time we met the Borg, the choice was to either destroy them or be assimilated.

"There is one other extremely significant fact Mister Prilch somehow forgot to mention. A few years after we destroyed that hub, the Borg amassed an armada of thousands of vessels. Using previously undetected subspace tunnels, they entered the Alpha Quadrant. They did not come to assimilate. They came to annihilate. They attacked dozens of planets, destroying many of them. The Federation was engaged in an existential struggle. There was no doubt that the Borg were intent on wiping out every living being. Had we failed, the Borg would now control vast areas of the Alpha, Beta, and Delta Quadrants.

"We did not fail, nor did we *destroy* the Borg. During the invasion, one of our vessels, the *Titan*, discovered an ancient civilization and a *species* that called themselves the Caeliar. They were catomic beings, effectively immortal, and had evolved to a point where they were composed entirely of programmable matter. They existed in a gestalt, a shared communal reality where all were one while absolutely retaining their individuality. Through that encounter, Starfleet learned that the Caeliar had unwittingly spawned the Borg thousands of years earlier. That act had been accidental, but also a result of a contact between the Caeliar and the Federation's forerunner, over two hundred years ago. In a way, our ancestors were as responsible for the existence of the Borg as the Caeliar. The first Borg, created on a distant planet deep in the Delta Quadrant, were hybrid life-forms born when a single Caeliar, near death, effectively merged with an officer of the United Earth Starfleet in order to sustain its existence.

"Despite the Caeliar's intensely xenophobic nature, one of our captured Starfleet officers, Captain Erika Hernandez, worked tirelessly to help the Caeliar understand their greater responsibility to the universe in regards to the Borg. Ultimately the Caeliar chose to use their technology, which was advanced beyond the Federation's, to *transform* the Borg. They were able to make contact with the entity that had always been at the heart of the Collective, the essence that was incarnated countless times as the Borg Queen. They were able to contain her and, once her control of the Collective was severed, welcomed all of the Borg into their gestalt.

"The Borg were not destroyed. They evolved. They *became* Caeliar. The Federation witnessed that moment. We were essential in bringing it to pass. But we were not its instigators. And in the days between the beginning of the Invasion and that moment, the Federation lost sixty-three billion citizens, several planets, and hundreds of vessels.

"Once it was done, the Caeliar advised us that they intended to pursue what they called their 'great work' beyond the borders of our galaxy.

"The fleet I command has returned to the Delta Quadrant with many objectives, but the primary one has been to confirm that the Caeliar and the Borg are truly gone. Although there is much territory left to be explored, everything we have seen thus far leads us to believe that they are."

Janeway paused to check the faces of the panel members. For once, even Emem was at a loss for words.

Finally Rigger Meeml found his voice. "If what you say is true, my people, all people of this quadrant, are in debt to your Federation and these Caeliar."

"Everything I have said will be confirmed by the logs that should have been transmitted to you by now," Janeway assured him.

"We look forward to reviewing them," Meeml noted.

FIFTH SHUDKA

"Sixty-three billion?" Cin asked softly.

"Yes, Presider," Chakotay replied. He then removed a padd from his jacket pocket and offered it to her. "I anticipated Admiral Janeway's intentions. This padd contains all of the fleet's reports and logs on the Caeliar."

Cin accepted the padd hesitantly, almost as if she feared to touch it.

"Are you still willing to allow this trial to continue?" he demanded.

Admiral Janeway began to speak again, and Cin returned her eyes to the screen, her golden skin paling visibly.

MANTICLE

Admiral Janeway's words had produced the exact effect she had intended. The Neyser essences masquerading as Kashyk, Odala, Veelo, and Dhina appeared stricken, while Rigger Meeml's eyes held a new respect for her. He had likely been co-opted like the others, but something in him, a distinct lack of animus, suggested that he *might* not.

Thus far, her plan seemed to be working, but the riskiest part was still to come.

"If I may continue to beg the panel's patience, there is one other critical piece of intelligence I believe the *Kinara* and the Confederacy should learn before any verdict is rendered," Janeway said, again addressing herself to Meeml.

"Rigger Meeml," Kashyk interjected. "This is nothing but an attempt on the admiral's part to stall for time. She is toying with this panel, and it will end now."

Meeml fixed his silver eyes on Kashyk, clearly offended. "We are each permitted to question the admiral," he said pointedly.

"What is your specific question?" Kashyk asked, his unflappable courtesy straining.

Meeml settled his eyes on Janeway again. "What other critical intelligence would you share with us, Admiral?"

Kashyk seemed ready to protest further, but Janeway rushed into the opening Meeml had provided. "Thank you again, Rigger Meeml. The intelligence of which I speak is more recent than the Borg Invasion. Almost as soon as the fleet I now command returned to the Delta Quadrant to begin its explorations, they encountered a cooperative collection of species known as the Indign."

"Like the Borg?" Meeml asked.

"No," Janeway replied. "The Indign were composed of six distinct species, one of which was humanoid, called the Neyser. Each Neyser functioned in coexistence with the five other species. They communicated telepathically and over time had developed a deep reverence for the Borg. Unlike most civilized species, they did not recognize the threat the Borg posed. They believed the Borg's collective existence was the pinnacle of sentient achievement.

"They were an aggressive species when it came to defending their territory. They sought to please the Borg in all they did, hoping to one day be worthy of assimilation. Most of their technology, however, was not on par with ours, or *yours*, if my analysis of our recent battle is correct.

"They did possess, however, one unusual weapon. They sent it to *Voyager*, hoping that it would destroy the ship. It has taken some time, but it is possible that the Indign are about to succeed."

"I don't understand," Meeml said. "What sort of weapon was it?"

"It was a canister that contained the consciousness of an ancient Neyser."

"Rigger Meeml," Kashyk interjected. "If you insist upon listening to the ramblings of a desperate woman, I will indulge you, but this tribunal will stand in recess until the admiral agrees to either directly address the charges against her or any panelist offers a question specifically related to those charges."

"Inspector—" Meeml began.

"The transmission will be terminated until the recess has concluded," Kashyk ordered.

VESTA

At some point during Admiral Janeway's remarks, both Captain Farkas and Doctor Sal had risen to their feet. They stood side by side, arms crossed over their chests, watching in fascinated dread as Janeway slowly began to turn the tables on her accusers.

The moment the word *Indign* had fallen from her lips, Farkas realized that the admiral's plan was far more ambitious than any of her fellow officers had suspected.

It was also far more likely to result in Janeway's death.

"Excuse me, El'nor," Farkas said softly, and moved swiftly toward the door.

As soon as she entered the bridge she heard "Kashyk" ordering the termination of the transmission. His face loomed large on the main viewscreen, and immediately after the order had been given, the image began to flicker.

"Jepel!" Farkas bellowed.

"One moment, Captain."

It felt like an eternity, but seconds later, the image stabilized.

"Mister Roach, take us to red alert, extend our shields around *Voyager*, and order the *Galen* to stand ready."

"Aye, Captain," her first officer replied.

FIFTH SHUDKA

"Why has the transmission resumed so quickly? And who are the Indign?" Cin demanded of Chakotay.

Now that he truly understood Kathryn's strategy, Chakotay was both shocked and impressed. He'd been right that she intended to use the truth as her weapon. He just hadn't figured on the size of the weapon she'd selected.

"My people are keeping the channel open, Presider. We suspected that the *Kinara* would be unwilling to share all of the proceedings with the Confederacy, but we wanted to make sure that you and the rest of the *Kinara* didn't miss a moment of it."

"An interesting precaution," Cin noted.

His thoughts now racing to keep abreast of what was about to devolve into a highly unstable situation, Chakotay said, "Presider, I already know the story Admiral Janeway is about to tell. It is my belief that once she's done, your interest in maintaining the cease-fire will have vanished, and if you do intend to attempt to rescue the admiral, you're going to have to move quickly."

"Captain Chakotay, I sincerely apologize for the actions of my first consul that led to the admiral's capture. I have ordered General Mattings to marshal every resource at our disposal to make this right. Over the past ten hours, a hundred CIF vessels have entered the area under cloak of our protectors. Thirty are in position to move immediately on the *Scion*. Another ten have surrounded your Federation vessels and will defend them to the death. The others stand ready to destroy the remaining nine *Kinara* vessels. The *Third Calvert*, now under the general's command, will take point in the operation intended to board the *Manticle* and retrieve your admiral and her security officers."

Chakotay released a deep sigh of relief.

"That should work," he conceded.

MANTICLE

"I don't give a *fij* who hears the rest of her story, Inspector," Meeml said, "but I intend to listen to every word of it."

Kashyk looked to Odala, and only when she nodded slightly did Janeway continue.

"At the time of our encounter, the Indign possessed eight of these canisters: eight separate individuals. It is our understanding from the Neyser, who later provided us all of the intelligence we have on 'The Eight,' that these individuals had, long ago, attempted to secure immortality for themselves. They were capable of transferring their consciousness from one person to another, and once a transfer was complete, they effectively controlled that individual. They could not be killed. The threat they posed to ancient Neyser society was so great that they were captured and incarcerated for what was meant to be eternity.

"The entity that was sent to *Voyager* was unintentionally released and took control of a hologram, a medic in our sickbay. Her name was Meegan McDonnell. Because she is a hologram, she has the ability to change her appearance at will. Initially, the entity that possessed Meegan pretended to offer *Voyager*'s crew assistance. She claimed that her only purpose was to facilitate communication between the crew and the Indign. She then proceeded to steal one of our shuttles, retrieve the other seven canisters that the Neyser held, and depart the area.

"We were unable to follow her, but for the last several months, we have searched for any clue that might guide us to her. I believe we have finally found her."

"Where?" Meeml asked.

"Here," Janeway said, casting her eyes over the rest of the panel. Kashyk's face had paled. Dhina's and Veelo's eyes darted between one another and Kashyk's. Odala, on the other hand, seemed completely composed, *amused* even. Her eyes held Janeway's, almost daring her to continue.

"Can you prove this?"

"For now, my only evidence is circumstantial. But there are other simple scans my people and probably yours can perform that would confirm my suspicions. The foundation for these suspicions is quite solid and based largely upon the presence of the Vaadwaur, Turei, Devore, and Voth among your *Kinara*."

"What do you mean?"

"I was surprised to learn that the Vaadwaur and the Turei had become allies," Janeway went on. "The enmity that existed between them was so old and so deep, there was nothing I or my people could do to mend it when we first encountered them. Indeed, as the record shows, I intentionally exploited it to ensure my ship's survival. Both species displayed unwarranted hostility toward us, but their hatred for one another was the only thing that could surpass their desire to take my ship and kill my crew. There was nothing I could imagine that would have convinced them to become allies with one another, let alone any other species.

"The Devore, likewise, were an intensely aggressive species, hostile to outsiders, particularly those that did not share their disdain for telepaths. They did not form alliances. They conquered. They, too, were an unlikely candidate for joining your *Kinara*.

"None of these species, apart from the Vaadwaur, had any immediate designs on expanding their territory. They had more than enough to deal with to sustain their current holdings. The only thing they had in common was a bad first contact with the Federation through *Voyager*. To find them here defied explanation until several of my officers reported significant concerns to me.

"Some of the species that are part of the Federation are telepathic and empathic. Several serve the fleet. They have detected what they call 'divided minds' within Inspector Kashyk and, quite likely, several of the others present here.

"If Meegan successfully released other Neyser into the bodies of high-level Devore, Vaadwaur, and Turei officers, and baited those they led with the opportunity to exact revenge on the Federation, that could easily account for their presence here. Even the Voth did not seem to hold lesser species in high enough regard to consider alliances. *Nothing* short of intervention like I have described could have brought them here."

For the first time, Janeway saw fear on Rigger Meeml's face. Whether it was for himself, or of the others, she could not say.

"This is absurd," Kashyk finally blurted out. "This is nothing more than a blatant effort by the prisoner to divide her accusers."

"No," Janeway said softly. "This is an opportunity. Technically, the holographic matrix that 'Meegan' now possesses is Federation property. It is very advanced and not something we can allow to be exploited by others.

"You may execute me. But the Federation fleet will be obliged to continue engaging the *Kinara* in negotiations, or battle, until that technology is returned to us, or we are certain of its destruction.

"The *Kinara* has indicated that they have long-standing grievances against the Confederacy. The presider of the Confederacy has already stated that she is willing to negotiate with you to put an end to the conflict that has beset this region for years and to grant you access to the streams the Confederacy now controls. The *Kinara's* newer members, the Turei, the Voth, the Devore, and the Vaadwaur, may share the same goal, but my suspicion is they have other motives for joining this alliance and, whatever they are, could complicate your agenda."

Janeway turned again to Odala. Unlike Kashyk, Dhina, and Veelo, she remained completely calm. "It would be easy to allow this situation to dissolve into further conflict and loss of life. We could fight one another to the bitter end. We could allow transgressions from the past on all sides to blind us to the possibilities of a better future.

"But that is not the only potential outcome. The Federation's highest goal is the peaceful coexistence of all sentient spacefaring races. Anything we can do to facilitate this, any diplomatic aid we may offer, we stand ready to give. We are not here to conquer, to coerce, or to annex territory. We are here to explore and to learn.

"Please, let us help you."

FIFTH SHUDKA

"Is this true?" Presider Cin demanded of Captain Chakotay.

"Yes, Presider," he replied. "It has been confirmed by reports of two of our telepathic and empathic officers. It is the most logical explanation for the presence of the Vaadwaur, Turei, Devore, and Voth among the *Kinara*. The only thing these four species have in common is their shared mistrust of the Federation.

"The Neyser entity that possessed our hologram was thousands of years old. When she found herself alone in unfamiliar territory, she used the only data at her disposal to cobble together a group of some of the most powerful species in the quadrant. She might have been able to sway a single one to her cause if her diplomatic skills were sharp enough, but the only way all four would join her efforts is if she took control of at least one high-ranking official among them."

"But if she is a hologram, how can she survive or exist outside of one of your holodecks?"

"A long time ago, we acquired an extremely advanced piece of technology that can contain and project an entire holographic matrix. That technology was duplicated and is at the heart of her program."

"Which one is she?" Cin asked.

"We believe the entity we refer to as 'Meegan' is currently projecting herself as the Voth minister. This suggests she probably had to kill the real Minister Odala, and it is likely the Voth aren't even aware of it."

Chakotay looked back to the screen to see Kashyk raise a weapon and point it toward Meeml before the transmission began to distort as if suddenly jammed.

Cin did not waste another moment before activating her comm system. "General Mattings," she ordered, "disperse your protectors. Your first priority is to board the *Manticle* and ensure the survival of Admiral Janeway. Destroy any ship in the vicinity that hinders your efforts."

"Understood, Presider," Mattings replied.

"General, this is Captain Chakotay."

"Good to hear from you, Captain. I'm too busy to chat at the moment."

"General, I wonder if you would be interested in continuing our officer-exchange program," Chakotay said.

After only a moment's hesitation, Mattings asked, *"Which officer did you have in mind?"*

"Me."

Mattings chuckled. *"Your transporters or mine?"*

"Mine," Chakotay replied, and tapped his combadge, requesting transport to the *Calvert.*

Placing a light hand on Chakotay's arm, Cin said, "Is there a reason you did not tell me as soon as you came aboard that you suspected the *Kinara's* leaders had been compromised by these Neyser?"

"When I first came aboard, all I knew for sure was that you had asked the commander of our fleet to help you open diplomatic relations with the *Kinara* and when the battle turned against you, your people sold her out to save your own lives."

"And now?" Cin asked.

"My commanding officer just ordered me to do everything in my power to forget our past misunderstandings and find a peaceful way to resolve our differences. She chose to trust you with the truth. I may not always agree with her orders, but *as long as she lives,* I will follow them."

Cin nodded. "Understood."

Chakotay felt the transporter take hold. The next thing he knew, he was standing inside the command center of the *Third Calvert.*

"Welcome aboard, Captain Chakotay," Mattings greeted him.

4

EARTH ORBITAL CONTROL

Cadet Icheb had arrived early for his new internship, a requirement of all cadets in their final year of study at the Academy.

Most days he found it hard to believe he was *still* a cadet, after the disaster of his first internship. Prior to returning to the Delta Quadrant, Admiral Janeway had advised him that she had personally requested Icheb be posted with Starfleet Medical. Seven was due to arrive there shortly and the admiral wanted Icheb nearby in case Seven had need of him.

After multiple attempts to contact Seven had gone unanswered, Icheb had illegally gained access to the classified division where he believed Seven was working. He had covered his tracks well, and his academic advisor had wanted to believe that Icheb's unauthorized security breach was the mistake he claimed.

Still, Icheb could not pass a superior officer at the Academy without wondering if the truth of his deception had finally come to light and his career with Starfleet was over before it had begun.

The only other consequence he had suffered was the termination of his post with Starfleet Medical. This had not surprised him, but it had added to his anxiety for Seven.

Icheb was no more suited to operate transporters than he had been to match requisitions and supplies, but he accepted his new post as the punishment it was, no doubt, intended to be.

It could have been much worse.

The cadet allowed this thought to steady him as he entered the secondary transporter operations bay that would be his station several hours per week for the remainder of the academic year. He was startled when the first face he saw upon entering was one he knew well: Commander Tom Paris, *Voyager*'s first officer.

Paris was chatting amiably with a lieutenant commander who had clearly not taken Starfleet's mandate to maintain one's physical conditioning at near peak levels to heart. Ruddy faced and sporting at least a week's growth of white facial hair, the commander was fifteen kilos above optimum for his frame, and faint beads of perspiration dotting his forehead suggested that his cardiovascular system was suffering as a result. He was also holding a bottle of bright green liquid with a festive bow fastened around it.

Both officers greeted him cheerfully as soon as they caught sight of him.

"Here he is now," the heavyset officer said.

"I told you he'd be on time," Paris remarked.

As required, Icheb stood at attention and announced himself. "Cadet Icheb, reporting for duty, sirs."

"And a stickler for regulations, I see," the lieutenant commander added.

"At ease, Cadet," Paris said, stepping toward him and extending his hand. "It's good to see you again."

Icheb accepted Paris's hand, saying, "I was not aware you had returned from the Delta Quadrant, Commander."

"I came back with Seven and Doctor Sharak," Paris said. "I had a personal matter to attend to."

"I trust your family is well," Icheb said, genuinely concerned.

"B'Elanna and Miral are fine," Paris assured him. "And if all goes well, I'll be back with them a few months before our family gets bigger. B'Elanna is going to have another baby: a boy."

"Congratulations, Commander. That is wonderful news," Icheb said. "Please pass along my regards to them."

"I will," Paris promised. "And now, permit me to introduce you to your new taskmaster, Lieutenant Commander Rob Blayk."

"Sir," Icheb said, nodding sharply.

"Tom says you'll be capable of running this transporter room in a few days. I hope he's right."

"I look forward to learning all you have to teach me, sir," Icheb said.

Paris's smile faltered. "Blayk here is an old friend, Icheb. Our dads served together, so he's always been like a *much older* brother to me."

"Not that much older," Blayk insisted, punching Paris's upper arm with his brick-like fist. "Just don't ever make the mistake of playing pool with him, Cadet."

Icheb tried to relax, to allow the easy banter between the two officers to calm him, but something in Paris's presence here was unnerving.

"Excuse me, won't you?" Blayk asked, starting toward the door behind Icheb, still holding the bottle that was likely a gift from Paris. "I need to hit the head." Fixing his eyes briefly on Icheb, he said, "We're off rotation for the next three hours, so I can get you oriented. Unless Earth is suddenly invaded, no one is going to transmit any orders our way. Don't touch anything until I get back."

"Of course not, sir," Icheb said.

Paris's eyes held the same convivial cheer until the moment the door behind Blayk swished shut. Instantly, his demeanor shifted and he removed a padd from the pocket of his jacket.

"A letter from home," Paris said softly.

Icheb was stunned. Paris could not mean his planet of origin. That was in the Delta Quadrant and no one on Brunali would have cause to contact him.

But he couldn't mean . . .

Icheb accepted the padd with hands that were suddenly shaking.

"I asked Blayk to request you," Paris said quickly. "He's a nice guy who owes me lots of favors. That letter is personal, for your eyes only. Your family needs your help. I know you're capable of what we require. I also know if mistakes are made, your career is over. We wouldn't be asking if we had another choice."

"Seven?"

Paris nodded.

Icheb's heart began to race with a combination of relief and fear. From the first moment, years earlier, when he had expressed interest in studying at the Academy, every single crew member aboard *Voyager* had gone above and beyond the call to assist him in reaching that goal. Why now, when it was finally within reach, they seemed determined to scuttle it, he could not understand.

Except that he did.

Something was wrong. Seven was part of it. And she was the only real *family* he had ever known. Seven had risked her life to save his more than once. Everything he was or ever would be, he owed to her, and to the officers on *Voyager* who had taken the terrified former Borg boy and set him on the path to becoming a man worthy of their respect.

Icheb knew that whatever Paris was asking of him would be in the service of Starfleet's values, whether or not it fell absolutely within their regulations.

It wasn't that he looked forward to, once again, betraying the Academy's honor code. It was simply that his heart would not allow him to betray his family if they needed him.

"I will do my best, sir," Icheb said.

Paris nodded. "I know."

RUNABOUT *COLEMAN*

Thus far, Commander Briggs had been as good as his word. Twenty-four hours after Seven had freed herself from stasis and *negotiated* the release of Riley's people, the *Coleman* had been designated for their use and readied for launch from McKinley Station.

Seven knew accommodations would be tight on the runabout. She transported aboard and was instantly assaulted by thirty-three pairs of eyes. These belonged to the former adult residents of Arehaz and all of them were wary. Most of the thirteen children of the former Borg were too young to take note of her arrival. Several squawked in protest from their parents' arms. Seven recognized the two oldest children, around three years of age, who had become Miral Paris's playmates for a short time aboard *Voyager*. One boy held tight to a worn, stuffed serpent.

A man dressed in the same gray utility trousers and shirt all had been issued once they were brought out of stasis rose from one of the four long benches that had been added to the runabout's rear cabin as Seven started through the unhappy throng.

"Seven of Nine?" he asked.

Without intending to, Seven pulled his name from his mind. "Mister Nocks," she greeted him.

"Where is Doctor Frazier?" he demanded.

"Riley has agreed to remain at Starfleet Medical for the next few weeks. You need not fear for her safety. That is my responsibility now."

Keeping his voice low, Nocks said, "You'll forgive me if I don't find that particularly comforting."

Seven resisted the defensiveness that rose automatically within her. It was much too soon to expect trust from any of these people. "I was unaware that Starfleet Medical would remove you from Arehaz. The moment I learned of it, I took appropriate actions to secure your release. I am taking all of you to a safe place. From there, I will work to find a more permanent home for you, but in the meantime, you must trust me."

Nocks shrugged. "We will go where you take us for now. The rest . . ."

"Will take time," Seven finished for him. "I know."

The transporter sounded behind Seven as Nocks continued, "We can't stay like this for long," indicating the extremely cramped conditions of the ship.

"You won't have to," the cheery voice of Commander Tom Paris assured him. "Give us just a few minutes to check in with our crew, and we'll be under way."

"How far away is our next *temporary* home?" Nocks asked bitterly.

"Not far," Paris said kindly, placing a reassuring hand on Nocks's shoulder. "I know you've been through hell. That ends very soon. Excuse us, please," he added, taking Seven firmly by the elbow and guiding her forward past the benches.

"Seven!" a familiar voice shouted as soon as she had crossed the threshold and entered the runabout's cockpit.

Before she could reply, Naomi Wildman practically knocked Seven over with the force of her embrace. Seven had not been expecting to see the young cadet and glanced furtively at Paris as she accepted the girl's affectionate hug.

"Don't suffocate her, honey," a soft male voice suggested.

As Naomi stepped back, still keeping hold of both of Seven's hands and staring up at her with mingled relief and adoration, Seven nodded to the Ktarian man seated at the pilot's station. "Hello, Greskrendtregk. Thank you for agreeing to assist us."

He smiled faintly in reply as Seven turned to Naomi and said, "Cadet Wildman, why are you not at the Academy?"

Naomi flushed. "I'm taking some time off," she replied, stung.

Seven immediately regretted her tone. She had been Naomi's mentor and friend for years, ever since as a very young child Naomi had insisted on following Seven through *Voyager*'s halls pretending to be a Borg. The affection she felt for the girl ran as deep as any Seven had ever known. She had not intended to embarrass Naomi.

Naomi's father did not hesitate to deflect Seven's question. "I decided that Naomi and I were overdue for a little quality time," he said simply. Seven did not doubt this was true, but also understood that more was going on here than she understood. All of the letters she had received from Naomi after entering the Academy spoke of her excitement and the challenges she was facing. Seven had never doubted her ability to meet them. Naomi was bright, disciplined, and a very hard worker.

There was no place for Seven to move that would afford them any privacy, so she simply lowered her voice and looked directly into Naomi's eyes.

"Are you well?" Seven asked.

Naomi nodded. "I'm better now. Icheb and I have been so worried about you."

"Why?"

"We thought you were sick."

Comprehension struck her. Admiral Janeway had indicated

that Icheb would be assigned to Starfleet Medical for his internship. Given how close the two former children of *Voyager* were, it only stood to reason that her inability to make contact since her return to Earth would have caused them alarm.

"I am so sorry," Seven said, pulling Naomi close again and allowing her to settle in her arms. Finally she felt some of the girl's tension begin to release. This time, when she pulled away, she offered Naomi a warm smile. "I have been unable to make contact. Otherwise, I would have been in touch much sooner."

"It's okay," Naomi assured her.

"Are you certain your coursework will not suffer for the next few weeks? We do not know when you will be able to return to Earth."

"I have a few assignments to work on while I'm here," Naomi said. "And I don't know . . ."

"Don't know what?"

Noami inhaled deeply. "I may not want to go back," she finally admitted.

Seven gently readjusted the long strawberry-blond braid that had fallen over Naomi's shoulder, tucking it back. "It sounds like you and your father have much to discuss," she said, smiling again.

"I wouldn't mind talking to you about it, too," Naomi suggested.

"As soon as this mission is complete, we will," Seven assured her.

This clearly cheered Naomi, who nodded and moved back to the navigator's seat next to Gres.

"We need to get to work on those sensor modifications," Paris suggested.

"Understood," Seven agreed, and quickly located the operational control panel. "Have you finalized our transporter protocols?"

Paris nodded sharply. "Icheb will need a few hours. We'll set our course out of the Sol system in the meantime. Take it nice and slow."

"Icheb?" Seven asked, her displeasure evident.

"We don't have that many friends here as talented as he is," Paris noted.

"He is still a cadet," Seven insisted.

"I pulled some strings to get him assigned to orbital control," Paris admitted. "He just has to find us a window. He can do this."

"If he should be discovered—" Seven began.

"Would you trust anyone else?" Paris asked.

Seven considered the question. Sadly, the answer she was forced to give was, "No."

ALDEBARAN III

The third planet in the Alpha Tauri system had once been home to a small Federation colony. It had come of age in the twenty-third century when Starfleet had decided to build a major shipyard there. A hundred years later, the planet's orbital facilities rivaled those found on Earth, and Aldebaran III was home to a population of billions.

The major cities were teeming with native and alien life. New Kerinna was one of dozens where a tourist could find luxurious lodgings, eat exotic food, and indulge in any form of business or pleasure they might desire.

New Kerinna had also been the focal point for an outbreak linked to the catomic plague a year earlier and was home to one of the major quarantine facilities affiliated with the Benevolent Daughters Hospital.

Aldebaran III had seen its share of devastation during the Borg Invasion. Most of the casualties had come from the Starfleet vessels that blockaded the planet to protect the billions living on the surface. The few areas of New Kerinna that had suffered aerial attacks had been cleared and reconstructed. The planet was a vital center of commerce, and its inhabitants had spared no effort to return the city to its former glory.

Anyone arriving at the Bemdeer Transport Station in the center of New Kerinna's historical district would never have known that the Borg had entered the Alpha Tauri system intent on its destruction a year and a half earlier. It was business as usual for the eight massive museums collected within a twenty-block area, along with the restaurants, hotels, and markets that served the center of tourism.

Bemdeer was unusually crowded when Wildman and Doctor Sharak transported down after securing the *Goldenbird* at an orbital dock. They had been warned when they approached that a six-kilometer area surrounding the Old Aberdeen District had been sealed off three days earlier and remained inaccessible even to residents until further notice.

Bemdeer was the station nearest Old Aberdeen, where the Benevolent Daughters Hospital was located. Even in the mid-afternoon, it was packed with weary travelers, many of whom carried large bags and cases, probably holding whatever personal possessions they had collected before their hasty evacuations. From here, they were being routed to the suburbs surrounding New Kerinna, and several public notice terminals listed dozens of additional temporary residence sites that had been swiftly established to serve the displaced.

While Sharak searched the public feeds for any information on the cause of the evacuation, Wildman approached the few uniformed Starfleet officers she could find. To a man, they told her exactly the same thing. *"No one without clearance from the Federation Institute of Health is currently allowed in the restricted area of the city. Anyone attempting to enter the restricted area will be removed, by force if necessary. There is no word yet on when the travel and occupancy restrictions will be lifted. At this time, Starfleet Medical and the Institute of Health are evaluating an outbreak of Jendarian flu. We appreciate the public's cooperation in halting the infection's spread."*

It was not difficult for Wildman to read between the lines of this rehearsed speech. The good news was that the public seemed to accept the precautions and concurrent inconvenience and moved steadily through the transport station without resistance.

Wildman finally found Sharak speaking to a young man in civilian attire who seemed more frustrated than most.

"They say they've sent her my messages, but I don't know," Wildman overheard as she approached.

Doctor Sharak had to be as alarmed as Wildman was by the situation, but was employing his most compassionate bedside manner with the young man. He interrupted gently to introduce Wildman when she arrived at his side.

"Lieutenant Wildman, this is Mister Herens. He is a student at Aberdeen University and was evacuated from his dorm three days ago. He is most concerned about his twin sister, who had reported to the campus infirmary that day. Apparently she was suffering from a mild cold."

"Everyone is saying it's the flu," Herens interjected. "But I've never seen an outbreak of the flu cause anything like this."

Wildman attempted to smile reassuringly. "The Jendarian flu is a unique strain," she advised Herens. "It is extremely contagious. Your local public health directors are simply trying to contain it."

"Is it fatal?" Herens asked.

"Not when treated immediately," Wildman assured him. "I'm sure your sister will be fine."

"In the meantime, you should avail yourself of one of the temporary relocation facilities," Sharak suggested. "If your sister has not arrived for transport in the last three days, it is unlikely she will do so."

"Those relocation facilities probably have dedicated comm lines with all of the local medical centers," Wildman added. "They'll have more information for you than you'll find here."

Herens considered both of them dubiously. "You're both Starfleet. They probably told you to say that."

"We are Starfleet officers," Wildman said. "But we came here on personal business and are not working with any of the local authorities. I'm just telling you what I'd tell any friend in your situation."

Herens nodded, chagrined. "I'm sorry. I'm just so worried about her."

"I understand," Sharak said, placing a hand on the young man's shoulder. "Try not to worry."

"Do they just take anyone at these relocation facilities?" Herens asked.

"Anyone who can prove they reside in the evacuated area. You have your student ID?"

Herens nodded.

Wildman pointed out a nearby lieutenant standing at one of the public information terminals. "He'll help you," Wildman suggested.

Once Mister Herens was out of earshot, Wildman pulled Sharak toward the nearest line of those awaiting transport off the planet's surface. Their eyes held the same fear, but they remained silent until they had returned to the *Goldenbird*.

"I've never heard of the Jendarian flu," Sharak admitted.

"It's a lethal strain that was eradicated a hundred years ago," Wildman reported. "It's a good cover story, but you and I both know it's not the truth."

"No," Sharak agreed.

The *truth* was that Ria had a counterpart on Aldebaran who had likely installed within the Benevolent Daughters Hospital a device similar to the one Wildman and Sharak had found on Coridan. Sharak had successfully neutralized it before it could release the catomic plague. The one meant to target the citizens of New Kerinna had likely been detonated without discovery. There was no telling how many people might have suddenly been infected by the plague, but based on the city's population and the size of the restricted area, casualties were easily going to be numbered in the thousands, if not tens of thousands.

"We're not going to be able to speak with anyone at that hospital, let alone get access to their patient records," Wildman noted.

"No."

"We need a new plan."

"Yes."

"Temba. His arms wide," Wildman said.

Shaka. When the walls fell, Sharak thought.

5

MANTICLE

Inspector Kashyk," Minister Odala snapped as he aimed his sidearm at Rigger Meeml.

"No one is watching," Kashyk retorted. "This charade is over."

Meeml rose to his feet and began to shout something, but the sound was quickly lost in the screech from Kashyk's weapon. Janeway's gorge rose as Meeml disintegrated from the center of his body outward, flailing helplessly for the few seconds it took for him to be completely vaporized.

"Franribkesh!" Odala shouted.

Janeway did not understand the word, but its effect on Kashyk was instantaneous. His entire body tensed, his shoulders hunching forward as his weapon fell to the floor. He grabbed the sides of his head with both hands. His face was clenched in a spasm of agony.

"Was that . . . ?" Veelo asked of Odala.

"Silence," Odala ordered.

Kashyk's breath came in short gasps as he fell to his knees. Lifting his head so that his eyes could meet Odala's, he begged, "Lsia . . . please . . ."

Pitiless black stones glared back at him.

Kashyk's chest began to heave. Ragged breaths tried to force their way out of his mouth.

"What have you done?" Janeway demanded.

"Would you have preferred I allowed him to kill you?" Odala asked.

Janeway stepped toward Kashyk and bent low, searching his face. Suddenly his eyes opened, darting about the room, wide with terror. When they found Janeway's, they settled.

"K . . . Kath . . ." He struggled for every sound.

"Kashyk?" Janeway asked.

"Atwaon," Odala said.

Kashyk's eyes closed again, and the tension gripping his body began to dissipate. Veelo and Dhina stepped down from the platform and rushed to his side, helping him to his feet.

He shuddered again. The eyes that found Janeway and moved swiftly back to Odala were filled with rage.

"You dare?" he demanded.

"I gave you that form, Emem," Odala replied coldly. "Never forget that I can take it from you whenever I wish."

"She cannot be allowed to live," he insisted.

Janeway found her voice again and directed it toward Odala. "To whom am I speaking?" she asked.

When Odala did not immediately respond, Janeway said, "Tell me who you are and what you want. Let's start there."

"Kill her," Emem shouted.

Instead, the form of the Voth minister began to shimmer and dissipate. It was replaced by the figure of an extremely tall woman with long black hair wearing a form-fitting ensemble composed of narrow layered strips of reddish-brown leather. Her eyes were dark green. "I am Lsia of the Seriareen," the woman said in a much warmer and richer voice than the Voth minister's.

The floor beneath them shuddered.

Lsia pressed a button on the console before her and with Odala's voice said, "This is Minister Odala. Report."

No response came, and the ship shook again as the unmistakable pounding of weapons impacting shields sounded around them.

"It sounds like your ship is now under attack," Janeway said.

"The Confederacy?" Lsia asked.

Janeway shrugged. "I told you that for us to proceed, we had to be honest with one another. I know you tried to disrupt the transmission, but if my people did their job properly, and they usually do, both the Confederacy and the rest of your *Kinara* heard every word I said and just watched you execute Rigger Meeml."

"Seal the doors to this chamber," Lsia ordered Veelo, who moved immediately to obey. To Janeway, she said, "If this ship is destroyed you will die. We will not."

"The moment I agreed to turn myself over to you, I figured my odds of surviving this were long. On the off chance I miscalculated, tell me why you've done this. Tell me what you want, and I will do whatever I can to help you if we all survive the next few minutes."

The clatter of weapons firing at the chamber door was added to the symphony of regular percussive booms followed by continued bucking of the deck.

Lsia smiled sadly. "Would you believe me if I told you that we just want to go home?"

THIRD CALVERT

Ranking General Mattings usually preferred bloodless victories. Today was an exception to that rule.

His forces had been humiliated by the *Kinara*. For that, the *Kinara* must burn. He could not argue with their tactics. Withholding their most powerful vessel, the *Scion*, until the fight was well under way was a dangerous choice, but it had worked to the *Kinara's* advantage.

Once.

Now that the CIF had all the requisite intel at their disposal, grinding the *Kinara* to dust was a simple matter of the appropriate allocation of resources.

A sight I hunger to see.

As his third detachment moved into formation to attack the *Scion*, her cannons rotated and opened fire.

On the *Manticle*.

"Sweet Source at sundown," Mattings cursed. "JP Mantz, order the second detachment to protect the *Manticle*. Encrypted transmission to LG Swenn. Destroy the *Scion*."

"It looks to me like he's already trying," Captain Chakotay noted.

Mattings focused his attention on the quadrant of his screen that showed the third detachment flying close target runs around the *Scion* like a swarm of *gnetz*. Her shields had yet to show any weaknesses, but that would change soon enough.

He hoped.

Quadrant one of his display showed the *Lightcarrier* and *Denizen* now trading fire with the Turei and Vaadwaur vessels who had departed their post at the Gateway. The latter were about to lose that engagement. The remaining two quadrants showed a flurry of fire between the CIF and the ships flanking the *Manticle*, and the cordon of vessels surrounding the Federation ships, far from the center of battle.

"General," a voice called from tactical.

"Report, JC Leveti."

"The *Scion* is—"

But before he could finish Mattings watched as the massive Voth ship cleared a path by ramming its way through the CIF line, accelerating as it moved toward the *Manticle*.

"Order the fourth detachment to take the three unID'd moving on the *Manticle*'s flank. Send the fifth to help LG Swenn."

A small explosion along the *Manticle*'s rear propulsion array caught the general's eye.

"Captain Chakotay, I swore to rescue your admiral, but she hasn't made my job any easier."

"She does that a lot," Chakotay noted.

As the deck began to vibrate, Mattings instinctively grabbed the edge of his control panel. A sharp crack indicated their shields had just taken a beating, but most of the status bars glowed gold with only a few edging into the orange.

"The Turei and Vaadwaur ships have been destroyed, sir," Leveti reported.

Mattings watched as five of his finest moved to intercept the *Lightcarrier*. The *Denizen* was belching flame from her underbelly, her course erratic.

"The *Lightcarrier* is trying to flee, sir," Leveti said.

"Let them go," Chakotay suggested.

"I don't think so, Captain," Mattings replied.

"That was Rigger Meeml's ship," Chakotay insisted. "His men just watched him die. The rest of his people should be told what happened here."

"When his ship never returns home, his family and friends can assume the worst," Mattings said.

"You don't know yet how many more ships they might have or *who* is really controlling them. It looks to me like the original *Kinara* members are attacking their newest allies, the ones we know were compromised by Meegan. They're *helping you*. A gesture of goodwill could go a long way toward making future negotiations easier. They don't have to be your enemy."

Mattings sighed. Vengeance was one thing. But Chakotay had a point.

"Let the *Lightcarrier* go," Mattings ordered.

"Now, hail the *Manticle*," Chakotay offered.

"I don't want to talk to them," Mattings replied. "I'll save their sorry backs for the sake of your admiral, but that's as much courtesy as I can possibly extend right now."

"May I?" Chakotay asked.

"It's your breath to waste, Captain."

Chakotay looked about the command center of the *Calvert*. Mattings obliged him by ordering Mantz to contact the *Manticle*.

"The Gateway has been cleared of enemy ships, General," Leveti advised. "The *Denizen* has been destroyed."

"Have those detachments fall back. What monster forged the alloys of the *Scion*?" he asked.

"No response from the *Manticle*," Mattings heard his communications officer confirm. This didn't surprise him. Mattings wondered if it surprised Chakotay.

A single Devore vessel was all that remained now of the *Kinara*, apart from the *Scion* and *Manticle*. The space between the two larger ships was filled with two CIF detachments making slow but steady progress. Several weak areas had finally begun to show in the *Scion*'s shields and his men were exploiting them mercilessly.

"Another direct hit on the *Manticle*," Leveti reported. "Her shield strength is below one-half. The other Devore vessel has been destroyed."

Finally, a huge burst of green flame shot up from the aft section of the *Scion*.

"It's about damn time," Mattings said.

Suddenly, perhaps cognizant of the futility of her efforts, the *Scion* accelerated, passing the *Manticle* and clearing a path through her CIF attackers. She seemed to shudder momentarily before engaging her faster-than-light propulsion unit. Her body appeared to elongate before she vanished before the general's eyes. A number of CIF vessels caught in the resulting shockwave tumbled out of control like falling stars.

"Order the second through fifth detachments to stand down with my gratitude and compliments," Mattings said. "Order the first to surround the *Manticle*."

"General, the *Manticle* is signaling her surrender and requesting parlay."

"Tell them to drop whatever is left of their shields, take all of their weapons offline, and prepare to be boarded." To Chakotay he said, "Let's go get your admiral."

MANTICLE

The door was sturdier than it looked. The internal seals Veelo had activated showed no signs of weakening as the sounds of disruptors and pounding continued. Admiral Janeway had moved toward the far side of the platform and taken hold of it as the ship rocked and bucked, tossed about by the waves of enemy fire now loosed upon her.

Lsia remained near her with enviable sea legs. The ship's motion did not appear to disturb her at all. Emem, Veelo, and Dhina had formed a tight semicircle near the door, their weapons raised, ready to attack the first person to breach the door.

"You said you wished to help us, Admiral," Lsia said softly. "Is that still true?"

"I suppose it depends on who comes through that door,"

Janeway replied. "You led the Devore, the Turei, the Vaadwaur, and the Voth here under false pretenses. You may need to answer to them for that."

"You understand that *we can't die.* They can kill these forms and if they do, we will simply choose others."

"Solving nothing," Janeway agreed bitterly.

"You wanted to end this without further bloodshed. This is your chance."

Janeway looked to the others.

"Hand over your weapons, and I'll see what I can do," Janeway said.

Lsia nodded, and moved to collect her companions' sidearms. Kashyk was the last to surrender his, and did so grudgingly.

"One more question," Janeway said.

"Yes?"

"You took seven canisters from the Neyser. By my count, four remain. Where are they?"

"Three," Lsia corrected her. "Sipho, Ruscho, and Phiel remain contained. The fourth, Xolani, was lost when I first attempted to release him. I fear he never survived the transfer from his last form into containment."

"Are they on board the *Manticle?*"

Lsia paused, then said, "I left them on an asteroid."

"Near New Talax," Janeway said, smiling faintly in anticipation of her next conversation with Lieutenant Barclay and making a mental note to add a commendation to his file.

"Yes," Lsia confirmed.

"Take cover," Janeway suggested as she moved to stand alone directly in front of the door.

Chakotay knew that transport via protector was completely safe. That didn't mean he enjoyed it. He could only manage to keep his stomach calm as he moved through open space by keeping his eyes focused on his boots and extending his arms out to the sides, allowing his fingers to graze the edges of the wave form that was carrying him.

After a few unsettling minutes of travel, he found himself inside a large shuttlebay. An old acquaintance awaited his party, flanked by four men. It was the first time Chakotay had ever seen any Devore officers unarmed.

General Mattings and six of his security officers were already standing on the deck when Chakotay's protector released him.

"Commander Chakotay?" the lead Devore officer greeted him.

"It's captain now, Mister Pratt."

Pratt was a portly man, well past his prime. He had taken more pleasure than most of his counterparts in petty humiliations during Devore inspections. Chakotay might have relished seeing him like this, his uniform scorched and blood trickling down the side of his face, had he not been conscious of how much now depended upon Pratt's goodwill.

"Captain," Pratt said.

"This is Ranking General Mattings of the Confederacy Interstellar Fleet's *Third Calvert*. His was one of many ships that just risked themselves to protect the *Manticle*."

"I suppose you want our thanks?" Pratt sneered.

"That won't be necessary," Mattings replied. "Where is Admiral Janeway?"

"The tribunal chamber was sealed from the inside just after hostilities began. My men are trying to force the door now."

"Is she still alive?" Chakotay asked.

"We believe so."

"And the others?"

"I've known for months that something was wrong with Kashyk," Pratt said. "His obsession with this alliance was completely out of character, despite the possible benefits. It's good to know now that I wasn't wrong."

"Is *he* still alive?" Chakotay demanded harshly.

"Just as long as the door holds," Pratt replied.

"We need to move now, General," Chakotay said, starting toward the bay doors. "Mister Pratt, order your men to hold their fire if they breach the chamber before we get there. We aren't certain, but we believe that the Neyser consciousness that took your inspector is capable of transferring itself to anyone it wishes. Killing Kashyk and the other officers they took will only result in additional loss of life."

"Does the general intend to let us live once you have secured the admiral?" Pratt asked, expending serious effort to keep pace with Chakotay.

"Every time you speak, I find that I am less inclined in that direction," Mattings replied.

Pratt nodded, started to speak again, and thought better of it.

The constant pounding on the door had become so regular it was shocking when it finally ceased. The silence came just a few minutes after the ship stopped shaking around them. The battle was clearly over but Admiral Janeway had no idea who had won.

A crackle of static over the room's comm system preceded the sound of a voice Janeway remembered almost as well as Kashyk's.

"This is Adjunct Inspector Pratt of the Devore Imperium. We have surrendered to the Commander of the Confederacy Interstellar Fleet and are assured that the survival of every life-form within the chamber and aboard this ship is contingent upon the condition of Admiral Kathryn Janeway. For all our sakes, I hope you people are wiser than I believe you to be."

"Mister Pratt," Janeway said, hoping he could hear her.

"Admiral Janeway, is that you?"

"Yes."

"Can you release the door?"

Janeway looked to Lsia, who nodded to Veelo.

As Veelo released the interior seals Janeway said, "Advise your officers to keep their weapons down when they enter."

"Is the chamber secure?" Pratt asked.

"It is," Janeway replied.

Finally, the doors slid open. General Mattings entered first, Chakotay a few steps behind with his phaser low. They were followed by four of the general's men. Two more remained outside, their weapons trained on Pratt and his officers.

"General Mattings, how good to see you," Janeway said. Three of the five aliens who had originally comprised the tribunal stood in a cluster behind her. A tall woman Mattings had never seen stood with them.

"Admiral," Mattings greeted her warmly. Chakotay moved swiftly past him, stopping just short of Janeway and taking her hands in his. She offered him a tight smile and nod, which he returned before guiding her gently back to stand beside him and Mattings.

"Who was in charge here?" Mattings demanded of the others.

"I am," the strange woman said, stepping forward.

"I don't recognize you," Mattings said.

Her body shimmered briefly, then solidified again as the Saurian female Mattings knew as Odala.

"That's really disturbing," Mattings said softly.

She repeated the trick, resuming her previous form. "I am Lsia of the Seriareen. Admiral Janeway has graciously offered to assist us in our future negotiations with the Confederacy."

At this, Mattings laughed aloud.

"You are now prisoners of the Confederacy. There is nothing to negotiate," he said.

"We defeated you once on the field of battle, General. You have now claimed a single victory over us. But surely you do not believe that all the forces I command were present here today?"

Mattings raised a hand to rub the back of his neck. "Let them come," he said. "We just turned seven of your ten ships to dust. We'll do the same to any enemy vessel that approaches the Gateway again."

"General Mattings," Janeway interrupted. "There is no cause on either side for further bloodshed. And despite your victory, these individuals continue to pose a serious threat to any they encounter. They have advised me that they came here seeking access to your space because their ancient homeworld is part of your territory."

"Seriareen?" Mattings asked.

"Seriar," Lsia corrected him.

"Never heard of it," Mattings said.

"That doesn't surprise me," Lsia said. "Nine millennia have passed since last I saw her."

"Be that as it may," Mattings said, "you led a fleet of vessels against the Confederacy, and that comes with only one penalty. It's my understanding that we'll need to be careful about how and where we execute you, but your fate was sealed the moment you opened fire on my people."

"General, the Federation has a vested interest in these prisoners," Janeway said. "Lsia inhabits technology we consider proprietary. And I've witnessed exchanges that suggest that the individuals they possessed may still be aware of and fighting their current condition. You cannot execute them for actions they did not willingly take. They are victims here and their rights should be considered."

"Admiral?" Chakotay asked. His obvious relief at finding her unharmed seemed to be giving way to confusion.

"Captain Chakotay," she replied, "would you be so kind as to collect Lieutenants Psilakis and Cheng?"

Chakotay's jaw clenched as he nodded and turned to Pratt, who directed him down the hallway.

Once he was gone, Janeway continued, "I need to speak with your presider. Until I do, my fleet will take these prisoners into custody. We have technology that will permit us to prevent them from transferring themselves into anyone else and our medical staff will work to determine if there is a safe way to separate them from their current hosts."

"That's not going to happen," Mattings said, his voice cold as stone.

"Why not?" Janeway asked.

Mattings was shocked. "Admiral, I witnessed more than enough of your *so-called* tribunal to satisfy myself that these people are unworthy of calling themselves civilized, let alone law-abiding. They don't deserve our mercy, or yours."

Janeway considered Mattings evenly. He hadn't spent enough

time with her yet to get a sense of her personal power, but an extended gaze from her hard blue eyes was beginning to educate him. "I appreciate your position, General, but the Confederacy's are not the only interests that deserve consideration here."

"I just brought twenty thousand of my finest officers here to rescue you, Admiral," the general admonished her. "Your courage in ordering your ships into the fight that claimed the *Lamont* and forty others was laudable. Given what I've learned of your people over the last several weeks, it was also unsurprising. When you agreed to become the *Kinara*'s prisoner, I made a personal vow to see to it that you survived that choice. It should never have been asked of you. Presider Cin was unaware that her first consul had already begun discussions with the *Kinara* behind her back. He thought you were the one preventing him from getting his hands on the Federation's technology. One conversation with me would have set him straight. Your Federation is defined by its sense of honor and duty. Captain Chakotay would have probably destroyed your ships before he let Dreeg set foot on them again, let alone take any of the technology he wanted for the consortium."

"Probably," Janeway agreed. "But all of that is in the past. The situation has changed radically, and accommodations must be made."

"Fine. You can discuss those with the presider. In the meantime, I have to take these people into custody."

"Respectfully, I can't allow you to do that, General."

Mattings paused, unable to believe the admiral's defiance.

"You don't strike me as a man who retreats when things get hard," Janeway continued. "I don't either. This is a critical moment in our relationship. We must be able to trust one another."

"They were going to shoot you down like a diseased *deng*, Admiral," Mattings insisted. "Why are you trying to protect them now?"

"Because it's the right thing to do. Neither of us knows what forces they might still have prepared to move against us. One wrong move now, on either of our parts, and this thing devolves into armed conflict."

"We're ready for that."

"That's not the point," Janeway insisted. "We do everything we can to avoid firing our weapons. Military engagement is a course of last resort. That's easy to forget when you've been hurt, General. I know the losses they inflicted on you still burn deep. I've stood where you are standing too many times. We make choices in the heat of battle and tell ourselves after the fact that we had no other option. But every time you allow yourself to settle your conflicts by force, you add to the chaos rather than containing it.

"There is another path. It's the harder one. But it is the only way through this moment that is not guaranteed to end with a larger body count."

"Whatever these people want, they want it from *us,* Admiral," the general said. "I know that you feel responsible for that hologram. But her days of causing trouble are over. We'll see to that. There's no reason for you risk anything on our behalf."

"Of course there is," Janeway countered. "Peace is not a naturally occurring phenomenon. It is dragged kicking and screaming from competing agendas. It requires compromise. It requires faith. And it requires trust."

"The peace you want to create here could also require your life. Are you honestly willing to give that for beings you only met less than two cycles ago?" Mattings demanded.

"Yes," Janeway said simply. "What are you willing to give, General?"

Mattings considered the question. For the Confederacy, he would gladly lay down his life. For Admiral Janeway and Captain Chakotay, he might do the same. But those who had attacked the Gateway, those who had taken lives of his fellow officers on the field of battle, for them, he could barely find the strength to offer mercy, let alone quarter.

But Janeway's raw nerve, her determination, and her belief that from the wreckage around them some sort of peaceful solution might be found, touched a chord within him.

Only a few weeks ago, Mattings had expressed to Captain Chakotay his fear that what the Confederacy had built could be destroyed by the continuous attacks upon her by outsiders. What he had not said aloud, and barely acknowledged to himself, was that the appearance of the Federation fleet had done more to feed that fear than the growing numbers of hostile ships attacking the Gateway.

His inner strength had been rooted in the belief that the Confederacy rested at the pinnacle of potential sentient achievement. They did not plead with others for acceptance. They did not compromise their values. They were the envy of all civilized species they encountered. Even the Borg had failed to wipe them out. *Others* looked to them from afar and strove to be worthy of acceptance by the unconquerable Confederacy of the Worlds of the First Quadrant.

The cognitive dissonance that was created when he was forced to accept the vastly superior technology the Full Circle Fleet possessed had been painful, but soon quelled. Tools were simply tools and the Confederacy's were more than equal to the tasks required of them.

Much harder to silence were the doubts that arose when he considered how much further the people of the Federation had traveled in half the time his Confederacy had existed. The space the Confederacy claimed wasn't one-third of the area held by the Federation in the second and fourth quadrants, and they were already exploring beyond that into the first and third.

Was it possible that the Confederacy was no more than a parochial, backwater power? Were they ultimately doomed to burn through the resources they could hold in their distant corner of the galaxy without ever even tasting all of the wonders the Source had created?

That the people of the Federation hadn't even expressed the slightest arrogance when it was obvious how greatly their accomplishments dwarfed those of his people only added to his humility.

Mattings could never say this aloud. But he couldn't ignore it either.

Was *this* how they had managed to come so far in such a short time? Was the leap Admiral Janeway was challenging him to risk with her, this willingness to take up the cause of people who had been intent on publicly executing her only a few minutes ago, utter foolishness? Or was it truly the price her people's greatness demanded?

Finally, he replied, "I'm not a diplomat, Admiral. And I'm not willing to lay down my life for these strangers, but I might be willing to risk it to see what you can create from this mess. My understanding of compromise is that all sides walk away equally unhappy."

"What do you suggest?" Janeway asked.

"I can transfer the prisoners to a neutral space where the Confederacy and your fleet can observe them at all times."

Janeway smiled warily.

"My men will secure this ship while you and the presider figure out how we move forward from here."

"I would suggest that once the *Manticle* has been disarmed and repaired, you send her back to Devore space. Those who witnessed what happened here should let anyone else looking for a fight know how they fared against the CIF."

"Don't push it, Admiral." Mattings smirked.

"You may not be an official diplomat," Janeway said, "but you do an awfully good impersonation of one, General."

"Then we have a deal?"

"We do."

6

EARTH ORBITAL CONTROL

Icheb would normally have found Commander Blayk's company boorish. Given the data he had hastily absorbed from the padd Paris had given him and the understanding that the transporter protocol revisions Paris had requested needed to be implemented before Icheb's first shift had ended, Blayk's incessant, inane prattle was maddening.

"Have you ever been to Marseille, Cadet?" Blayk asked through a wide yawn.

"No, sir," Icheb replied as he pretended to continue running transport simulations. His station had been taken offline for his orientation. It would take mere seconds for Icheb to re-activate it, but clearly Blayk did not suspect that Icheb knew how to do that.

"Oh, it's a great city," Blayk said, stifling a second yawn.

Icheb only nodded as Blayk launched into a lengthy dissertation on Marseille's many merits, highlighting the bars and cafés with the most attractive staff.

The controls were familiar. Icheb had first learned standard transporter operations aboard *Voyager*, and B'Elanna Torres had personally instructed him in dozens of esoteric applications she had devised. At the Academy, he'd suffered through two additional basic survey courses and had aced the requisite exams.

Lieutenant Paris had requested more than just a simple transport of several individuals from a nearby runabout, however. He had also asked that Icheb delete all records of the transport once it was complete.

Altering the contents of transporter logs was never permitted, but the basic required programming had been part of his coursework to enable any officer to determine if the logs had been subjected to tampering. This had given Icheb all of the insight he required into the many ways there were to hide any trace of a transporter's use.

The only complicated request Paris had made of Icheb was the last. It involved eliminating the ability of the transporters to lock onto a specific signal for the foreseeable future without a personal command override. Hacking the main database was risky, but also well within Icheb's abilities. It was, however, a dangerous proposition.

It was not difficult to imagine why Paris would have asked

that Seven's transporter signals be disrupted. It was essential that she not be detected once she was taken off the runabout. She required the ability to move unrestricted and invisible for several days. But, should she require emergency transport, only Icheb would be able to provide that, and he would only be present to do it for a few hours each week. Had Icheb been able to discuss this further with Paris, he might have suggested a few safer alternatives. As it was, he could only obey and hope for the best.

This would not be possible as long as Blayk was present. Icheb fully expected that Blayk would require another short *break* during their first few hours together. When the commander had returned from his initial absence, he no longer held the bottle Paris had given him. Blayk's breath, however, suggested that he had sampled it liberally prior to depositing it into his personal locker. His eyelids had begun to droop only a few minutes into his orientation presentation and almost as soon as Blayk was satisfied that Icheb grasped the basics of transporter control, he had settled himself onto the chair set before the panel, leaning his back against the wall and crossing his arms over his belly.

Finally, after receiving Icheb's assurances that he would ask for Elayne should he ever visit the Bistro Marmont in Marseille, Blayk seemed to have exhausted conversational topics, and a merciful stretch of silence began while Icheb pretended to continue his simulations. He was, in fact, searching for access to the master database.

A grating inhalation caught Icheb's attention. He turned to see Blayk's eyes closed and his mouth hanging open.

Icheb froze. If Blayk would only nod off for a few minutes, Icheb could execute Paris's request.

Unfortunately, Blayk snorted himself awake seconds later and, after wiping his mouth, grinned sheepishly at the cadet.

"Sorry about that," Blayk admitted. "I don't know why I'm so tired tonight."

Icheb knew. Among the notes in Paris's padd was confirmation that the Aldebaran Ale he had given the commander as a thank-you gift was spiked with a mild sedative. Paris clearly knew his old friend's weaknesses and was leaving nothing to chance.

"There is no need to apologize, Commander," Icheb assured him. "If you require a short break, I will continue to familiarize myself with the system."

Blayk considered the proposition. "We're still off rotation," Blayk said. "Five minutes," he finally decided, settling himself back against the wall. "I just need five minutes."

"I will advise you when five minutes have passed," Icheb offered.

"Good man." Blayk smiled and winked before closing his eyes.

Icheb actually required fifteen minutes, but he did not expect to be chastised for allowing Blayk a slightly longer nap. As soon as the commander's breath had settled into a deep, slow, loud rhythm, the cadet set to work.

Eight minutes later, he signaled the *Coleman*.

COLEMAN

"We're ready," Paris said, relieved.

"Icheb?" Seven asked.

"Standing by for our signal. I'll advise the embassy. You're sure the sensor modifications are complete?" Paris asked.

Normally, Seven would have simply nodded, but given her fatigue, she quickly re-checked her work and, thankfully, found it satisfactory. "The modifications are set. Even after we have departed, scans will indicate the presence of forty-nine life-forms."

"Okay," Paris said. Turning to Gres, he asked, "Which course did you choose?"

"Beta," Gres replied.

"Any reason?" Paris had given the Ktarian three possible routes, all of which would bring the runabout within range of several densely populated worlds—*Paris hoped*—Briggs might believe were good choices for the refugees from Arehaz.

"It's close to Ktaria," Gres replied. "I'm more familiar with the area and have identified a few places you didn't suggest where we could easily 'get lost' if we need to."

"Under no circumstances are you to risk taking fire," Seven admonished Gres. "You will abide by Starfleet regulations at all times."

"Even if they intend to board us?" Gres asked.

"Just tell them the truth," Paris suggested. "You and your daughter are on a family vacation. I offered you the use of this runabout. You and Naomi were the only passengers who left the Sol system. You had no idea your sensors were malfunctioning."

"I'd just as soon avoid that conversation if at all possible."

Paris nodded. "I'll let you know the second it is safe for you to return."

Gres smiled. "Whatever you're planning, I hope it works."

"So do I," Paris agreed. "Seven?"

"Signal Icheb."

TAMARIAN EMBASSY
PARIS, EARTH

Approximately five minutes later, Seven materialized in a large room with high ceilings from which hung several intricate lights. They were beautifully designed decorative arts, probably ancient, with several branched arms dripping with large crystals. Unfortunately, they gave off very little in the way of illumination. There was an unmistakable dampness in the air, tinged with a sour smell. This and the absence of windows suggested that the room was below ground level.

Several mismatched chairs, stools, and benches lined the walls, which were adorned with paper in a metallic pattern of floral sprays that was visibly peeling away, in some sections, by the sheet. At the far end of the room, several long tables had been set up. One was piled high with blankets and pillows. One contained large dispensers filled with water, a huge tureen from which steam was rising, baskets filled with thinly sliced bread, and several plates of fruit.

Standing beside the "buffet" were two Tamarian individuals, one male, one female. Both were dressed in long, dark robes draped with single sashes pinned with dozens of small, reflective ornaments. Their heads were slightly larger than most humans'. A bony spine began at the bridge of their two long nasal slits and ran over the top of their skull. Two smaller ridges ran parallel above each aural opening. Their flesh was brown and their eyes were extremely kind.

The refugees had grouped themselves in small clusters of families and several threw uncertain glances at Seven as she made her way toward the Tamarians.

Commander Paris reached the female a few paces ahead of Seven.

"Ratham?" Paris asked, extending his hand.

"Yes." The woman nodded stiffly as she took it. "Please permit me to welcome you to the Tamarian Embassy on behalf of Ambassador Jarral." At this, she gestured toward the male who smiled openly at his new guests.

"Lakam. In early spring," Jarral said.

"I am Commander Paris and this is Seven," Paris began. "It is very kind of you to allow us to bring our friends to your embassy," he added slowly, as if that would help. Although Seven agreed that the embassy was the best possible hiding place for the refugees, the fact that only Ratham would be able to translate for the Tamarians until Doctor Sharak returned meant that the next several days were going to be a struggle for both sides.

"You accompany Sharak," Ratham said. "You may request anything you wish of us and, if it is ours to give, you will have it."

"Thank you," Paris said.

"Gialee. At Crasa's door," Jarral said to Ratham.

"Of course, Mister Ambassador," Ratham replied. Turning to Paris, she said, "It is a formal moment."

Paris looked to Seven in confusion.

"A formality?" Seven suggested.

Paris shook his head, still uncomprehending.

Seven stepped forward and addressed herself to Jarral. "Mister Ambassador, on behalf of the thirty-three adults and thirteen children most recently inhabiting the planet of Arehaz in the Delta Quadrant, I formally request that the Children of Tama grant them asylum until an imminent threat to their safety has been eliminated."

Jarral nodded toward Ratham, who said, *"Feriar. At Waleesh. With hands open."*

"Tama. Filled with mercy," Jarral finished for her.

"Your request is granted, Miss Seven," Ratham translated.

"Solotep. At midday," the ambassador said loudly, gesturing broadly for them to approach the food.

"Please, eat," Ratham translated, this time, unnecessarily.

A few individuals glanced toward the tables, but no one moved.

"We do not have all we would like to give you," Ratham said, clearly struggling with the words. "This room was not in use, and we have made it a home for now. It was once for dancing. The Children of Tama do not celebrate as humans do. We dance under the stars. But it was the largest here. We will do better tomorrow. We have requested sleeping mats for all. They will come soon."

"This will suffice," Seven said. "You are most kind and generous and we are in your debt."

Ratham smiled. "When will Sharak return?"

"We don't know," Paris replied honestly. "Soon, we hope."

"Solotep. At midday," Jarral said again, gesturing hopefully to the refugees.

Seven turned to see more distrustful glances directed toward her. Squaring her shoulders, she moved back to one of the larger groups.

"Welcome to the Tamarian Embassy," she began. "The Children of Tama are not members of the Federation. They have enjoyed diplomatic relations with the Federation for several years now, and some of their citizens have begun to learn our language, although, as you can see, it is difficult for them.

"You will be safe here. Technically, you are not on Federation soil, although the embassy is located in Paris, on Earth. The Tamarian people have granted you asylum. You cannot be removed from this place without the ambassador's approval, and he will not give that approval without my authorization. Should you step foot outside the gates that border the embassy, you forfeit its protection.

"Resources are limited at this moment. This location was hastily arranged, and over the next few days, Commander Paris will work with the ambassador to make it more comfortable for all of you.

"You may move throughout the embassy as needed, but you will observe any restrictions the ambassador's staff imposes. Also, for now, you will not venture outside of this building. There are substantial grounds surrounding the embassy, but the fencing is quite old and you could easily be seen through it. It is our intention to keep your presence here a secret for as long as possible. Dozens of other embassies line the street where this building is located and foot traffic is heavy during the day."

Finally, Nocks stepped forward. "We understand. Thank you, Seven," he said.

"Please make your home here," Ratham said.

The sound of a lovely stringed instrument began to float among them. Several turned to a corner of the room near the tables, where three more Tamarians sat, unnoticed in the dimness until now. One played a small harp, drawing rich sounds from it using the unusual tip of his long thumb. A second soon picked up the melody on a short flute, and the third accompanied them with tinkling bells.

The melody was simple. The music warmed the room, and soon individuals began to break from the group, led by Nocks, toward the tables.

Paris pulled Seven aside. "Don't worry," he said. "I can fix this."

"It is not perfect, but it will do."

"You won't recognize this place in a few days," Paris assured her. "Tonight will be rough, but it's better than stasis, right?"

"Yes," Seven said, a smile tugging at her lips.

"Icheb's shift ends in a few minutes. Are you still planning to leave tonight?"

"Yes," Seven replied. "I require solitude. That will be impossible to come by here."

"You also require safety, and this is about the only place we can guarantee that."

"I must go, only for a short while," Seven insisted.

"Are you going to tell me where?"

"I don't know if that's wise."

"Humor me, Constance."

Seven sighed. "When we separated from the fleet, the admiral suggested I visit her mother. I do not believe anyone would think to look for me there."

"They might," Paris said. "She's family."

"I was given ten days. Nine remain, and I don't intend to be there long. Briggs is undoubtedly monitoring the runabout and given the falsified life-form readings, will assume I am still on board."

"He's despicable, but he's not an idiot. He's going to see through that ruse eventually," Paris warned.

"Hopefully, by the time he does, it won't matter."

Paris nodded. "Give Mrs. Janeway my best, won't you?"

"Of course."

"If you're not back in three days, I'm coming after you."

Seven nodded, tapped her combadge in a prearranged signal, and seconds later, felt the transporter take hold of her.

7

STARSHIP DEMETER

And there?" Overseer Rascha Bralt asked.

Commander Liam O'Donnell, *Demeter*'s captain and one of the Federation's most esteemed botanical geneticists, scanned the latest sensor display of the Ark Planet's third-largest land mass. "We seeded those plains with a resilient hybrid grass. The growth rates have exceeded even my expectations. But do you see the rise in the *malmut* herds? They're herbivores and apparently they reproduce like rabbits. That population has grown by eight percent in as many weeks. They'll keep the grasses in check. And at least four other species appear to be migrating into the area. That is an example of *healthy* competition, as opposed to what we saw when we first scanned this planet," O'Donnell said.

Turning, O'Donnell checked Bralt's face. To his satisfaction, the typically garrulous Confederacy Overseer of Agriculture was speechless.

Actually, that had been Bralt's default state since they had arrived in orbit of the Ark Planet, or the last *lemm*, several hours earlier.

O'Donnell and his ship had been dispatched by Admiral Janeway to accompany the overseer on a tour of the Confederacy's most productive agricultural worlds. While Bralt had extolled the virtues of their enhanced growth rates, their orbital weather-control stations, and the speed with which their produce was delivered to the appropriate markets within the Confederacy, the commander had been forced to hold his tongue in the interest of maintaining the potential for an alliance between the Federation and the Confederacy.

The accomplishments of Bralt's people were impressive. They were also shortsighted and lacked sufficient diversity to sustain the population of those planets in the event that the markets for their limited produce fell or failed entirely.

The farmers on Femra, the first world Bralt had shown O'Donnell, were rich and growing richer every day. As an object lesson to his XO, Commander Atlee Fife, O'Donnell had asked if *Demeter* might visit a world to which the markets were currently not so kind. The overseer had grudgingly agreed and Fife's tour of Vitrum had opened the young officer's eyes to the pain a market-based economy could inflict on the unfortunate. Vitrum's people, once as prosperous as those on Femra, were barely eking out an existence. The vast majority of the population was starving while their land, in desperate need of nutrients and repurposing, lay fallow.

Bralt had tried to convince O'Donnell and his crew that such privation encouraged the people of the Confederacy to strive daily to better themselves. Many of the inhabitants of Vitrum had accepted this pretty fiction. Bralt had opined that the residents of those worlds could not afford what they required to replenish their soil and make it fertile once again. O'Donnell had wondered what Bralt would do if he realized that entire planets, like Vitrum, could be returned to productive states within weeks using technology the Confederacy already possessed and at a fraction of the cost Bralt had estimated.

Toward that end, O'Donnell had offered to show Bralt the Ark Planet. This was a world more than ten thousand light-years from the First World, located in a region of space the Confederacy's ancestors had pulverized five centuries earlier. The wave forms, or "protectors," they had used to destroy the planets whose resources they required had eventually rebelled when they came to appreciate the presence of life-forms on those planets. In an unprecedented act of defiance, the ancient protectors had begun to rescue the life-forms on planets targeted for destruction and relocate them to the Ark Planet. While their motives had been pure, their understanding of the basics of biology, ecology, and genetics had been sorely lacking.

When *Voyager* had answered a distress call from an ancient protector, they had found the Ark Planet on the verge of dying a most unnatural death. Too many species the protectors had transplanted were unable to survive in their current habitats, and much of the planet already refused to support any life apart from some very hearty fungi. Working with the protectors, *Voyager*'s and *Demeter*'s crews had revived the planet, providing it with several necessary bacterial life-forms, relocating several populations to more suitable habitats, and terraforming otherwise uninhabitable continents.

During their relatively short journey, O'Donnell had shown

Bralt their initial scans of the Ark Planet. Now Bralt was forced to confront its miraculous renewal; a process that had taken O'Donnell's people all of six weeks.

Finally, Bralt sighed deeply and stepped away from the science station, focusing his attention on the bridge's main viewscreen, where the vibrant green-and-blue world spun beneath him.

"The protectors did *all* of this?" Bralt asked.

O'Donnell nodded. "There were, of course, some basic elements we provided to them: seeds, bacteria, annelids. And we directed their efforts. We told them where to plant, where to move the various populations, where to alter weather patterns, where to dig. But they performed the work. Given all they've learned, they can now sustain this planet indefinitely."

"And you believe that our protectors could do the same?"

"They're the same technology, Overseer," O'Donnell reminded him. "You've just never imagined using them in this manner."

For reasons that completely elude me, he did not say aloud.

"And there is no question that utilizing the protectors as we did here would require investments of time and energy precious and valuable to your people. But even if profit is your ultimate goal, small loans of resources to farmers as industrious as Izly and Cemt could be repaid in months."

"With interest," Bralt noted, smiling.

Resisting the urge to punch Bralt in the nose, O'Donnell continued, "And millions of acres that are currently unproductive could return to feeding the people of the Confederacy." When Bralt did not respond, O'Donnell added, "You want your people to work, and they want desperately to contribute to the Confederacy. With the protectors' help, they could. They *will*."

Bralt nodded thoughtfully. Turning back to O'Donnell, he said, "Commander, when you first proposed this journey, I was skeptical. And had I not seen it with my own eyes, I would scarce have believed it."

I know, O'Donnell thought.

"I am ready to return to the Confederacy. We have much to discuss, and I hope you will continue to offer us guidance, should we choose to proceed along the path you have forged for us."

"We'd be happy to," O'Donnell assured him. Nodding to Fife he asked, "Is our return course plotted?"

Fife stood at the tactical station beside Lieutenant Url, his brow furrowed.

"Captain, long-range sensors show six ships approaching our position," Fife said. "Two are Turei, two Devore. We can't identify the others yet."

"I'm ready to go whenever you are, Atlee."

"We can't engage the slipstream drive within the system. At full impulse we're half an hour from safe exit coordinates, and we don't have that much time."

"Options?" O'Donnell asked.

"We could head for the system's star. If we modify our shields temporarily, we could hide near enough to survive the radiation and evade their sensors until they pass us by."

"Have they detected us?" O'Donnell asked.

Fife did not respond, which meant he did not have an answer O'Donnell wanted to hear.

"You should call for the ancient ones," Bralt suggested.

"The last time the ancient ones took control of our vessels, we barely survived our journey to the gateway," Fife said. "We need to return to Vitrum, where the *Jroone* awaits us."

"Ask them to hide you," Bralt said.

"They can do that?" Fife asked.

"It is a standard defensive protocol among the CIF," Bralt replied.

"Atlee," O'Donnell began.

"Summoning a proctor, sir," Fife said, nodding.

A few minutes later, Fife was hard at work dusting off his conversational skills. Given Doctor Sharak's unique facility with the visual "language" of the wave forms, he and Lieutenant Kim had taken point in most of the communication that had transpired between the Federation ships and the protectors during their work on the Ark Planet. Fife had observed them closely and was familiar with most of their standard protocols.

Four ancient proctors answered Fife's initial call. O'Donnell did not start to worry until Fife's second transmission resulted in the appearance of a sentry, one of the wave forms initially programmed to defend the space around the Ark Planet with deadly accuracy.

Fife continued to work diligently, however, and a few minutes later, a familiar hum tickled O'Donnell's spine.

"Our modified sentry is in place," Fife reported.

"And we're still alive," O'Donnell noted. "Well done."

"Two of the alien ships will be within range in nine minutes, sir," Url reported.

"In the meantime, perhaps you would join me in your mess hall, Commander?" Bralt suggested. "I am anxious to sample the berries and cream you told me about."

O'Donnell looked to Fife, who shrugged. "The proctors say we're cloaked, sir," he reported.

If they weren't, it would be Atlee's job to deal with *Demeter*'s tactical response. Aboard *Demeter*, O'Donnell and Fife shared command, each taking charge as dictated by their respective strengths.

"I can think of worse last meals," O'Donnell said, and gestured for Bralt to precede him to the bridge's exit. "Atlee, the bridge is yours."

"Thank you, sir," Fife replied, stepping down to the center seat.

Nine minutes later, the first vessels passed close enough to *Demeter* to read her hull markings without altering course or pausing to investigate. Four more followed in the next fifteen minutes.

Despite their newfound sense of security, long-range sensors continued to pick up additional ship movements through the system and Fife was forced to report to O'Donnell that it would be several hours at least before *Demeter* could safely return to the Confederacy.

STARSHIP GALEN

Lieutenant Reginald Barclay had made locating Meegan his only priority for months. Now that she had been found, he wanted to shift his focus to separating the Seriareen consciousness that had taken his hologram from the original program. He knew that "Meegan" was lost forever. But that didn't mean that the technology he had created should be left to the alien who had stolen it.

He was now forced to set this aside until his friend the Doctor was functioning optimally again. He'd been analyzing the Doctor's program for more than a day and *optimal* remained elusive.

Barclay had been chastised in years past for his affinity for holograms. Once, he had preferred their company to flesh and blood people. Counselor Troi, in particular, had worked tirelessly with Reg to assist him in forming deeper relationships with his fellow officers, and he counted many of the *Enterprise*'s and *Voyager*'s crew as friends.

But his affection for the Doctor was not evidence of relapse. The Doctor was a unique hologram. Although his original program design had been widely disseminated for multiple applications throughout Starfleet, the Doctor's experiences in the Delta Quadrant during *Voyager*'s maiden trek had allowed him to surpass his programming. Some of the alterations had been simple upgrades, but most were the result of constant interactions with the crew that gave him a deeper understanding of humanity than most holograms enjoyed. The Doctor was now much more than a collection of subroutines and processors. He was now a sentient being who just happened to exist as photonic energy rather than organic matter.

Barclay had been relieved to learn of Admiral Kathryn Janeway's rescue several hours earlier, but was surprised by her unheralded arrival at the *Galen*'s holographic lab.

"Admiral," he said, rising immediately to his feet.

"Hello, Reg," she said, smiling.

"Admiral, I . . ." he began, but faltered. Finally, he found a sticking place for his courage, embracing her with unreserved happiness. "Forgive me." She returned the gesture patiently.

"It's good to see you too, Reg. I'm due aboard the *Vesta* for a briefing but I wanted to check in. How is he?"

Barclay shook his head. "Hard to tell."

"Did Doctor Zimmerman's modification to the Doctor's memory centers cause his cascade failure?" Janeway asked.

"I don't think so," Barclay replied. "I'd run several diagnostics on the Doctor's program prior to the disruption Captain Chakotay witnessed and quite wisely interrupted. We might have lost the Doctor entirely if the captain hadn't shut his program down when he did.

"Now that I've read Doctor Z's file, the variances I found in those diagnostics make sense. They indicate that the new program was working as intended for the most part."

"For the most part?" Janeway asked.

"The purpose of the modification was to mitigate the Doctor's emotional distress given Seven's new personal circumstances by 'muting' the otherwise incredibly vivid memories of their shared experiences that were in his long-term memory files. Memories that produced intense emotional responses when accessed were segregated in a separate buffer. Any significant factual data was retained, but the memory could no longer be recalled in perfect detail. The Doctor wouldn't be able to replay or relive a segregated experience. At the same time, a program similar to an endorphin response was activated to ease any confusion the Doctor might experience by the 'loss' of a specific memory."

"The information contained in the memories remained intact, but they lost their impact," Janeway clarified.

"Yes. But the segregated memory buffer did not function as intended. Any time the Doctor accessed a previously muted memory, he should have been able to grasp the facts, without the emotional relevance. But the volume of memories transferred to the buffer was greater than Doctor Zimmerman anticipated. It overloaded and the muted files degraded rapidly. Many have been lost entirely. Understand, the Doctor has countless memories of Seven, a lot of them mundane. There's no danger that he's going to forget who she is, and her medical files were not subject to the modification, so he hasn't lost any significant data in that respect.

"In addition, none of the Doctor's other subroutines were

impaired by the modifications. He was functioning normally. To anyone who knew him well, he might have seemed a little off, more abrupt than usual, but I think that's because he was unaware of the modification. He must have sensed the change, but had no control over it. It would have frightened him, were it not for the dopamine effect easing the transition. And from time to time, when he tried to access specific memories that had already been lost, other similar memories were randomly accessed, creating a sense of confusion.

"As best I can tell, he was managing whatever internal dissonance the modification created. His work on the catomic plague is evidence that he was capable of continuing to function. There was some minor corruption in his ethical subroutines, but that was created by several attempts to reach conclusions regarding moral judgments in the sudden absence of all relevant data."

"So what happened?"

"I don't know," Barclay admitted. "Just prior to the onset of the cascade failure, there was an unusual energy surge from the holographic mainframe into his matrix. That could have resulted in the majority of the damage I'm seeing. If it did, we need to find the cause and repair it. Then we need to decide how to proceed from here."

"What are our options?"

"I've already repaired his program and begun to restore his unmodified long-term memories. He won't be himself again until that process is complete. I can't eliminate the modification. I'd have to rebuild his program completely and if I do that, we'd lose much more than his memories of Seven. But I should be able to expand and stabilize the segregated buffer so that all of the data transferred there remains intact and any new memories that are segregated won't be lost."

"Is the Doctor able to choose which memories are transferred to that buffer?" Janeway asked.

"Not right now. It's automated. Any memory of Seven that creates substantial emotional impact is muted and transferred."

"Could you change that?"

"How?"

"While I remain troubled by Zimmerman's methods, I do understand what he was trying to achieve. It wouldn't be the worst thing in the world if the Doctor's memory worked more like ours does. Over time, the emotional impact of traumatic experiences fades. This makes it easier for us to put them in a larger context, to gain the perspective required to accept the past and to release it."

"I could add an autonomous subroutine," Barclay realized. "Each time a memory was flagged to be transferred, I could allow the Doctor to decide whether or not to segregate it."

"Could you also give him the option to delete his segregated memories?"

"Do you really think that's wise? Even *we* can't do that."

"If the Doctor is going to continue to grow as a sentient being, it's essential that he have as much autonomy over his program as we can give him. That should include the ability to let go of the past when he's ready. Deletion is not a perfect solution, but it's the closest we can come given the technology we're working with."

"Okay," Barclay agreed.

"As soon as you reactivate him, I want you to bring Counselor Cambridge in to consult."

"Why?"

"His creator, his *father* in a way, essentially just assaulted him. By removing the Doctor's wishes from the equation, Zimmerman treated him more like a malfunctioning replicator than a sentient being. In addition, the Doctor has lost many significant memories and a great deal of emotional context surrounding one of the most significant personal relationships he's ever had. We can't fix that. And a few days ago, a power surge almost fried his matrix. He's been through a lot, and up until now, he's dealt with it alone. The nature of his existence has already been altered without his permission. We're going to give him more control over his program to soften the blow, but we need to make sure he's going to use that control responsibly. He's going to need help coming to grips with all of this."

"I agree," Barclay said, "but do you really think Counselor Cambridge is the right person to help the Doctor resolve these issues?"

"He's the best counselor in the fleet."

"He's also the source of the Doctor's distress. And to be honest, I don't think the counselor thinks as highly of the Doctor as he should."

Janeway shook her head. "Whatever the counselor's personal feelings, he will set them aside. He knows his duty. I will brief him and as soon as you believe the Doctor is ready, Counselor Cambridge will join you on the *Galen* to begin his treatment."

"Won't you require the counselor to continue assisting you with the Confederacy?"

"For now, this is a higher priority," Janeway replied. "Oh, and Lieutenant," she added, "I've only spoken briefly with the essence now inhabiting Meegan, but according to her, three of the original seven canisters she took are on that asteroid you found."

Barclay nodded. "Thank you for telling me, Admiral."

"You've done excellent work, Reg. Keep it up."

"I will, Admiral."

VESTA

Captain Chakotay awaited Admiral Janeway's arrival with Captain Farkas, Commander Glenn, and Counselor Cambridge. As the admiral dismissed her aide, Decan, at the door and entered the *Vesta*'s large briefing room, tension writ plainly on her face, he should have felt relief. Instead, for reasons he refused to examine too deeply, Chakotay found that he was steeling himself mentally for a new battle.

Captain Farkas was the first to step forward to greet the admiral. Janeway quickly took her hand and smiled reassuringly. After nodding to Glenn and Counselor Cambridge, she turned to face Chakotay. Their eyes met and with a single glance she read his trepidation and determination, acknowledged it with a subtle nod, and allowed the mask of command to once again fall firmly into place.

"We have a great deal to discuss," Janeway began. "Let's take our seats."

The group settled themselves around one of the room's three smaller tables that comfortably accommodated six. In a fairly radical departure from protocol, Captain Farkas had placed plates of fruit, cheese, and small sandwiches before them, along with tall glasses of water.

"I don't know about the rest of you, but I haven't eaten since yesterday," the *Vesta*'s captain noted. "Did the *Kinara* offer you a last meal before they escorted you into that farce of a tribunal?" she asked of the admiral.

"No," Janeway replied, reaching for a sandwich as the others filled small plates for themselves. "Delicious and much appreciated," she added after a few bites. Chakotay expected her to rise and replicate a cup of coffee before continuing, but to his surprise, she washed her quick meal down with water before nodding that she was ready to get down to business.

"Lieutenant Decan summarized the fleet's status as soon as I came aboard," Janeway began, "but I'd appreciate a quick report from each of you."

Farkas responded, "*Vesta* is at ninety-eight percent of nominal. To all intents and purposes, she is fully operational."

"So is *Galen*," Glenn noted.

Janeway nodded toward Glenn before her eyes settled on Chakotay. "*Voyager* is at least three days from completing repairs," he reported. "B'Elanna is coordinating with Lieutenant Bryce to replicate some of the larger components we need to replace the deflector dish, and the presider has also offered to supply us with any resources we might require."

"Free of charge?" Cambridge asked.

"For now," Chakotay replied.

"That's interesting," Farkas observed.

"And *Demeter*?" Janeway asked.

"Should have returned to the First World yesterday," Chakotay said, shaking his head. "Our last intelligence came from the CIF indicating that Commander O'Donnell had taken Overseer Bralt on board and activated his slipstream drive to make a quick run to the Ark Planet."

"Why?"

Chakotay shrugged. "You'll have to ask him that, Admiral."

Janeway exhaled, slowly tempering her frustration. "Decan mentioned a discovery the Doctor made regarding the catomic plague prior to being deactivated," she said.

Chakotay nodded. "During our mission to Lecahn, the Doctor studied all the evidence we have on the catomic plague. He is convinced, and his evidence was compelling, that Starfleet Medical may be using the plague as some sort of cover for their true intention: to weaponize catoms."

"That's quite an accusation," Janeway said, stunned.

"He re-created the plague," Chakotay continued. "He also discovered that the only potential cure lies in completely reprogramming catomic matter, something he assures me we are years from being able to do. Containment is the only viable option at this point."

"Then why did they need Seven?"

"To access her catoms," Chakotay replied.

"But *not* for her assistance in curing the plague," Cambridge added pointedly.

"Not according to the Doctor," Chakotay continued. "He was understandably upset when he first reported this to me. He asked that I find a way to forward his research to Seven, and I'd still like to do that."

"As would I," Cambridge echoed.

"Oh, we will," Janeway assured him.

Satisfied on this count, Chakotay asked, "Have you spoken with Presider Cin?"

"Yes," Janeway replied. "She's agreed to a joint meeting with myself and Lsia to discuss her request."

"What request?" Farkas asked.

Janeway sighed. "Apparently the Seriareen homeworld lies somewhere in Confederacy space. Lsia said that they came here hoping to convince the Confederacy to allow them to visit it."

"Huh," Farkas mused.

"If I didn't know better, I'd think that someone had been reading our personal logs and determined the best possible way to earn our sympathy," Cambridge said. "Oh . . . wait . . . that's exactly what happened, isn't it?"

"That is entirely possible," Janeway agreed.

"Did she happen to tell you where her other four friends are making their home?" Cambridge asked.

"She said three containers are buried near New Talax. The fourth was lost."

"You don't trust her, do you?" Chakotay asked.

"Not as far as I could throw her," Janeway replied. "She prevented whoever has taken Kashyk from killing me, but she stood by as he murdered Rigger Meeml in cold blood. She also insinuated that she still controls several ships that could enter this area at any time and resume hostilities."

"The *Lightcarrier* escaped during the battle," Chakotay said. "The original *Kinara* members will know soon enough that their alliance with Meegan, or *Lsia*, was a mistake. But most of the Turei, Devore, and Vaadwaur ships were destroyed. There's no one left to tell them they were duped into attacking the Confederacy other than the *Manticle*, but I'd be surprised if the Confederacy doesn't end up destroying the ship and executing her crew."

"I plan to take that up with the presider," Janeway noted. "Didn't the Voth ship escape as well?"

"Yes, and they might advise their new friends of developments here, but they might not," Chakotay observed. "When last seen they were trying to destroy their former allies."

"We have to be sure," Farkas said.

"Agreed," Janeway said, nodding. "In fact, that's going to be part of your job, Captain Farkas."

"Part, Admiral?"

"As soon as you are ready, you are to take the *Vesta* to the Ark Planet to find *Demeter*. You will relay my order to Commander O'Donnell that he return Overseer Bralt immediately."

"And if he's not there?"

"Go back to her last known coordinates. If she hasn't returned or made her way to the First World by that time, you will abandon the search."

"Admiral?" Chakotay asked.

"I doubt the Skeen, Karlon, Emleath, or Muk will return any time soon, and if they do, it won't be to aid their former allies," Janeway said. "But that might not be true of the Turei, Vaadwaur, Devore, or Voth, especially since they know we are now working with the Confederacy against them.

"You'll start with the Turei," Janeway advised Farkas. "You will provide them with copies of the transmissions of my tribunal and our records of the battle that followed. Hopefully that will convince them to reconsider their allegiance and abandon their mission."

"And then we'll share the good news with the Vaadwaur?" Farkas asked.

Janeway nodded.

"What about the Devore and the Voth?" Farkas asked.

"I'm not sending the *Vesta* alone into either of those territories."

"We're coming in peace, with critical intelligence for them," Farkas reminded her.

"We'll have to find another way to share that intelligence," Janeway said. "I'm hoping that the Devore and Voth will hear of it from the survivors of the battle. In both cases a direct assault is simply too dangerous."

"I tend to agree," Farkas said, "but they could be Lsia's most powerful assets."

"I know she convinced them to follow her here, but I will be amazed if she can hold on to them now that her secret is out. I'm just as concerned that the Devore and Voth will send reinforcements to finish off Lsia and those she corrupted. Time will tell," Janeway said.

Farkas nodded.

"Once you've made contact with the Turei and Vaadwaur, you are to return to the rendezvous point and transmit the Doctor's findings to Seven."

"It may be too late by then, Admiral," Cambridge interjected.

Janeway turned to face Cambridge. "Counselor, how well do you know Seven?"

The admiral saw embarrassment pass over his face and immediately wished she'd phrased the question differently, but Janeway forged ahead. "Seven probably already knows what the Doctor has found. She's likely a few steps ahead of all of us right now. We will honor the Doctor's request, but don't underestimate Seven's abilities. She's one of the most brilliant individuals I have ever had the pleasure to know."

"You'll get no argument from me on that, Admiral," Cambridge said.

"And then?" Farkas asked.

"It is my hope that this matter will be resolved by then." Janeway ordered, "You'll either find the fleet, or some word from us waiting there for you. Barring that, return to New Talax and transmit a full report of our status to Command and await further orders from Admiral Montgomery."

"*Vesta* is not coming back to the Confederacy?"

"We're not going to solve this through force of arms. We're outnumbered, outgunned, and unable to completely trust any of the other players on the field. We will do what we can to assist Lsia until we are able to either separate her from our hologram and the others from the bodies they have taken, or determined that to do so is impossible. Once that's done, so is our work here."

"If that's how you really feel, Admiral," Chakotay said, "why don't we simply ask the Confederacy to turn the Seriareen over to our custody and leave as soon as *Voyager* is repaired?"

Janeway turned to him. "I did. They intend to execute them, which strikes me as dangerous and short-sighted."

"Dangerous?" Cambridge asked.

"The Neyser told you that these entities were immortal, and

Lsia confirmed it. We may kill the bodies of their current hosts, or destroy Lsia's holographic generator, but the essences would simply attack the nearest available host and pick up where they left off," Janeway replied.

"Could we transport them into the middle of a singularity and take our chances?" Cambridge asked.

"Even if that would work, their current hosts are innocent," Janeway argued.

"You don't know that," Chakotay said. "Maybe they agreed to become hosts."

"I *saw* Kashyk," Janeway admitted. "At least I think I did. I believe he's still in there and still fighting."

"And still the Federation's enemy unless I missed a memo," Cambridge said.

"Yes, but we don't *execute* our enemies," Janeway replied.

"Unlike the Confederacy," Chakotay said. "You haven't heard my report on Lecahn yet, Admiral."

"It didn't go well?" Janeway guessed.

"The Seriareen aren't the only ones out here who don't seem to struggle with cold-blooded murder."

Janeway began to massage her forehead. "What happened?"

"We came under attack by a group called the Unmarked. They're from the planet Grysyen, a member of the Confederacy that seems to have some valid and disturbing issues with the central government. I captured the crew of one vessel that made a suicide run on *Voyager*. I interrogated them briefly and advised Mattings that I would release them to his custody if he would assure me that they would be able to air their grievances and receive a fair trial. He recaptured them and executed them on the spot. The CIF calls them terrorists. I call them . . ."

"Maquis?" Cambridge asked.

Chakotay shook his head. "To hear them tell it, they are citizens of the Confederacy that tried to work through proper channels and are now being mercilessly oppressed. I'm not sure who is in the right, but the general's choice solved nothing."

Silence descended for a few moments. Finally, Janeway said,

"I am under no illusion that the Federation will be able to form an alliance with the Confederacy anytime in the foreseeable future."

"Then we should move on," Chakotay argued. "We're wasting time and resources here better spent continuing our investigations of the rest of the Delta Quadrant."

"*Voyager* can't fly right now and *Demeter* is AWOL," Janeway reminded him. "And I gave my word to Lsia that I would help her."

"You said whatever you needed to in order to survive while you were their prisoner. No one is going to hold you to that now."

"The Confederacy might," Janeway noted.

Chakotay shrugged. "So we need to buy ourselves a little time. We can keep up the pretense of good faith negotiations for a few days, devise a means to hold Lsia and the others, capture them if we must, and be on our way."

Janeway considered the proposition, but shook her head. "No," she said simply.

"Due respect, Admiral, why not?" Chakotay asked. "None of these people are our friends or allies. They've demonstrated varying levels of barbarity and deception from day one. We're not here to bring peace to the Delta Quadrant. We're here to explore. We've investigated the potential for an alliance and found it to be impossible. We are responsible for ending any threat the Seriareen pose, and this is the best way to do that without further conflict."

"Do we embrace deception?" Janeway asked.

"We prioritize *our* safety and *our* needs," Chakotay clarified.

Janeway looked to the others. "Thoughts?" she asked. "Speak freely."

"I'm with Chakotay on this one," Cambridge said quickly. "We did everything in our power to find common ground with the Confederacy. Our fleet is too small to take on the CIF should they refuse to release the Seriareen. If we have to embellish the truth to get what we need, so be it."

Glenn asked, "Are you absolutely certain, Admiral, that no exchange of technology between us and the Confederacy will be possible?"

"I fear not," Janeway replied.

Glenn nodded somberly. Chakotay did not know what the young commander might have been hoping for but she quickly resolved herself to reality. "It's entirely possible that in the time it will take to repair *Voyager* we'll know *Demeter*'s status. Once that's settled, I agree, we should move on," she finally said.

Janeway turned to Farkas. "Captain?"

Farkas clasped her hands and brought them to her lips, her elbows resting on the table. She looked past Janeway, lost in thought for a few moments, then said, "I see your point, Captain Chakotay, and a couple of days ago, I tried to make a similar case. But not now. This isn't just about who the Confederacy has shown themselves to be, or the depravity of the Seriareen. It's about who we are. Admiral Janeway spent the day staring down the business end of a disruptor and still managed to destroy the *Kinara*'s alliance simply by telling the truth. She asked everyone in earshot to open themselves up to the possibility that by working together, we could find a way through this that might be acceptable to all parties concerned. That took strength, character, and courage. The admiral stood there and made a case for the values that lie at the heart of our Federation and the principles we all agreed to uphold when we joined Starfleet. If we run now, we may survive, but who are we? When the Confederacy tells others about us, what will they say? Will they remember us as technologically advanced liars? Will they encourage others to trust us?

"*Voyager* made a lot of hard choices the first time she was out here. We're here to correct misconceptions, not create new ones.

"If we're going to go down, I'd prefer we do it fighting the right battle. I know this isn't the one we came looking for, but it's found us. We're in too deep to pretend our responsibilities are as cut-and-dried as you're suggesting. I don't know what it will cost us if we stay. But the admiral gave her word. And I'm not comfortable advising her to betray it or to negotiate in bad faith."

Janeway smiled faintly. "There is no question we must proceed cautiously. I will consider all you have said. Until then, we focus on our immediate concerns."

When no one raised further objections, Janeway dismissed Glenn and Farkas and asked Chakotay and the Counselor to remain behind.

After spending a few moments speaking privately to Counselor Cambridge, Janeway dismissed him and turned toward Chakotay. He had risen from the table and stood staring out the briefing room's long port at the numerous CIF vessels now patrolling the area.

"Chakotay."

He turned, but did not move to her. "Are you planning to resume your counseling sessions with Hugh?" he asked.

Janeway paused, wondering at his accusatory tone.

"Now that you mention it, that probably wouldn't be the worst idea. But I needed to speak with him now about the Doctor."

"How is he?"

"It's complicated," she replied. "Barclay is working on it. I want him to bring Counselor Cambridge in to assist him as soon as the Doctor is ready."

"Why?"

"There's only so much Reg can fix. Some of it, the Doctor needs to work through the old-fashioned way."

Chakotay waited for her to continue. Finally, he said, "You're still not going to tell me what's really going on with the Doctor."

"This isn't about us, Chakotay. Please don't take my silence as evidence of a lack of trust. To share more than I have might be embarrassing to the Doctor. I respect him too much for that. At some point, when he's had a chance to find some peace, he may be willing to discuss it with you. I will encourage him to do so. But I won't betray his confidence."

"Okay," Chakotay said. "Is there anything else?"

He might not have intended that question to sting, but it did.

"It's been quite a day," she managed. "I thought we should

take a few minutes to talk. Obviously, we both have a lot on our plates, so if you'd rather not . . ."

Chakotay shook his head. "Of course I . . ." he began, then paused, searching for the right words. "I don't understand your insistence on *helping* Lsia. Are you more worried about our technology, or about Kashyk?"

"I beg your pardon."

"I know you were fond of him. I know how much his betrayal hurt you. But not every soul you encounter is yours to save. Even if you can separate him from the Seriareen now wearing his face, do you honestly believe he wouldn't try to kill you, the first chance you gave him?"

"That isn't the point. The Seriareen are a new life-form. We've never come across anything like them. It is our duty to learn all we can about them. And who is to say that assisting them now with the Confederacy might not lead us to a better solution than simply tossing them out an airlock or watching General Mattings do it for us."

"They tried to kill you, Kathryn. I had to stand by helpless and watch, hoping you knew what you were doing."

"They were trying to use me to drive a wedge between the Federation and the Confederacy."

"And if it hadn't meant losing you, that wouldn't bother me. You know an alliance is impossible, but part of you still wants it, don't you? Are you trying to prove something to Command or just hoping that the writing on the wall is going to change?"

"What's wrong with you?" she demanded. "I appreciate what you've been through, but you're out of line."

"Where's the line, Kathryn? I'll follow your orders. I always have. But I won't stand here and watch you throw away our lives in the name of pride. What was I supposed to think when you turned yourself over to be executed without so much as a backward glance?"

Janeway took a few breaths to calm herself before responding. "I don't think I'll ever know how much of my choice to turn myself over to the *Kinara* came from a sense of duty to the fleet, or the existential horror I felt seeing *Voyager* seconds away from annihilation when I knew I had the power to stop it."

"You ordered us into battle, Admiral. Don't do it again, unless you're prepared to live with any outcome."

Janeway shook her head in disbelief. "I thought you understood how this has to be. I decided once that loving you while serving as your commanding officer was too much to risk. You convinced me I was wrong. This was a bad day. But we're going to have those from time to time. If we can't accept them and move on, this isn't going to work."

"You keep saying that. You keep questioning this choice we've both made. And just when I think we've settled the issue, you pull back again. You're right. *That isn't going to work.*

"If you want me to support your decision to put this fleet at a greater risk than I believe is necessary or wise, you need to give me more than platitudes about duty and honor. I need to know in my bones that you are as committed as I am to keeping our people safe. Your insistence on aiding Lsia and continuing to court the goodwill of the Confederacy smacks of recklessness. We don't need to prove anything to them. They have been weighed, measured, and found wanting."

"What if Lsia is telling the truth?"

"I don't care. She could have asked us for help the first day we met her. Had she done so, we would have done whatever we could to assist her. But she didn't. Instead, she spent months building a fleet big enough to destroy us and to force her way into the sovereign territory of the Confederacy. What do you think she intends to do if she finds her homeworld?"

"I don't know," Janeway admitted. "I asked you to stay because when I go to speak with her in a few hours, I wanted you to come with me. When that conversation is over, I'll have to make a decision. I wanted your input, but I felt it might be more constructive if it was informed by your direct impressions."

Chakotay paused, clearly surprised. "Oh."

"I'll advise you when I'm to depart," Janeway said, turning to go.

"Kathryn."

"I'll be transferring to *Voyager* when *Vesta* is clear to leave. Please ask Lieutenant Kim to prepare quarters for me," she added before continuing out the door.

8

INDIANA

It was the middle of the night, local time, when Seven arrived at the end of a long dirt road that led to Gretchen Janeway's home. Prior to her departure from the fleet, Admiral Janeway had told Seven that if she needed anything, she should contact her mother. The two women had met several times during Seven's years on Earth, the last at Admiral Janeway's memorial service.

Even with the invitation, Seven could not conscience rousing Gretchen from her sleep. She had no intention of availing herself of Gretchen's generous hospitality for several hours and chose to turn off the road well before it reached the large house that rested on the southern edge of the vast property.

To her left, behind the house, the moon lit a large, freshly planted vegetable garden. Beyond that, rows of fruit trees in bloom stood in straight lines for several hundred meters. Seven sought out a well-worn path east of the orchard. Admiral Janeway had brought her this way the first time Seven had visited Gretchen's home. Carved through tall grass, the path led to an ancient willow tree that figured prominently in the admiral's childhood.

Seven had no difficulty locating the tree, its limbs overflowing with pale pink flowers. Seating herself at its base, rather than attempting to balance on a large low limb the admiral had favored, she rested her back against its solid, reassuring trunk.

She could easily have closed her eyes and allowed sleep to over-take her within minutes.

But there was simply too much to be done.

In some ways, the land reminded her of her aunt Irene's farm. Here, as there, it was relatively easy to forget that anyone else inhabited the planet. The low moaning of the wind stirring the fragrant grass was not intrusive. It added to the necessary sense of isolation.

Breathing deeply, Seven turned her attention to the mental defenses she had erected as soon as she had left Starfleet Medical. In the moments immediately following her release from stasis, Axum had been able to enter her mind and speak at will. She knew this would come in handy eventually, but had needed to put some distance between them as she arranged for the trans-port of Riley's people. The feeling of being constantly observed was unnerving.

Now she needed the walls to come down. In the past, this visualization might have been challenging. Meditation was an art form that required patient practice to master, and she had not devoted herself to it with appropriate rigor. But her new awareness of her catoms seemed to make up for her lack of dili-gence. Almost as soon as she decided she wished to speak with Axum and Riley, they appeared vividly in her mind's eye.

For the last several weeks, she and Axum had shared a con-joined thought space made manifest by Axum's catoms. If she returned to stasis, Seven did not doubt she would find herself there again in the living quarters she had mistaken for a Starfleet facility. As the only conscious one of the three of them, however, she found she had more control over their shared environment. She placed them near her, standing in the tall grass.

"Where are we?" Riley Frazier asked immediately.

"The home of one of Annika's friends," Axum replied, clearly uninhibited by Seven's request that he refrain from pulling infor-mation she had not directly shared with him from her mind. It was no longer necessary, but would still have been a polite gesture on his part. As Axum's need to master his catoms grew,

however, so did his disregard for any barriers both Seven and Riley would have preferred remain between them.

"Are you well?" Seven asked aloud.

"The Commander has continued to test our catoms," Riley said. *"But the pain is better. Axum has shown me how to separate from it. It is still there. But I no longer seem to mind that it is there."*

"That is good," Seven said. "The Commander agreed to refrain from testing the catoms of the rest of your people for the time being."

"They are safe now," Riley said, not a question.

"They are," Seven confirmed. "But we must make the Commander's need to use their catoms irrelevant."

"How?" Riley asked.

"If the others will not open themselves to us, we can still use our catoms to access theirs. The sensation would be briefly disorienting, but soon enough they would come to accept its necessity," Axum suggested.

"We do not require them to aid us at this time," Seven said firmly. "We will not violate their minds or bodies. They have suffered enough."

Both Seven and Riley felt a wave of disapproval wash over them, but Axum did not verbalize his disagreement for the time being.

"It is, however, essential that the three of us continue the work Axum has begun by testing the limits of our catomic abilities," Seven continued.

"To what end?" Riley demanded. *"While I do not share the distaste of my companions for catomic contact, I worry that the more we interact in this manner, the harder it will become to sever our present connection. Our catoms appear to be acting in accordance with our wishes, but—"*

"Catoms are meant to bridge the divide between thought and matter," Axum interrupted. *"That they exist in discrete organic containers is irrelevant to them. We are not forcing our individual catoms to do anything. They are leading us toward their most efficient and powerful state. Our only task is to open ourselves up to this reality and accept it."*

Neither Riley nor Seven responded immediately. Finally, Riley said, *"You see the problem?"*

Seven did. Axum was convinced that all individuals who had been left with functioning catoms by the Caeliar were intended to exist in some sort of new, small gestalt. That this would so horrify Riley, who had forced her own people back into a linked state using Borg technology long before the Caeliar transformation, was as ironic as it was understandable. She knew this monster's name and precise dimensions.

Both Riley and Seven understood the value of individuality. Those who remained with Riley after the transformation to care for their young children who had been born free of Borg technology had come to cherish theirs as well. Axum's experiences for several years prior to the gift of the Caeliar and in the months that followed had been more difficult. He had lived for too long as a Borg who retained the memories of his life prior to assimilation. His daily existence had been torture. That had been compounded by the personal attention of the Borg Queen, who had attempted to drive Axum to suicide once he had destroyed his scout vessel and set course for a Federation facility. She had all but succeeded.

Axum had few memories of individuality that were not accompanied by intense psychological torment. That he was seeking to use his catoms to re-create a joined state, one which unconsciously gave him a perverse sense of comfort, was hardly surprising.

It was also unacceptable. But this was not the time for that conversation.

"If you do not wish to assist me, Doctor Frazier, I will understand," Seven said. "It may make the work ahead more challenging, but you should not participate against your will."

Seven felt the conflicting emotions with which Riley was struggling. She was relieved when Riley said, *"Explain your intentions."*

"While I have no desire to seek interaction with the catoms of the rest of your people," Seven began, "we must learn if it is possible for us to contact and affect the catoms that have been removed from our bodies."

"They are ours," Axum said. *"Their location beyond our physical bodies is irrelevant."*

"Commander Briggs is modifying them and injecting them into test subjects under the auspices of using them to cure the catomic plague. If we can neutralize them without his knowledge, we can end the threat they pose to those who are receiving them."

"And once we have mastered our own catoms, we can seek out the others that have mutated," Axum realized.

"One step at a time," Seven cautioned him.

A blinding light struck Seven's face with the force of a physical blow as a feminine voice tinged with familiar steel said, "I don't know who you are or what the hell you think you're doing out here, but you'd better get up and . . . Seven?"

"Mrs. Janeway," Seven replied, clambering to her feet. Despite the sudden interruption, her link with Axum and Riley remained present and strong. Raising a hand to assure Janeway's mother that she meant no harm, Seven said, "I will speak with you again as soon as possible."

"Do not fear, Annika. We will comply," Axum said. The intensity of his pleasure at Seven's request chilled her as much as it comforted her.

Gretchen had stepped closer and was almost upon her when she felt Axum and Riley slip from her conscious mind. "Why don't you speak with me right now?" Gretchen asked. Sweeping her hand beacon across the grass beyond the tree, she added, "Are you alone out here?"

"I apologize for appearing here without prior contact or your permission," Seven said. "I have come alone."

Gretchen nodded. "All right, then." Seven noticed for the first time that in one hand, the octogenarian held a phaser. Gretchen deposited it in the pocket of the long, suede jacket she wore over her nightclothes. She then extended her free hand to Seven, who took it and shook it lightly.

"Did you just come to visit the old willow tree?" Grechen asked, bemused. "Kathryn said you might be stopping by, but I figured you had come and gone from Earth by now."

Seven steeled herself internally. She believed she could trust Gretchen Janeway implicitly, and she was about to learn if she was right. "It is a rather long story," she began. "I need to disappear for a few days. Starfleet is currently unaware of my location, although a trusted fellow officer knows where I am. Your daughter suggested I come, but I arrived so late I did not wish to wake you."

"Well, I'm up now," Gretchen said with a smirk. "I can offer leftovers and a warm bed for the rest of the night. You can tell me now or never what's brought you here. Kathryn trusts you, so I trust you. And anything you need from me that I can provide is yours."

"Thank you, Mrs. Janeway."

"If I've told you once, I've told you ten times, Seven. It's Gretchen."

"Gretchen."

"Let's get inside."

Seven fell into step beside her as they made their way back to the house.

"It was your voice that woke me," Gretchen said. "I know all of the sounds of this place at night by heart. And I guess I don't sleep as deeply as I used to."

"Again, I apologize for waking you."

"Don't," Gretchen said. "I'm happy you're here." Smiling openly, she added, "It's nice to be needed."

STARFLEET MEDICAL

"Hello, Jefferson."

"Good afternoon, Naria," the Commander greeted his patient. *More than his patient.*

Naria was his most stunning scientific accomplishment. That no one else could ever know of her existence did not disturb him. Glory had never been a consideration. His duty to science ranked well above the esteem of his peers, and Naria's existence had long ago transitioned from an end result to a necessary tool in rising to that duty.

His ultimate goal was to use his gifts for research and esoteric scientific applications, cultivated over years of industrious labor to safeguard both Starfleet and the Federation.

Naria was a critical component in his work. That he felt pride in her existence was understandable. She was physically stunning to behold. Long jet-black hair framed a well-proportioned face. Her skin was a light lavender hue at the moment, but was most beautiful in its natural state of tranquil pink. She was draped in a patient's gown, but beneath that gown was a well-toned frame any human woman would have envied and many men would have coveted.

To the Commander, she was his child, his creation. *Never an object of desire.* She was also characteristically tense, as was customary during these sessions.

The bio-suit he wore made communication through subtle visual clues difficult, but as always, he did his best to calm her as he removed a hypospray from his case.

"Will it hurt?" she asked for the thousandth time.

"Only a little," he assured her.

This time, he had cause to believe those words. Seven had not intended to leave him with enough information to make much progress until she returned eight days from now. But even the few clues she had dropped about the nature of the catoms—whose potential he was striving to unlock—had been enough to suggest dozens of new approaches in his work.

Naria lay down, awaiting the administration of the hypo.

The Commander took a deep breath, rechecked her vitals one last time on the display panel to his left, and lifted the hypo to her neck.

Her initial reaction was instantaneous. The flesh of her face began to ripple—usually a bad sign—and soon the effect spread down her limbs. Confusion registered on her face, followed by fear.

"Jefferson?" she gurgled.

Faint alarms began to sound as one vital system after another was stressed beyond its normal capacity. Fifteen seconds after the injection had been given, Briggs stepped back, readying himself to step through the airlock to the lab's exterior controls, where he could quickly and efficiently eliminate all evidence of his latest failure.

At the nineteen second mark, the alarms ceased. Perplexed, the Commander stepped closer to Naria and realized that her skin had stabilized. In fact, it had shifted from lavender to a light shade of rose.

"How do you feel, Naria?" he asked.

A lazy smile spread across her lips.

"Fine," she replied.

Before the Commander could commence the necessary diagnostics, a beep sounded through the comm system of his suit.

"Observation to the Commander," a confident male voice said.

"Go ahead."

"The Coleman *has departed the Sol system. We will continue to track her progress as requested."*

"Life signs?" the Commander asked.

"All present and accounted for."

"The shadow?"

"In position and ready to transport Coleman*'s cargo aboard on your order."*

"Very good," the Commander said, closing his comm link.

Should Seven keep her word, there would be no reason to modify their agreement. It pleased him that thus far, she seemed to be doing just that. It elated him to think that if Naria remained stable, and he was able to duplicate these results, Seven's promised assistance might no longer be required.

"Without my help, you will never achieve that goal," Seven had assured him.

How he longed to prove her wrong.

GOLDENBIRD

Doctor Sharak stared in horror at the statistics on the data panel before him. Unwilling to risk discovery by contacting the capital city's central hospital on Ardana directly, he could only rely upon the same information that was available to the general public to confirm his hypothesis and extrapolate the most likely consequence of his actions on Coridan.

Sadly, the outbreak of a deadly strain of the "Rurokimbran virus" on Ardana less than a day after the devastation by the "Jendarian flu" on Aldebaran III could not be considered coincidental, nor could its cause be doubted. Both outbreaks were flimsy covers for the truth that devices—similar to that Ria had attempted to use on Coridan to disseminate the catomic plague—had been planted on Ardana and Aldebaran, and had released their deadly contents without discovery.

Sharak did not know why he had assumed that the threat of potential exposure would have stayed Briggs's hand. The series of events that had unfolded on Aldebaran and Ardana so soon after Coridan had to arouse suspicion in even the dullest of statisticians.

Clearly, Briggs did not care. Agents like Ria had obviously been inflating the infection rates on Aldebaran and Ardana just as Ria had on Coridan. They had also likely terminated themselves shortly after Sharak had made his report to Starfleet Medical. And Doctor Frist had clearly not seen fit to warn the hospital administrators on Ardana or Aldebaran to search for devices similar to those found on Coridan.

Tens of thousands of people had already died in the new outbreaks. The models of infection rates Sharak had constructed posited as many as fifty thousand on each world would die before the quarantines would slow the rates of infection.

Any medical professional would have cringed at the possibility of causing such losses. *Had Briggs lost control of Ria's counterparts? Were they acting alone now? Had they always been?*

These were questions only they could answer. Proof of their existence and their species was the evidence Sharak required to bring this devastation to a halt. Clearly nothing less would move Doctor Frist to take appropriate action.

It seemed all too likely now that he would never find that proof. Nor could he contact those affected directly to tell them what to look for or where to look. He was no longer authorized by Starfleet Medical to work on this classified project in an official capacity. Should he make direct contact with the hospital administrators, they might do more than refuse to meet with him or transfer data about their staff and patients to him. They might order him and Lieutenant Wildman detained.

Until this moment Sharak had believed his cause to be right and his efforts essential. These results forced him to question that belief.

To his left, Lieutenant Wildman dozed fitfully in her chair. She had spent the last day programming their ship's sensors to search for Planarian life signs in New Kerinna. Had a baseline existed in her anthropological databases for Planarians, this would have been simple. Instead, Wildman had been forced to extrapolate from their computer's analysis of the Planarian genome the most likely markers that would distinguish a Planarian from the millions of other life-forms in the city. Her first several attempts had failed.

Should the sensors succeed, there was only one road open to them: a road that could easily lead to arrest, conviction, and loss of their Starfleet commissions.

Lemross. At Illashanta. Would the story of Lemross's catastrophic hubris one day be more rightly cited by the Children of Tama as, *"Sharak. At Aldebaran"*?

A series of trills roused Lieutenant Wildman. Her eyes jerked open, but she lifted her head slowly, massaging the back of her neck prior to focusing on her display.

"How long was I out?" she asked groggily.

"Almost an hour," Sharak replied.

"That explains it," Wildman said, groaning slightly as she tried to work the cramps from her neck.

She stared silently at the display for a few moments, then turned to face him.

"Are you ready to go?"

Sharak's stomach fell. But he could not deny the small sense of relief that accompanied her words. Both had already agreed that should the sensors fail to provide meaningful data this time, their only recourse was to return to Earth, turn all of their current data over to Doctor Frist's superiors, and hope for the best.

"I am," Sharak said, nodding.

"I'll get the bio-suits," Wildman said, rising from her seat.

Sharak stood, his thoughts suddenly running in unruly circles. He peered at her display screen.

There, a single green blip rested over what appeared to be an apartment complex on the outskirts of the evacuated sector of New Kerinna.

"Does this mean another Ria is still alive?" Sharak asked as he moved quickly to join Wildman at the storage pods in the rear bay of the ship.

"It means that organic material consistent with the Planarian genetic markers has been detected," Wildman replied. "Who or what that might be, we won't know until we get down there."

Sharak nodded. His doubts subsided in a new rush of adrenaline. *Uzani. With fists closed.*

9

VOYAGER

As acting first officer, Lieutenant Harry Kim had more than enough to worry about. With the ship in crisis, the problems of one hundred forty-six people were now his. And nobody's problems right now were trivial. Every choice might be the difference between life and death. Kim had once believed he would thrive in this crucible. As it was, he was barely keeping his head above water.

The sheer tonnage of work might have been more manageable had his mind not insisted on betraying him every time he sat down for more than a minute.

Captain Chakotay had left the bridge half an hour earlier. During that time Kim had fielded six personnel requests, revised the next day's duty roster to accommodate four injured crewmen who had just been released from the *Galen*, scanned the most recent engineering and tactical reports, and was ready to move on to the nineteen new items that had appeared in his queue in the meantime.

His unruly subconscious chose that moment to revisit a point it had been trying to make for the past three days.

You should be dead right now.

Kim was not being maudlin, nor was he depressed. He might be suffering some version of post-traumatic stress, but it was not intense enough for him to seek treatment.

This certainty stemmed from a split second Kim had experienced on the bridge just before the battle at the Gateway had ended.

The bridge crew had been jolted in their seats when the main deflector was hit. It was one of those bone-rattling impacts that results in a few seconds of shock before you realize that you are still breathing and must refocus your attention should you wish to stay that way.

The last three years spent at tactical had given Kim a new internal chronometer. Its tempo was based upon the relationship between damage to the ship, current vulnerability, and the demonstrated strength of hostile weapons. Kim had not been standing at tactical when the *Scion* fired the shot that took out the deflector dish. But his internal clock had immediately begun to count the fractions of seconds remaining in Kim's life as soon as he had recovered from the moment of impact. No matter how he had tried to fudge the numbers, his clock would not be swayed.

We're going to die, it reported. There was nothing to be done about it. Had he been standing a post on the *Scion*, he might have taken one inhalation between the shot that disabled the dish and the killing blow. Given the ferocity of the battle at that moment, there wouldn't even have been time to think. Twenty-five CIF vessels had already been destroyed by the *Kinara* at that point. *Voyager* had entered the battle late, but on the wrong side if survival was the goal. Once their shields were down, they were defenseless. Half a second had determined their fate.

The final shot had never come. Kim had later learned about the *Shudka*'s call for a cease-fire and Admiral Janeway's choice to accept the *Kinara*'s terms of surrender.

But that shouldn't have mattered. The presider would have had to make the call *before Voyager* suffered that blow, and although the CIF's potential for victory had been negligible at that point, as long as the Federation's ships could still engage, it remained a possibility. *After Voyager* had been hit, that changed. But had she waited that long . . .

No matter how he looked at it, *Voyager*'s survival simply made no sense to him.

Kim knew what he had to do in order to quiet this disturbing thought. He needed to spend about eight hours studying every moment of the engagement at the Gateway and running numerous simulations projecting possible outcomes. Had he not been acting first officer, he would already have done this. Because he did not have that time to spend, his mind pestered him without cease, and his only choice was to force this thought down every time it rose unbidden.

Six new people required immediate responses from Kim in the time he had just wasted deciding that he didn't have time to wonder why he was still alive. As soon as he had focused his mind firmly on the padd in his hand, a call came from *Galen*, advising him that Lieutenant Barclay wanted a word.

Kim didn't want to distract the rest of the bridge crew, and he assumed Barclay's request might be related to the Doctor's current issues, which were not for public consumption. Captain Chakotay was in his quarters, so Kim ordered Lieutenant Devi Patel to take the bridge and retreated to Chakotay's ready room.

"Go ahead, Reg," Kim ordered as soon as the door shut behind him.

And please make it quick, he thought.

"I've been reviewing Voyager's *power distribution patterns for the last two weeks, and I've discovered something I hope you can explain,"* Barclay began.

This was not Barclay's job, but also not beyond his expertise. Curious, Kim asked, "Why?"

"There are several corruptions to the Doctor's program I couldn't account for until I discovered some odd power surges in the main holographic matrix that date back more than a month."

"Did the Doctor cause them? I know he wasn't happy with sickbay's data storage capabilities and power regulation. Did he accidentally break something?"

"I don't think so," Barclay replied. *"I designed the programming upgrades the Doctor required and installed them myself. They weren't the issue. On at least nine separate occasions, I've discovered large, unintended power transfers, most of which targeted holographic systems. I know they have a discrete power source, but these surges seemed to originate from other systems and were rerouted by the central computer to the holographic mainframe."*

Kim pondered this in silence for a moment. He was as well versed as Barclay in *Voyager's* holomatrix interfaces. He had rebuilt dozens of them by hand during the dark days of the Hirogen's occupation of his ship. The entire system had been upgraded when *Voyager* was refitted for her return to the Delta Quadrant, but the basics had remained the same.

"Could our interactions with the protectors have affected the system?" Kim asked.

"Possibly, but they seem to be occurring too *randomly for one system or interaction to be the sole cause. I'm going to send you my reports. You should review them with Nancy and B'Elanna. It may be nothing, but I'm pretty sure now that one of those surges caused the Doctor's near cascade failure."*

"How is he?"

"Much better," Barclay assured him. *"His program has been restored. There are just a few issues left to resolve."*

"Glad to hear it," Kim said. "I'll take a look at those reports."

When, he did not know, but like everything else, it was added to the list that never seemed to get any shorter.

"*Thanks, Harry.*"

"Anytime," Kim said, signing off.

You really should be dead right now.

Kim suddenly wondered if this was simple curiosity about a tactical probability, or a wish.

TWENTY THOUSAND KILOMETERS FROM THE GATEWAY

When General Mattings had advised Admiral Janeway that he could create a holding facility for the prisoners in neutral territory, she had assumed he was referring to a civilian ship that he could temporarily press into service.

The possibility that she would find herself facing Lsia while floating in empty space had never crossed her mind.

The general's solution had been to program protectors to create static cells for each of the four Seriareen. They were spaced too far apart for any to be visible to the others.

A separate protector had been created in which Admiral Janeway, Captain Chakotay, and Presider Cin now sat on invisible, yet surprisingly comfortable, indentations within the wave form. General Mattings stood at attention behind them. Their protector had merged with Lsia's to facilitate this conversation, although a barrier remained between them that Lsia could not breach.

Lsia stood facing them, still in the form of the tall humanoid woman Janeway had seen aboard the *Manticle.* Apparently prisoners didn't get invisible chairs. It was impossible to look down without becoming disoriented. But Janeway had focused her attention on the Seriareen and by doing so, she could keep her stomach calm. Janeway also appreciated the fact that Lsia appeared every bit as disconcerted by her surroundings, or lack thereof, as she was.

Janeway admired the general's ingenuity. Nobody enjoyed an advantage here. They were all in the same transparent boat.

Presider Cin sat to Janeway's left, Chakotay on her right, his game face in place. Janeway allowed Cin to begin the conversation. "You indicated to Admiral Janeway that you believe your homeworld to be located in Confederacy space," she said. "We have double-checked our records. There are no worlds now called Seriar, nor do our histories mention your world or your species. Who are the Seriareen?"

"I am Lsia. Devore Inspector Kashyk is called Emem. Magnate Veelo of the Turei is called Tirrit, and Commandant Dhina of the Vaadwaur is Adaeze," Lsia replied. "We are almost all that remains of the Seriareen."

"Didn't you say there were eight?" Cin asked of Janeway.

"One was destroyed, and the other three are still contained a long way away from here. We will retrieve them in due course," Janeway advised her.

"Can you tell me exactly where your home was?" Cin demanded.

"Thousands of years ago, the stars that now surround us lit but a small fraction of our territory."

"The canisters that contained your essences were held by a species that called themselves the Neyser. They told us you were their ancestors," Chakotay said.

"We were," Lsia said. "Seriareen space was vast, extending over tens of thousands of light-years and consisting of almost half of what you call the Delta Quadrant, or First Quadrant," she added, nodding toward the presider. "Before we fell, those that allied themselves against us took the designation *Nayseriareen*. I believe 'Neyser' is a bastardized version of that word."

"How could you possibly have held territory that vast?" Janeway asked. "We've seen a fair bit of the Delta Quadrant in our travels and this is the first we have heard of your civilization."

"You have already discovered the means by which we conquered and ruled," Lsia replied. "You call them subspace corridors or streams. Many have claimed them in our absence. What time has forgotten is that *we* created them."

"How?" Chakotay asked as Presider Cin blanched at this

revelation. The people of the Confederacy believed in an all-powerful entity they called the "Source," and one tenet of their faith was that this Source had carved the subspace tunnels that allowed them to escape the Borg and build their civilization around the First World.

"Technology," Lsia replied. "The tools we used to carve the corridors were the first target of the Nayseriareen. To defeat us, they had to eliminate our ability to travel vast distances in periods of time no starship could match.

"Once, the corridors were open to all that offered allegiance to us. Our enemies shattered our alliances by destabilizing as many corridors as they could find, ultimately capturing and destroying our technology."

"But they couldn't kill you?" Chakotay asked.

"The Seriareen possessed many forms of advanced technology as well as unique telepathic abilities. Our natural life spans were very long compared to yours and most of the species we encountered. Continuity of leadership added stability to the territories we ruled. We came to believe that this stability could only be enhanced by extending our lives even further. After exhausting all medical means to sustain our bodies indefinitely, we accepted that eventually all physical beings would die. But our essence did not have to. We developed the ability to transfer our consciousness at the moment of our death to other beings."

"Did those beings resist?" Chakotay asked.

Lsia shook her head. "You assume it was something to be feared. For those who would receive an ancient consciousness, it was something to be celebrated. Consciousness transfer was seen as a means to share in immortality. Contests of strength and intelligence were held to select those best suited for transfer. The lucky few who were chosen were envied by their peers."

"Why few?" Janeway asked.

"Sustaining one's consciousness in a new form is difficult and a skill many attempted, but only the strongest mastered. Millions trained themselves to undergo transfer, but a very small percentage survived the process. If it could be successfully accomplished once, it became easier. But still, by the end, only a few thousand existed that had lived more than one lifetime. We were the undisputed leaders of the Seriareen. We were exalted."

"You make it sound like you were gods," Chakotay said.

"To many, we appeared as such," Lsia agreed. "In addition to hunting us to extinction, the Nayseriareen developed means to inhibit telepathic essence transfer," Lsia went on. "They were able to destroy whatever form we inhabited while simultaneously preventing us from moving immediately to a new form."

"I don't suppose you'd care to tell us how they did that?" Mattings asked.

Lsia smiled wanly. "To be honest, I never knew. By the time I realized it was even possible, it was too late to ask."

"How many did the Nayseriareen capture?" Chakotay asked.

"I don't know," Lsia replied. "When I escaped and took your hologram as my new form, I was shocked and deeply saddened to learn that only seven others remained with the Neyser. The ancient ones who hid The Eight believed we were the last. I have no idea what may have happened to the others."

Janeway exchanged a worried glance with Chakotay before saying, "So you have come back to try and reclaim some of the space that was once yours?"

"No," Lsia replied. "So many years later, any claim we might make would be dismissed out of hand, and rightly so. We were unable to hold what was once ours. It was taken from us by superior forces and, ultimately, lost to them as new powers rose to take their place."

"You sound surprisingly resigned to your fate," the presider noted.

"Thousands of years of contemplation of your life in a very small, dark place does wonders for one's perspective," Lsia said wryly.

"If that is so, why have you joined forces with species that have a history of unprovoked attacks on the Confederacy's Gateway?" Mattings demanded.

"When I was first freed, I set about attempting to discover

how much of the Seriareen's past glory remained intact," Lsia admitted. "I soon realized that only a fraction of the subspace corridors had survived. No species I encountered even remembered our names. I first sought out the Turei and Vaadwaur, given the descriptions of those encounters from *Voyager*'s logs. They were not the most reasonable of species. I was forced to take extreme measures in order to learn how much of our subspace network remained intact and the identity of those controlling it.

"I first learned of the *Kinara* from the Turei. I decided that before I attempted to join forces with the *Kinara*, who have actually extended their explorations almost to the network's known limits, I would have to strengthen my negotiating position. The *Kinara* respect strength and numbers. The Confederacy was winning their conflict with the *Kinara* through attrition, so I brought Rigger Meeml forces he couldn't refuse to gain his trust."

"Did Rigger Meeml speak the truth when he indicated that the *Kinara* only wished to explore the Confederacy's corridors and to access resources beyond their territory?" Cin asked.

"He did."

"And did you share his goals?" Janeway asked.

"Yes, and no," Lsia admitted. "The only way to confirm the limits of the subspace network was to access the Confederacy's streams. But I have no interest in anything that lies beyond Confederacy space. Based upon the *Kinara*'s astrometrics charts, it is very likely that Seriar is within the space now claimed by the Confederacy. As I have been unable to discover anything of my people's fate since my incarceration, I hope to find the answers I seek there."

"And then do what?" Janeway asked.

"I do not believe we could resume residence there," Lsia admitted. "Fighting throughout my planet's system was fierce and terribly destructive. Many of the weapons used rent savage holes in the fabric of space and subspace. Even thousands of years later, I doubt time has repaired all that was damaged.

"You might think me sentimental," Lsia continued, "but before I can look for a new road down which to guide those of us who remain, I must know how the old road ended."

Janeway looked to Chakotay and Cin, both of whom seemed to share the same healthy skepticism.

"If all you wanted was information, you might have simply asked," Mattings noted.

"Forgive me, General, but it is my understanding from the *Kinara* that your Confederacy refused to even discuss the desires of races you deemed inferior until we amassed a force capable of defeating you on the field of battle."

"In the past that might have been true," Cin allowed. "But I have committed myself and my people to a new, more open path."

"Still, many questions remain unanswered," Janeway noted.

"Such as?" Lsia asked.

"One member species of the Federation shares something in common with the Seriareen," Janeway began. "The Trill are a joined species, a humanoid host and a symbiotic life-form that merges with that host to create a new individual. The host retains a certain amount of autonomy, but the symbiont brings the memories of each past host to the joining. The *continuity* you spoke of is assured in this way. It is an unusual arrangement, but our long association with the Trill has given us a certain appreciation for the fact that a species could develop a desire and reverence for the process of transferring actual consciousness from one generation to the next, and that those receiving the transfers would accept the loss of complete individuality in exchange for what they consider an enhanced existence.

"Based upon what I have seen, however," Janeway continued, "your hosts remain conscious of your presence within them and seem incapable of offering resistance."

"Once a transfer is complete, the memories, consciousness, the very *essence* of the host, is displaced by ours. Some vestige of it remains, but it cannot resume control of its body while we inhabit it, and we remain trapped within it until its death."

"While we were aboard the *Manticle,* you spoke a single word that allowed Inspector Kashyk to temporarily subsume Emem," Janeway said. "Another word from you put an end to that struggle."

"During the ritual of transfer, which I performed for Emem, Tirrit, and Adaeze, ancient words of power are invoked as triggers to alert the transferring essence in the unlikely event a new host becomes unstable. Those words are unique to each transfer and temporarily halt the integration. What I did—*to stop Emem from murdering you, Admiral*—was to briefly loosen his hold upon the host. Emem was forced to struggle for control with an unwilling host, distracting him from his previous intention. But even had I not reversed that command, Kashyk would never have survived Emem's release. There is simply not enough of him left, and what little remains has probably been driven mad by his new reality. Emem would have sought refuge in another body—probably *yours*—and Kashyk's body would have died."

Janeway wasn't sure if she didn't believe this, or simply didn't *want* to believe it.

"I don't expect you to understand or approve of our history," Lsia continued, "but I speak the truth when I say that the ancient Seriareen welcomed the transfers, even though it meant the loss of their individuality and autonomy."

"This isn't the first time you have told us the story of your people's past," Chakotay interjected. "You painted a very pretty picture of the Indign's history for Captain Eden before you betrayed us and stole our shuttle."

"I told you enough of the truth to eliminate the need for hostilities between yourself and the Indign," Lsia argued. "I was displeased to find the Neyser, pale reflections of their once-great ancestors, living in cooperation with so many lesser species. One does not wish to judge unfairly, but I felt they had devolved to a point where nothing I could offer them would be met with anything other than fear. They believed we were monsters. They had no memory of who we really were or all we had once achieved."

"If they were descendants of the Nayseriareen who once defeated you and incarcerated those among you capable of consciousness transfer, I'm not sure what you could have told them to make them trust you," Chakotay observed. "And clearly their ancestors had reasons for defying you as they did."

"It came down to power and fear," Lsia said. "As long as enough of us retained the ability to conquer death by taking the bodies of our enemies and turning them to our will, we were the undisputed masters of all we beheld. Some of the Nayseriareen wanted to control what we had created. Others simply could not abide the existence of any they perceived as such a great threat."

"We're going to have to take your word for that," Janeway observed. "My concern is not with your ancient enemies. By taking the bodies of Inspector Kashyk, Magnate Veelo, and Commandant Dhina, you have effectively murdered those individuals, have you not?" Janeway asked.

"Yes," Lsia agreed.

"You cannot simply choose another host, should a willing one exist?" Chakotay asked.

"Not while our current hosts live," Lsia replied. "And the longer we inhabit a host, the more receptive it becomes to us."

"But you are not alive," Chakotay noted. "You are a hologram."

"I know," Lsia snapped. "The same principle applies, however. Should the holomatrix I now inhabit be damaged, I would simply be forced to transfer myself to the next nearest form to continue existing. And bear in mind," she added, "that physical proximity is not required to complete a transfer. Once freed from a host, we are all adept at sustaining ourselves in a disembodied state until a new prospect is found."

"How comforting," Mattings said.

"If you require our guarantee that we will not transfer ourselves to any others, adding casualties to those already claimed, you have it," Lsia said. "As long as you allow us to continue to live in the bodies we have taken, we will not seek out new ones."

"Would you be willing to submit yourselves to complete physical examinations?" Janeway asked. "None of you have possessed the bodies you now claim for long. We might be able to find a way to safely separate you from those you have taken against their will."

"And transfer us where?" Lsia asked.

"If technology similar to that you now occupy could be duplicated, you might no longer require living bodies," Janeway suggested.

Lsia paused. Finally she said, "We would be willing to explore that possibility once we have learned the fate of Seriar."

Nodding, Janeway turned to Presider Cin. "Do you have any other questions, Presider?"

Cin started to speak, but paused, looking to General Mattings. His face was inscrutable, but Janeway sensed something unspoken passing between them.

"No," she finally said.

"Very well. Thank you for your honesty, Lsia," Janeway said. "The presider and I will confer and advise you as soon as possible of our decision."

"Thank you, Admiral. Presider," Lsia said, inclining her head to each in turn.

10

TAMARIAN EMBASSY
PARIS, EARTH

It had been more than a year since Julia Paris had received an invitation to tour the embassy of a Federation world. When Owen was alive, such requests were common. Although the spouses of Starfleet's admiralty had no official duties, they were the unofficial backbone of Starfleet's diplomatic efforts. On countless occasions they would be called upon to host small, informal gatherings of alien ambassadors and their staffs. By opening their homes to visiting dignitaries, they often did more to cement new friendships and open minds and hearts to the realities of Federation life than the diplomatic corps achieved in months of formal meetings.

Julia had never visited the Tamarian Embassy, though she believed Owen had when it was first established. The incredibly short notice she had received was a little rude, but not unwelcome.

That the invitation should come so close to the end of the day was odd, but given the time difference, she realized she would be meeting with the Tamarian ambassador tomorrow before the start of his work day.

When she arrived at the embassy's doors, Julia was immediately welcomed into a lovely sitting room by an aide of the ambassador who spoke only enough Federation standard to make it clear that she was expected and should wait. The furnishings were well-worn antiques. Julia believed this embassy had once belonged to the Ferengi, but suspected they had found it insufficiently garish.

She was struggling to remember who might have occupied it between the Ferengi and the Tamarians—*surely* not *the Cardassians*—when the double doors before her opened and a uniformed Starfleet officer entered.

Julia rose automatically before she recognized her son's face. The sight of it almost put her back in her seat, but she rallied and steadied herself. She did not, however, move to close the distance between them.

"Hi, Mom."

"What is the meaning of this?" she demanded. "Is it your intention to turn our personal family issues into a diplomatic incident?"

"Nope. I asked you to come here because I need your help."

"At the Tamarian Embassy?" she asked, incredulous.

"Yep."

Julia shook her head. "I was invited by Ambassador Jarral."

"He knows you're here. He's downstairs. He asked me to brief you, as his grasp of Federation Standard is nonexistent, and the one decent translator we have available right now has her hands full."

Julia felt trapped. If Tom was speaking the truth, leaving now would be considered a great insult. If Tom was lying, perhaps it was a good thing that the ambassador did not understand their language, because his ears would burn when he heard the dressing-down she was prepared to give her son.

Tom seemed to watch these thoughts drift through her mind. Finally he said, "Over the last few weeks you said a lot of things I found hard to accept, but the hardest was that you had no idea who I was anymore. I didn't bring you here to re-litigate anything or to make you change your mind. I asked you to come because I don't know how else to handle a problem it is now my duty to solve.

"I don't know how to *tell* you who I am anymore. But maybe I can show you."

His words struck her heart like a dull blade, but she nodded for him to continue.

"Do you remember when I told you and Dad about a group of former Borg we found in the Delta Quadrant, the ones who used us to reestablish a neural link between them so they could create a cooperative existence?"

An unwelcome shudder flew down Julia's spine as much at the memory as her son's casual use of the word *Borg*.

"I do."

"A few months ago, *Voyager* returned to that planet to see if the cooperative had been absorbed into the Caeliar gestalt. The vast majority had, but forty-seven remained behind. Some of them had reproduced in the interim, and their children could not join the gestalt, as they did not possess Borg technology. At their request, we relocated them to a planet deeper in former Borg territory."

"They still thought of themselves as Borg?" Julia asked, horrified.

"No," Tom replied. "They had come under attack by a group of local thugs who had claimed their world as a relocation center for aliens whose ships they made a habit of stealing.

"When we left them on Arehaz, we assumed we'd seen the last of them. Shortly after we left, Starfleet Medical dispatched a ship with slipstream capabilities to collect them and bring them to Earth."

"Why?" Julia asked, finally intrigued.

"Shortly after the Caeliar transformation, a new plague arose on three Federation worlds. Starfleet Medical believes it was caused by Caeliar catoms. Every individual we have discovered who was Borg but did not join the Caeliar appears to possess a limited quantity of these catoms. They replaced whatever Borg technology existed in them at the time of the transformation.

"Officially, Starfleet Medical relocated the people of Arehaz to Earth in order to study their catoms because there are only a few known sources of them in the galaxy."

"Seven of Nine?" Julia asked.

"Yes. And one former Borg drone discovered in the Beta Quadrant. An old friend of Seven's named Axum."

"Am I to understand that the Federation has now asked the Tamarians to house these people while they study them?"

"Not exactly," Paris said. He took a deep breath before he continued. "Seven was ostensibly brought to Starfleet Medical to consult with the physicians working to cure the plague. Only they didn't do any consulting. They simply took samples of her catoms and placed her in stasis. They did the same with these people."

"Are their catoms the source of this plague?"

"No. We still don't know where it came from, but none of them have ever set foot on the affected worlds. Seven believes that the physicians and scientists assigned to the classified project at Starfleet Medical are doing more than trying to cure the plague. They are attempting to learn how to program catoms, and the methods they are using are unethical, immoral, and illegal."

Julia felt the blood rush from her face. "Can you prove this?"

"Do I have to?" he asked.

It was a lot to take on faith, but even Julia could not see her son risking his career and his life on a hunch that was based on shoddy intelligence.

"Someone at Starfleet Medical lied to these people. And the experiments being conducted with their catoms are incredibly painful, both to them and to the test subjects. Seven was able to force the project's leader to agree to release them into her custody. Until we can expose his inappropriate actions and satisfy ourselves that they are safe, we will not return them to his care. The Tamarians have granted them asylum."

It comforted Julia to know that Starfleet Medical was at least working with Seven on this issue. But she still had no idea why Tom would have brought her here.

"A few things before I take you downstairs," Tom said, interrupting her thoughts. "Most of what I just told you is classified."

"You know you can trust me, Tom," Julia began, but paused when she saw his face harden.

No, he didn't, she realized.

"Also, these people have been through hell in the last several months. I hoped by bringing them here we could offer them a temporary respite. The Tamarians mean well, but their resources are limited. I can't do what needs to be done here without attracting unwanted attention."

"But I can," Julia realized.

"If you are willing."

Julia considered the proposition. Technically, she wasn't doing any more for her son than she would have gladly done for Owen in years past. She might actually be doing the Federation a great service; something that mitigated the confusion she felt at Tom's present display of temerity.

She remained uncommitted as her son ushered her down the halls of the main floor and into the bowels of the ancient building. She was shivering by the time they reached the landing that led to what had once been a ballroom and now was little more than a vast, dank holding cell.

She greeted Ambassador Jarral and his translator, a Miss Ratham, cordially, but from the moment she entered the room, her eyes were captured by the faces of the men, women, and babies surrounding her.

The adults were little more than walking skeletons. Their children were painfully thin as well, and many were clad only in rough and filthy approximations of diapers. A few toddlers careened about, their faces, hands, and chests slick with the juices of chunks of fruit they carried with them as they explored. Older food stains were congealed on their bodies.

The worst part was their eyes. They were almost feral and deeply wounded.

Julia knew too well that many Federation citizens were now living in desperate conditions. That any would be forced to do so on Earth was as unthinkable as it was unconscionable.

Their needs were obvious. They required food, clothing, beds, suitable furnishings, and access to anything and everything Julia could get her hands on to make it possible for them to live comfortably for as long as they were guests of the embassy.

She had not walked among the refugees of Arehaz for more than five minutes before the only choice available to her became crystal clear. An unusual feeling stirred within her and filled her with a heady sense of energy she hadn't felt in more than a year.

Julia Paris was *needed* once again, and there was only one response to need. Moving to her son's side, she whispered to him, "You should move on to whatever other duties your current mission requires."

"Are you sure?" he asked.

"Oh, yes." Without another word, she returned to Miss Ratham's side as a list began to take shape in her mind.

ALDEBARAN

The *Goldenbird*'s transporters released Doctor Sharak and Lieutenant Wildman in a clearing surrounded by dense foliage on the outskirts of a public park. Wildman had routed their transport signal through the local station inside the quarantine area to give it the appearance of legitimacy, although close scrutiny would betray its unofficial nature. *If they were wrong about the Planarian life signs, or detected by Starfleet security . . .*

Rilna. At Abossu, Sharak chided himself internally. Personal concerns were no longer a priority.

Clad in bulky biohazard suits, they moved deeper into the trees that skirted the park and bordered the quarantine area. A level-ten forcefield had been established around the quarantined perimeter, as Starfleet wanted to make sure that no one would gain access.

Sharak was sweating profusely before they reached the rocky hill that ran behind the building they had targeted. Their ascent was painstakingly slow but by the time they had reached the crest and could see the building only forty meters in front of them, an adrenaline rush gave Sharak the strength to follow Wildman's brisk pace as she approached the rear doors.

Thankfully, they reached the door unobserved. From this point forward, their only hope of escaping further detection was their suits. Every individual working within the perimeter would be wearing them, and their comm signals had been falsified to read as medical technicians from Benevolent Daughters.

As with every other building in the area, the door locks had been automatically disabled to allow for ease of access by official personnel in the event reluctant residents attempted to resist evacuation.

Sharak slipped into the multilevel stone edifice behind Wildman and followed her through a labyrinth of halls to the unit on the first floor they sought. The only sounds they heard beyond the shuffling of their feet were Sharak's heavy respirations and the pinging of Wildman's tricorder.

Sharak was somewhat relieved to find the door to Unit 117A open. This suggested their quarry was not present. Most likely, if she had followed Ria's example, she was deceased. But traces of her DNA would be more than sufficient and easier for Sharak to gather undisturbed.

Once they had entered and the door shut behind them, Wildman offered Sharak her tricorder and removed her phaser. They moved slowly, Wildman taking point, through the unit's four small rooms and found nothing beyond common residential furnishings and a few unremarkable personal effects in the bed-room and single bathroom. None of them were the source of the readings the tricorder stubbornly insisted were present, but apparently invisible.

"I don't understand," Sharak muttered when they had returned, empty-handed, to the living area.

"Hang on," Wildman said, studying the room's longest wall. After a moment, she traded her phaser for the tricorder and began to run it along the wall. She unexpectedly hurried out the main doorway, saying, "Stay here." When she returned, she again retuned her tricorder and ran it over the few pieces of fur-niture closest to the wall.

"It has to be here somewhere," she muttered to herself.

"What?" Sharak asked.

"Aha," Wildman replied, digging her hands into a dead pot-ted plant that was suspended in the corner of the room above an end table next to a short sofa.

"What?" Sharak asked again.

"It's a small holographic generator," Wildman replied, remov-ing a panel from inside the plant's metallic pot. "There's a four-meter differential between this wall and the next load-bearing wall in the adjacent unit. Something's back there, and it's been hidden by this false wall. It's such a small discrepancy you'd have to be looking for it to ever notice."

Sharak estimated the wall was less than three meters across. What a twelve-square-meter space might contain that would be useful to him, he could not imagine, but he tightened his grip on the phaser automatically as Wildman succeeded in jamming the holo-emitter and the wall before him disappeared.

"*Shaka*," Wildman said triumphantly when a landing and staircase was revealed. Sharak looked at her, curious, as she added, "*When the walls fell?*"

This forced an inappropriate chuckle from the doctor. "Not at all," he said. "I will tell you the story when our work here is done."

Wildman again took the lead and the phaser as they made

their descent. Sharak silenced the tricorder's audio alerts. They had become so frequent and loud he found them more disturbing than helpful.

The stairs ended at a door-sized opening. Wildman paused before stepping into it and studied the tricorder's small display. A large space, more than fifty square meters, lay past that threshold, some sort of basement where the building's schematics indicated none should exist. A soft bluish light spilled from it onto the landing.

Wildman activated a small SIMs beacon around her left wrist and, crossing it over her phaser hand, turned her body to enter the doorframe with her right harm extended.

Sharak moved behind her and barely had a moment to register some of the room's contents—three tall bio-containers filled with murky liquid and bio-masses of various sizes, a long table, and what appeared to be a medical examination suite—before he was momentarily blinded by a bright orange light. The whine of a phaser accompanied it and was soon joined by the sound of Wildman's weapon returning fire.

Sharak threw himself back toward the safety of the stairs and waited as Lieutenant Wildman fought an unknown assailant for both of them.

Shaka, he cursed silently, praying he would still have a chance to tell Wildman that story.

INDIANA

"There you are," Gretchen Janeway said as the shuffling of feet at her back door alerted her to Seven's return from the willow tree. Seven had explained that, when necessary, the artificial matter the Caeliar had left in her body allowed her to go longer than many humans without rest or food. Clearly, Seven expected to do whatever she was doing out there for several hours and did not wish to cause Gretchen undue worry.

Almost two full days after Seven had left the house, restored by a few hours of sleep and a hearty breakfast of fruit and freshly baked muffins, Gretchen was planted before her kitchen sink staring through the window that looked out over the garden and orchard, straining for any sign of Seven's return. Over Seven's protests, Gretchen had sent her out with a picnic lunch and several jugs of fresh water. *But two days later . . .*

She hadn't seen Seven approach from the path that ran along the edge of the pumpkin patch, but she could easily have taken the long way around the far side of the orchard. She might be a little disoriented. It wasn't as if this was her home.

"Hi, Mom," a familiar voice greeted Gretchen as she turned toward the kitchen door.

"Phoebe."

Her youngest daughter paused in the doorway, staring at her mother strangely.

"Who else were you expecting?" Phoebe asked.

"No one, dear. How lovely to see you."

Seven's unexpected arrival had thrown Gretchen off her routine. She and Phoebe had standing dinner arrangements once a week, but her daughter's imminent arrival had been forgotten until this moment.

"So what's new?" Phoebe asked as she moved to the fridge to pour herself a glass of tea.

Gretchen did not reply immediately. It was possible Seven would not disturb them for the next few hours and that Phoebe might come and go without ever learning of her visit.

But if Seven suddenly appeared at the back door . . .

Gretchen sighed. She did not want this conversation, but once she had agreed to allow Seven to stay, it had become unavoidable.

"An old friend of Kathryn's came by."

"Who?"

"You remember Seven?"

Phoebe's eyes widened. "Isn't she part of Kathryn's fleet?"

"Yes, but she's returned to Earth for a special mission."

"What does that have to do with you?"

"It's complicated, dear."

"Is she in some sort of trouble?"

"I don't think so," Gretchen lied.

"Mom."

"Sweetheart, it isn't your concern. How are things at the gallery?"

"Is she still here?"

"Yes, but . . ."

"Where?"

"Phoebe . . ."

"Where is she?" Phoebe demanded. "It isn't enough that Kathryn went back out there? Now she's sending her officers here for you to look after?"

"I offered, darling."

"Why?"

"The same reason I welcomed every stray housepainter and lute player and Kilgarian fruit pastiche construction artist you ever brought here," Gretchen replied sternly. "Kathryn is my daughter. Her family is my family."

Phoebe's eyes narrowed. "Why did you wait until now to tell me?"

"You barely have a civil word for me these days when the subject is your sister. I won't have you making a spectacle of yourself in front of those Kathryn holds dear just because you can't forgive her."

Phoebe dropped her head, appropriately shamed by her mother's words. "Seven hasn't done anything to apologize for. I'm sure I can find a few civil words for her."

"Neither has your sister."

"I want to see her," Phoebe said.

"I don't think that's a good idea right now."

"Where is she?"

"She took a walk." *Two days ago*, Gretchen did not add.

"Then I'll do the same. I think some fresh air would do me good right now."

Without another word, Phoebe hurried out the back door. Gretchen grabbed a jacket from a peg on the wall by the door and followed.

Gretchen didn't know if it was habit or instinct that set Phoebe's feet toward the willow tree, but she reached it well before Gretchen could catch up with her.

She found Phoebe standing completely still about fifteen meters from the tree as the light of day faded around them.

Gretchen followed her daughter's gaze and saw Seven seated much as she had first found her beneath the tree.

Wait, Gretchen thought as she drew closer.

It took her a moment to accept what her eyes were trying to tell her. Phoebe's unusual stillness suggested she was sharing the same strange vision.

Seven was cross-legged with her hands resting on her knees. Her eyes were closed, her back was straight, and her chin was slightly lifted. Her lips might have been moving but no sound came from them.

But she wasn't exactly *sitting.* Seven's entire body floated about half a meter above the ground.

The food and water Gretchen had sent sat untouched on the ground below her.

"Mom?" Phoebe asked when Gretchen finally reached her.

"It's all right, darling," Gretchen whispered. "Come back inside."

Seven remembered the night sky of her childhood, remembered lying on her back in fragrant fields beneath a blanket of stars—far too many to count, let alone name.

She no longer needed to count them.

She knew them.

Each star arrayed before her was a catomic molecule. Those that were hers emitted a soft gold light. Riley's flamed violet. Axum's flared in harsh green shades.

The rest cast fainter white light. These had once belonged to SevenRileyAxum but had been removed from their bodies. They drifted aimlessly across the darkness seeking definition.

SevenRileyAxum ignored them for now. Instead, they focused their attention on the few molecules in sight emitting a sickly reddish hue.

RileyAxum followed Seven's intention and moved with her to intercept the nearest red star. SevenRileyAxum reached for it as one and reminded it that the alterations recently made to its structure were in error. Those alterations were not of them. They had been imposed by another.

Each star knew its proper form. Its instinct was to revert to that form when damaged. SevenRileyAxum removed the errant commands and stray additions, restoring lost fragments until red was transmuted once again to white.

Almost as soon as one was restored to brilliance, several more began to sicken. SevenRileyAxum moved purposefully among them, never faltering, never wearying; their conjoined efforts renewed their strength with each reversion.

Together, they created/restored/beheld perfection.

11

VOYAGER

Commander B'Elanna Torres could not remember the last time she had slept for more than three hours straight. A normal schedule left her exhausted thanks to the extra energy she was expending creating an entirely new person within her body. The emergency repair schedule she had drafted and Lieutenant Conlon had implemented had been borderline cruel.

Thankfully, it was also about to end.

Four hours earlier, *Voyager's* new deflector dish had been installed and only twelve hours of tests remained before it would be fully operational. Torres intended to oversee all of those tests personally, but as she was already running on fumes, she was seriously considering taking a short break before the dish was brought online for its final tests.

Her internal debate ended when she began to hallucinate.

From the auxiliary control panel where she was working, she had an unencumbered view of the main doors of engineering. It didn't matter that this was the middle of gamma shift. Twice as many personnel as was normal for alpha shift were constantly moving in and out, and the doors were left open to accommodate the traffic.

One moment, she was aware of only constant motion in and out of the doorway from the corner of her eye. The next, a small figure stood still at the door clutching a blanket to the side of her face. Her wide eyes explored the vast engineering room, clearly searching for something.

Miral?

But that wasn't possible. Miral was a sound sleeper and was only halfway through the eleven hours of rest she required each night. Even if she had awakened unexpectedly, Torres's holographic nanny, Kula, was programmed to contact B'Elanna. Kula could not leave the Paris family's quarters, except to be transferred to a holodeck, and would never have allowed Miral to wander out on her own.

"Mommy!" Miral shouted as soon as her eyes found her mother.

Miral hurried toward Torres, Ensign Bash following quickly behind. "I found her wandering the halls on deck three," Bash reported.

"Thank you so much," Torres said, dropping to a knee to embrace Miral. The child's firm hug convinced Torres she wasn't imagining her presence, but simultaneously sent a wave of panic coursing through her body. Torres had taken every precaution she thought necessary to ensure that Miral was always attended to while she was working. That she could end up *wandering the halls* was terrifying.

"What happened, honey?" Torres asked gently, determined not to allow Miral to see her fear.

"Kula is gone, Mommy."

It was hardly the first time a holographic system had malfunctioned on *Voyager*, but the safeties Torres had installed with

Kula's program should have alerted her to the problem well before Miral ended up alone.

"Nancy," Torres called as she rose.

"Lieutenant Conlon is on holodeck one," Ensign DuChamps advised her in passing.

That's right, Torres remembered. Harry had wanted her to look at something Barclay had reported. *But she should be back by now.*

"Let's take a walk, sweetie," Torres said to Miral.

"I'm sleepy," Miral whined.

"Okay," Torres said, lifting the girl into her arms. Sometime in the next few weeks, she wasn't going to be able to do this anymore. Miral had grown so much taller and despite the fact that she still wanted to be treated like a baby from time to time, was now very much a little person, all sharp knees and elbows and no longer the soft little ball Torres could easily hold comfortably.

Torres treasured the burden as she made her way to the main holodeck. There she found Lieutenants Conlon and Kim amid a holographic apocalypse.

She was grateful that Miral had fallen into a light sleep on her shoulder, because the sight was as frightening as it was disorienting. Dozens of holographic characters standard to a variety of programs were visible or *partially visible.* Sections of them stood or lay in pieces all about the room. It looked as if someone had tested a new *bat'leth* on them, severing heads and limbs and rending torsos at will. All that was missing was the blood, although faint sparks emanating from various unnatural tears was disturbing enough.

"What happened?" Torres asked as soon as she reached Conlon and Kim, who were standing over the room's control panel.

"Hell if I know," Conlon replied, clearly nearing her wits' end.

"Reg reported some strange power surges in the holographic systems," Kim said. "I finally got around to checking his readings, and this is what I found."

"Nobody has used the holodecks in days," Conlon added. "No one's had the time."

"Did this all happen at once?" Torres asked.

"No," Kim replied. "The first surges go back more than three months, but most of those didn't target the holodecks. Then they started accelerating in frequency."

"And I can't tell you why, so don't ask," Conlon said, frustrated.

"What you see here occurred in the last four days," Kim reported. "It started just before we reached Lecahn."

Miral stirred and started to lift her head. "Are the other decks in the same shape?" Torres asked, gently caressing Miral's neck.

Conlon and Kim nodded together.

Torres did a few quick mental calculations and ordered, "Lock it down for now. Get back to main engineering and finish up the tests of the new dish. Once it's online, we'll get a team down here to sort it out. Until then, nobody accesses the holodecks."

"Reg thinks these surges damaged the Doctor's program. They might be indicative of a larger problem," Kim noted.

"I'm sure they are," Torres replied. "But we can't spare anyone to deal with it now."

"What happened to Miral?" Conlon asked, as if she had only just noticed the child.

"Kula's program was affected as well," Torres replied. "I'm going to try and restore a backup for my quarters. That will take me the rest of the night."

"You need to get some rest, too," Conlon noted, obviously concerned.

"I need my . . ." Torres growled as she turned away, but stopped short of finishing the thought aloud. Harry and Nancy understood better than anyone the strain of her current predicament. But they couldn't really *know* how hard the last few months had been.

Her daughter needed her. The son growing in her body needed her. *Voyager* needed her. The whole damn fleet needed her.

Torres needed to find a small, dark, cool place to close her eyes for a few hours, while someone else shouldered some of the burdens she was struggling to carry alone.

I need Tom, Torres thought grimly, refusing to allow the tears forming in her eyes to fall.

GALEN

The last time Counselor Hugh Cambridge had spoken with the Doctor, they had argued. Cambridge had taken the Doctor to task for betraying Seven's confidence. The Doctor's responses had ranged from cutting sarcasm directed toward Cambridge, polite indifference to Seven's current status, and brief impassioned flares of temper indicating how much he still cared for Seven.

Even Cambridge had been able to see at the time that there was something odd about the Doctor's behavior. The last hour spent in Lieutenant Barclay's company had cleared up much of the counselor's confusion.

Apparently the Doctor had been so distraught over Seven and Cambridge's budding romantic relationship, he had contacted his creator, Doctor Lewis Zimmerman, and requested his counsel. Zimmerman had taken it upon himself to modify the Doctor's program in an attempt to help the Doctor deal with these intense "feelings" without doing permanent damage to his program or his personal relationships.

Zimmerman had focused on the fact that when humans experience emotional traumas, time becomes a natural aid in the healing process. Memories, no matter how vivid, fade over time as they move from short-term to long-term memory storage within the mind.

Or they should, Cambridge thought bitterly. Often as not, traumatic events led to a wide range of neuroses, and the mind's ability to sublimate painful memories was interrupted. "Posttraumatic stress disorder" was a general term for many psychological anomalies that indicated the mind's natural healing processes were not functioning properly.

Cambridge wished Zimmerman had thought to consult

another doctor, or another *human*, before tinkering with the Doctor's memories so haphazardly. Cambridge's sense of Zimmerman from Barclay was that the holographic-design genius lacked sufficient normal human interaction to make him cognizant of, let alone fluent in, the realities of human emotional processing.

Human memory, its power and its flaws, was significantly more complicated than the experience of it suggested. Time did not simply heal all wounds. The perspective that came from living beyond pain, realizing that one could continue to exist despite trauma, and new positive experiences were critical to the healing process. Zimmerman had tried to do an end-run around those essential steps.

If the Doctor had been nothing more than a collection of subroutines and processors, it might have worked.

"I have completely restored the Doctor's program," Barclay said, once he had summarized Zimmerman's modifications. "As long as we can protect him from overloads like the one that caused the most recent cascade failure, he should be fine."

"I'd hardly call the intensely narcissistic, passive-aggressive, manipulative individual I've come to know as the Doctor *fine*, but we won't quibble about that right now," Cambridge noted.

Barclay rose from his work station and faced the counselor indignantly. "When Admiral Janeway suggested that you try to help the Doctor come to terms with the modifications, I told her I did not believe you were an appropriate choice. The Doctor may be all of those things. But he is also one of the most compassionate, warm, and brilliant people I have ever known."

"I—" Cambridge began, but Barclay cut him off.

"You will not insult him. You will not embarrass him, and you will not judge him."

Cambridge stepped back, shocked by this sudden display of intensity from the normally fragile and unassuming Barclay.

"You will, to the best of your abilities, *help him*. If you feel inadequate to that task, tell me now and I will find another way to assist the Doctor."

Cambridge shook his head, smiling faintly. "I'm accustomed to a certain amount of irrational protectiveness from the members of *Voyager*'s crew who shared seven years together in the Delta Quadrant. They are, and always will be, much more than fellow officers. The emotional context of their relationships mirrors familial ones rather than professional ones. You weren't part of that crew, but you seem to have embraced the Doctor as fiercely as his oldest friends."

Barclay's face reddened. He seemed unaware that Cambridge was complimenting him. "I was familiar with *Voyager*'s crew long before I had the pleasure of meeting them. When they returned home, the Doctor and I began to work closely together on a number of projects. He is my closest friend."

"Those feelings do you credit, Lieutenant," Cambridge assured him. "And the Doctor is fortunate in his friends. While my experiences with the Doctor have not been as universally positive as yours, I do not wish him ill. Believe it or not, I have as much invested in his emotional equilibrium as you do."

"Because of Seven?" Barclay asked.

Cambridge felt his own pain struggle to surface, but kept it at bay. "I do not believe Seven will ever return to our fleet. That said, she would be devastated should the Doctor suffer permanent damage, particularly if she knew she was part of the cause. I will offer the Doctor my best. For his sake, and hers, I can do no less."

"For *duty's* sake, you can do no less," Barclay corrected him.

Okay, we'll go with that, Cambridge thought. "Of course," he said aloud.

"I have already briefed the Doctor fully on the events of the last few days as well as the nature of the modifications to his program. He understands now what has happened. He is expecting to speak with you. I want you to do that here, where my diagnostic programs are most easily accessed."

Cambridge nodded, and Barclay activated the Doctor's program.

As soon as he appeared, the Doctor looked to Barclay. "Hello, Reg," he said.

"Counselor Cambridge is here," Barclay said gently.

"Yes, I can see that," the Doctor said, shifting his gaze to Cambridge's face. The counselor noted a hardening of the Doctor's features, but that was not unexpected.

"I'll leave you to it," Barclay said, offering Cambridge a final stern look before he departed.

The two faced each other with several meters between them. After a short silence, the Doctor said, "I assume Reg has briefed you?"

"Yes," Cambridge replied.

"Had Admiral Janeway not ordered me to participate in these sessions with you—" the Doctor began.

"Me neither," Cambridge interjected.

"Really?" the Doctor said, evidently surprised. "I imagined you would enjoy finding yourself in this position."

"What position is that?"

"Power," the Doctor replied. "I am no longer free to hide thoughts and feelings from you that I would prefer remain private."

Cambridge exhaled slowly. "Doctor, nothing you have ever thought or felt about me was hidden."

The Doctor's face assured the counselor that he had unintentionally added insult to injury.

"When were you first activated, Doctor?" Cambridge asked.

"Eleven years, two months, twenty-nine days ago."

"And have you ever met an eleven-year-old who was at all challenging to read?"

"No," the Doctor admitted.

"Nor have I," Cambridge said. "You care deeply for Seven. Your concerns about her choice to enter into a relationship with me were well founded. I am hardly a textbook example of maturity or emotional stability. My personal relationships tend to be rather fraught and usually end badly. While your response to this situation was a little extreme, the insights upon which it was based were wise beyond your years and perhaps even prescient."

The Doctor accepted this grudgingly.

"I know you don't remember the conversation, but do you think it was possible that you asked Doctor Zimmerman to alter your memories?"

"No," the Doctor insisted. "Had I suspected it was possible, I would have refused to allow him to make the modifications. Upset as I was, I have faced emotionally and ethically challenging situations in the past and managed to survive. I did not doubt my ability to rise to this one as well, although apparently my creator did not share that confidence."

"Pain is a problem for most people." Cambridge shrugged. "Avoidance is common. What Doctor Zimmerman did in the name of relieving your suffering was really nothing more than salve for his own conscience. He identified a shortcoming in his programming and decided to rectify it. Very few parents can endure the sight of their children's pain. Only the strongest develop the ability to witness it without interference, allowing the child to develop its own critical coping mechanisms. Adolescent rebellion has as much to do with a child's need to test boundaries as their developing sense that they must learn to survive without their parents."

"At least we agree on that much," the Doctor noted.

"Before you spoke with Doctor Zimmerman, had you accepted the reality that Seven would likely never reciprocate your feelings for her?"

"Long ago," the Doctor replied.

"Then why was your reaction to our relationship so intense?"

The Doctor raised a droll eyebrow in Cambridge's direction.

"It was more than my unsuitability as a potential partner," Cambridge insisted.

"No, it wasn't."

"It had to be."

"Why?"

"Because on my worst day, I've got nothing on this man Axum, into whose arms you thrust her so eagerly. He is a victim of sustained abuse. Being Borg was horrific enough, but at least *while* Borg, he didn't know better. Seven and Admiral Janeway then freed him to live for years as a conscious victim of pure evil. The Borg Queen drove him to attempt suicide and since his rescue, he has apparently suffered only slightly less at the hands of Starfleet Medical. It will take him years to process all he has endured, and if you think he's going to be a stable and loving partner in the meantime, we may have larger problems with your program to address."

"If you are so certain that Axum will be unable to sustain a relationship with Seven, why are you convinced she will not return to the fleet?"

Cambridge lifted his head to the heavens in search of patience. After a deep breath he replied, "Seven is an extraordinarily stubborn and capable woman who feels responsible for Axum's current condition. She will not rest until she is certain he can survive without her, and that day will never come."

The Doctor scrutinized Cambridge in silence. Finally he said, "I think it's possible you underestimate her."

Cambridge laughed bitterly. "Well, you have more experience in that regard than I do."

The Doctor bristled. "I have never treated her as anything less than—"

"Than a hapless victim in need of a firm guiding hand?" Cambridge finished for him. "Come now, Doctor. Isn't Seven almost as much *your* creation as you are Doctor Zimmerman's?"

"Of course not," the Doctor replied, stricken.

"Think back as best you can to the early days and months," Cambridge suggested. "You were her mentor, weren't you?"

"One of many."

Now it was Cambridge's turn to raise an eyebrow.

"You believe I have somehow infantilized Seven?"

"While love remains a deep and disconcerting mystery, I don't think it is surprising that I was the first man Seven chose to explore her sexuality with. I had never seen her as less than an adult. I had no desire to parent her. Her innocence was part of her charm, but hardly the most alluring part."

The Doctor shook his head slowly. "I honestly don't know,"

he finally allowed. "When I think of Seven now, I don't *remember* how I used to feel. I see her in flashes, fragments of moments, but the emotional context has vanished. I can no longer access the data required."

For a fraction of a second, Cambridge found himself envying the hologram.

"How do you suggest we proceed?" the Doctor asked.

"Can we start by sitting?" Cambridge asked.

After a moment, the Doctor nodded. "Yes."

FIFTH SHUDKA

It had taken Presider Cin almost two full days to advise Admiral Janeway that she had made a decision on the Seriareen matter.

Within hours of their last meeting, General Mattings had advised the admiral that the *Manticle* had been stripped of its weapons and tactical systems, and its crew had been released from their holding cells. They had departed the area at best possible speed but it was hard to guess how soon they might bring word of their defeat back to the Devore.

Apparently determining Lsia's fate had been more difficult. Mattings stood beside Cin's desk as she welcomed Janeway and Chakotay to the *Shudka*.

"I am willing to accept your assurances that you can contain any threat posed to my people by the Seriareen and am ready to release them to your custody," Cin said as soon as Chakotay and the admiral had taken their seats.

Chakotay should have felt a certain amount of relief when Presider Cin issued her verdict. But it surprised him too much for that. He would have bet anything that after their last conversation, the Confederacy would have opted to execute the prisoners over Janeway's objections. But somehow, Cin's decision didn't feel like progress.

"You are unwilling to grant them access to your territory in order to determine whether or not their homeworld still exists here?" Janeway asked.

"It does not," Cin assured her. "Any investment of resources spent confirming that would be a waste. Our time and yours is much too valuable for that."

"Should my people find any evidence of Seriar's location using independent data, would you permit my vessels to search for it?" Janeway asked. "We would, of course, restrict ourselves to any streams you designate or bypass them completely and use our slipstream drives to conduct our research."

Cin's eyes hardened. "*Voyager* and *Galen* are holding position outside the Gateway. You've indicated that the *Vesta* was dispatched to locate *Demeter*. While we expect one of your vessels to return our overseer of agriculture to us, at this time, there is no need for any other Federation ships to return to the Confederacy. Should your travels bring you back to this area of space at some future point," Cin hastened to add, "we would hope you would alert us to your presence. We will always value your friendship and appreciate the opportunity for future cultural exchanges."

"Just not *at this time*," Janeway confirmed.

"Your visit has been more disruptive than I had anticipated," Cin said. "We have learned a great deal and are grateful for all you have shared with us, but we require time to consider all that has transpired."

"May I speak frankly, Presider?" Janeway asked.

"That has never been a challenge in the past," Cin observed.

"Is this choice the result of internal pressures you are receiving from the Market Consortium?"

"Hardly," Cin replied. "My former first consul is gathering support to turn me out of office, but this is not an attempt to secure my political future. I have weighed all of the options before me and determined the course I feel would be best for my people."

"This isn't about politics," Chakotay guessed. "It's about faith, isn't it?"

Cin's tentacles stiffened visibly but she did not reply immediately.

"Faith?" Janeway asked.

"If Lsia was speaking the truth, *if* the Seriareen did use some ancient technology to create the streams, that revelation casts doubt on the very foundations of the Confederacy's faith in the Source," Chakotay clarified. "I don't doubt your ability, Presider, to weather the coming political storms, but you are unwilling to risk the chaos that might result should this story become widely known."

"It would be an intensely destabilizing force to our society," Cin acknowledged.

Chakotay turned to Janeway. Not that long ago, their thoughts and actions had been in perfect accord. Most conversations had happened in shorthand. There was simply no need for two who knew each other as well as they did to speak when a gesture or even a glance communicated their intentions so completely.

That effortless connection had been disrupted when Kathryn left the fleet. Since her return, he had glimpsed it, but begun to doubt that they could recapture it. They seemed to constantly be finding themselves at cross-purposes.

But not now. The edges of Kathryn's lips curved slightly upward, mirroring his. He had been the first to grasp the truth behind Cin's reticence, but once he had hit upon it, Kathryn had seen the only possible rebuttal as clearly as he did. She also understood that of the two, *he* was, by far, the better choice to give voice to that rebuttal.

Go ahead, he almost heard her think.

He paused. Cin had just given him what he wanted. Once *Demeter* was recovered, the fleet could depart the Confederacy, their prisoners in hand, and resume their current mission. Chakotay had decided after speaking directly with Lsia that the wisest course of action was to collect the remaining canisters from New Talax and send all of the Seriareen back to the Alpha Quadrant, where the resources existed to safely study them and perhaps rescue their hosts. He had never wanted to see them executed, but hadn't expected the Confederacy to be so accommodating.

The problem was that Cin's decision to simply wash her hands of a complicated problem because of parochial, ignorant fear, revealed Chakotay's inclination as little better. Hoist on his own petard, Chakotay began by shifting his gaze to General Mattings. "Do you agree with the presider's decision?" he asked.

Mattings's shoulders tensed visibly. "It is not my place to question the presider's choices," he began. "Personally, if I may?" he asked of Cin.

She nodded for him to continue.

"While the potential impact of the Seriareen's claims would be disruptive, I think we owe it to ourselves to see if they are speaking the truth."

"Their truth would make lies of the beliefs that have built and sustained our Confederacy," Cin argued.

"No, they wouldn't," Chakotay said simply. "I have yet to encounter a system of faith that can long endure when its followers insist upon clinging to literal interpretations of its tenets. I have seen many, however, that may begin with the literal, but evolve in the light of scientific discovery and scrutiny to something much richer. You look to the Source for guidance and truth. My people have a larger, more eclectic pantheon of spirits that offer the same deeper insights into the mysteries of existence. Whether or not the Source actually carved the streams of the great river is as irrelevant as whether or not a raven impregnated a woman with a child that demanded the stars, the moon, and sun as playthings and then threw them out of the smokehole of its cave into the heavens.

"Your people have understood for centuries that *something* beyond the normal experience of day-to-day life calls them to live with compassion and respect for one another. The Source brings a sense of order to the chaos all around you. Does it matter if it built the streams through its own divine purpose or inspired the hearts and minds that built the technology to serve that purpose?"

"It matters a great deal if the hearts and minds belonged to megalomaniacal aliens who claim the Source's powers for their own without offering credit or even thanks to the being that inspired them," Cin argued.

"Does it?" Chakotay asked. "Is the Source so fragile that it requires gratitude? Or is it beyond such petty, temporal needs? The Source *is*, just as the gods of my fathers *are*, whether we worship them or not. They don't need us nearly as much as we need them."

Cin's eyes shifted under Chakotay's gaze, finally settling upon those of General Mattings.

"Do you agree, General?"

Mattings nodded somberly. "I admit, my faith has never been all my parents desired, but it has sustained me through some very dark times. To *know* more would not diminish that. To understand the Source as a living entity, still capable of and intent upon revealing itself to us, might actually bring our people closer to it. To refuse to even ask the questions doesn't feel right. Are we the Source's children, only capable of walking in limited light? Or does it call us to live in the full brilliance of enlightenment? That the Seriareen did not know the Source does not trouble me. They were warped by their own selfish desires and dared to call their arrogance truth. But they were ultimately brought low. You fear what they might show us. I wonder what we might show them."

Cin sighed deeply. "I *am* afraid," she began, but stopped herself. Finally she said, "But policy should not be born of fear."

"No, it shouldn't," Janeway agreed.

"What do you suggest?" Cin asked warily.

The admiral smiled and made her proposal.

An hour later, the logistics had been settled. Janeway and Chakotay were escorted to the *Shudka*'s shuttlebay, where their craft was waiting to ferry them back to *Voyager*.

Once their course was set, Janeway said simply, "Thank you."

Chakotay nodded, then asked, "Why is this so much harder now?"

Janeway shrugged. "We know the Confederacy too well to trust their motives."

"I wasn't actually talking about the mission."

"Oh."

After a lengthy silence, Chakotay said, "Do you think we made a mistake?"

Janeway turned and met his eyes. "No."

Chakotay felt the knots in his stomach loosen ever so slightly. "Okay," he said.

The last few minutes of their journey back to *Voyager* were spent in amicable, if heavy, silence.

VESTA

"Anything?" Captain Regina Farkas asked of Ensign Jepel, her operations officer.

"Long-range scans remain inconclusive, Captain," Jepel replied.

Given the fleet's history at the Ark Planet and the developments at the Gateway over the past few days, Captain Farkas had opted to survey the system *Demeter* had returned to from deep within the cloaked parsec of space that was the purview of the ancient protectors. Backtracking along *Voyager* and *Demeter*'s previous course exiting the system would have likely put her ship directly in the path of a number of vessels that were now traveling with concerning regularity through the area.

The new ships followed a predictable path, beginning at the termination of a transwarp corridor several million kilometers outside the cloaked area and moving briskly past the Ark Planet's system. Farkas had no idea where they were going. Should they approach the Gateway they would be destroyed. Once the Confederacy had all but decimated the *Kinara* it stood to reason that their reinforcements would recon the area. They probably had some new rendezvous point beyond the long-range sensor capabilities of the CIF vessels at the Gateway and were regrouping.

All of the vessels detected thus far were Turei, Vaadwaur, and Devore. Farkas hoped that the *Lightcarrier* had succeeded in apprising the Skeen, Karlon, Muk, and Emleath of the truth about their allies and that everyone had seen the last of them, at least for a while.

It had taken several extra hours, but Farkas had patiently spent them allowing her ship's sensors, modified with enhancements installed by *Voyager*, to render accurate astrometrics readings of the cloaked parsec. The captain ordered the slipstream engine on a course that would bring them within scanning range of the system but beyond the notice of anyone else traveling through the area.

As soon as they had arrived, they were scanned by a local protector. Apparently that scan designated them as friendly, and *Vesta* had otherwise been left alone as they began their search for *Demeter*.

"Captain," Malcolm Roach, Farkas's first officer began, "I wonder if we are going about this the wrong way."

"I am, as always, open to suggestions, Commander," Farkas replied.

"If we assume *Demeter* arrived safely within the system, the protectors would be aware of it."

"One would think."

"Perhaps we should simply ask them for any intelligence they have on *Demeter*."

Farkas grinned. "We have all of Lieutenant Kim's communications protocols loaded. I'm a little wary, however, of the potential response. They might give us a set of coordinates, or they might initiate direct telepathic contact. I'd just as soon avoid the latter. But if we ask, we don't get to choose how they answer."

"Too much information could be unpleasant," Roach agreed. "But given the wave forms' cloaking capabilities, we might not have another choice. We could be right on top of them as we speak and not know it."

"If *Demeter* is out here and they detected us, I imagine *they* would initiate contact," Farkas said.

"What if they can't?" Roach asked. "They could have come under attack and been damaged."

"And we don't exactly have the rest of our lives to wait, do we?" Farkas asked rhetorically. After a moment's consideration she said, "Jepel, let's summon a local protector and see if they feel like talking."

"Aye, Captain," Jepel acknowledged.

A few minutes later, a protector emerged several thousand kilometers from the ship as requested, and Jepel transmitted an image of *Demeter* to it. The moment the transmission was received, an additional protector emerged, and Farkas's seat was jolted as it surrounded *Vesta*.

"What did it say, Jepel?" Farkas demanded.

"Nothing," the young Bajoran replied.

"Then we'll just hope for the best," Farkas said as the ship began to move toward the Ark Planet's system. They had almost achieved the protector's equivalent of warp speed when the ship slowed in preparation for moving into orbit around the planet. Seconds later, Farkas watched as *Demeter* seemed to appear out of nowhere just a few thousand kilometers to port.

"We found her," Jepel reported.

"Yes, I can see that, Ensign." Farkas smirked. "Open a channel."

"Commander O'Donnell is already hailing us," Jepel replied.

Demeter's captain appeared no worse for the wear and genuinely happy to see Farkas. "*Hello,* Vesta," he greeted Farkas jovially.

While Farkas was relieved, she was also cognizant of the wrench O'Donnell had thrown into the fleet's works by pulling this little stunt.

"I'm assuming you have a very good reason for being here, rather than back at the First World, where you were expected days ago, Commander," Farkas said.

"*I do,*" O'Donnell confirmed. "*Do you want to hear it, or should I just begin composing my epitaph?*"

"I'm all ears, Captain," Farkas replied, "but you'll want to finish that before your next report to Admiral Janeway."

Over the next few minutes, O'Donnell briefed Farkas on all that had transpired at Femra and Vitrum. Overseer Bralt interrupted on several occasions to express his wonder at the fleet's work with the

Ark Planet and his gratitude to O'Donnell for opening his eyes to many uses he had never suspected possible for the protectors.

Commander Fife then provided Farkas with a complete tactical update of the alien traffic they had detected near the system that delayed their departure.

"So you've been sitting here cloaked for the better part of two days looking for a safe window?" Farkas asked.

"*Yes*," Fife replied.

"Is there any reason you didn't ask the protector cloaking you to carry you to a safe departure point before you engaged your slipstream drive and returned to the Confederacy?"

Fife's eyes were already much too large for the rest of his face. At this, they widened impossibly as the commander turned to O'Donnell, clearly hoping for rescue.

"*In the first place, I didn't know they could do that. More important, we've made good use of our time, Captain,*" O'Donnell assured her. "*Overseer Bralt raised a number of salient questions about our work here and now has all of the data he could possibly require to begin implementing some of our protocols back in the Confederacy.*"

"But you are ready to leave now?" Farkas asked.

"*Absolutely,*" O'Donnell confirmed.

"Good. I'm going to send you a complete report on the rest of the fleet's actions since we lost contact with you. You'll need it before you speak with Admiral Janeway."

"*I cannot tell you how I've anticipated that moment, longed for it, really,*" O'Donnell teased.

Farkas chuckled. O'Donnell could be maddening, but she had grown to appreciate his wit.

"Captain, our sensors have picked up another vessel approaching our position," Kar reported from tactical. "They exited the transwarp aperture one minute ago and are following their predecessor's course."

"We'll sit tight for a few minutes and then ask our protectors to facilitate our departure," Farkas ordered.

"Aye, Captain," Kar replied.

"*Commander Fife,*" an unfamiliar voice reported from off screen.

"*Yes, Lieutenant Url,*" Fife replied.

"*Our database identifies the incoming vessel as Voth.*"

A chill crept up Farkas's spine. She'd only seen one Voth ship up close and the *Scion* had made quite the first impression.

"Commander Fife, have any of the previous vessels passing through paused to scan the area?"

"*No, Captain. Most of them come under brief attacks from the protectors, counter them, and continue on their way.*"

Farkas found her admiration for the wave forms increasing. She knew there was more to them than they'd probably ever have time to learn. Their recent encounters with the new ships now moving regularly through their little corner of the universe might have taught them the futility of such efforts. But apparently undaunted, they continued their quixotic attacks, honoring their original programming despite the probability that their actions would prove useless.

"Let's hope the Voth do the same," Farkas noted.

Silence descended upon both ships as the massive Voth vessel approached the system. For a few seconds, it appeared the two Federation ships had dodged the incoming bullet.

As soon as the protectors began their assault, however, the ship slowed. It easily dispersed the attacking wave forms but did not immediately resume its course.

Instead, it slowly turned and began to move directly toward the Ark Planet.

"Damn," Farkas cursed under her breath.

12

STARFLEET MEDICAL

The Commander did not understand the latest set of data before him.

Modification 247-RF-N651-A was the first he had

inserted into Naria's system that had not been rejected entirely. His initial presumption was that he had finally succeeded in programming the catoms he had injected into his subject to adapt themselves to Naria's organic systems. All of the readings he had taken immediately following the injection clearly showed the tagged catoms within her system, and all of her vital signs remained normal seventy-two hours later.

But with each hour that passed, the number of catomic molecules present diminished. The few that remained appeared to have altered their configurations significantly, suggesting that they were reverting to the same neutral state they had displayed prior to his modifications.

The Commander could not rule out the possibility that the catoms were behaving this way *because* of the modifications he had made. Several control tests would have to be administered to confirm or deny this thesis.

He did not, however, believe this to be the case.

Every instinct the Commander possessed advised him that the catoms he had modified had been altered by an external force: *Seven of Nine.*

How she might be doing this, he could not yet imagine. That she would make the attempt did not surprise him in the least.

The bargain he had made with her had not been explicit on this point, but he could not help but see it as a betrayal.

Seven must be made aware of his displeasure.

Toward that end, the Commander first contacted Lieutenant Slue of the *McFarland.*

An hour later, after receiving Slue's report, he contacted Doctor Frist.

COLEMAN

Every muscle in Gres's body was tense. His chair had been turned to face the rear of the runabout, as had Naomi's. Both sat silently as officers from the *McFarland* scanned every millimeter of the runabout with their tricorders. The lieutenant who had hailed the *Coleman* just outside the Tyree Nebula, a young, fresh-faced Bolian called Slue, observed their work while casting sidelong glances at Gres and Naomi.

Finally, an ensign moved to Slue's side and offered him his tricorder to substantiate his report. "There are no traces of DNA that do not belong to the pilot or the cadet."

"How is that possible?" Slue demanded.

"I don't know, sir," the ensign replied.

Slue turned a hard face to Gres, who completely understood the lieutenant's frustration. After Tom, Seven, and the refugees from Arehaz had departed, Gres and Naomi had scrubbed the runabout from stem to stern to remove any evidence of their former passengers' presence. Neither Tom nor Seven had thought to request this precaution. Naomi had suggested it to Gres during the first few hours of their flight, and he had readily agreed.

"Let's go over this one more time," Slue said.

"Gladly," Gres replied. "Commander Tom Paris, a dear friend of our family, offered me use of this runabout to take my daughter on an extended vacation to Ktaria. She's never seen my homeworld, and my wife and I decided that was long past due. I would have taken my own ship, but Sam was using it. I didn't want to pass up the opportunity when Commander Paris presented it to me."

"Was Mister Paris ever aboard this ship?" Slue demanded.

"Briefly," Gres acknowledged. "He stopped by to see us off."

"Was Seven of Nine, also known as Annika Hansen, ever aboard this vessel?"

"She came to say hello to me," Naomi offered. "I'd been trying to reach her since she returned to Earth several weeks ago. It was the first chance she'd had to make contact. She left with Tom."

"Neither of them left any genetic residue," Slue noted.

"They were only here a few minutes. I'm not sure either of them touched anything," Gres said.

"Your route to Ktaria has been indirect," Slue noted.

"There's a lot out here I wanted Naomi to see," Gres said.

Slue obviously knew he was being lied to. He just couldn't

prove it, nor could he explicitly state his suspicions. If Gres was telling the truth, to ask about the refugees would be to reveal classified information to a civilian and an Academy cadet.

"You will hold position here until I advise you further," Slue ordered. When he and his team transported back to the *McFarland*, Gres heaved a pent-up sigh of relief.

Naomi offered him a tight smile in return.

"What do you think they'll do?" she asked softly.

Gres shrugged, lifting a finger to his lips to caution her.

Half an hour later, Slue advised Gres that he was free to return to his previous course. When the *McFarland* was no longer visible on the *Coleman*'s sensors, Gres instigated a sweep of the ship for any device that might have been planted on board by Slue's crew. Two bugs were detected. Gres left them in place, but made sure Naomi understood that every word they said going forward would be monitored.

Finally, he said, "You know, we have been away quite a while. If you'd rather just go home, I'd understand."

Naomi shook her head. "I've never seen Ktaria. We're almost there. I think we should stick to the plan."

"Are you sure?" Gres asked, deeply touched. Both of them knew that at this point Tom and Seven's ruse was over, at least as far as they were concerned. The safest thing to do now would be to return the ship to Earth and put the whole thing behind them.

"I am," Naomi said. "I'm really enjoying spending time with you, Dad."

"Me, too," Gres said.

STARFLEET MEDICAL

"Thank you for responding to my summons so quickly, Commander Paris," Doctor Pauline Frist said as soon as he entered her office.

"I'm always happy to do what I can to help Starfleet Medical," Paris replied cordially.

"I'm afraid I have a rather disturbing report for you," Frist continued.

Paris nodded, keeping his face neutral. Several possibilities for her urgent request to see him flew through his mind. He had remained in constant contact with the Tamarian Embassy over the past few days, but had not visited since his mother had arrived. His presence there would raise suspicions, though he had no reason to believe that Commander Briggs was aware that Riley's people were not aboard Gres's runabout.

Yet.

"My last report to you indicated that Seven remained in stasis in our quarantine facility."

"Yes, it did," Paris agreed.

"I have just been advised by the Commander that Seven was removed from stasis and temporarily released from the quarantine area."

Just been advised? Paris found that hard to believe but decided to play along.

"I see," he said.

"We have lost contact with her," Frist continued as her brow furrowed. "She had agreed to depart only briefly, and that request was granted on the understanding that she return within forty-eight hours."

Not according to Seven, Paris thought. *She was given ten days, not two.*

"Although she appeared to be free from contamination when she was revived, the Commander was adamant that she return for additional testing to confirm this."

That, Paris knew, was a lie.

"Seven agreed to these terms, but is now more than twenty-four hours past due."

Paris nodded sagely.

"She has left us no choice. The Commander has asked me to issue a public health alert. Starfleet will immediately begin a search for her. The moment she is found, *and she will be found*," Frist said with emphasis, "she will be returned to the quarantine facility."

"That sounds like a reasonable precaution," Paris offered.

Frist paused, studying him in silence. "I take it she has not contacted you?" she finally asked. "The Commander was under the impression that she might already have done so."

Confusing as this conversation had become, it had also been quite instructive. Either Doctor Pauline Frist was a world-class liar, or she had no idea what Briggs was really up to. She had not mentioned the refugees or the runabout. *Does she even know about them?*

"Commander Paris," Frist demanded, "has Seven contacted you in the last three days?"

"No," Paris lied. If Frist was toying with him, his goose was already cooked and on the table. But if Briggs had decided to keep her in the dark, Paris dared not risk directing her toward the light switch just yet.

"Should she make contact, you are hereby ordered to advise me immediately. If I learn that you have or obtain knowledge of her whereabouts and do not report them immediately, you will be subject to disciplinary action, including a possible court-martial."

Finally, Paris understood.

This was not Doctor Frist interrogating him. This was Commander Briggs *using* Frist to send him a message. He knew about the runabout. He knew he had lost access to both Seven and his catomic goldmine. Seven had frustrated his plans, and he was now altering the terms of their agreement. This wasn't even a warning shot. Seven had fired the first volley and the Commander was returning it in kind.

Poor Doctor Frist probably had no idea that her job over the past year had really been to act as cover for Briggs. In a way, that was a good thing. Paris sincerely hoped that when the list of names of the officers complicit in Briggs's transgressions was finalized, it would be short. He was not so fond of Frist that he worried overmuch about her presence on that list. But he continued to hold out hope that the vast majority of those connected with this project were not willingly debasing themselves or their oaths to Starfleet by knowingly assisting Briggs in egregious unethical behavior.

"You can count on my full cooperation, Doctor," Paris advised her.

"I expect nothing less, Commander," Frist said.

"Is there anything else?"

"Not at this time."

Paris left her office swiftly, his thoughts racing. He could no longer risk following Seven to Indiana, for Gretchen Janeway's sake as much as Seven's. But Seven needed to know how quickly the rules of the game were changing. Sharak and Wildman had not reported in for several days. He could have used their help but had no idea when they might return. Gres and Naomi had promised not to get in touch unless they were taken into custody, and Paris dared not cast any further suspicion on them by making contact. The risk to the career of any other officer he tried to bring into their conspiracy was too great. Who else could he ask?

Only one person came to mind.

ALDEBARAN

Lieutenant Samantha Wildman was hardly a crack shot, but the combination of adrenaline and fear of imminent death focused her thoughts and steadied her arm.

She couldn't see her attacker, but the shots she was evading were only coming from one place: the farthest, darkest corner of the room. Using the tables for cover and cursing her need of the biohazard suit, Wildman continued to fire, advancing toward the shooter.

What felt like hours but was actually only a few seconds later, a sharp cry met Wildman's ears, followed by silence. Wary of a ruse, Wildman called out, "Doctor, scan the room for life signs."

Her eyes remained glued to the corner of the room, but she heard Sharak shuffle back to the entrance.

"One life sign, seriously injured," Sharak finally reported.

"Get behind me," Wildman said, and once he had joined her, they made their way with slow, deliberate steps toward the corner. They were still a few meters away, just beyond a standard medical diagnostic table, when her beacon illuminated their quarry.

She was seated on the floor attempting to curl herself into a fetal position, her face wracked with pain.

The pain was not shocking to see. What halted Wildman in her tracks was the woman's face.

She was Ria's identical twin.

Much of her exposed flesh was a deep shade of purple, but it was generously covered with swirling black lines.

"Show me your hands," Wildman ordered.

The woman lifted her eyes to Wildman's. With effort, she raised her empty right hand and swept it forward, readjusting herself against the wall. The phaser she had fired was on the floor, not far from what should have been her left hand. But her left hand, her entire left arm, and much of her left shoulder were gone.

Wildman had set her phaser at its highest stun setting. Even a direct hit should not have caused the damage she was seeing.

As Doctor Sharak stepped closer to examine her, Wildman played her beacon farther into the corner, and her stomach revolted at the sight of the severed arm resting near the wall. It was more densely blackened, but its fingers continued to move. They appeared to be seeking to climb the wall.

"What is your name?" Sharak asked kindly.

The woman coughed, spat a thick pink glob of something to the floor beside her, and fought for each breath. Undeterred, Sharak said, "Help me."

Wildman understood and quickly pocketed her phaser so she could assist the doctor in lifting the woman to the diagnostic table.

Once she was settled, the doctor began to search the nearby tables and drawers.

"What are you looking for?" Wildman asked.

"Anything I can give her for the pain," Sharak replied.

"No," the woman murmured.

"Why not?" Sharak asked, returning to her side.

"Interfere . . . with healing," she managed.

Sharak nodded. "Is there anything I can do for you?"

The woman seemed to study his face for a moment.

"Jefferson?" she asked.

"I am Doctor Sharak," he replied. "What is your name?"

The woman's eyes closed, though her ragged breathing continued.

A faint scratching sound Wildman could not place nagged at her, but she turned her attention to the rest of the room. Between her and the door were three large biometric chambers. All were filled with a bluish fluid, and each contained life-forms at different developmental stages. One was only a few inches long and looked like a small tadpole. The second was the size of a young child with dark hair that already reached her shoulders. The third appeared to be fully grown and, again, identical to Ria.

Wildman moved to a terminal near the chambers and activated it. There were no security measures in place. She quickly located the controls and began to navigate through a treasure trove of data.

"Her name is Anari," Wildman advised Sharak. "And these are her . . ."

"Sisters," Anari offered.

Wildman didn't need to ask if the woman was a Planarian. The data before her confirmed her species as well as the developmental progress of six others who had been "grown" within this lab. Despite the fact that Anari's creation was a violation of Starfleet's long-standing ban on eugenics, Wildman could not deny her fascination. She could easily spend the next several weeks studying the information on this terminal and the rest of her life marveling at this amazing species.

She could find no immediate references to Commander Briggs, but Anari had already spoken his name. If she survived, she could testify to the link between them.

"Amazing," Wildman heard Sharak say.

"I know," Wildman added.

"You must see this, Lieutenant."

Wildman moved back to Sharak's side. He had found the controls for a bright overhead light, and it now cast its harsh glow over the exam table. Even with her naked eyes, Wildman could see the black flesh where Anari's arm had been severed beginning to sprout new pink replacement tissue. Anari's face had relaxed, and she seemed to have fallen into a deep sleep.

"We need to contact someone," Sharak said.

"We will," Wildman assured him. Turning back, she noted the presence of several small cases on the table between her and the biometric containers. All were marked with the insignia of the Benevolent Daughters Hospital.

Wildman carefully released the locking mechanism on the first and lifted the lid. Within it rested a single hypospray. A small display panel embedded in the interior lid was activated and quickly displayed the status of the hypo's contents. As soon as she read it, Wildman stepped back involuntarily.

"We have the plague," she advised Sharak.

He turned and studied the case just as she had. Finally, he stepped forward and carefully closed the case's lid.

"We have more than that," Sharak noted. "We have everything we require to expose Commander Briggs."

Wildman nodded, wondering at the sudden silence in the room. Anari continued to regenerate. The biometric tanks emitted a low hum, as did the light above the diagnostic table.

The scratching sound, Wildman realized. It had finally, mercifully ceased.

Sharak had moved to the opposite side of the bed and was inspecting Anari's regenerative progress more closely while simultaneously scanning her with their tricorder. A shadow of movement over his shoulder caught Wildman's attention. Once again, she lifted her wrist beacon.

The arm that had rested on the floor near Anari was now hanging by its fingers from a control panel embedded a meter and a half up the wall. Three fingers held it in place as two others played over the active buttons lighting the panel.

A soft, regular alarm began to sound. The shift in the color of the display from green to red suggested that the low beeping sound should be taken as a warning.

Wildman swallowed her disgust and moved toward the panel. Small digital numbers were displayed and were counting backward from two minutes and fifty-one seconds.

"Doctor!" Wildman shouted as she turned and roughly grabbed the back of Sharak's suit.

"Samantha, what are you—" he blurted as the tricorder in his hands fell to the floor.

"Run!" she shouted over him, forcing him around the side of the diagnostic bed and toward the room's only exit.

INDIANA

For the past twenty hours, Gretchen and Phoebe had sat an exhausting vigil. After returning from the willow tree to the relative normalcy of the kitchen, Phoebe had refused to leave her mother's home until Seven awoke from whatever state she had entered.

Between tirades against her sister and Starfleet, Phoebe had retreated to her father's office and begun a search of Federation records on exotic alien meditative practices. So far, nothing explained what they were witnessing.

Both had nearly jumped out of their skins when the front doorbell rang. With Phoebe at her heels, Gretchen had answered the door, only to greet a completely unexpected visitor.

"Julia?"

"Hello, Mrs. Janeway. I'm sorry to disturb your dinner hour, but I'm afraid I have come on urgent business. May I come in?" Julia Paris asked.

Gretchen nodded wordlessly, stepping back to allow the old acquaintance to enter her home. Only then did Julia see Phoebe. "Miss Janeway, isn't it?" she asked, extending her hand.

"Yes, Mrs. Paris," Phoebe replied, returning the gesture and shaking Julia's hand firmly.

"The artist?"

"Yes."

Julia's polite façade remained firmly in place, but a hint of steel tinged her voice as she said, "It is urgent I speak with your guest. Is she still here?"

"You mean Seven?" Phoebe asked.

Julia looked to Gretchen in a way that made her wonder if there was some special protocol that the parents or spouses of Starfleet officers were expected to observe that she had forgotten.

"Do you and your daughter understand that no one else should be made aware of Seven's presence here?" Julia demanded.

"We do," Gretchen began.

Phoebe quickly responded over her, "Why not? Surely no one sent here by my sainted sister would ever be involved in any activities that would bring shame to her family or put them in any danger."

"Phoebe, please."

"Phoebe," Julia began calmly, "has Seven shared with you the reasons for her visit?"

"Of course not. She's like everyone else in Starfleet. She does whatever she wants, and the rest of us are expected to stand by and live with the consequences."

"Phoebe, that's not fair," Gretchen chided her.

"When are you going to stop defending her?" Phoebe demanded.

"Who? Seven?" Julia asked.

"Kathryn," Phoebe replied. "She invited Seven here, and now we're trying to figure out who we should contact."

"You will contact no one," Julia ordered. "I came here to speak with Seven, and once she has heard my message, I am certain she will return with me. You will forget any inconvenience her visit might have occasioned and go on with your lives as if she had never been here. If you are questioned about her presence here by anyone, including Starfleet, you will feign ignorance. Seven's life and the lives of many whom Kathryn holds dear depend upon your silence. Surely that is not too much to ask from her family."

"Of course it isn't, Julia," Gretchen insisted. "Phoebe wouldn't do anything to hurt Kathryn or her friends."

Julia's appraising glance rested on Phoebe for a long moment. Finally, she said, "Phoebe Janeway, you come from a family that has given Starfleet and the Federation some of its brightest lights. Your father and your sister dedicated their lives to securing yours and mine. But for their efforts, and those of thousands like them who choose to stand between us and the darkness, we would not be here having this conversation. We would long ago have fallen to any number of hostile forces determined to exterminate our way of life. You must never doubt this."

Phoebe started to retort, but Julia continued, "Spare me your selfish prattling about how much you have suffered. Your father and sister died serving the greater good. Powers beyond comprehension returned your sister to us. The only appropriate response is gratitude, and the only acceptable action is your continued support."

Julia paused, shaking her head. "I know how easy it is to forget that when you are in pain. Don't allow that pain to guide you. Don't make mistakes for which you might never have the opportunity to atone." Turning back to Gretchen, she said, "Where is Seven?"

"This way," Gretchen said.

They walked to the willow tree in silence. Seven remained as Gretchen had last seen her. Although Gretchen feared to get too close, Julia seemed to accept with complete equanimity the fact that a woman in a lotus position was floating above the ground. She moved to stand directly in front of Seven and, tapping her gently on the shoulder, began to say her name softly and urgently.

"Seven? Seven?"

It took a few moments, but finally Seven's eyes fluttered open. Gretchen had imagined that the moment the spell was broken,

Seven would tumble to the ground. Instead, she brought her feet down gracefully and stood as if she had just risen from a very comfortable chair. Her cheeks had good color and her eyes were bright. She even appeared well rested.

"I am sorry to disturb you, Seven," Julia began. "Tom sent me."

"I know. We must go," Seven said. Turning to Gretchen, she stepped forward. "Thank you for your hospitality, Mrs. Janeway."

"Anytime," Gretchen said, and meant it.

13

VOYAGER

You're kidding me, right?"

Ensign Aytar Gwyn was *Voyager*'s best flight control officer. She was half-Kriosian, and Paris had long ago concluded that she flew by a sixth sense. Commander B'Elanna Torres wasn't surprised by the young woman's analysis of the area of space *Voyager* was preparing to explore. It was displayed with dispiriting clarity on the astrometrics lab's large viewscreen.

"No," Torres replied. "Lsia has provided Admiral Janeway with intel on Seriar's location. Based on a number of calculations, including the intersection of those six streams you see there, just outside the affected area, *this is it.*"

Running a hand through her short aquamarine hair, Gwyn asked, "Can we even call that space?"

Lieutenant Kim spared Torres the explanation. "Lsia told the admiral there was heavy fighting between her people and the Nayseriareen with advanced weapons near Seriar. She doubted the damage to subspace would have repaired itself since then."

"So the admiral is okay spending at least a year out here navigating this mess?" Gwyn demanded.

"We're all hoping you can shave down that estimate a little for us," Torres noted, although she didn't think it was far off.

The first time Torres had studied this region was several weeks earlier, while *Voyager* was en route to Lecahn and she and Conlon were trying to produce a map of all of the streams running through Confederacy space. Initially, she had thought this vast dark spot on her charts was another cloaked area, similar to the one that surrounded the Ark Planet. It covered several sectors, and its outermost border was near the edge of Confederacy territory in that area. Clearly the CIF already knew what Torres now realized. It wasn't cloaked space. It was space that had been laid waste by terrible weapons, filled with subspace instabilities and exotic radiation, and no sane spacefaring folk would risk entering it.

Gwyn stepped back from the display, crossed her arms at her chest, and inhaled deeply. Closing her eyes, she stood motionless for a long moment. Torres looked to Kim, who could only shrug.

Abruptly, Gwyn stepped back up to the console that controlled the lab's display. She started to place her hands on the controls, then lifted them, saying, "Can one of you highlight anything in the area that might once have been a subspace corridor?"

Torres stepped to Gwyn's side. "Why?" she asked, even as she began to run the appropriate calculations. "None of them will be stable enough at this point to utilize. I doubt the CIF even has the appropriate frequencies."

"Yeah, I wasn't thinking about entering them," Gywn said. "I was just curious."

"Ensign," Kim interjected, "Captain Chakotay and Admiral Janeway need a briefing in the next half hour. We don't have time for curiosity right now."

"Look," Gwyn said, pointing to the huge screen before her. "Do you see that?"

Kim had no idea what she was pointing to. More than a hundred stars, planets, and streams were displayed before them.

"What?" Kim indulged her.

"That system a few light-years above the intersection of those streams," Gwyn replied. "The one inhabited planet there is Grysyen."

"And?" Kim asked.

Torres suddenly understood what Gwyn might be getting at, and why Harry didn't. "When we engaged the Unmarked at Lecahn, while you were still on the *Twelfth Lamont,* the ship whose crew we captured was able to catch up with us by executing a maneuver I'd never seen. They were from Grysyen."

"They bounced," Gwyn said. When both Torres and Kim shot her the same confused look, she continued, "Those corridors require an access key, a precise harmonic resonance that allows a ship to slip inside. The *Frenibarg* transmitted a frequency to open the stream just before it accelerated, at a distance of about ten thousand kilometers from the point of ingress. Then they cut their engines completely. Their momentum carried them toward the corridor but instead of pulling them in, they just bounced across the instability between normal space and subspace that exists once a corridor has been opened."

Torres smiled at Gwyn in admiration. Kim appeared horrified at the thought.

"What?" Gwyn demanded. "I'd never seen a ship move like that. I spent the next week studying our sensor readings until I figured out how they did it. It looked like fun."

Torres returned her gaze to the astrometrics display and inhaled sharply. While there were no stable streams displayed, dozens of fragments were present that appeared to be permanently open.

"I'd bet my life this is where *Frenibarg*'s pilot learned that maneuver," Gwyn said.

"You're not suggesting we try the same thing?" Kim asked.

"How long do you want to spend in that mess?" Gwyn asked. "If we try to navigate around all of the various instabilities out there, we could spend the rest of our lives at one-quarter impulse and still never find that planet. This way, if we find sections of corridors that remain stable enough, we can make up a lot of time."

As Harry paused to consider this, the doors to the lab hissed open.

"Commander, Lieutenant, Ensign," Lieutenant Conlon greeted them.

"Hi, Nancy," Torres said. "What's up?"

Conlon extended a padd to Torres, saying, "I've analyzed all of the power disruptions Lieutenant Kim discovered. *Voyager*'s systems weren't the only ones affected. One of our shuttles suffered similar surges. None were bad enough to damage any of the systems that weren't holographic. It appears the source is the bioneural interface regulators. At some point we are going to have to go in and replace all of the affected regulators, but the surges have stopped for now, and I've programmed the main computer to advise us if any new ones are detected. I was also able to restore the holodecks."

"The crew is going to be happy to hear that," Kim said, smiling.

"Is there anything else?" Conlon asked.

Torres considered Conlon's brisk report. They had both passed their wits' end days ago, but now that all of the major repairs had been completed, Nancy should have started to unwind a little.

Of course, Torres knew how she had felt when *Voyager* was damaged while she was her chief engineer. She *had* believed it was similar to what a parent might feel watching someone hurt their child, right up until she'd had Miral and understood that the two sensations were nothing alike. One induced anger and frustration; the other, primal madness.

"Our flight controller thinks she might have figured out a way for us to use the subspace corridor fragments in this wasteland we are about to explore to cut time off our work." Turning to Gwyn, she said, "You need to show Lieutenant Conlon all of your research and together run simulations before we decide to try it."

"Understood," Gwyn said eagerly.

"Of course," Conlon said, nodding.

Torres looked to Kim. He was studying Nancy's face, disconcerted. Conlon hadn't made eye contact with him since she'd entered the room. The fleet chief engineer made a mental note to speak to Harry about it later. She knew the two of them had been seeing each other, but Harry needed to understand the distance Conlon required right now. She'd shouldered the responsibility for getting *Voyager* repaired over the last several days and had rightly devoted herself entirely to it. You didn't just shut off that kind of focus or drop your defenses the moment the work was done. For the next several months, every time the ship made an unexpected move beneath her feet, Conlon would feel the impact that almost destroyed the ship. Torres would too. But she'd been down this road enough times to know what was happening to Conlon. This had been Nancy's first major test as *Voyager*'s chief engineer. She'd passed with flying colors. She just didn't know it yet.

"Come on, Harry," Torres said. "Let's leave these two to their work. We have to brief the captain and fleet commander."

"Sure," Kim said, nodding to Conlon, who returned a tight smile before focusing entirely on Gwyn.

GALEN

Three days into their work together, the Doctor and Counselor Cambridge were making progress in fits and starts. Neither trusted the other enough to listen without judgment or speak without first rallying their defenses. But despite this, they had stumbled across a few insights.

Cambridge had already indicated that he believed the Doctor was ready to resume his normal duties, although their sessions would continue to be part of the Doctor's daily schedule.

The counselor sat across from the Doctor, his left leg crossed over his right, swinging like a metronome set at its widest interval. The Doctor had detected an inverse relationship between the counselor's level of frustration and the speed of his incessant ticking: the slower the pace, the shorter his patience. At the moment, the motion was almost glacial.

They had spent the last hour discussing a new sense of despair the Doctor had begun to experience. Counselor Cambridge considered this progress. The Doctor was clearly moving rather briskly through the requisite stages of grieving the man he had been when his memories had remained intact and accepting the man he now was.

The Doctor was disinclined to celebrate this progress.

"Have you considered the possibility, Doctor, that your creator has, perhaps inadvertently and in the most ham-handed way possible, given you an experience that, in time, might enhance your ability to empathize with your organic patients."

"I already—" the Doctor began.

"To *better* empathize," Cambridge allowed.

"I really don't see how that's possible."

"None of us are perfect. Now that includes you," Cambridge said.

The Doctor started to reply, but paused as he calculated the statistical probability that the counselor could actually be complimenting him.

"You possess an encyclopedic understanding of ways in which an organic body can be damaged. By the time most physicians acquire that amount of knowledge, they have also accumulated a lifetime's worth of personal challenges, losses, and pain to go along with them. I *know* you have also faced your own fair share of difficulties. You have lost friends you held dear. You have loved with and without reciprocation. Didn't I read in your record that you once created a holographic family for yourself to better understand the human condition and interpersonal relationships?"

"I did," the Doctor replied, suddenly wishing that *this* was one of the memories Doctor Zimmerman had thought to mute. While he did not consider the experiment a failure, the Doctor would forever be tormented by the death of his holographic daughter. He had learned soon enough that *real life* came with enough painful eventualities. Seeking them out in the name of personal betterment was unnecessary. *Why rush the inevitable?*

Of course, now it might be possible to add Belle's memory to my segregated file, the Doctor suddenly realized. It only took a fraction of a second for him to dismiss the notion. He had lost too much of himself already. He would not willingly part with more.

"But you have never really been physically injured, have you?"

"I suppose not," the Doctor said. "Past damage to my program was repaired. The insights that came from facing personal challenges diminished the regrets for lapses and unintentional transgressions."

"You learned from your mistakes."

"Like everyone else."

"And now, *finally*, like everyone else, you find yourself damaged, with no perfect fix. Numerous conditions exist that our medical technology cannot reverse. You treated Seven's aunt. Her Irumodic Syndrome is one of the most difficult to witness, given the slow mental degradation that accompanies it. You counseled Seven to accept the unacceptable because there was no other choice. There was no way to repair Irene's brain.

"Likewise, your *brain*, for lack of a better description, has now been damaged. Your memories are a casualty of that damage."

"You believe I should accept my current condition?"

"I believe that rather than simply wallowing in the loss, it might be helpful for you to consider what you have gained in this unusual transaction."

"I'm sorry, Counselor," the Doctor said. "I'll try to wallow more quietly."

"You'll have to forgive my inability to pity you, Doctor," Cambridge said. "Admiral Janeway's decision to alter Doctor Zimmerman's modification and allow you to control the segregation and deletion of your current and future memories is a boon the rest of us should have long ago demanded of the gods."

"Are you suggesting, Counselor, that if you could remove your memories of Seven, you would?"

"If you'd asked me that question a few months ago, I might very well have said, 'Yes,'" Cambridge admitted.

"What has changed?"

"I've had sufficient time to accept the choice she made and to recognize that it was probably inevitable; perhaps *not so soon,* but ultimately."

"And how did you come to this acceptance?"

"I tried drowning my sorrows, but the buggers learned how to swim," Cambridge smirked. "Now I meditate."

"You . . . *meditate?*" the Doctor asked in disbelief.

"Why is that so hard to believe?"

"Isn't the practice usually born of a desire to achieve proximity to one's deity of choice? I find it difficult to believe you would acknowledge the existence of any being greater than yourself, let alone attempt to commune with it," the Doctor replied.

"For some, the practice is devotional, not unlike prayer. For me, it is a mental discipline. By eliminating extraneous thoughts and sensations, and entering a state of alert relaxation, I am able to separate my emotional responses to a thought from the thought itself. The insights that arise when I am able to achieve this detachment never fail to surprise me."

"Hmm."

"What?"

"I now have that ability, thanks to Reg's autonomous protocol."

Cambridge shook his head. "You have the ability to permanently separate emotion from specific memories. *Thought* and memory are not the same thing. One is present tense. One is past. Were you capable of achieving a meditative state, you might find it unnecessary to even contemplate using your new gift. You might be able to find the equilibrium your creator was so determined to force upon you *without* losing the vibrancy of your normal memory storage process."

"And how would I do that?"

"Practice."

The Doctor's brow furrowed.

Cambridge sat forward, uncrossing his legs. "I'm going to give you an assignment, Doctor. For the next few days, I want you to set aside some time to actively relax. Eliminate external stimuli as best you can. Clear your mind. Maintain that state for as long as you can. A few minutes will suffice at first, but the longer you can go, the better."

"Counselor, I really don't think . . ."

"Are you afraid?"

"I most certainly am not."

A low, clucking sound began to chirp through the counselor's closed lips.

A sharp, merciful trill sounded from the door.

"Come in," Cambridge and the Doctor said in unison.

Lieutenant Barclay entered. "Hello, Doctor, Counselor. I am sorry to interrupt."

"It's all right, Reg," the Doctor assured him.

"Admiral Janeway just came aboard. She'll be departing again for *Voyager* when she's done with Commander Glenn. She wants the counselor and me to accompany her." Barclay swallowed hard. "Meegan is being transferred to *Voyager*'s brig as we speak."

Cambridge rose to his feet. "Thank you, Lieutenant. I will return as soon as I am able, Doctor, and you and I can resume our work."

"Counselor?"

"Yes?"

"May I . . . I mean, I would very much like to go with you."

"Why?"

"I'll be resuming my duties as *Voyager*'s temporary CMO tomorrow. I may as well report now."

Cambridge sighed wearily. "Why?" he asked again.

The Doctor paused. Thus far, Cambridge had refused to accept anything less than the truth from the Doctor's lips. "I need to see for myself what she has become," he finally admitted.

"Doctor," Barclay interjected, "every analysis I've done of my files and the last readings I took of Meegan suggest that none of her personality subroutines survived. The holomatrix remains, but Meegan is gone."

"I understand," the Doctor said. "But I still need to see her."

Cambridge considered him, *almost* compassionately. Finally he shrugged, saying, "I see no medical reason to deny your request. But I am curious."

"It's one thing to be told a person has died. It's something else to see their corpse," the Doctor said.

"Have you always been this morbid?"

"I require . . . closure," the Doctor finally said.

"Closure or revenge?" Cambridge asked. "You understand I'm not philosophically opposed to either."

"I don't know," the Doctor admitted.

"Do you have any objections?" Cambridge asked of Barclay.

"No," Barclay replied.

"Then let's not keep the admiral waiting, gentlemen," Cambridge said.

"Both Tirrit and Adaeze have agreed to permit any tests you require, Commander, but you will observe the security protocols I have ordered at all times," Admiral Janeway advised Commander Glenn. "Under no circumstances will you remove the prisoners from their cells or deactivate the anti-psionic field surrounding them."

"Lieutenant Velth will be working with our security chief, Lieutenant Bamps, and we will post only organic guards outside their cells," Commander Glenn assured her. "It's a shame we can't use our holographic security team for this, but given what happened to Meegan, I just don't think it's wise."

Although *Voyager* would have been Janeway's first choice for holding all of the Seriareen prisoners, she didn't want to pass up the opportunity for a qualified doctor to settle the question once and for all as to whether or not the Seriareen's possession of Veelo, Dhina, and Kashyk was permanent. Glenn was the best choice for that.

General Mattings had asked to take custody of Emem for

the duration of their joint mission to locate Seriar, and Janeway had agreed. In what would likely be the only real exchange of technology between the Confederacy and the Federation, Janeway had provided the general with an anti-psionic force field generator. It would prevent Emem from launching any sort of telepathic attack on the *Calvert*'s crew should the opportunity present itself.

The general had departed for Confederacy space once Presider Cin had agreed to allow *Voyager* and *Galen* to join the *Third Calvert* in searching for Seriar. As soon as he returned, Emem would be relocated to his brig, and the three ships would set their course.

Janeway nodded. "I'm going to bring Lieutenant Barclay back to *Voyager* for the next few days, just to confirm his findings about the possibility of separating Lsia from our hologram. He doesn't think we can do it. I'm hoping that because Dhina and Veelo are living beings, there might be a way even though Lsia swears that there isn't."

"I'll do my best, Admiral."

"I know you will."

"But even if I can, would you really risk providing them with holographic bodies like Lsia's?" Glenn asked.

"It's troubling on so many levels," Janeway acknowledged. "If you find it is possible to separate the Seriareen from their current hosts while saving the lives of the hosts, I might be just as inclined to return them to stasis canisters similar to the ones they were in when you first encountered the Indign."

"I'll check our records and talk to Benoit about re-creating them, just in case," Glenn said. "Is there any chance I might have the Doctor's assistance?"

"I'll talk to Counselor Cambridge," Janeway said. "Reg tells me he's once again functioning within normal parameters. The problem is, it's a *new* normal, and I want to make sure he's adjusted to it as best he can before I ask too much of him."

"Having something other than his own problems to focus on might help," Glenn suggested. "We'll be keeping pace with

Voyager once we set course for Seriar. Since our communications restrictions have been lifted within the Confederacy, there's no reason I couldn't consult with him while I work," Glenn said.

"As long as the counselor agrees," Janeway said.

"One more question, Admiral."

"Go ahead."

"I know we're not going to be able to do anything to change the state of medicine in the Confederacy, at least in the short run. But after I finished going through the material ownership decrees you requested I research, I spent some more time looking at some of the central library's other records."

"To what end?"

"I just wanted to see if there was anything there that might help Doctor Kwer or her clinic."

"Did you find anything?"

"Not yet, but with your permission, I'd like to keep looking."

"As long as it doesn't interfere with your other duties."

"Of course not, Admiral," Glenn said.

"Velth to Captain Glenn."

Glenn tapped her combadge. "Go ahead, Ranson."

"The prisoners have been secured."

"Admiral Janeway and I are on our way," Glenn advised.

VOYAGER

Lsia had found the sensation of being suspended in open space surrounded by an energy field intensely disconcerting. For this, she was grateful. Since she had taken this holographic form, she had experienced nothing similar. She had believed that as long as she was trapped in this holomatrix, she was damned to a half-existence, one where she understood the feelings various situations should provoke, but would forever remain insensate of them. Every hour she spent enclosed in that invisible cage had produced ever-increasing, visceral fear. This had been progress, in a manner of speaking.

Perhaps this form had more to offer than she once thought.

Her new home was no larger than her previous prison. Its only furnishing was a long bench that ran along the back wall. A shield of visible light separated her from the rest of the brig, which contained four other empty cells.

She had not spoken to any of the others since they had turned themselves over to General Mattings. Tirrit and Adaeze were older than Lsia, having survived more than a dozen transfers each. Little could shake them. Emem was another story. He was only two transfers into immortality when he had been captured and contained. His shattered hopes for Admiral Janeway's tribunal and the loss of their allies could easily have driven him to extreme anxiety by now. She hoped he had used the last few days in patient reflection, analyzing his mistakes and learning from them.

She knew him too well to believe this likely. Soon, it wouldn't matter.

Captain Chakotay, a tall man with coloring similar to her own and an intricate black design on his forehead, entered the brig, moving to stand directly across from her. She had found his questions in their last interview revealing. He trusted her less than any of those present. He had likely counseled against accepting her request for assistance. It was a pity that his voice had not carried the day.

She lifted her shoulders and chin. She was his prisoner. *For now.*

"Welcome back to *Voyager,*" he greeted her.

"It is a definite improvement over my previous quarters," she said.

A faint smile of acknowledgment vanished from his lips before it was fully formed. "My crew has reviewed your data and believes they have discovered the likely location for Seriar. It is, as you feared, in an area of unstable space. We are formulating strategies for safe navigation through the area, but should we find it too dangerous, we may not be able to offer you the assistance you hoped for."

"You don't strike me as a man who runs from danger," Lsia observed.

"I do when it's avoidable," he countered. "I'm as curious as the next, but I'm more than willing to live without answers if it means protecting my ship and my crew. Unfortunately for you, my ego isn't quite that fragile."

"So I see."

They were interrupted by the arrival of Admiral Janeway, the ship's counselor, the holographic doctor, and Lieutenant Barclay. Of the four, Barclay was the only one that approached her cell with any trepidation.

He was right, of course, to still fear her. The rest were fools not to.

"Hello, Lsia," the admiral said once she had settled herself beside Chakotay.

"Have the others been released from their previous holding cells?" Lsia asked.

"Tirrit and Adaeze are now aboard the *Galen*. Emem will be transferred to the *Third Calvert* as soon as General Mattings returns," Janeway replied.

"Where has he gone?" Lsia asked.

"I don't know," Janeway admitted. "But he is expected back by the end of the day. I can assure you that Emem is quite safe and remains in what appears to be good health."

Emem has not yet done anything stupid. Excellent.

"I'll advise you of our progress," Janeway continued. "You will remain here during our explorations but a comm panel has been installed in your cell and should we require your input, it will be activated in order for you to communicate directly with our bridge officers."

"Can't I—" she began. "That is, I am understandably anxious to be among the first to see Seriar when we arrive there."

"This cell has been equipped with a special anti-psionic field. You have said that you cannot transfer out of your current host until that host is destroyed, but just in case, we've taken this extra precaution. This is the only location on the ship where we can be assured that you are completely contained and for now, I'm afraid you will have to remain here."

"I understand."

Janeway nodded to Chakotay and together they moved to speak quietly to Barclay, the Doctor, and Cambridge. Lsia could not hear their conversation, but after a few minutes, the admiral and Chakotay departed. The Doctor looked to Cambridge and Barclay, and both of them retreated toward the door, giving the Doctor and Lsia as much privacy as was possible in the small space.

"Hello, Meegan," the Doctor said.

"I am Lsia, of the Seriareen," she replied.

"There is a question I'd like to ask you," the Doctor said.

"Yes?"

"When you took Meegan, when you invaded her program, was she frightened?"

"No," Lsia assured him. "I searched through every potential host at my disposal as soon as I was released. Of those present, she was the least capable of offering resistance. I sensed her unique nature, though I did not understand at the time what it was to be photonic. There was more to her than her simple programming. There was a spark, a faint essence, still unformed, and a vast blank canvas that welcomed my presence."

"That blank canvas was a series of buffers in her program intended to house her developing sentience," the Doctor said.

Lsia considered him. She did not expect his forgiveness. She had used him cruelly before departing *Voyager* the first time. But he was the only other individual in the universe now who might actually understand her, and with his help, she might more quickly develop the intensity of feelings he was currently displaying.

With a thought, she shifted her appearance, reverting to Meegan's original form. She hoped this might comfort him.

He smiled quizzically at her. "Never do that again," he warned. "She was an innocent. You are a monster. You don't deserve that face."

Stung, she resumed her Seriareen form.

The Doctor nodded, turned, and left the brig.

14

TAMARIAN EMBASSY

When Seven and Julia materialized in the foyer of the Tamarian embassy, Commander Paris was waiting for them. A smile of relief lit his face, giving it an almost boyish appearance.

"Mission accomplished," Julia announced.

"Well done, Mom," Paris congratulated her. There was an awkward moment where he almost embraced her, but Julia retreated, saying, "I need to check on the children."

Paris nodded, staring after her for a moment before returning his undivided attention to Seven.

"How did it go?" he asked. "No, wait. Everyone should hear this."

"Everyone?"

"Our long-lost adventurers have returned."

Paris led her into a small sitting room just off the entryway where Doctor Sharak and Lieutenant Samantha Wildman were standing before an unlit fireplace. Sharak moved toward Seven immediately.

"Harath. The sun blazing," he said.

"It is good to see you again too, Doctor Sharak," Seven said, intuiting his meaning. "Lieutenant Wildman, I trust you are well," she inquired.

The petite blond woman stepped forward, extending her hand. "I've been better," she noted.

Seven nodded in understanding. While she appreciated the Wildman family's willingness to assist her, she understood well how their lives had been disrupted over the last several weeks.

"We can't stay long," Paris reminded them. "Sharak and Sam transported directly to the embassy as soon as their ship was in range, bypassing orbital control. I'm sure Doctor Frist will want to speak with them, given recent developments, but my presence here as the doctor's commanding officer shouldn't arouse any suspicion as long as we keep this brief."

"Do you intend to return to Starfleet Medical, Doctor?" Seven asked.

"Only if I am forcibly detained and ordered to do so," Sharak replied. "I believe you will be surprised when we tell you what we have discovered. Commander Paris already told us what Briggs did to you and the others. Added to our discoveries, the picture of the Commander becomes damning indeed."

"Of course, we can't prove any of it," Wildman noted bleakly.

"Tell me," Seven said.

The four seated themselves around a low coffee table. Refreshments had been laid out before them, but Seven had no appetite. It should have been impossible. She had not eaten in three days. It seemed, however, that the more she used her catoms, the more energy she had.

Doctor Sharak and Lieutenant Wildman took turns recounting their journey to Coridan, the discovery of Ria, and their suspicions that Commander Briggs was exploiting his discovery of the Planarian genome in the worst possible manner. Evidence existed to establish Ria's connection to the patients on Coridan who had fallen to the plague, but it was decidedly tenuous. No evidence had been discovered to confirm that she had planted the device in the hospital that would have dispersed the plague more widely had it not been detected and disabled. No one present doubted Ria's culpability.

Wildman's frustration became clear once they had described what had happened on Aldebaran. Anari's lab had contained all of the evidence necessary to expose Briggs. Much of the data had been scanned into Doctor Sharak's tricorder while he studied Anari's early regenerative processes. Unfortunately, he had dropped that tricorder in his haste to evacuate the lab, and it, along with any trace of Anari's existence, had been vaporized by a small but terribly efficient explosive. Starfleet security had descended upon the building immediately and Sharak and

Wildman had barely escaped detection in the immediate confusion as the *Goldenbird* transported them aboard, and they set course at maximum warp for Earth.

"It might take them a few days to connect you two to the explosion," Paris said once they had lapsed into silence. "But they're going to figure it out pretty quickly, and we're going to have to explain ourselves."

"I know," Wildman agreed.

"It is helpful, nonetheless," Seven noted. "Briggs insisted to me that he had not *killed* anyone during his experiments. The unique regenerative properties of the Planarians explain how he could assert this truthfully, despite what I witnessed. He justifies his actions to himself by believing that as long as one of them lives, it doesn't matter how many he destroys."

"Have you learned anything that might help us make a case against him?" Paris asked hopefully.

"Not directly," she replied. "I have spent the last several days working with Axum and Riley. Together we were able to detect and neutralize all of the catoms that were extracted from our bodies. Commander Briggs can no longer use them to experiment on anyone."

"Okay," Paris said dubiously. "But doesn't he still have the catoms from the rest of Riley's people?"

"He promised not to use them," Seven said.

"Briggs used Doctor Frist to send me a message this afternoon," Paris said. "He's had Frist issue a public health alert on you, Seven. If you are found anywhere, you will be immediately apprehended and taken back to Starfleet Medical."

"He knows I am no longer on the shuttle," Seven realized.

"That's my guess."

"What about Gres and Naomi?" Seven asked.

"I didn't want to risk contacting them," Paris admitted.

"You don't have to," Wildman interjected. "Gres's mother just sent me a message. She can't believe how much Naomi has grown."

"They made it to Ktaria," Paris realized, relieved.

"Yes."

"Your husband is a very smart man, Samantha," Paris said.

"I know."

"Okay. Between all of us, we've figured out a lot of what's going on. Briggs is clearly using the catomic plague as a cover for some other research. If he hadn't sent some of his minions to artificially inflate the number of plague victims, that wouldn't necessarily be a problem. He's probably not the only person in Starfleet who would like to see us master catomic matter."

"He violated every tenet of medical ethics when he re-created a Planarian," Wildman interjected. "That kind of work was banned after the Eugenics Wars. Everything else he's done pales in comparison to that transgression."

"But right now we have no way to tie him directly to either of the Planarians you discovered," Paris argued.

"Even if our testimony doesn't count for anything," Wildman said, "Seven just said he's also experimenting with Planarians inside of Starfleet Medical. Where are they coming from? Even if nobody else has seen them, there has to be some sort of trail. He's getting them in there somehow."

"All it took was a little digging and two of his agents terminated their work, destroying all evidence of their existence," Paris cautioned. "I have to believe he's ready to do the same here if he thinks he's about to be discovered. You already told Frist about Ria. So *he knows* we know. We have to find some concrete link; otherwise no one will believe what he's done."

"The only other proof is inside his lab," Seven said. "He has terminated operations on Ardana. He will do the same here soon enough, if he has not already done so."

"Are you ready to go back?" Paris asked.

"No," Seven replied. "Axum, Riley, and I have just begun our work. The next step is to attempt to reach the catoms that were not original to our bodies. We all believe this is possible, but we were not successful before I had to sever our communication."

"How long do you think it will take you to find those other catoms, and where do you plan to look?" Paris asked.

"*How* do you plan to look?" Wildman asked.

"It is difficult to explain," Seven replied. "Our catoms seem to recognize intrinsically that they are part of something greater, connected to all other catoms. But once we attempted to search outside ourselves, there was simply too much data to process. I need a way to focus our efforts. I need to know how the plague actually began."

"Does anybody know that?" Paris asked.

"Commander Briggs leads the project. He will know as much as anyone in Starfleet," Seven replied.

"Then why not return now and confront him?" Paris asked.

"Once I return, I am at his mercy once again. He could easily render me unconscious without returning me to stasis. If he inhibited my neural activity it would be impossible for me to continue to connect with Axum and Riley."

Paris nodded. "That only leaves us one choice."

"What?" Sharak asked.

"Admiral Montgomery," Paris replied.

A moment of silence followed. Seven was the first to break it. "I beg your pardon?"

"He's the admiral in charge of our current mission. Admiral Janeway commands the fleet, but he's her superior, which makes him *our* direct superior here on Earth. We go to him, tell him everything we've learned, and let him figure out how best to proceed."

"Will he assist us?" Sharak asked.

"How well do you know Kenneth Montgomery?" Wildman said simultaneously.

Seven had already decided. "No."

"Seven?"

"Even if Icheb transports me to Starfleet Command, I will be identified as soon as I arrive there. I will be taken back to Starfleet Medical before we reach the admiral's office."

"I could talk to him in advance," Paris offered. "I could ask for a guarantee that you would be protected."

"You would be asking him to disregard a public health alert," Seven insisted. "In my experience, Admiral Montgomery is, first and foremost, a follower of rules. He does not disregard orders lightly, nor is he a man who has demonstrated sufficient appreciation for ethically murky situations. He is our last resort, not our first."

"I disagree, Seven," Paris said. "We need help. All we can do now is run out the clock on your agreement with Briggs. Doctor Sharak *needs* to report his recent activities or come under suspicion."

"He reported them to *you*," Seven said.

"And now *I* am obligated to report to my superiors in turn," Paris retorted. "The longer we delay this, the worse we all look. We know we're doing the right thing, but nobody else does. All any of us have to lose is our commissions. When Briggs is discovered, they're going to put him in a very dark, deep hole somewhere, and no one is ever going to hear from him again. He's going to fight like hell to protect himself, and throwing all of us in front of a firing squad won't trouble him in the least.

"The fleet we serve with is under a magnifying glass right now, given our early losses," Paris continued. "We have to do this by the book. Both Captain Chakotay and Admiral Janeway expect it of us."

"I will not go," Seven insisted.

"Okay," Paris agreed. "The rest of us are reporting to Montgomery's office first thing in the morning. With the ambassador's permission, I think we should all remain here until it's time to go."

"I will see to it at once," Sharak said, rising.

Wildman excused herself, leaving Paris and Seven alone. Seven wasn't angry with Tom. She understood his choice. Seven also suspected she knew how Montgomery would respond, and the idea chilled her.

Both turned as Ratham hurried into the room. The look on her face brought both of them to their feet immediately. "Help," she said urgently.

Commander Paris knew what to expect when he entered the basement room that had been transformed by his mother in a matter of days. He had already seen the fruits of her labors. Seven paused for a moment in shock before following Ratham through the large double doors.

The ancient chandeliers and sconces had been replaced with four long rows of hanging lights. These made it possible for some areas of the room to be bright as day, while others were considerably dimmer. The far wall was now lined with double bunks, each containing thick, soft mattresses and clean linens. The rest of the room had been divided into different areas, some for relaxing on sofas and chairs, some for solitary pursuits, and a large section in the center had been cleared and filled with toys and games for the children. Nearest to the entrance, one large table had been assembled that could accommodate the entire group for family-style meals. Several platters of fruit, nuts, and flatbreads were available. Most of the refugees had already lost the gaunt appearance they'd had when they first arrived. The walls and floors had been scrubbed, and all of the refugees wore new, clean clothing.

"Your mother?" Seven asked softly as she hurried to keep pace with Ratham.

"Is amazing, yes," Paris agreed.

They found Julia Paris sitting on the edge of one of the bunks, her face contorted in concern. Nocks stood beside her, and a small group of adults was gathering while others distracted the children who were not yet asleep.

Groans interspersed with violent spasms of pain came from the bunk's resident, a middle-aged woman with thick, dark hair. Black wisps were plastered to her face, which was generously beaded with sweat.

Seven forced her way through the crowd and addressed Nocks. "What happened?"

"I don't know. Jilliant had just gone to bed. She sat up, screaming. It's only been a few minutes. Something she ate?" he asked.

"I don't think so," Seven said.

Julia rose and allowed Seven to take her place as Doctor Sharak entered the hall and came rushing toward them. Paris raised a hand to hold him back as Seven took both of Jilliant's hands in hers and closed her eyes.

A few moments later, the woman's pain seemed to subside.

Her breathing calmed and her eyes opened, staring up at Seven's face in mingled fear and wonder.

"Get her some water," Seven ordered.

Several rushed to comply as Nocks asked, "What did you do?"

"It's all right," the woman said weakly.

"Jilliant?" Nocks asked.

"It's gone now. She made it go away."

"Seven?" Nocks demanded.

Seven squeezed Jilliant's hand and smiled kindly at her before rising to face Nocks. "All of you gave samples of your catoms to Starfleet Medical before you were placed in stasis. I had an understanding with Commander Briggs. He has been experimenting with my catoms, as well as those of Axum and Riley. He was not to use any of yours for his ongoing work."

"What does this—" Nocks began.

"He is no longer honoring our understanding," Seven said. "Once he has modified catomic particles, he injects them into living subjects. Once they begin to acclimate to their new environment, the previous owner experiences the same sensations as the test subjects. I have endured this many times already.

"With proper instruction, all of you can be taught to control your responses to these attacks. The pain will still be present, but you will not *feel* it."

"How?" Nocks asked, wary.

"Riley told me that you had all agreed not to explore your catomic natures. I'm afraid the Commander's actions have made that choice unsustainable, unless you wish to subject yourselves to his experiments."

Nocks looked ready to punch something or someone. Paris moved to one side of Seven as Sharak stepped to the other.

"What have you done to us?" Nocks asked, horrified.

"I have done nothing," Seven replied. "This was the work of the Caeliar and the result of our choice not to join their gestalt. I have spent a great deal of time beginning to understand what that means. I am ready to share what I know with all of you. And should anyone else be attacked as Jilliant was, I will assist them in moving beyond the pain. If we work together," Seven assured him, "the Commander will be unable to harm any of us."

"There is *no* us!" Nocks shouted. "We are individuals now."

"Individuals who face a common threat," Sharak noted.

"I have no wish to strip anyone of their individuality," Seven said. "I would no more part with mine than I would expect you to part with yours. But *together* we are stronger than any individual."

"I know what we were *together*," Nocks spat harshly. "We were freed from that, but you would lead us back there, Seven of Nine."

"I have no intention of leading you anywhere," Seven insisted. "I will not force you or anyone to comply."

Nocks pushed his way past Seven and seated himself beside Jilliant. "It's all right," she assured him. "It wasn't like before."

"What wasn't?" Nocks asked.

"The gestalt," Jilliant replied.

"What is she talking about?" Paris asked Seven on a whisper.

"In order to assist Jilliant, I had to bring her into the joint thought-space Axum, Riley, and I have created," Seven said. "Axum believes that eventually, all of us will join him there."

"Is that your belief?"

Seven shook her head. "But I'm not sure how to prevent it either."

15

VESTA

As the Voth ship continued its scans, Captain Farkas considered her options. She had been ordered to share the fleet's discoveries about the Seriareen and the *Kinara*'s fate at the Gateway with the Turei and Vaadwaur. Avoiding the much more dangerous Voth seemed like a wise precaution.

It was also no longer possible.

As soon as the Voth ship began emitting anti-proton bursts, Farkas began to worry that they suspected the presence of cloaked vessels. When tachyon surges followed, that fear was confirmed. Something had tripped their sensors, and they were hunting for the source.

Jepel was constantly revising his calculations indicating how soon the Voth ship would pinpoint their location. With each minute that passed, roughly another five minutes was shaved off his estimates.

Farkas was worried about her ship, but much more concerned about *Demeter*. They couldn't initiate a slipstream jump from their current orbit of the Ark Planet, and for them to ask their protector to move them to a safe location would only increase the speed with which they were discovered.

The captain was also reviewing everything she had read about *Voyager*'s initial encounter with the Voth and her ship's records of the *Scion*'s capabilities. She had little doubt that the Voth would eventually come to appreciate the intelligence she had to share with them. The trick was living long enough to make that happen.

Her best chance was risky, if not rash. Its odds of success topped out at around forty percent. Not good. Just the best she could do.

She quickly relayed the outlines of a plan to Commanders O'Donnell and Fife. Their jobs would be relatively easy compared to hers. Timing was essential to this effort, and Fife assured Farkas he would wait until the last possible moment to act. They did not bother wishing her luck. They merely nodded grimly, in unison. Farkas smiled at this, marveling at how far these two had come in such a short time together.

Regina Farkas then ordered the *Vesta*'s self-destruct protocol to commence on a delay under a single circumstance, added an unusual trigger, locked out any overrides, and gave the bridge to Commander Roach.

Moments later, as she jogged lightly toward the transporter

room on deck three, the hairs on the back of her arms rose. *Vesta* had just shed her protector.

No turning back now.

"Captain Farkas, we have opened a channel to the Voth ship and begun transmitting standard friendship greetings," Commander Roach reported.

"Very good, Commander," she replied.

Entering the transporter room, Farkas hurried to the platform. Roach had already relayed her transport coordinates, and the officer on duty stood ready. The moment she was in place, she ordered, "Energize."

She could have sworn her gut lurched as the transport effect began to take hold. *Get a grip, Regina,* she thought, tightening her fingers around the only weapon she was taking with her: a padd.

Finally, the sight of Lieutenant Kerscheznsky hunched over his control panel vanished and was immediately replaced by a glorious vista.

Commander Roach did not expect the Voth to respond to their hails. He agreed with his captain that they would likely refuse to lower themselves to speak with any inferior species. He only hoped they would not immediately open fire.

He sat calmly in his seat, trying to convey the same poise his captain always displayed, even under the most challenging of circumstances. He hadn't served with Farkas long, but had already come to regard her as one of the finest officers in Starfleet.

The moment the bright blue beam shot forth from the Voth ship, Roach smiled.

Damn, Farkas was good.

"All hands, secure stations and prepare to welcome boarding parties," Roach ordered.

Commander Liam O'Donnell had made some truly terrible decisions in his life. He tried to keep them in perspective. When they were set alongside his list of accomplishments, the scales remained slightly tipped toward the good.

Should Captain Regina Farkas and her crew lose their lives because he had needed to prove a point to Overseer Bralt, that calculus was going to change dramatically. He doubted anything he might do in the future would ever make up for it.

Alana, he thought.

She had died years ago after a tragic miscarriage, but she had never really left him.

No, that's not true.

He had never really let her go.

From that day to this, he had carried her so close that their constant conversations in his head had become as normal, as *real*, as any he shared with the living.

Alana, he thought again.

She didn't answer. She might have already decided that this time, he'd gone too far. He had endured her silence in the past, knowing that she would return as soon as he had once again earned the privilege of her company.

He racked his brain, trying to remember the last time they had spoken.

Has it really been that long?

She'd advised him well during his confrontations with Captain Chakotay following their initial discovery of the Ark Planet. *But since then . . .*

He'd been so busy, so preoccupied with his duties, and had become so accustomed to seeking out the counsel of his crew, that he'd somehow fallen out of the habit of taking every concern first to her.

He couldn't even remember when, let alone how, that had happened. Only that it had. And now, when he needed her again so desperately . . .

"Alana," he whispered.

"Captain O'Donnell," Fife advised, "*Vesta* has been transported aboard the Voth ship."

"Have you communicated our request to the protectors?" O'Donnell asked.

"Aye, sir."

"Stand by."

"Are you all right, Captain?" Fife asked.

No, he realized, but nodded anyway.

Captain Farkas hadn't been specific when she asked Jepel to find the best spot on the Ark Planet for her pending negotiations: warm, dry, and far from large wild animals had pretty much covered it.

Jepel had outdone himself.

The sand beneath her boots was fine and white. The waves rolling toward the shoreline were tranquil and reassuring. The water extending as far as her eye could see was so clear that near the coastline, it was the palest green. Several reefs dotted the ocean floor. It was past midday, local time, but the sun had just begun its descent and bathed the beach in radiance, softened by a fierce, fresh breeze.

Should her crew die now at the hands of the Voth, she would always regret not being with them. But there were worse places to spend her final moments.

Instead of dwelling on the glory around her, she shaded her eyes and lifted them skyward.

"Anytime, Liam," she said aloud.

Finally, she clearly discerned a black dot on the horizon, speeding toward her. It arrived less than a minute later, a single Voth male wearing a vibrant blue uniform draped with a large metallic chain.

The moment the protector that had brought him here released him, he fell to his knees on the sand before her. Fear filled his eyes, but rather than kiss the ground—a clear desire once he ascertained his physical safety—he stumbled, attempting to rise to his feet.

Cognizant of the importance of first impressions, Farkas extended a hand to him to help him up.

"How do you do, sir," she said, taking a little of his weight. "I am Captain Regina Farkas of the Federation *Starship Vesta*." As she brushed away the sand he had transferred to her hand on her pant leg, she added, "You're here because you refused to answer my ship's hails. You and I really need to speak. After your ship assumed orbit around this planet, this was the only way I could think of to make that happen."

"Human," he spat. "Always deception."

Tapping a bracelet he wore, he said, "Thulan to *Vival*. Respond."

When no signal sounded, he tapped the device again furiously.

"Right now both you and I are invisible to our respective ships. Some local friends of mine have cloaked this beach and our presence here is undetectable."

"More treachery."

"Not at all," she said. "I know your people and mine didn't get off to a great start. Despite that, I've just put myself and my crew at great risk to facilitate this meeting."

"Capturing me will not further your aims. My crew will act on its last orders whether I am present to carry them out or not."

"Did those last orders include capturing my ship and taking it into one of those vast holds I've heard so much about on your city-ships?" Farkas asked.

He seemed taken aback.

"Let's try this again," Farkas said. "I'm Regina. You're Thulan?"

He nodded, grudgingly.

"Hello, Thulan. The moment you transported my ship into your hold, the *Vesta*'s self-destruct protocol was armed. It is set to a ten-minute delay to give us some time to talk, but as my first officer is no doubt advising your second-in-command right now, it will activate should our sensors detect any energy wave consistent with your transport devices. I know *Vesta*'s a lot smaller than your *Vival*, but between her mass and the considerable ordnance she's carrying, *Vesta*'s destruction within your ship should guarantee that *Vival* suffers some very serious damage should you try to remove her from your vessel's belly and send her back to open space."

"She's a bomb," Thulan realized.

"With a short fuse. I'm the only officer who can order that protocol rescinded, and I'm going to have to do it in person," Farkas added apologetically.

"Why have you brought me here?" Thulan demanded.

"Several months ago, your First Minister Odala did something I'm guessing many of your leaders found odd. Rather than continuing the xenophobic tendencies for which the Voth are famed, she coerced her fellows into joining an alliance of several alien species called the *Kinara*. The purpose of that alliance was to take down an even bigger alien alliance, The Confederacy of the Worlds of the First Quadrant. I'm not sure what she promised you, but she probably said that this was critical for your people because my Federation had recently dispatched a rather large fleet of ships to the Delta Quadrant with more powerful propulsion systems than the *Starship Voyager*.

"Odala then sent a few small ships out to investigate our communications relays and when her intelligence was confirmed, those ships began meticulously destroying key relays in order to eventually destabilize the whole network."

Thulan crossed his arms over his chest.

"You haven't contradicted anything I've said yet," Farkas observed.

"Go on," Thulan replied.

"The *real* First Minister Odala would never have been able to conscience such an alliance with inferior species, let alone allocate resources to the *Kinara*. The *real* First Minister Odala was murdered by an alien we know as Lsia of the Seriareen. Lsia is a hologram. She can take any form she wishes. She has probably been impersonating your minister since the first day she gained access to Odala. I can't guess as to what form she took at that time. I only know what the result was."

"Are these Seriareen part of your Federation?"

"No, sir. The whole story is a little complicated for the few minutes of life both of our crews now have left to them. This padd contains all of the intelligence we have on Lsia and her people, their history, and their current goals. It also contains sensor readings from a battle that took place a few days ago near the Gateway to the Confederacy. Your ship, the *Scion*, took a beating during that engagement, but was able to escape. I'm assuming you're here because the *Scion* has yet to report in."

Thulan's silence confirmed Farkas's guess.

"You have a choice to make. I'm not here to turn millions of years of Voth doctrine on its head. I'm not here to ask for a new beginning between our people, although I wouldn't mind it. I'm here to help you. Are you going to let me do that, or are we both going to spend the rest of our lives on this beach wondering what we should have done differently?"

Thulan shook his head. "I haven't understood a decision the first minister has made for months," he said, extending his hand to accept the padd she held out to him.

"I'd read quickly," Farkas suggested.

VOYAGER

General Mattings had been looking forward to boarding *Voyager* since the first moment he'd laid eyes on her. Like all of the Federation's vessels, her lines were sleek and graceful and turned his thoughts to art rather than technology. He'd rarely seen the two exist so comfortably together.

His first peek inside her consisted only of a quick walk from the transporter room through several gray, nondescript halls, into a small elevation device and down a short hall into a briefing room containing a midsized utilitarian table and several soft chairs. Not everything he had imagined, but he was growing more accustomed each day to frustrated expectations.

Captain Chakotay and Lieutenant Kim greeted him cordially, offering him a beverage before taking a seat at the table. Admiral Janeway was on her way to join them. Mattings wanted to request the strongest drink the replicators—he'd heard so much about—could produce, but settled for a spiced cider the captain suggested. It had a nice bite, but did little else to calm the general's nerves.

"What did you think of our transporter, General?" Lieutenant Kim asked politely. Kim was a good man and was clearly hoping to set the general at ease. Chakotay was also a good man, comfortable on his ship, but still less so in the general's presence.

"My journey was over before I knew it," Mattings admitted. "Extraordinary. It didn't even tickle."

Kim smiled and looked to Chakotay, who did not. Although the two of them had enjoyed several productive exchanges since the battle at the Gateway, it was clear that Chakotay still harbored serious misgivings about the general and the Confederacy he served. He hoped that was about to change.

Admiral Janeway entered, greeted the general warmly, and took the seat beside him at the table. Her aide was with her and provided the admiral with a small data tablet and a cup of something dark and steaming before taking his place at the far end of the table.

"I apologize for my absence," the general began.

"No apology is necessary," Janeway assured him. "In the interim we have completed preparations for our upcoming joint mission and taken custody of three of the Seriareen prisoners."

"My men are welcoming Mister Emem on board as we speak and have reported no difficulty integrating your anti-psionic technology into our security systems," Mattings reported. "But I'm afraid my apology is going to have to stand, Admiral."

She looked puzzled until he said, "You see, I've just returned from Grysyen." These were the first words the general had spoken that clearly sparked Captain Chakotay's interest.

"Why did you go there?" Chakotay asked.

"Two reasons," Mattings replied. "Captain Chakotay is the first officer I've ever met to describe the Unmarked as anything other than terrorists. It would have been easy to blame his error on cultural differences, but I've come to know him quite well over the last few months and found it difficult to dismiss the passion with which he argued for the lives of the four individuals he captured at Lecahn.

"I know it doesn't matter now, Captain, but what I saw at

Grysyen convinced me that you had the right of that discussion, and my actions, while proper based on my orders, were misguided."

Chakotay bowed his head, taking this in. Finally he nodded at the general.

"I visited the planet's surface. I was appalled at what I found there. What I learned convinced me that the CIF's actions there were not based on any real understanding of the circumstances, the needs of our citizens, or compassion. I've ordered all tactical operations in the system halted until a thorough review can be conducted. It's going to take a long time to make things right on that planet, but if I have anything to say about it, we will."

"Will the presider approve?" Chakotay asked.

Mattings shrugged. "She's fighting on every front right now. Normally this wouldn't even see the surface of her desk. Dreeg would have seen to that. She'll allow me to make my case, and I believe she'll agree with my assessment."

"That's good to hear, General," Janeway said. "But you indicated that you had *two* reasons for going."

"The presider didn't lie when she told you that nothing in our records exists regarding the Seriareen or Nayseriareen. But there are worlds, like Grysyen, whose writings have been less widely dispersed over the years, given their controversial nature. Grysyen is the closest Confederacy world to the wastes where we believe Seriar might be found. Grysyen's academies contain millions of documents that never made it to our central database. I spoke with a number of scholars, asking for records that might confirm what Lsia has told us."

"Did you find any?" Janeway asked.

"I found more than I cared to know," Mattings replied. "A lot of it was fragmented. I'm told that's common when the records in question are so ancient. The historians on Grysyen have long referred to the period we're talking about, between five and ten thousand years ago, as the 'dark times.'"

"They were that bad?" Kim asked.

"What little we know of them was, but I believe the term

is meant to convey the paucity of data available more than any judgment on the people or their actions."

"Were there explicit references to the Seriareen or Nayseriareen?" Janeway asked.

"No. But there were many tantalizing and suggestive ones. There are myths about sacrifices to powerful gods who demanded the bodies of the youngest and strongest. Those children 'died to themselves' but were reborn as gods."

"That does sound vaguely familiar," Chakotay agreed.

"There's an epic ballad that tells the story of a boy who had fallen in love with a girl. The gods came for him and tried to take him, but he refused their gifts. He died fighting them, but never succumbed."

"So perhaps not all of the Seriareen's hosts were as excited about their new lives as we've been led to believe," Chakotay said.

"I don't read a lot of love poetry, Captain," Mattings admitted, "but that was my conclusion as well."

"Still, the presence of these artifacts does give credence to Lsia's story," Janeway observed.

"The strongest support came from another, very unlikely place," Mattings continued. "You have to understand that when my people came here, armed with their faith in the Source and ready to convert all who intended to join us, old ways were set aside in favor of our new revelations."

"That's not uncommon," Chakotay said.

"The Grysyen people's reputation as upstart troublemakers also makes sense in hindsight, as do the lengths the Consortium has gone to maintain this fiction. Their Science Academy contains records going back thousands of years prior to our discovery of the planet," Mattings admitted. "Among those records are detailed descriptions of experiments done to create the protectors."

"What?" Kim interjected.

"My people first discovered the technology we use to create protectors on the last *lemm*, as you know," Mattings replied. "I never knew we had any idea where that technology originated."

"On Grysyen?" Chakotay asked.

"As best I understand it, the few spacefaring races that existed at that time had already discovered the streams, although none of them credited the existence of the streams to the Source. The streams we use now are a small percentage of those that originally existed. Some had been destroyed, as Lsia said. But many others simply collapsed. There weren't enough protectors left to sustain them. The ancient inhabitants of Grysyen pooled their resources and expertise and found a solution."

"They learned how to make new protectors, to stabilize the streams," Kim guessed.

"It looked like they had some help from another alien species that wasn't local," Mattings said. "Eventually, they set out to map the rest of the existing streams and apparently, once they were too far from this area to utilize the technology they'd left here, they re-created it on other worlds, like the last *lemm*.

"We don't know why the inhabitants of Grysyen abandoned this work," the general added. "We only know that by the time we arrived, they had."

"Once the problem was solved," Kim suggested, "they might have simply turned their attention and efforts elsewhere."

"A choice that left them ripe for conquest when the Confederacy came calling," Mattings admitted sadly.

"Did anything you discovered contradict what Lsia has told us?" Janeway asked.

"No," Mattings replied.

"Very well," she said.

"I'll be honest, Admiral. I went there hoping to prove her a liar."

"I wouldn't have been the least bit surprised if you had, General," Janeway acknowledged. "That said, I think we're ready to proceed. Captain Chakotay will brief you on our analysis of the wastes. We both believe that the risks inherent in traversing the area are too great for both of our ships to venture in. *Voyager* is prepared to take the lead in our initial investigations."

"Why don't we make that decision when we've both had a chance to take a good look, Admiral," Mattings suggested.

"Fair enough," Janeway agreed.

"But even if we could identify the source of any individual engram, how would we segregate it?" Commander Glenn asked.

The Doctor considered the question carefully. He'd been reinstated as *Voyager's* CMO that morning and spent most of the day consulting with Glenn. The Commander had already subjected Tirrit and Adaeze to a battery of tests, and while their neural scans distinctly showed the presence of multiple engrammatic patterns, she was correct that determining which individual engrams were essential to each of the essences now sharing a single body was not possible with their technology.

"Wouldn't the weaker ones most likely belong to the host, while the stronger ones are part of the invading consciousness?" the Doctor asked.

"Yes, but we're talking about a fluid process. We all hold thoughts in our minds for fractions of seconds. 'Weakness' as you are describing it might as easily point to the significance of the thought as its origin."

"And we are talking about essences that had multiple previous hosts. Some of the weaker signals might have carried over from former victims."

Glenn shook her head. The Doctor could see her weariness. *"I'd hoped this analysis would reveal the tapestry of these minds,"* she said. *"I thought I'd be looking at individual threads we could follow and remove."*

"Instead, you're looking at a cake," the Doctor agreed. "The eggs, flour, and sugar are still there, but once the cake is baked, you can't remove the eggs anymore."

"I know this isn't what Admiral Janeway's hoping to hear," Glenn noted.

"The admiral knows how to deal with disappointment," the Doctor reminded her as a soft alarm began to sound on the Doctor's data panel.

"What's that?" Glenn asked.

The Doctor sighed deeply, shaking his head. "I'm afraid I am going to have to sign off for a few hours."

"Why?"

"It's part of my *treatment*," the Doctor replied, his disdain for the word clear. In response to Glenn's puzzled look he continued, "Counselor Cambridge believes it is essential that I engage in brief periods of rest. During these times, I am not permitted to work on medical issues—except in the event of an emergency, obviously."

"What are you supposed to do?"

"Meditate," the Doctor replied.

"And the thought of that fills you with anxiety?" Glenn asked kindly.

"I suppose," the Doctor admitted.

Glenn smiled. *"Would you like a little help?"*

"What did you have in mind?"

"I spend a fair amount of time meditating daily," she replied. *"It's an active process, intended to clear and focus the mind. It is incredibly effective and restorative."*

"Hm."

"My first experiences were with guided meditations. One of my teachers would help me settle and focus my thoughts. From there, I learned to enter a meditative state without external cues."

"I appreciate the offer, Commander, but I know how busy you are."

"I've been at this for twelve hours straight, Doctor. I could use a short break as well. Come on, let's give it a try."

After a few more half-hearted protests, the Doctor relented. At Glenn's instruction, he dimmed the lights in his office, locked the door, assumed a supine position on the deck, and closed his eyes.

Glenn's voice quickly became the only exterior sensation of which he was aware. She spoke in a calm, low tone, asking him first to imagine a pristine lake bordered by soft grass bathed in warm sunlight.

The Doctor soon realized that much as he tried to focus only on her words and the images they evoked, other thoughts would intrude. She counseled him to simply observe these thoughts without following them. Eventually, his imaginary mental landscape became his sole focus. He was only vaguely conscious of Glenn's voice. All other mental processes ceased.

Half an hour passed before the Doctor realized how effective Glenn's guidance had been. She brought him out slowly, and by the time he was sitting up inside his darkened office, all anxiety at the prospect of engaging in Cambridge's "treatment" was gone. He thanked Glenn profusely and she promised to work with him daily and forward him some other meditations she found particularly helpful.

The Doctor rose and increased the illumination of his office to a standard setting. He turned back to his desk and was momentarily disoriented to see himself sitting before his data screen, tears streaming down his face.

"She's dead. I failed her."

This was a memory. The Doctor had not accessed it since he was deactivated, but the black curtain in his mind behind which his "muted" memories now lived had been pulled back ever so slightly. The Doctor was reliving an experience he'd had shortly before the cascade failure that had destabilized his program. *Or was this shortly after?* He did not know. Fortunately, he did not feel the same emotional distress he was observing. Simple awareness of this fact allowed the memory to fade. As soon as the connection was made, the Doctor found himself alone again in his office.

Conscious that he should record this event in his personal log, and actually looking forward to sharing it with Counselor Cambridge, the Doctor moved toward his desk.

A tall male alien with deep-red-tinted flesh stood before him. *"Release me!"* he bellowed. A strange short sword rested in the alien's hand. Distant crashes and booms echoed all around them.

The Doctor did not hesitate. He stepped toward the figure, took the sword, and plunged it into the alien's chest.

Commander B'Elanna Torres knew better. She should be sleeping, but her brain was not cooperating.

Miral had been in a rare terrible mood at dinner. Torres had assumed Tom's absence was to blame until, while tucking Miral in for the night, the little girl had revealed that Nancy had forgotten their ice-cream date. The chief engineer had become quite close to Miral, especially since Tom's departure, spending several free hours distracting the child, but those free hours had disappeared from everyone's schedule when the deflector dish was destroyed. Conlon had promised to make it up to Miral this afternoon, but apparently she'd forgotten.

Torres didn't blame her. The computer indicated that Conlon was in her quarters, but she wasn't answering hails. She'd probably already turned in for the night. Torres had broken down and replicated delicious sundaes for both of them, which they finished off in bed. Mollified, Miral had fallen asleep.

Torres had then decided that the quickest path to joining Miral lay in reviewing the last few days of engineering reports. The fleet chief had already received verbal updates, but she was required to sign off on the written ones as well. One or two at the most should dull her mind sufficiently and sleep would soon follow.

It didn't.

The first report contained the full analysis Conlon had completed on Harry's mysterious and destructive power surges. Conlon's conclusions were reasonable, just not probable, given the supporting data. It seemed the lieutenant had taken a few shortcuts in her analysis, particularly when it came to the issues of the affected shuttle. That wasn't like Conlon. *Of course, it wasn't like she had nothing else to do*, Torres told to herself.

Torres was so focused on the report that she barely heard the chime at her door. Only when Harry began to knock softly and call her name did Torres ask the computer to grant him access.

"Hey, Harry," she greeted him as he crossed to her replicator, ordered a synthetic ale, and settled himself on her sofa, putting his feet up on the coffee table. Realizing he intended to stay, she began, "Is everything okay?" meaning to follow it quickly with *because I have a ton of work to do*.

But Kim's forlorn face stilled the words. Rising from her workstation, she moved to sit across from him.

"What's going on?" she prodded.

"Nothing," Kim replied. "Want to watch a little TV?" he asked, nodding to the antique set that had been a fixture in Tom Paris's personal quarters even before he and Torres were married.

"It'll wake Miral," Torres replied. "She'll probably think Tom's back. He's the only one who ever watches it with her. She misses him a lot."

Kim nodded. "She's not the only one."

"Oh, come on," Torres said. "*Acting first officer.* That's huge for you. And you're doing a great job."

"Yeah, but my work-life balance is suffering," Kim noted.

Torres smirked. "What's that?" she teased.

Kim shrugged. "It's my fault. I'm giving it everything I have. I can't do less. But I also can't shut it off. Tonight I made a special effort. Nancy and I haven't had dinner in days. But by the time I got to her quarters, she was already asleep."

"I think the exhaustion has finally caught up with her," Torres agreed. "She forgot a date with Miral today."

"Miral and Nancy are dating now?" Kim asked.

"Yep. And the kiddo is stiff competition, so you'd better step up your game."

"I can't compete with that face," Kim conceded.

Torres laughed lightly. She hadn't done that in a while, and it felt good.

"Why aren't you asleep?" Kim asked.

Torres nodded toward her desk. "Reports."

Kim brought his feet to the floor and started to rise. "I'll leave you to it so you're not up all night."

"What are you going to do?" Torres asked gently.

Kim shrugged. "I think I'll spend the next few hours trying to figure out why we're not all dead."

"Huh?"

"It's been bugging me for weeks. I need to review the tactical logs of our battle at the Gateway. Looks like I finally have some time."

"What are you looking for?"

"The answer is probably in the *Scion*'s rate-of-fire indices. I just remember *knowing* that right after the dish went, we were dead too. But the Voth held their fire."

"No, they didn't," Torres said. "The *Shudka* called for a cease-fire. The *Scion* was honoring that."

"There wasn't time," Kim argued. "The cease-fire order came several seconds too late to save us. But there might have been a power drain or delay or *something* else going on. They destroyed, what, thirty other ships in five minutes? Why were we spared?"

"Harry, that's a really depressing thing to be fixating on when . . ." Torres began, but a new thought caused those words to trail off. Rising quickly, she returned to the report she had just been reviewing, the one where Conlon blamed their power surges on faulty bioneural interface regulators.

Torres read for a few minutes in silence until Kim interrupted. "What is it?"

She lifted her face to him, but her eyes were glued to the blank wall over his shoulder. "We're on our sixth generation of bioneural gel packs. System integration errors have been nonexistent since the third upgrade. There's nothing wrong with the interfaces."

"Apparently there is now," Kim corrected her.

"No, there isn't. But Nancy is right. The regulators are the weakest interface point, and you *have* to get past those in order for the surges we detected to affect other systems."

"Right. The regulators malfunctioned and the surges spread," Kim said. "I still can't figure out how they affected our holodeck's segregated power supplies. It's not as if they are disconnected from the rest of the ship. They're just a discrete system."

Torres sighed, shaking her head. "Forget the holodecks for a second. The first surge detected was in the *Van Cise*."

"So?"

"That was the shuttle Neelix returned to us. The one Meegan stole. We rebuilt most of the central processing and power distribution systems when Neelix brought it back to us. I always assumed she was in such bad shape because of what the Talaxians did to her to get her flying again. But they didn't give us their engineering reports. For all we know, they didn't even touch the primary systems. We were all focusing on the data cores that were completely fried apart from the logs Neelix was able to restore."

"Did you replace the gel packs?"

"All of them," Torres replied. "So they all had brand-new regulators that wouldn't have come from the same stock as the ones on *Voyager* that have been in use for almost a year now."

"Maybe we have a bigger problem with the regulators than we thought: a design issue."

"The moment the shuttle was returned, our diagnostic scanners were connected to it via hard lines; anything on that shuttle could have moved into our primary systems," Torres offered.

"But there are buffers in those lines that screen for any unusual signals. Nothing showed up at the time, did it?"

"No," Torres agreed. "But we weren't looking that closely, either."

"What do you think was on that shuttle?" Kim asked.

"Something that could live in the gel packs until it found a way to move into our primary systems," Torres replied. "A virus, maybe."

"Something meant to destroy the ship?" Kim asked.

"No," Torres insisted. "If you're right, and the *Scion* spared *Voyager* after disabling us completely, that means *they wanted us alive*. Meegan ordered them to hold their fire."

"Lsia."

"Whatever. If *she* wanted the ship intact it would only be because there is something of value here, something she *sent back to us* on that shuttle."

Kim nodded thoughtfully. "I'm going to—"

"Review those tactical logs," Torres finished for him. "And I'm going to go over those shuttle diagnostics again."

"Should I wake up Chakotay?"

"Not yet," Torres said. "Not until we know what we're dealing with."

16

STARFLEET HEADQUARTERS
SAN FRANCISCO

Commander Tom Paris took it as a good sign that shortly after his arrival at Admiral Montgomery's office, he, Doctor Sharak, and Lieutenant Wildman were ushered inside by his aide. That optimism endured until the moment he saw the admiral's face.

"Commander Paris," Montgomery began, "I trust you've been keeping yourself out of trouble while enjoying your liberty?"

Paris smiled tightly. "As I'm sure you're aware, Admiral, an issue has arisen regarding a civilian assigned to the Full Circle Fleet, Seven."

"I am," Montgomery confirmed. "She was briefly released from her duties at Starfleet Medical and has failed to report back in a timely manner. Starfleet security is now scouring the surface of this planet for any sign of her. It appears her last recorded transport was performed by a cadet with whom I know you are familiar. The transport logs in question show signs of tampering. While no blame has yet been assigned, Cadet Icheb has been relieved of his post until the matter can be resolved. We both know Seven and Icheb are very close. It will be a great disappointment to his Academy advisors should it be confirmed that he has been assisting her in evading our personnel."

Paris accepted this body-blow stoically, keeping his face completely neutral. "Admiral, I have prepared a full report for you, outlining Seven's experiences while at Starfleet Medical. She has made a number of troubling discoveries of which I believe you should be aware."

"Save it, Commander," Montgomery said briskly. "Doctor Pauline Frist has already briefed me thoroughly on the matter. I know you are aware of the nature of Seven's assignment, and

I know you understand how seriously we take *classified data*. Seven's actions thus far are unsupportable, although sadly, not at all out of character. She has been given far too much authority in the past, despite her civilian status, and that's going to end as soon as she is found."

"Admiral, if you would read my report, or just allow me to present the highlights," Paris attempted.

"Starfleet Medical and the Federation Institute of Health are currently engaged in a desperate attempt to contain a deadly and highly infectious plague caused by Caeliar catoms. *Anything* and *everything* they deem necessary to complete this work has been authorized by their superior officers and neither you, nor I, nor Seven are in any position to question their actions. Just because you do not see the full picture doesn't mean that those directing Starfleet Medical's efforts are not well aware of their moral and ethical boundaries. I can you assure you that they are acting well within the law and working tirelessly to secure the safety of all Federation citizens."

"Admiral—"

"Mister Paris," Montgomery cut him off, "I'm going to ask you this once. Are you currently aware of Seven's whereabouts?"

Paris swallowed the lump that had formed in his throat but did not reply immediately.

"I'm going to take your silence as a yes," Montgomery said. "You are hereby ordered to return her to Starfleet Medical immediately. Should you fail to do so, you will be subject to disciplinary action, including possible court-martial."

Turning his fierce gaze toward Sharak and Wildman, the admiral continued, "Where have you two been? Your last report to Doctor Frist was very disturbing. You claimed that some hospital volunteer on Coridan was responsible for infecting some of the patients there with the plague and also attempted to disperse the plague more widely. The authorities on Coridan have thoroughly investigated these claims and found nothing to substantiate them or directly link them to the individual you identified, who was apparently killed in a tragic accident.

"After adding to the incredible workload of the hospital's

staff, you advised Doctor Frist that you were headed to Ardana but you never arrived there. You were, however, apparently sighted on Aldebaran a few days ago by a student, and a vessel registered to Lieutenant Wildman's husband was recorded as being in orbit of the planet for almost three days."

"We chose to investigate Aldebaran rather than Ardana, given its proximity to Cordian," Wildman offered weakly.

"Without advising any of your superiors of a change in flight plans?" Montgomery demanded.

"Yes, sir," Wildman replied.

"Do either of you know anything about an explosion that occurred in a residential area within the quarantine district at New Kerinna?" the admiral asked.

Now it was Wildman's turn to hold her tongue.

Sharak interjected softly, "Admiral Montgomery, there are a number of pertinent facts that Doctor Frist has failed to bring to your attention."

"There are only a few facts that concern me right now, Doctor Sharak. Paramount among them is the *fact* that Starfleet is still in the process of recovering from the loss of billions of Federation citizens. Not only is it *not* within my purview, but it is not my inclination to question the actions of any individuals who are now devoting themselves to securing the Federation's future and preventing any similar losses."

It was now clear to Paris that Doctor Frist had chosen, even in the light of Sharak's evidence, to protect Commander Briggs and was attempting to preempt any effort to cast doubt upon his work or motives. It was also clear that Montgomery was not going to place himself or his career on the line by defending the actions of a few renegade officers. *He sees what he wants to see.*

"I don't know what kind of games you people think you're playing or what authority you believe you have been granted to engage in these reckless activities, but they end now." Montgomery continued, "Doctor Sharak, you will return to your quarters at Starfleet Medical until further notice. Lieutenant Wildman, you have a post that you have deserted. If you expect to keep it, you will return to it at once and I will leave any disciplinary actions to your direct superiors. Commander Paris, you already have your orders. As soon as Starfleet Medical is ready to release Seven, or advises us that she cannot be released in the near future, I will let you know."

Sharak looked ready to object, but a glance from Paris silenced him.

"I advised Admiral Janeway before she assumed command of the fleet that all those under her would be expected to comport themselves appropriately in the future. You are not the only officers she commanded whose past choices raise serious questions about your fitness to serve. It appears she has not communicated the seriousness with which we take our sacred trust or the scrutiny under which you are all being observed. I hope I've made that clear."

Paris said, "Thank you, Admiral," before following Sharak and Wildman out of his office.

No one spoke as Paris led Sharak and Wildman out of Starfleet Headquarters. Foot traffic was heavy this time of morning. As soon as they had cleared the stone benches and hedges that lined the wide entrance, Paris diverted them onto the short grass toward a cluster of flowering trees that dotted the landscape.

Once they had reached relative seclusion, Paris quipped, "I think that went well, don't you?"

"Tom," Wildman chided him.

"Seven was right. When *isn't* Seven right?" Paris asked rhetorically.

"What are our options now, Commander?" Sharak asked.

"Depends," Paris replied. "Do you like serving in Starfleet?"

"Not at the moment," Sharak replied honestly.

Wildman smiled and placed a hand on Sharak's shoulder. "What he's trying to say is that we have no options. I have to get back to my post, and you have to return to your quarters until further notice."

"I cannot do that," Sharak said simply.

Wildman moved to stand directly in front of Paris. "I know you're disappointed, Tom, but there's nothing more we can do. Briggs and Frist have beaten us to the punch. For all we know, Montgomery and everyone else at his level already know what Briggs is doing to unlock catomic programming and have decided that security trumps ethics."

"I refuse to believe that anyone who has taken the Starfleet oath could possibly condone intentionally infecting innocent individuals with a deadly plague, let alone re-creating an extinct species for the sole purpose of using them as lab rats," Paris said coldly. "Montgomery doesn't know what's going on. The problem is he *doesn't want to know.* He's right that the officers in question do not fall under his purview. They're not technically his responsibility. He's going to hide behind his plausible deniability and let someone else take the fall for their actions when it all comes out, which it will eventually, just not soon enough to save us, Seven, Axum, Icheb, or Riley's people."

"*If* we follow his orders—" Wildman began.

"Briggs and Frist have told Montgomery just enough to make them sound cooperative and make us look like we're running around half-cocked," Paris cut her off. "Briggs obviously let the runabout go. To admit it exists is to open himself up to accusations by the refugees from Arehaz. We already know Gres and Naomi are fine. But once Icheb's actions are fully revealed, his career is over. He never graduates. He will never tell anyone that *we* asked him to tamper with those logs or perform the illegal transports. Seven might try to take full responsibility for that. But I've been at the Tamarian Embassy a lot and once it is revealed that the refugees are there, I'm done. I don't go back to the fleet. I don't get to see my son born. He's two and Miral is five before I lay eyes on either one of them again. They'll definitely link you two to the explosion on Aldebaran, and there go your careers along with mine."

"Tom."

"I'm so sorry, Sam," Paris said.

"It's all right. I wanted to help. I still think it was the right thing to do. This is all going to come out at some point, and we will be vindicated. Until then, we have to lie low."

"What about Miss Seven?" Sharak asked.

"I'll talk to her," Paris said. "She won't give up Riley's people, and as long as your embassy will have them, they're safe. If Seven goes back now, maybe she can find a way to expose Briggs from within. If she doesn't go back, Axum and Riley probably become unfortunate casualties of the catomic plague, and she's not going to be able to live with that."

"Forgive me, Commander," Sharak interjected, "but Admiral Montgomery cannot be the final word in this matter."

Paris shrugged. "He'll already have filed a preliminary report with Admiral Akaar. The CNC is the only one above Montgomery, and you can bet if we try to go over Montgomery's head, Akaar won't even take the meeting now."

"What about the president?" Sharak asked.

"Of the Federation?"

Sharak nodded. "Starfleet is hers to command, is it not?"

"Technically, but . . ."

"And she is a personal friend of Miss Seven's, is she not?"

"Yeah. I already played that card with Frist," Paris admitted. "But you don't just walk into the Palais and request a meeting with the President of the Federation. Nothing gets in front of her eyes that hasn't been vetted by ten levels of staff beneath her, including Akaar. It's just not how things are done."

"Then Seven should go to the president," Sharak suggested.

"Now that Icheb's modifications have been discovered and disabled, the moment Seven steps off the grounds of your embassy she will be detected on Federation soil and detained. Shortly thereafter, she will be returned to Starfleet Medical. There's no way to get her in front of President Bacco."

"Seven could ask the president to meet with her at the embassy," Sharak suggested.

"The president of the Federation does not visit foreign embassies without a year of diplomatic negotiations. Tamar is a friend of the Federation but not a member. That complicates matters more than you or I could imagine."

"Then I will go," Sharak said.

"You'll never get a meeting with her."

"I will make the request and remain there until she agrees to see me."

"You will remain there until Starfleet security escorts you out of the building and arrests you," Paris corrected him.

"You and Seven should do what you can," Wildman said. "But I have to get back to my lab."

"I know," Paris said. "I'll get in touch with Gres and as soon as I do, I'll let you know."

Wildman nodded and turned to Sharak. "You've done well, Doctor. You fought the good fight. It's just not our fight to finish."

"*Shaka*," Sharak said softly.

Wildman smiled sadly. "*When the walls fell.*"

"They took a thousand years to build," Sharak said.

"What did?" Paris asked.

Wildman shushed him and looked back to Sharak as he continued.

"Shaka had ruled his people justly and wisely. His ancestors had built the first wall that surrounded his kingdom. Each successive generation added to its size and majesty. Our people did not fly among the stars in those days, but the walls would have been visible from space by the time Shaka took the throne.

"Tama sent a messenger to Shaka. He had already united all of his children outside the walls. Tama was the father of all. No walls could change that. He asked Shaka to tear them down. Shaka laughed. No one would ever rule over him. His walls would see to that.

"Shaka killed the messenger and sent his body back to Tama. Then he waited for Tama's army to arrive. No army came. Only Tama. When he reached the northern face, Tama took a single breath and blew.

"The walls fell.

"Shaka failed to stand against Tama because no one can stand against Tama. He *is* the father of all, no matter what we choose to call ourselves, what colors our armies wear, or how high the walls appears that divide us from one another. We are all one. No wall is stronger than the truth."

Wildman nodded. *"Temba. At rest,"* she said softly and opened her arms.

Sharak embraced her, saying, *"Ubaya of crossed roads."*

"Sharak on the ocean?" Wildman asked.

"His sails unfurled."

Without another word, Sharak turned and was soon lost in the crowds moving in and out of headquarters.

"What's he going to do?" Paris asked.

"What he has to," Wildman replied. "What I might, if I didn't have Gres and Naomi to worry about."

Paris shook his head. "I'll go give Seven the bad news."

TAMARIAN EMBASSY

Night was better than day. Night was cool. Night was safe. Night was freedom.

This had always been true. In the caves it had always been night, and Shon had been free to run as far as he wanted. He never wanted to run farther than the sound of his mother's voice, but then he had been a child.

Now he was big. Bigger. *Big enough.*

Night on his home planet was long. The days were too hot to run, and mother had needed him to play with the babies. At night, he was free to explore the world outside the tents. It felt familiar. It felt safe.

Night was not as long here. Nothing was safe. But Shon still needed to run. It was always day inside. There was always light. Shon had found stairways. They led to closed doors. He had found small rooms. One of those rooms was filled with dusty boxes and books. It had a window. Shon had climbed the boxes to look out the window. Outside there was room to run. He saw it through the window.

He waited for night to come again.

The window had been easy to open. He was almost too big to slip through it. But he had.

Shon breathed the cool air of night. For the first time in a long time, he felt free again.

He kept to the shadows at first. He ran between them. When no one came to call him back, he ran farther. He found the end of the building. The high fence was so far away. He could run to it and back in no time.

He did.

He did it again.

He laughed in delight.

No one came to call him back.

The third time he reached the fence, he stopped to catch his breath. A shadow fell over him.

"Hello, there," a voice said.

It was not his mother's voice.

Shon turned and looked up. A tall man stood there. His eyes were silver, like the moon. Shon started to run, but the eyes held him.

"And who might you be?" the voice asked.

The man stepped closer to the fence, and suddenly Shon saw his face. He didn't like it. It reminded him of his stuffed serpent.

"Don't be afraid," the voice said.

Shon was.

Shon ran. He scurried back inside the window and slammed it shut.

He didn't tell his mother what he'd done or about the man with the voice.

17

VESTA

Thulan turned out to be one of the more reasonable and discerning aliens Captain Regina Farkas had ever met. It had aided matters considerably that Farkas had presented him with the answers to questions that had plagued him and many among the Voth leadership for months. As first minister, there was little that fell outside Odala's power to command. Although she had made a compelling case for countering the objectives of the disruptive Federation, joining the *Kinara* had been a bridge too far for most of her subordinates. A thorough forensic analysis that had been completed after the *Scion* had left to join the *Kinara* had revealed faint, telltale transporter signals between Odala's private chambers and a Voth scout vessel. Odala's body had never been recovered, but the signal's artifacts pointed to its final resting place in deep space.

After accepting Farkas's intelligence gratefully, Thulan had returned the favor, offering Farkas the one thing she had requested, beyond the lives of her crew and the continuing existence of her ship. As the captain had suspected, there was a *Kinara* recon point several light-years from the Ark Planet, closer to the Gateway but still within the space the protectors cloaked. Thulan had given her the coordinates and a warning. The Turei and Vaadwaur were both species of limited resources and imagination. He doubted they would believe Farkas's intelligence. He also assured Farkas that this small, mutually beneficial contact changed nothing between their peoples. The *Vesta's* captain was willing to live with that, as long as the unprovoked attacks on the Federation communications relays ended. Thulan agreed. Farkas couldn't help suggesting that if the Voth ever changed their minds, they use those comm relays to signal the fleet. Thulan did not believe that day would ever come.

The *Vival* had departed, continuing their search for the *Scion*, and *Vesta* set course for what remained of the *Kinara's* fleet.

Long-range sensors soon painted a cheerier picture than Farkas had dared hope would be found.

"Six vessels, two Vaadwaur, four Turei, all holding position, bearing three-one-one mark two-four," Jepel reported. "They are all among the smallest of these species' vessels."

"Helm, approach at full impulse. Let's give them a nice, long look at us," Farkas ordered. "As soon as we're in range, Jepel, go ahead and send out a friendship message and a request to share our data with them."

A few minutes later, the small fleet appeared to scatter. It was soon clear, however, that they were moving into attack formation.

"Are we really going to have to do this the hard way?" Farkas sighed.

"Going forward, may I suggest that designation be restricted only to operations that include arming our self-destruct mechanism while inside an alien vessel?" Commander Roach asked.

Farkas laughed in genuine surprise. "Mister Roach, you just made a joke while on duty."

"Aye, Captain."

"Only took you a year."

"I used to be such a quick study," Roach said with feigned chagrin.

"The lead Turei vessel has armed its weapons, Captain," Kar reported from tactical.

"Sienna, I want them disarmed, not destroyed."

"Understood, Captain."

A few minutes later, two of the Turei vessels had lost the use of their shields and weapons and two had suffered sufficient damage to break off their attacks. The Vaadwaur ships were considerably smaller and had held back, though they had both suffered minor damage from Kar's first surgical strike.

Throughout the brief conflict, Farkas had continued to transmit messages on all frequencies indicating that she had simply come to share information that was vital to them.

Finally, the pale gray-blue face of a Turei officer who introduced himself as Frim appeared on *Vesta*'s main viewscreen.

"Mister Frim," Farkas greeted him. "I am Captain Regina Farkas of—"

"We know who you are," Frim said.

"The intelligence I've brought is for your edification, as well as that of your Vaadwaur allies. I'd like to bring one of them into this conversation as well."

Frim shook his head in disgust. *"Hail them, if you like. Our communications systems have suffered some damage recently."*

Jepel did so, and in response, the cool and appraising face of

Vaadwaur Section Leader Tiqe joined Frim's. Tiqe was clearly feeling a little superior. Behind him, his small ship appeared to be fully operational while Frim's bridge was a darkened mass of belching smoke and debris.

"Mister Tiqe, thank you for joining us."

"The Vaadwaur learned long ago to respect the tactical capabilities of your Federation," Tiqe said placidly.

"I apologize for damaging your ships, but you left me no choice."

"What terms do you demand for our surrender?" Frim asked.

"A few minutes of your time," Farkas replied congenially. She then presented both of them with the same data she had provided to Thulan about Lsia, The Eight, and the battle at the Gateway. While both were clearly interested in what she had to say, Frim did not appear ready to accept her words at face value.

"Why should we believe this report?" Frim demanded.

"Because we are both still alive to hear it," Tiqe replied for Farkas. *You ignorant buffoon,* was clearly implied by Tiqe's tone.

"You don't have to take my word for it," Farkas said. "I am now transmitting to you our ship's logs of the battle at the Gateway, as well as written reports detailing our encounters with the Indign and the Seriareen. In addition, I am sending our most recent intelligence regarding the Borg. Once you've had a chance to review it, I hope you will better understand the Federation's presence in the Delta Quadrant, as well as our intended goals. We do not wish to instigate hostilities with any local species or claim any territory. We have come here to explore and when we can, to clear up any misunderstandings that arose during the *Starship Voyager*'s first journey through your space."

"More Federation lies," Frim said.

"To what end?" Farkas asked. "I sincerely hope you will accept what I've given you in the spirit in which it is intended. Even if you don't, you should be aware that your alliance with the *Kinara* is over. The Skeen, Karlon, Muk, and Emleath vessels that joined yours in attacking the Gateway were destroyed or retreated, leaving the Devore, Voth, Turei, and Vaadwaur to the mercy of the Confederacy. A Devore and Voth ship both survived the battle at the Gateway, and I'm assuming they had the location of this recon point but neither came here to provide you with this critical intelligence. They are busy tending to their own. You should do the same. Should we meet again, I expect that you will remember this act of goodwill on our part."

"The Vaadwaur will, Captain," Tiqe assured her.

Seconds later, his ship rattled around him and he looked away from the viewscreen in alarm.

"What the—?" Farkas began.

"Two of the Turei vessels have opened fire on their Vaadwaur *allies,*" Kar reported.

"Are you serious?" Farkas asked as the channel between all three vessels was cut.

"The Vaadwaur ships are returning fire," Kar added.

"Mister Hoch, fall back. As soon as we're clear, set course for New Talax and engage our slipstream drive."

"Aye, Captain," Hoch said.

Farkas turned to Roach. "Did you see that coming?"

Roach thought for a moment. "I'm surprised their alliance lasted this long," he observed.

"Fair point," Farkas agreed.

DEMETER

"Overseer Bralt, we are so relieved that you have returned," EC Irste said.

"Thank you," Bralt said, smiling benevolently.

Commander O'Donnell had hailed the *Fourth Jroone* the moment *Demeter* was in range. They had waited too long for news of their overseer of agriculture. In a few minutes, they would be in transporter range, Bralt would return to the CIF vessel, and O'Donnell would set course for the last known coordinates of the rest of the fleet, just outside the Gateway.

"Shall I dispatch a protector for you?" Irste asked.

"That won't be necessary," Bralt replied. "Commander

O'Donnell and his crew have provided us with a great deal of intelligence on the capabilities of our protectors. I intend to test some of the theories immediately. You will remain in orbit of Vitrum, and as soon as we join you our tests will commence."

"I beg your pardon, Overseer," O'Donnell interrupted, "but I cannot join in those efforts. I have been ordered to take my ship to the fleet rendezvous. I will bring this request to the admiral's attention, and with her permission, will return as soon as I can."

Bralt frowned. "I understand, Commander," he began. "I did not intend for your ship to make contact with the protectors for us. The *Jroone* can do that. But I was hoping you would observe our efforts and offer any guidance you feel would be appropriate."

No. The only possible response was on the tip of O'Donnell's tongue. It hung there, ready to fall from his lips.

"Commander," Fife interjected. "A few more hours at this point couldn't do much harm, could it? *Vesta* is aware of our intended destination, and we could use the CIF's communications system to send word of a brief delay to the fleet. Given what this might do to further relations with the Confederacy, I can't imagine that the admiral would disapprove."

O'Donnell turned to Fife's expectant face. He knew what the young officer was thinking. On Vitrum, hundreds of thousands of men, women, and children were living in abject poverty. That could change in a matter of weeks. Every minute they delayed was one more minute of needless suffering.

How dare you put the face of a hungry child in front of me and order me not to feed him?

Fife had hurled this insult at O'Donnell the first day he'd visited Vitrum's surface. It had wounded O'Donnell. Ordering Fife to return to *Demeter* immediately had been one of the hardest things the commander had done in a long time. But it had cleared the way for their breakthrough with Overseer Bralt at the Ark Planet.

Alana, O'Donnell thought.

As expected, she did not answer.

A spasm of fresh pain shot through O'Donnell's heart.

I don't need her to answer.

She hadn't abandoned him. She would never do that. He had lived too long apart from others. His self-imposed isolation had been intentional. Alone, he had been free to create a world inside his mind where she had never died. No, *where the consequences of her death had been avoided.*

That isolation had come to an end when he had assumed command of *Demeter.* Forced into the land of the living, he had accidentally and unintentionally, little by little, opened himself up to the counsel of others. They had not replaced her. No one would ever do that. They had simply helped make possible a transition that should have happened years ago.

O'Donnell nodded to Fife. "Three hours."

Fife nodded. "Would you care to return to your quarters? I will advise you when the *Jroone* is ready to begin."

O'Donnell shook his head and settled back into the command chair. "No."

"Are you all right, sir?" Fife asked gently.

"Yes, Atlee. I am."

VOYAGER

"What am I looking at?" Admiral Janeway asked as she studied the holographic display suspended before her eyes in the center of the briefing room's conference table.

Captain Chakotay, Counselor Cambridge, and Lieutenants Kim, Conlon, and Barclay were all giving the fleet chief engineer their full attention. The Doctor glanced at the display, recognized nothing significant, and continued to record Commander Torres's explanation for future reference, while focusing the majority of his attention on a different concern.

He had replayed the two memories that had emerged after his meditation session several hundred times in the last few hours.

The first memory was troubling in that he had obviously been experiencing a level of distress far beyond any he could imagine even should he learn that Seven had actually died. He could not fathom reaching the level of despair he had witnessed for *any* reason. The Doctor had believed his creator's modifications were limited. Now he was skeptical of that assessment. Zimmerman might have made the Doctor more "human."

Not that this was something he had particularly desired.

But Zimmerman had also made him *less* than he had once been.

"This display shows the virus's progress through our systems over the course of several months," Torres pointed out.

"We have no idea how long it waited in the shuttle's bioneural gel packs before it was finally released into *Voyager*'s systems," Kim noted.

"We'll never know for sure," Conlon added.

"It learned as it went. Its actions suggest intelligence, but since we can't find any trace of it now, we can't confirm whether or not it was organic, artificial, or a hybrid," Torres continued.

"It touched every major system on the ship," Janeway said, equally awestruck and disconcerted.

"But it seemed to take particular interest in our holographic ones?" Cambridge asked.

"We think that's where it overreached," Torres replied, nodding. "The holodecks were the last system it targeted. They aren't accessible through our primary processors, but there was a weakness in our security protocols that it managed to exploit."

"What weakness?" Janeway demanded.

"It's my fault, Admiral," Kim admitted. "The last time we lost control of the holodecks, several crew members were almost killed. I installed a personal code to act as a fail-safe so I would never be denied access again. Apparently even the engineers that did *Voyager*'s refit prior to the fleet's launch missed it."

Janeway sighed as Chakotay said, "I can see your reasoning, Lieutenant, but in hindsight . . ."

"I understand, sir," Kim said quickly. "Lesson learned."

Torres continued, "Once it had gained access and collected as much data as it required, it attempted to infiltrate the Doctor's program, causing his cascade failure."

"That explains a great deal," Barclay said. "It's a relief, isn't it, Doctor?"

At the sound of his name, the Doctor turned automatically to Barclay, but with no idea what an appropriate response might be. He decided to go with, "It is," and when Reg smiled, he returned to his musings.

The second memory was more viscerally frightening than the first. It was also different in one major respect. Whereas in the first memory the Doctor was able to watch himself from outside his program, he experienced the second without detachment. An alien he had never seen commanded him to "release him" and, without hesitation, the Doctor killed him with a sword. His ethical subroutines would not allow him to take a life except in the act of self-defense. But this was not self-defense. It was more like following an order. But the Doctor was not programmed to accept orders from anyone outside his current chain of command, and even then, as he had recently learned, he could resist orders if he found them ethically troubling.

This was simply not something the Doctor would or could imagine himself doing. *So why did he remember doing it so vividly?*

When Barclay had listed the various subroutines that had displayed minor corruptions, his ethical subroutines had been among them. *Could that corruption account for his actions? Could this be part of a lost memory, or was his program beginning to unravel in a new and unexpected way?*

The Doctor understood that if one could question their sanity, they could not be considered to have lost it. Part of him wished to confide in Reg or even Cambridge. But to do so was more terrifying than the memories. *What if this was something they could not fix?*

The Doctor had rarely had cause to contemplate his mortality. He found the process paralyzing.

"We think the complexity of the Doctor's program was simply too much for it to absorb," Kim continued. "It then attacked several other less-advanced holograms, but apart from corrupting their programming, it didn't permanently damage them."

"Where did it go next?" Chakotay asked.

"Once I initiated full diagnostics of the holographic system, it seemed to have disappeared," Conlon said. "But it could have been designed to destroy itself once its work was complete or if it was in danger of detection."

"What work?" Janeway asked.

The display shifted to a dense string of programming code. "We found this file buried in our backup systems," Torres said. "If activated, it would essentially slave all of our systems to a single terminal on the bridge and allow the individual who enters the appropriate authentication code to take control of the ship: navigation, communication, weapons, you name it. It's voice-activated, so all it needs is the proper code word, and we would all have been at the mercy of the person who activated the program."

"Do we know what that code is?" Janeway asked.

Torres nodded. "Hax."

"What's a hax?" Janeway asked.

"Nothing as far as we know," Conlon replied. "There are no matches in the database. It could be a proper name or simply a code word."

"As soon as we found the program, we isolated it, and extracted it," Kim reported. "It no longer poses any threat to us."

"Who created it?" Janeway asked.

"It appears that the virus did. It gathered the data it required, slowly, over time, built the program, and left it for us like a ticking time bomb," Conlon said.

"If it completed its work, why did it move on to the holographic systems?" Barclay asked.

Torres shrugged. "As it stands, the program was capable of controlling every system apart from our holograms. That might have been its last target, but it never successfully acquired all the data it needed. Its contact with our holograms might have damaged it too greatly for it to continue to function."

"But why would it need our holograms?" Barclay asked.

"Lsia might," Chakotay said, as if it should have been obvious. "She understands better than most the capabilities of our holograms. They are the perfect host for the Seriareen. They never die. They can take any form they wish. She must have intended to bring the rest of The Eight back here so she could transfer them into holograms like herself."

"That would never have worked," Barclay noted. "Meegan's holographic matrix was unique. Even the Doctor's probably wouldn't have survived an attempt to integrate an outside consciousness. Meegan was a perfect candidate, given the amount of empty space in her buffer meant to support a developing sentience. No other hologram would have been a viable candidate, nor would they have been able to exist outside our holodecks without mobile emitters."

"She couldn't have known that when she stole our shuttle and ran," Chakotay said. "Is it possible that this *virus* might have been one of Lsia's companions?"

"Aren't they all accounted for?" Kim asked.

"If we're taking her word for it," Chakotay replied, "but I'm not sure that's a good idea."

"I don't see how it could be," Torres said. "I'm still amazed Lsia was able to survive within a holographic matrix, but Meegan's design was unique. Our bioneural systems mimic organic processes in some ways, but they aren't complex enough to support a consciousness. And it would have had to leave those gel packs and move through our power systems before relocating into *Voyager*'s bioneural systems. I'm not an expert on the Seriareen, but I don't see an individual consciousness surviving that process with enough of itself left intact to create that program."

"But a virus could?" Janeway asked dubiously.

"Yes," Torres assured her. "It had to be simple enough to survive, probably in some dormant state, until it was transferred to *Voyager*. That's when it really began its work. We have the results. We know it did happen, even if we don't know exactly how."

"Either way, it's gone now," Conlon reminded them. "We've

scanned every system, multiple times. There's no place left for it to hide."

"Does this program bear any resemblance to the one Admiral Batiste created to take control of our systems?" Chakotay asked.

"Yes," B'Elanna replied. "It's more complicated, but it's not hard to imagine that Lsia built on what she learned from him."

"We were never sure how closely they were working together," Chakotay said. "I guess now we know."

"We do," Janeway agreed. "This is excellent work. We could have been in serious trouble at a most inopportune moment. You are all to be commended. I don't think it's likely that this virus could have found its way to *Vesta*, but *Galen* should be checked before we enter the wastes and begin our search for Seriar."

"Do you still think that's wise, Admiral?" Chakotay asked.

Janeway looked to him, but did not immediately respond. "Doctor, I received Commander Glenn's latest report on her analysis of Tirrit and Adaeze. Do you agree with her findings?"

Once again, the Doctor's focus was pulled back to the briefing. "Her findings?"

"She is convinced that it would be impossible to separate the Seriareen from their current hosts," Janeway said.

"Yes," the Doctor agreed. "As it stands, there is no way to segregate the alien consciousness from the host. Should they depart of their own accord, we could certainly try to revive the hosts, but we can't force them apart."

"What about those words Lsia indicated were meant to sever the connection in the event the host was unstable?" Chakotay asked.

"Even if we knew all of them, we still might lose the hosts. The more troubling question is where would the Seriareen go once released?" the Doctor asked.

"Commander Glenn and her chief engineer, Lieutenant Benoit, have created new containment canisters, like the ones the Neyser used. Obviously, we can't test them, but we have them standing by," Janeway reported.

"I would suggest we place them inside the holding cells currently housing the prisoners," Chakotay said. "Just in case."

"Agreed," Janeway said. "In fact, I want Tirrit and Adaeze aboard *Voyager* before we enter the wastes. Our brig is more secure than the temporary holding cells we created on the *Galen*. I'd bring Emem here as well if I didn't think General Mattings would take it as an insult."

"I don't mind risking that," Chakotay noted.

"For now, it's not worth it," Janeway countered.

Chakotay reported that they were on course to arrive at the border to the wastes within the hour. The Doctor rose from his seat as soon as they were dismissed and hurried out the door.

The Doctor had just reached the turbolift when Counselor Cambridge tapped his shoulder.

"Where were you just now?" the counselor asked.

"The briefing," the Doctor replied, stepping into the lift.

Cambridge followed quickly and raised an apologetic hand to Kim and Conlon before they could step inside. He then ordered the lift to deck five. As soon as the doors closed, the counselor said, "No, *I* was at the briefing. You were somewhere else."

"Counselor, recent alterations to my program notwithstanding, I am more than capable of giving adequate focus to a number of issues simultaneously. If you like, I could repeat for you verbatim every word spoken at the briefing. I could alter my vocal subroutines to imitate the speakers to heighten the realism of the presentation. Nothing said during the meeting apart from Admiral Janeway's direct questions about my work with Commander Glenn was relevant to me or my duties."

The lift reached deck five and the Doctor set a quick pace as he exited. Cambridge followed, undeterred.

"You understand why we hold these briefings, don't you, Doctor?" he asked.

"Even for you, that's an asinine question," the Doctor retorted.

Ignoring the insult, Cambridge said, "Whether the subject under discussion directly intersects with your current duties or not, your participation is requested when it is believed you might have something to add that would not have occurred to any of the other senior officers."

"You think I don't know that? I've served as a senior officer longer than you've been on a starship," the Doctor said sharply.

"If you know it, why did you fail to give the briefing your full attention?" Cambridge pressed. When the Doctor didn't immediately respond, Cambridge added more gently, "Did I return you to duty prematurely?"

"Is that a threat?"

Cambridge shook his head. "It's an honest question. You've been through a great deal in the last several days, and while I am as anxious as any to see you once again contribute, if you require more time to process your new status quo, you should take it."

"I have done everything you asked of me," the Doctor said, his voice rising. "I have answered every question you asked, I have tried to accept my new limitations, and I have engaged in your proscribed rest periods."

"How's that going?" Cambridge asked.

"Very well. Commander Glenn assisted me earlier today, guiding me through a simple meditation. It was quite rejuvenating."

Cambridge seemed surprised at this. "Really?"

"Really."

After a short pause, Cambridge said, "You understand, my only concern is for your well-being."

"I do. Do you understand that good intentions are no substitute for experience? You and I have not served together long. Our recent discussions, while helpful, have not been sufficient for you to pretend to grasp all there is to know of me. You have raised some valid points, and your suggestion that I try to rest my program has been surprisingly effective. But you are no more perfect than I am. Sometimes your observations may simply be wrong."

A faint smile passed over the counselor's lips. "Wrong?"

"It happens to the best of us."

"Would you care to share a specific example, beyond my apparent overreaction to your demeanor during the briefing?"

"Certainly. You are wrong about Seven."

This took the counselor aback, and he paused to digest the accusation while crossing his arms at his chest.

"How so?"

"You have decided that her former attachment to Axum will outweigh all other considerations, including her affection for you, and that she will choose to remain with him rather than return to the fleet."

"He was her first love," Cambridge said bitterly. "Her physical cues when speaking of him are incredibly powerful. They were divided by circumstance. Fate has remedied that. Even setting her sense of obligation to him aside, I would be amazed if she did not find the prospect of exploring the potential of their relationship in the *real world* both irresistible and temporarily satisfying."

"He was *Annika's* first love," the Doctor corrected him. "Seven is not Annika. Seven has become an entirely new person in the years since she met with Axum in Unimatrix Zero. She has experienced realities that go so far beyond the mundane as to defy description. Annika never existed beyond the few years of life she lived before assimilation. The version of her that Axum knew has not existed for years. Seven's rejection of the Caeliar is the surest indication that her past no long defines her future possibilities. And against all logic, reason, and evidence of taste, *Seven chose you.* She shared with you something she had withheld from many a better man. Her choice to go to Axum's aid had nothing to do with you. Your choice since then to assume the worst of her merely indicates your deep-seated insecurities and inability to grasp exactly what you've been fortunate enough to find with Seven. *You* are as surprised as I am by her choice in romantic partners. I would suggest you reconsider, because *she will return.* And when she does, you had best be prepared to answer for your lack of faith."

The counselor was, for once, speechless. The Doctor added, "Now, if you will excuse me, I have work to do."

Captain Chakotay remained seated as the briefing room cleared. Admiral Janeway waited until the room was empty before moving to sit beside him. It was ridiculous to feel as if he was speaking to her for the first time, but Chakotay found himself framing his thoughts as carefully as if that were the case.

"Assuming B'Elanna is right, and that Lsia intentionally sent an advanced virus to *Voyager* to study our systems and plant that file, we are now, officially, at a disadvantage."

"How so? We found the program before she could activate it. I'd say we're ahead of whatever game she thinks she's playing," Janeway observed.

"We have assumed, until now, that she was surprised to find us negotiating with the Confederacy." Chakotay went on. "Her first move was to attempt to sever any potential alliance between us and them by using that tribunal to cast aspersions on you and the Federation. Had she succeeded, we would have been taken off the board, and she would have been free to try and convince or force the Confederacy to explore these wastes in search of Seriar."

"Yes."

"But this casts doubt on those assumptions," Chakotay stated. "If she always hoped to return to *Voyager* and utilize that program, why would she have risked losing that opportunity by almost destroying our ship and then trying to humiliate us in front of the Confederacy?"

"Like any skilled tactician, she probably set many contingencies in place initially," Janeway suggested. "She might have feared that *Voyager* would begin to search for her, as you would have, had the fleet's encounter with the Children of the Storm gone differently, or had the Omega Continuum not been an issue. Had you found her before she could cement the alliances she required to face the Confederacy, having access to our primary systems would have come in handy."

"Don't you think she took your victory over her a little too well?" Chakotay asked.

"She's not an idiot. She's lived we don't know how many lifetimes. Defiance was no longer an option. She might not have expected our willingness to assist her. She's learning more about us at the same time we're learning more about her."

"Do you honestly believe we're going to find a planet in the middle of those wastes that has eluded detection by the Confederacy for five hundred years?"

"I don't know what we're going to find out there," Janeway replied. "I know that whatever it is, it's valuable enough to her to warrant extreme measures. I also know that if we don't take this opportunity to find it, the Confederacy will."

"Presider Cin would have been happy to let the matter drop," Chakotay reminded her.

"General Mattings wouldn't," Janeway insisted. "He strikes me as a man who doesn't like unanswered questions. There is nothing to prevent him leading a force out here to explore the area. And given all the presider is facing politically, she might not have the time or the political capital to deny his request. If Mattings made a case for the potential value of any discovery out here to the Market Consortium, they could do whatever they wish, even over Cin's objections."

"It's their space, Kathryn," Chakotay said. "Whatever is out here belongs to them and ultimately, they will have to decide what to do with it."

"Agreed. But Lsia and her people could aid them in understanding what they find. We're simply facilitating that and hopefully eliminating what could become a flashpoint for future conflict."

"And risking our ships and our crews in the process."

Janeway bowed her head. "Nothing we do out here comes without risk."

"That's true, but when we risk, it needs to be for good reason. I hate to sound callous, but what's in it for us?"

"Maybe nothing," Janeway said. "Aren't you curious?"

"Definitely. I'm also afraid that we are underestimating her. I'm afraid that she's thought this through twenty moves out, and no matter how good we are, we aren't going to be able to find every trap she's set for us."

"As long as she and the others remain behind the anti-psionic field, they cannot threaten us."

"We could suffer power losses. Those fields could fall. Hell, if the ship were somehow destroyed, she and the others could simply abandon their current hosts and find the next nearest living beings to possess."

"Chakotay, you may be right. But I will not lead this fleet guided by my fears. Fear is helpful when it leads us to act mindfully. But if we're going to let it run the show, we should go home now."

Chakotay considered this. "I don't understand why I can't shake it off anymore."

Janeway placed a hand over his. "For the first time in our lives, we want more than to survive the day. Somewhere out there in the as-yet-undefined future is a dream we both share of a life beyond answering to duty. There's nothing stopping us from letting all of this go and stepping into that future. But as long as we're here, *this* has to be the only moment that matters. Living for that future will damn us as surely as retreating into our past."

Chakotay smiled. "That's what I had to learn when I lost you. How is it possible I forgot that lesson the moment you came back to me?"

"Apparently I'm a terrible influence on you," Janeway teased.

Turning his palm, Chakotay twined his fingers around hers, and he lifted her hand to his lips. "That must be it."

"I'm not in a hurry to leave this life," Janeway said. "And I don't want to see any of our people suffer for our command decisions. But I think we've proven that together, we're reasonably formidable."

"Together, then?" Chakotay asked.

"Always," Janeway replied.

18

PALAIS DE LA CONCORDE
PARIS, EARTH

D octor Sharak had followed his orders. He had returned to his temporary quarters in San Francisco immediately following his conversation with Commander Paris and Lieutenant Wildman. From there, he had spoken for several hours with Ratham and Ambassador Jarral. The ambassador had transmitted the appropriate requests through his diplomatic channels, and in the middle of the night, local time, first thing in the morning in Paris, Sharak had transported there and entered the Palais, certain that, within hours, he would be granted a few minutes of President Bacco's time.

He had been right about the wait. Six hours later he had been politely refused an appointment and been assured that the president would make time to meet with Ambassador Jarral as soon as her schedule permitted. Sharak hadn't been deterred. He had spoken to three undersecretaries, including one with direct access to the president's chief of staff, before it had been suggested that if he did not leave the premises, he would be escorted out.

This had been more shocking than insulting. Obviously, it was impossible for the president, or her staff, to understand the seriousness of his request or the intelligence he had come to provide based upon the tepid language Jarral had used to cloak the request. But that shouldn't have mattered. If the president was truly the mother of her people—as Tama's political representatives embodied him as father—no request from any of her children should have been met with such dismissive disdain.

There was still so much about the Federation that eluded Sharak.

Even as the day was drawing to a close, there were still a number of people standing outside the main entrance to the Palais behind a low blockade. These were press representatives eager to engage the president and her staff. The moment any high-level official was seen, they were immediately bombarded with questions. Some paused for brief exchanges, while others hurried on their way. Sharak distinctly heard the term "Typhon Pact" thrown about liberally during these brief, vociferous discussions.

Consumed with these thoughts and overwhelmed by his ineffectualness where the need was so great, Sharak slowed his steps. He *should* go immediately to the nearby embassy. Ratham and Jarral would be anxious to learn the results of his efforts. He was in no hurry to disappoint them.

"Excuse me, Doctor Sharak, isn't it?" a melodious male voice inquired.

Turning, Sharak beheld a Cardassian wearing a meticulously tailored suit in deep green and brown colorations. He smiled pleasantly at the doctor, and his eyes held Sharak's intensely. Although Sharak had encountered few members of this species during his time in the Federation, he could not help but feel an immediate sense of trepidation. He understood the Federation's long history with the Cardassians to have been somewhat fraught, and he was immediately on his guard.

Either the man was accustomed to this or keenly sensitive to it. His smile widened as he bowed his head, saying, "It is always an honor to meet a Child of Tama. I have had the pleasure of speaking several times with your Ambassador Jarral. I never fail to find those conversations enchanting."

Sharak nodded warily.

"Forgive my presumption, but I was advised that you had become quite proficient with Federation Standard. If I was misinformed, permit me to begin again. *Zima. At Anzo.*"

"You were not misinformed, sir," Sharak said quickly, though he was curious to know how much of his language this man might have troubled himself to learn.

"Garak," the man said, clearly pleased. "I am Elim Garak, the Cardassian Ambassador to the United Federation of Planets."

"I am Doctor Sharak," the doctor replied as cordially as he could.

"Yes. Your reputation as a man of great ability and honor precedes you," Garak said, inclining his head again.

"I apologize," Sharak began. "I have never heard your name before."

"There is no reason why you should have," Garak assured him. "I was once but a simple tailor, exiled from my home. The challenges of the last several years have seen my star rise to unexpected heights. But like you, I fear not high enough to serve my people as well as I would wish."

Sharak understood Garak's words well enough, but could not help but sense that he was missing many deeper insinuations.

"I spent most of this day like you, my dear doctor: hoping to be granted a few minutes of President Bacco's time."

"I see."

"As I'm sure you appreciate, the president is an extremely busy woman. I have not taken her lack of attention to heart and neither should you," Garak continued. "But, in my admittedly limited experience, I have found that there are times when a direct assault cannot be expected to bring about the desired result. Like most who occupy positions of great import, President Bacco only has time to concern herself with issues that her staff perceives as priorities."

"That appears to be true," Sharak ventured, wondering why the Cardassian ambassador should trouble himself to spend any time at all speaking with him, let alone offering him advice. In fact, Sharak was unsure if this was Garak's intention or simply the ambassador's unusual means of passing the time.

"I understand you are a physician, but I wonder, have you any interest in gardening?"

"No," Sharak replied, taken completely off guard by the abrupt change of subject.

"It is a passion of mine," Garak said, his smile returning. "I first learned to love watching living things grow and bloom at my father's knee."

"I see," Sharak said, although he didn't really.

"Above all, it taught me patience. Seeds do not flower

overnight. They require attention, fertile soil, water, light, shade, depending on their preferences. Above all, they must be planted in the right place. This is true of many things. Should you desire to gain the ear of President Bacco, may I suggest you consider utilizing the incredibly rich nutrients available here to plant your seeds?"

"I do not understand what you are suggesting, Mister Ambassador," Sharak replied.

"Permit me," Garak said. Stepping closer to a small circle of reporters busy comparing notes, and raising his voice to a surprising level, Garak continued, "I cannot help but see this gesture on the part of the Children of Tama as evidence of both your extreme generosity and resourcefulness. There are many so-called friends of the Federation who have yet to demonstrate the same level of compassion as your people. With so many displaced by the Borg Invasion, it might seem appropriate for those with resources to offer them willingly to those in need. However, too many have failed to answer this call. The *Children of Tama*," he said with great emphasis, "are to be emulated. To have taken the most vulnerable among us, the *children* of alien species, into your care and to house them in your embassy is simply heartwarming. I, for one, am humbled in the face of such selflessness, and I truly hope that many others who currently enjoy the Federation's protection will choose to follow the path your people have forged."

Sharak's eyes widened in alarm. The focus of every member of the press within earshot suddenly fell upon him. Within seconds, he and Garak were surrounded by the ravenous throngs, and small recording devices were pointed in his direction. An invisible signal seemed to move like wildfire among them, alerting them to the presence of fresh prey.

"Excuse us, ladies and gentlemen," Garak said as soon as their attention was assured. "I fear I have embarrassed my Tamarian friend by the effulgence of my praise." Taking Sharak firmly by the arm, Garak then directed him through the reporters and remained by his side as they crossed the street and headed briskly toward the Tamarian embassy.

The press followed at a reasonably respectful distance. Although Sharak had remained silent throughout this odd scene, Garak whispered conspiratorially, "No thanks are necessary, Doctor Sharak. We both represent nonaligned powers and, as such, have many common interests. I look forward to learning how they might intersect, and until then, I will do everything possible to further your goals, as well as Cardassia's. I do hope we meet again, soon, Doctor."

Sharak looked up and found that in their brief walk, they had reached the gates of the Tamarian embassy. Sharak hurried inside as the crowd that had followed him began to surround the building, peering through the fence and searching for any confirmation that Garak had spoken the truth.

Commander Paris's report of his meeting with Admiral Montgomery had not surprised Seven. Every interaction she'd ever had, or heard of, with Admiral Montgomery had revealed the consistency of his character and its many weaknesses.

She and Paris had turned their attention to practical matters. They had successfully made contact with Gres and been assured that he and Naomi were well and would be on their way to Earth soon. Naomi was making the most of her first visit to Ktaria.

Without the data Seven required from Commander Briggs—about the earliest incarnations of the catomic virus—there was little she, Axum, and Riley could do to eliminate the wider threat. Briggs had continued his experiments with the catoms extracted from the Arehaz refugees and much of Seven's time, over the last day, had been devoted to helping them survive the initial experience and working in concert with Axum and Riley to neutralize the affected catoms as they had their own.

That she must return to Starfleet Medical was not in question. When and how remained unclear. Seven was turning the question over and over in her mind while sharing a light meal with Jilliant and her infant daughter when the serenity she had come to associate with the embassy was suddenly shattered. The sound of heavy footsteps overhead was mingled with distant shouts. Ratham hurried into the basement and communicated in short, desperate phrases that the embassy had come under attack.

Seven rushed upstairs past a flurry of individuals moving in brisk shock to fortify the embassy's perimeter. A male Seven knew to be the chef and several domestic workers were being armed with small phasers and directed out the back of the embassy toward the garden along with the security detachment. Seven stopped at a small window to see the high iron fence surrounded by individuals peering through them and shouting questions at the Tamarians who emerged and took up silent posts at the gates.

She found Paris and his mother already in Ambassador Jarral's office. They stood around Doctor Sharak, who was seated and visibly pale.

"What happened?" she asked as she entered.

"*Lucsha. At Hion,*" Jarral replied tersely.

Sharak turned to face Seven, despair writ clearly on his face. "I am so sorry, Miss Seven," he said.

Seven took Paris's arm and demanded, "Tell me."

Paris sighed. "It appears we can all now add inciting a diplomatic incident to our résumés."

"Tom, don't be ridiculous," his mother interjected. "This isn't Doctor Sharak's fault."

Seven didn't understand, but her frustration was such that had she still possessed assimilation tubules, she might have injected them into Paris's neck at that moment to obtain the information she required.

"Doctor Sharak went to the Palais this morning to seek an appointment with President Bacco. He was rebuffed. When he left, he ran into the Ambassador to the Federation from Cardassia, Elim Garak," Paris explained.

Seven was familiar with Garak. He had attended some of the high-level meetings at the Palais during the Borg Invasion. She had not formed an unfavorable opinion of him, but could not say she trusted him.

"Mister Garak alerted the press to the fact that the Tamarian embassy is currently housing refugees displaced by the Invasion," Paris continued.

"How could he know that?" Seven demanded.

"I don't know," Paris replied.

"Ambassador Jarral," Ratham said softly.

Turning, Seven saw her standing in the doorway to the ambassador's office, her hands on the shoulders of a young boy clinging tightly to a stuffed snake. His eyes were wide with terror.

Julia Paris quickly moved to stand before the boy. Kneeling to meet him at eye level and placing her hands on his arms protectively, she said, "It's all right, Shon. No one is angry with you. Please, don't be afraid."

Shon stared at her but gave no indication that he believed her.

"Come and sit with me," Julia suggested tenderly. Moving to the floor and crossing her legs, she welcomed the boy into her lap and began to rock gently. After a few moments, he buried his head in her shoulder and began to sob. She shushed and hugged him, patting his back and assuring him over and over that all was well. Finally he looked up at her and said softly, "I wanted to run."

"Of course you did," Julia said. "Did you go outside?"

Shon nodded. "I waited until it was dark."

"What a good boy," Julia assured him. "When you were outside, did you see anyone?"

Shon nodded again. "A snake-man," he whispered.

"That must have been very frightening," Julia said. "But thank you for telling us. You are so brave." With strength Seven would never have suspected existed in Julia's tiny and aging frame, she took the boy's weight in her arms and rose to her feet. "Let's go find your mother, shall we?"

Ratham followed them out.

As soon as they had left, Jarral again turned on Sharak. "*Kadir. Beneath Mometeh.*"

"He is a child," Sharak said. "He could not have known better. But you are right. I should have."

The crowd outside the embassy must have been growing. Now shouts could be heard coming through the front windows.

"You will have to make a statement, Mister Ambassador," Paris said, clearly trying to reason his way through this. "For now, you could simply confirm what Garak said. It's actually the truth, though hardly all of it."

"*Kinla. At court,*" Sharak translated for Jarral.

"*Beeaze. Her staff broken.*"

"*The court full. The sun bright,*" Sharak offered.

"It won't take Briggs long to figure this out," Seven warned Paris.

"Nor will it take long for the president to demand that the refugees be turned over to Federation custody," Paris noted. "This is a nightmare."

"Thomas Eugene Paris, I am extremely disappointed in you."

Seven and Paris turned to see that Julia had returned. She stood still, framed in the arched doorway, her hands on her hips.

"That's okay, Mom," Paris said. "I am too."

"How can you fail to see the opportunity this turn of events has created for us?" Julia demanded.

Paris looked to Seven, then back at Julia.

"Huh?"

"Elim Garak is many things, but he is not stupid. Why he would choose to aid us remains a mystery. He might simply have been seeking an opportunity to publicly embarrass the president, or his designs may be more complex, but either way, he has now made it impossible for President Bacco to avoid addressing this issue."

"How do you know Garak, Mom?" Paris asked.

"Your father knew him," Julia replied. "Mister Garak has been complicating the lives of Starfleet officers for years now. He's infamous."

"I'm sorry, Mrs. Paris, but how, exactly, does this help us?" Seven interrupted.

Julia moved to stand between Seven and her son. "For the next two days, the embassy will be bombarded with requests for information, from the press and from low-level Federation diplomats. Ambassador Jarral will say nothing. Not only will his silence further whet the appetites of the Federation New Service, the stories they will spin from whole cloth will transform this from a minor, curious nuisance, to a potential diplomatic disaster. The Federation needs all of the friends it can get right now. Bacco will never risk insulting the Tamarians. At any other time of the year, she might make a personal call on the ambassador to clear this up, but she won't be able to do that before we make our move."

"*We?*" Paris asked. "What move are we making?"

"What is the day after tomorrow, Tom?" Julia demanded.

"Friday?"

"*April fifth,*" Julia said with emphasis.

A light went on in Paris's eyes.

"First Contact Day," he realized.

"Oh," Seven began.

Paris's mind was already whirring. "The Palais will be open for the reception. Bacco will be there receiving all of the guests."

"As will Admiral Akaar and the Vulcan ambassador," Julia added.

"Are you still invited to those things?" Paris asked.

"Of course," Julia replied. "I had intended to send my regrets this year. It is, without a doubt, the most tiresome event on the calendar. But under the circumstances, I will attend, and you will accompany me as my guest."

Paris exhaled slowly. "President Bacco won't want to talk to me."

"But would she dare publicly refuse a small request of the widow of one of Starfleet's most decorated officers?" Julia asked. "I think not."

Paris smiled wistfully at his mother. "You don't have to do this, Mom."

"Of course, I do," she corrected him. "You are my son and what I've seen over the last several days has more than convinced me that your love of Starfleet, the Federation, and her highest ideals is stronger than I or your father ever suspected. You are right. Seven is right. Admiral Akaar and President Bacco need to know that. They are the only ones who can intercede now."

"Even if you are able to speak with President Bacco and Admiral Akaar," Seven said, "you will have no proof to offer them."

"Actually," Paris replied, "if we time this right, we can give them more than proof. We can give them a confession."

"Ours?" Seven asked.

Paris shook his head. "The Commander's."

19

VOYAGER

The border dividing the wastes from the rest of Confederacy space was invisible. *Voyager*, *Galen*, and the *Third Calvert* held position in a swath of inky blackness, two light-years from the edge of the star system that contained the planet Grysyen and seven million kilometers from the nearest terminus of the six streams that intersected near that system. Surveying the darkness ahead on the viewscreen, a green Ensign Harry Kim might have assumed that journeying into the wastes would be relatively uneventful.

Lieutenant Kim knew better.

After Tirrit and Adaeze had been transported to *Voyager*'s brig, Admiral Janeway ordered *Galen* to hold position at their current coordinates. Lieutenant Lasren would provide regular progress reports to Commander Glenn until the exotic radiation and subspace ruptures ahead made communications impossible. Kim estimated that they would lose contact with *Galen* within the first four hours of their mission, if not sooner. In the event of an emergency, or *Voyager*'s and *Calvert*'s failure to return within the next five days, Commander Glenn had been given the harmonic resonance frequencies to the nearest stream and would utilize it to enter Grysyen's star system and request assistance from one of the dozen CIF vessels General Mattings had stationed there to provide long-overdue aid to the planet's inhabitants.

Ensign Gwyn had perfected the bouncing technique to both Commander Torres's and Lieutenant Conlon's satisfaction. She had spent the previous day refining her skills in simulations and demonstrating the particulars to the *Calvert*'s helmsman, EC Pluek.

In the final hour, Lasren and his counterpart on the *Calvert* synched their comm systems to allow for continuous contact. Lieutenant Aubrey reinforced *Voyager*'s shields with as many power sources as Lieutenant Conlon was willing to divert. Kim took the ship to yellow alert. Finally, both ships engaged their impulse engines at one-quarter speed and entered the wastes.

Within minutes, *Voyager* was bucking and jolting intermittently as Gwyn adjusted to the many new obstacles now in her path. The subspace ruptures in the area were easy enough to navigate, but the distortions of normal space where they intersected were more difficult to predict. Gwyn was flying more by feel than data.

The first two hours of exploration yielded little meaningful information apart from a few ancient pieces of debris and the certainty that at their current pace, they would be lucky to reach the coordinates Lsia had given them for Seriar within the week.

Kim was seated to Captain Chakotay's left, Admiral Janeway to his right. They spoke in low tones, interrupted frequently by the sound of General Mattings alternately encouraging and dressing-down his helmsman when he drifted too far from the course Gwyn was forging for them.

Just three hours in, Lasren detected a relatively stable section of subspace corridor. No key was required to open it. A point of ingress was clearly visible to sensors. Chakotay ordered Gwyn to execute her bounce. The flight controller, who had chosen a vivid shade of lavender for her hair this morning, set her approach course.

The sensation was similar to riding rough rapids. A certain amount of momentum was required to thread the needle between space and subspace, and for the first time since entering the wastes, *Voyager* reached full impulse.

Lieutenant Conlon was seated at the bridge's engineering control station and monitored her systems carefully as the ship bucked and rocked.

"Ensign Gwyn, hull stress is climbing," Conlon noted.

"She'll hold together," Gywn assured her chief engineer. "I need a little more speed for thirty seconds."

"Rerouting additional power to the impulse engines," Conlon advised.

"All hands, brace yourselves," Kim ordered.

With shocking suddenness, the constant tossing ceased in a single, violent whiplash-inducing impact. The force would have thrown several crew members from their seats had the momentum Gwyn had generated not eased the ship toward the currents of their targeted corridor.

In an odd moment where all motion on the bridge seemed to expand in slow motion for a fraction of a second, Kim felt his stomach lurch. The sensation passed and he was thrown back against his seat as *Voyager* began to accelerate.

Just as Gwyn had intended, they were riding the seam, still in normal space but propelled forward at speeds approaching maximum warp across the edge of the subspace corridor.

The flight controller eased them out of the maneuver as carefully as possible. It was a bumpy ride, but considerably less so than anticipated.

Finally she reported triumphantly, "We have cleared the corridor."

"All stop," Chakotay ordered. "Lieutenant Lasren?"

"Sensors indicate we are now four light-years from our last coordinates," the ops officer reported.

"Lieutenant Conlon?" Chakotay inquired.

"All systems nominal, sir," she replied.

"Shields holding at maximum," Lieutenant Aubrey offered from tactical.

"Excellent work, Ensign Gwyn," Chakotay noted as a short round of spontaneous applause erupted on the bridge. "One-quarter impulse, heading one-nine-one mark four. Let's clear the area for the *Calvert*."

"*Astrometrics to the bridge*," Torres's voice came over the comm system.

"Go ahead, B'Elanna."

"*Sensors read some sizeable chunks of debris out here. Some of it is younger than the pieces we detected when we first entered the wastes.*"

"Commander Torres," Lasren asked, "are you picking up—"

"*It's impossible to miss,*" Torres cut him off. "*Bearing two-six-nine mark three-one. We're getting some very unusual energy readings roughly one point eight light-years distant.*"

"How unusual?" Chakotay asked.

"*It appears to be a massive radiant field, but the nearest edge doesn't show the natural dispersion you would anticipate. It's almost as if the entire area is somehow being contained,*" Torres replied.

"It has to be massive for us to pick it up at this distance," Janeway mused. "B'Elanna, can you extrapolate its composition from here?"

"*It's all over the spectrum. We'll have to get closer for a detailed analysis.*"

"Do we want to get closer?" Chakotay asked.

"*Our intended coordinates are beyond the field; it appears to surround an area of several million kilometers.*"

"Are the readings being generated by a planet or star?" Janeway asked.

"*None like any we've ever seen.*"

"Captain," Lasren interrupted, "the *Calvert* is incoming. We lost our comm signal just after we impacted the edge of the sub-space corridor."

"On-screen," Chakotay ordered.

There was little to see until a faint, bright speck began to grow larger at a rapid pace. Almost as soon as it became easily identifiable as the *Calvert*, its motion altered radically, shooting directly up off the edge of the corridor, accompanied by two large, brief explosions.

"What the . . . ?" Janeway said softly.

"Lasren, was the *Calvert* just destroyed?" Chakotay asked.

A pregnant pause followed. Finally Lasren reported, "No, sir. I've got her. She's holding position bearing three-one-eight mark six."

"Distance?"

"Two point four million kilometers," Lasren replied.

"Set intercept course," Chakotay ordered, "maximum safe speed."

"Aye, sir," Gwyn acknowledged.

By the time they reached the *Calvert*, almost an hour later, it was clear that her first attempt at "bouncing" off a stream had not gone as well as *Voyager's*. Her belly was scorched and several small hull breaches were in evidence. Emergency force fields were holding.

General Mattings seemed shaken when his face appeared on the main viewscreen, his bridge officers even more so.

"What happened, General?" Chakotay asked.

"We caught a bad break," Mattings replied. *"A piece of debris from inside the corridor breached the seam and impacted us. We lost helm control temporarily, but EC Pluek pulled us out and stabilized our course. The good news is, we're still in one piece and within a few hours will have completed repairs sufficient to start heading back. The bad news is, we won't survive any additional shortcuts and cannot continue forward at this point."*

The general's disappointment was clear.

Janeway rose to her feet and approached the screen.

"Voyager" will continue on, General. We have detected an unusual energy field surrounding the planet's coordinates. We can investigate and report back to you."

"That's very kind of you, Admiral. If all goes well, you'll probably make it back to the rendezvous coordinates before we do.

"One more thing, Captain."

"Yes, General?"

"With our power systems in flux, I'm concerned about our prisoner. He appears to be behaving himself, but I'm not sure how long that will last if our anti-psionic field falls."

"We'll move into position and transport him aboard, immediately," Chakotay offered.

"Thank you."

Chakotay exhaled sharply, then turned to Janeway. He didn't say anything, but something clearly passed between them. Janeway smiled faintly and nodded to him before returning her gaze to the viewscreen.

"General," Chakotay said, "this was meant to be a joint operation between the Federation and the CIF. I understand if you feel the risk is too great to your ship. I'd like to return the courtesy you extended to us several weeks ago. The officer exchange program you initiated has only gone one way. I think we should remedy that."

Mattings smiled, his sharp teeth exposed to the fullest.

"Whom did you have in mind, Captain?"

"You, General."

Mattings bowed his head. Finally, he said, *"Give me a few hours to see if I can take you up on that offer."*

"Voyager out," Chakotay said.

The Doctor waited outside the doors to the brig for confirmation that Emem's transport from the *Calvert* was complete. Lieutenant Barclay stood beside him, shifting his weight from one side to the other nervously, cradling a small silver canister. The Doctor had been asked to confirm the prisoner's physical well-being. Barclay would transport the canister into Emem's cell. Similar devices already resided in the cells of Lsia, Tirrit, and Adaeze.

The Doctor hesitated to enter prematurely. He had already said everything he needed to say to Lsia. There was no reason to further salt the wounds.

He had always assumed that once Meegan was found, it

would be a simple matter to purge the alien consciousness and restore her program to its original settings. It had been difficult not to speculate about what might happen next. As much as he hated the idea that Meegan had been created to be his perfect mate, the longer he had contemplated her existence, the more curious he had become. It would be pleasant to pass the time with a kindred being. There was so much he could teach her.

That thought triggered a correlative fragment, and a recent memory was propelled from his short-term memory buffers into his primary processor. In their first session, Counselor Cambridge had accused the Doctor of seeing Seven as his "creation." While the notion was arguable in principle, the Doctor had dismissed it with relative ease. Seven had learned from every member of the crew in her early months on *Voyager.* The Doctor had certainly taken a primary role as her social guide, but he had never seen himself attempting to craft her into something she was not. Rather, he had used the experiences gained during his difficult early days of activation to ease Seven into her new life.

He had taken pride in her development. He had enjoyed their interactions. But he could no longer pinpoint the moment when his detachment had failed and Seven had become more to him than a student.

Would I have done the same to Meegan? he suddenly wondered. Was this the only way in which he was comfortable relating to women, or men, for that matter? How much of his sense of self had come from the belief that he was superior to those with whom he shared his existence? How would that change, given the permanent alterations to his program that Doctor Zimmerman had imposed upon him?

Was he even capable of meeting a potential partner on equal terms? Denara Pel came to mind, but she had been his patient— *a patient for whom he had created a perfect holographic body with which to interface rather than her actual phage-ravaged form*— before they had briefly explored a deeper relationship.

Horrified, the Doctor realized that Cambridge might have had a point.

"Riordan to the Doctor. Transport complete. You are clear to enter."

The Doctor shunted these dispiriting musings back into his memory buffers for future contemplation, nodded to Barclay, and led him into the brig. Ensign Riordan stood just inside the door, monitoring the energy fields that kept their prisoners secured.

Emem's cell was the third one on the Doctor's right, directly across from Lsia's. He noted Tirrit and Adaeze both seated in their cells as he passed them.

As soon as he came face-to-face with Emem, the Doctor was surprised by his initial response. It was easy enough to think of Lsia as herself, given the form she now wore. He had never known the Turei or Vaadwaur individuals the other Seriareen had taken. But the Doctor had gotten to know Kashyk rather well, and it was disorienting to see him again while knowing he was now an entirely different being.

"Ah, the Doctor," Emem greeted him.

"Welcome aboard," the Doctor said perfunctorily, raising his medical tricorder and performing a quick scan.

"I do hope the food on *Voyager* is as delicious as Kashyk's memories promise. The paste I was offered on the *Calvert* thrice daily was not worthy of that designation."

"What it lacked in taste, it made up for in nutritional value," the Doctor replied. "You've lost a little weight since the last time the inspector was aboard, but otherwise, you are the picture of health."

"I could have told you that."

"Reg," the Doctor said, nodding to the lieutenant.

Barclay placed the canister before the force field and stood back. "Go ahead, Ensign Riordan." It dematerialized seconds later and rematerialized inside Emem's cell. As soon as it did, the lid opened with a pop and a hiss.

"What is this?" Emem demanded.

For the first time since they had arrived, Lsia spoke. "Your new home, Emem, should you be foolish enough to die in that cell."

Polite, condescending Kashyk vanished as anger too great for the circumstances to warrant suffused his features. "Get it out!" he shouted. "We gave our assurances to your admiral that we would not seek new hosts among you. But you would force us against our will? Was this always your intention?"

"N-n-no," Lieutenant Barclay stammered. "This is a precaution, nothing more."

"Calm yourself, Emem," Lsia ordered. "We all have them. You'll find it gives you something quite stimulating to contemplate beyond the bare walls and energy field."

"Don't be a fool," Emem shouted. "They have lulled you into complacency with false promises."

"We are closer than we have ever been to Seriar," Lsia insisted.

"You have forgotten, haven't you?" Emem said. "*They are all Nayseriareen now.*"

"You have always been such a coward," the Doctor said as Emem's visage morphed before his eyes into that of a man with bronze skin, long, fine black hair, and chiseled, hard features, not unlike Lsia's.

The Doctor stepped back as all around him, warning alarms rang out. The deck rocked beneath his feet and shouted reports confirmed his imminent destruction. A control panel was beneath his hands. Bright red lights assaulted him, indicating multiple hull breaches and power drains.

"Release me."

The alien from his memory, Obih, stood before him, dagger in hand. *"The hax must survive."*

"Doctor, are you all right?" Barclay asked, placing a hand behind the Doctor's back to steady him.

The Doctor turned to Reg in confusion. He did not recognize the ship on which he stood. But it felt familiar. It was *his*. Emem was beside him and Lsia sat at a forward panel. And he was . . . he was . . .

"Doctor," Barclay said more urgently.

The Doctor closed his eyes, willing the sensation to pass. He tried to force his mind back to the tranquil lake Commander

Glenn had helped him visualize. By focusing on the small details, the feel of the earth beneath his body, the sound of lapping water, the heat of the sun, he slowly blocked out the unwanted memories. When he opened his eyes again, he saw Reg standing in the brig and Emem, once again, wearing Inspector Kashyk's face.

He turned to face Lsia. She considered him with clinical eyes, the same eyes that often evaluated his patients.

"Who is Xolani?" the Doctor asked softly.

Lsia smiled.

"Doctor?" Barclay asked again.

"Reg," he replied, "take me to sickbay and ask Counselor Cambridge to join us."

General Mattings was torn. He wished to personally guarantee the safety of his crew. But his direct EC, an experienced leader named Ralle, was capable of overseeing *Calvert*'s repairs and guiding her slowly out of the wastes, and as a ranking general, his responsibilities to his ship had to be balanced with those he owed the Confederacy Interstellar Fleet. Had Chakotay not offered, the general might have found himself begging for permission to join the Starfleet crew. His ego was grateful it had not come to that. It was absolutely necessary that at least one representative of the Confederacy participate in this expedition. He'd hoped to do it while aboard the *Calvert*. Now Mattings would be doing so as an observer, with almost no ability to act in the best interests of his people should theirs and the Federation's diverge. This was hardly optimal, but better than nothing.

These concerns were relegated to the rear of his mind the moment he was ushered into what Lieutenant Kim called the "astrometrics lab." The screen that dominated the room, and its vivid rendering of a vast quantity of local space, was stunning. The general had never considered his own tools crude or wanting. The more he learned of Starfleet's capabilities, the more he mourned the fact that a genuine alliance was now politically impossible.

There is so much we could learn from these people.

Admiral Janeway and Captain Chakotay welcomed him as he entered the lab. The fleet's chief engineer, a female called Torres who was clearly with child, was ordered to brief them. Mattings had become accustomed to the sight of Starfleet's female officers. The CIF did not have nearly as many, and none so young as most of those he'd met from the Federation. This was the only cultural idiosyncrasy of the Federation that the general found difficult to wrap his brain around, but he knew better than to suggest that any of the female Starfleet officers he'd met were less than capable of fulfilling their duties or might be better employed in other capacities until they were no longer fertile. Obviously the people of the Federation did not consider potential extinction a serious threat, even after the Borg had wiped out tens of billions of them. The Confederacy knew better, to their credit. Mattings genuinely hoped the Federation did not eventually learn how wrong they were the hard way.

"The first thing I'd like to bring to your attention," Commander Torres began, "is the composition of the debris we've detected. Most of the pieces we scanned were ancient—thousands of years old. These are not."

"Where did they come from?" Chakotay asked.

"At least one Devore cruiser and as many as three small Turei vessels," Torres replied.

"Lsia has already sent ships out here," Janeway realized.

As difficult as Mattings found this to believe, the evidence was impossible to refute. It was projected on that massive screen, larger than life.

Chakotay looked at Mattings. "How?"

Mattings sighed. "As you know, there are several streams that access our space other than the Gateway. We protect all of them, but the Gateway takes priority because it leads directly to the First World. If Lsia was telling the truth and her knowledge of the streams predates our own, it's possible she found some we haven't detected or was able to slip a few of her ships past our sentries."

"But if she could do that, why waste so much time and resources attacking the Gateway?" Chakotay mused.

"These ships couldn't handle the stresses of the wastes," Torres suggested. "They weren't destroyed in combat. They met their match when they tried to breach that energy field we're about to enter. Maybe one of the reasons Lsia decided not to destroy *Voyager* when she had the chance is because she already knew that the other ships in her alliance were incapable of helping her find Seriar."

"Then *Voyager* can't enter that field," the general said. "We need to take more time to study it. I won't have you people running the risk of destroying yourselves for us or the Seriareen."

"It's a little late now, General," Chakotay said wryly. Mattings welcomed the captain's return to form. He doubted after what had transpired at Lecahn that the two would ever again enjoy the easy familiarity that had marked their initial meetings. But, finally, Chakotay no longer seemed to see him as the enemy, and that was a step in the right direction.

"I don't think we're going to have the same problems the Devore and Turei did," Lieutenant Kim noted.

"Why not?" Janeway asked.

"The energy field is buffered by thousands of protectors," Kim said. "That's why the dispersal pattern at the edges is so unusual."

"Where did they come from?" Chakotay wondered aloud.

"The wastes are filled with subspace instabilities—places where normal space and subspace have been permanently inverted—which means any protector in existence has access to it," Kim replied.

"The composition of the field is similar to, though not an exact match for, the internal dynamics of a subspace corridor," Torres added. "We know that protectors in their natural state are drawn toward this energy. The Confederacy has been churning them out for hundreds of years; those who first discovered them and the means to create them, longer still. The protectors live in subspace, when they aren't being utilized in normal space. They could be attracted to this area, and nothing here would have to call them forth to allow them to enter it. The wastes contain thousands of open portals. All the protectors have to do is move through them at will."

"And given the way we saw the ancient ones develop, it's not a huge leap to suggest that they would act under their own initiative and come here if they detected it," Kim agreed.

"Can we communicate with these protectors?" Chakotay asked.

"We can try," Kim said. "But it probably won't be necessary. Should they misunderstand our intentions and attack, we know how to disperse them. All we really need to do is find an area of the field where they aren't present and slip past them."

"I've already found several good possibilities for that," Torres noted.

"And you're sure we can survive crossing that field?" Janeway confirmed.

"As long as our shields hold," Torres replied. "The Doctor should replicate hyronalin, and I wouldn't want to be out there in a shuttle or an escape pod. But *Voyager* should be fine."

Counselor Hugh Cambridge had been expecting the Doctor's call, though not so soon. The hologram's comments about Seven had been a calculated deflection. The Doctor was worried about something and must finally be ready to share it.

Whether the Doctor had been right about Seven was a matter the counselor was not inclined to explore. To hope was to become vulnerable and Cambridge's continued existence had long been predicated upon limiting his exposure to that condition.

He *was* surprised, however, when he entered sickbay and found the Doctor standing near a biobed at the rear of the suite behind a crackling energy force field. Lieutenant Barclay stood outside the field at the main data control panel.

"What do we have here?" Cambridge asked immediately.

The Doctor seemed to steel himself before he said, "I have a confession to make."

Cambridge stepped closer to the field. "Did you raise this force field for your protection or mine?"

"When you asked me to explore ways to 'rest' my program, I thought it was absurd. However, I did my best."

"You said your first attempt at meditation went well," Cambridge encouraged him.

"It did. What I experienced with Commander Glenn's assistance was unexpected. It is also not the point. *After* my meditation had concluded, I experienced two very vivid memories. I don't know if they were triggered by the meditation or not."

"What did you remember?"

"The first thing I saw was me, only moments before the energy surge that destabilized my program. I was suffering intense emotional distress at the thought of Seven's death, quite beside myself with grief."

"Literally?"

"Actually, yes. I saw myself from outside, almost as if it was through someone else's eyes. The second memory was not my own. In it, I saw an alien standing before me. He demanded that I 'release him' and at his request, I took the dagger he held in his hand and attacked him, slicing his chest open."

"And to what did you credit this extraordinary memory?" Cambridge asked.

"I didn't know," the Doctor replied, almost pleading. "Given the damage to my program, I had no idea what to think. It could have been an old holographic program, maybe a corrupted artifact from the ship's database."

"You didn't entertain the notion that it might have been a genuine memory?"

"*Not mine*," the Doctor insisted.

"And given all you've seen on the front lines of insanity we call the Delta Quadrant, it didn't occur to you that experiencing *someone else's memories* might be something you'd want to report?"

"I'm reporting it now."

"Because it's gotten worse, hasn't it?" Cambridge guessed.

The Doctor bowed his head. "A few minutes ago, I went to

the brig to examine Emem. It happened again. This time, I saw myself on an alien vessel that was under attack. I saw Lsia and the rest of them. The alien I 'killed' was called Obih. He was Seriareen. The memory was not mine. It was Xolani's."

"Xolani was one of The Eight," Barclay interjected. "Lsia told us he was dead, that his consciousness did not survive the transfer out of containment."

Cambridge crossed his arms at his chest. "So you have concluded that the energy surge Commander Torres described—her *virus*—was another Seriareen essence that was planted in the shuttle Lsia stole. He moved into *Voyager*'s systems when the shuttle was returned and eventually attacked your program."

"And took it over." The Doctor nodded. "I am Xolani," he said gravely.

Cambridge shook his head. Turning to Lieutenant Barclay, he said, "Drop the force field."

"No!" the Doctor shouted.

"Calm down, Spartacus," Cambridge insisted. "Lieutenant?"

"Do you really think that's wise?" Barclay asked.

"The Doctor isn't Xolani," Cambridge said.

"How can you know that?" the Doctor demanded.

"Because unlike you, I was actually listening to our last briefing. *After* Xolani attacked your program—and you are likely right about that—he moved on and attacked several other holograms. If you had become his host, that would not have been necessary. Some of his memories were clearly stored by your program during your brief contact with him. Lucky for us, we are forewarned that Lsia's agenda is even more complicated than we suspected. But you need to stop flagellating yourself so you can help us determine whether, as Commander Torres believes, this Xolani destroyed himself, or found another, more suitable host somewhere on this ship."

The Doctor considered this. Finally he said, "I would be more comfortable agreeing to this request if we could confirm that Xolani is not, in fact, sharing my program right now."

"Oh, for the love of . . ." Cambridge began, tapping his

combadge. "Counselor Cambridge to Lieutenant Decan. Please report to sickbay immediately and bring a security team with you."

"Acknowledged," Decan replied.

"A wise precaution, Counselor," the Doctor said.

"I didn't call him here to check on you," Cambridge said.

"Then . . . who?" the Doctor asked.

Cambridge turned to Lieutenant Barclay.

Lieutenant Barclay didn't know whether to be insulted or complimented by the counselor's accusation. Decan arrived within moments, along with an armed detachment of six officers. Once he understood the nature of the counselor's question, the Vulcan advised him that Reginald Barclay's mind was his own. Cambridge then ordered Barclay to lower the force field and Decan assured the Doctor that he sensed nothing unusual from his program.

As the group made their way to the astrometrics lab to put their commanding officers to the same test, Cambridge explained. "While I would have been surprised if Lieutenant Barclay had been compromised, it was possible. It was safe to assume, Doctor, based on your actions before the energy surge, that your program was functioning as best it can. Since then, Lieutenant Barclay is the only officer who has worked on your program and had you been housing an entirely separate consciousness, I can't imagine that it would have escaped his detection. Had *he* been taken by Xolani, however, he would likely have attempted to cast doubt upon you, particularly given the emergence of these new memories, in order to buy himself some time. He did not, but I had to be sure."

"By that logic, you might have easily come under suspicion as well," the Doctor suggested to Cambridge.

"Were I the imposter, do you think I would have brought one of the only people on the ship who could unmask me to sickbay?"

The discussion ended abruptly as the group entered astrometrics. Admiral Janeway, Captain Chakotay, Commander

Torres, Lieutenant Kim, and General Mattings were all present. Before the counselor responded to their obvious question, he waited for Lieutenant Decan to observe each of them silently for a few moments.

"Patience, please," Cambridge requested.

When Decan shook his head, Cambridge finally said, "It appears that the virus Commander Torres found was a Seriareen consciousness known as Xolani."

"What?" Torres demanded.

The Doctor quickly explained the chain of events that had led to this conclusion, to the mounting horror of everyone assembled.

Chakotay had just raised his hand to tap his combadge when Admiral Janeway said, "Wait."

"We need to take the ship to red alert, Admiral," Chakotay said. "Decan and Lasren should begin an immediate search. Nothing takes priority above finding this potential intruder."

"You're right," Janeway said. "But, you were also right when you suggested that Lsia is many moves ahead of us. It won't take long for rumors of this search to spread throughout the crew, possibly alerting this intruder to our suspicions and forcing him to take some precipitous action before we can find him." Turning to Decan, she said, "Begin your search with the senior officers. Captain, take Lieutenant Kim and the general back to the bridge, provide Lieutenant Lasren with a security team, coordinate with Decan. Lasren should start with the bridge officers. But let's do this *quietly*. It's our best chance of finding Xolani without tipping our hand."

Chakotay nodded. "Let's assume the worst for a minute. Let's say Xolani has compromised a key crewmember. If his intention was to turn control of the ship over to Lsia, he may already know we found his program and deleted it."

"He'd be looking for another way to accomplish his goal," Janeway said.

"And if he found it?"

Janeway said, evenly, "We analyze whatever modifications he's made."

"B'Elanna and Lieutenant Conlon are our best hope for finding a technological solution. Should worse come to worst, I'm going to leave that in your capable hands, Admiral."

Janeway smiled. "While you focus on our tactical response?"

"Yes."

"Agreed," Janeway said. "The only way to eliminate this Xolani is to force him out of the body he is currently inhabiting and back into containment. But as it stands right now, we can't do that without exposing the rest of the crew to possible possession."

"How many canisters did Commander Glenn give us?"

"Five. Lieutenant Barclay has the spare."

"Okay," Chakotay said.

"I'm going to have a little chat with Lsia," Janeway said. "There might still be time to convince her of the error of her ways and enlist her aid in separating Xolani from anyone he might have taken."

"Doctor, Counselor, Lieutenant Barclay, return to sickbay," Chakotay ordered. "I realize, Doctor, you've given up hope of separating Emem, Tirrit, or Adaeze from their hosts, but we're talking about one of our own. Whoever it is, they might not have been compromised for long. The general discovered some ancient references that suggested individuals might have had some success in fighting Seriareen possession. I'd be willing to bet that any of our people who were attacked would have resisted. If it's only been a few days or less, the consciousness might still be struggling to control its host. We have baseline scans on the entire crew. I want this thing removed from the body it has taken immediately."

"I will do my best, Captain," the Doctor said.

"Reg, Hugh," Chakotay added, "make sure nothing compromises the Doctor's program."

"Understood," Cambridge replied as Barclay nodded mutely.

Chakotay, Kim, and Mattings moved briskly to the doors. The Doctor and Cambridge followed. Janeway was speaking quietly to Decan. Barclay paused, waiting for their discussion to end.

"Decan?" Torres interjected softly as soon as the admiral

dismissed him. Barclay noted how pale and still her face had become. She looked like someone who knew they were about to receive terrible news.

"Yes, Commander."

"We're going to start your search in main engineering."

Decan looked to Janeway, who nodded.

With that, they departed, leaving Barclay alone with the admiral.

"Admiral," he began hesitantly, "I know you understand how dangerous Lsia is."

"I think I do," Janeway replied.

"I have already placed a containment canister in her cell. An intense enough electromagnetic charge within the cell would overload her holographic matrix."

"You're suggesting I kill her now?" Janeway asked.

"She's a hologram," Barclay replied. "The only part of her that's real *can't* be killed."

"But the charge would also disable her cell's force field and the anti-psionic field. If they fall, there's no way to ensure that Lsia's consciousness would move into containment. Any of us would become vulnerable."

"As plans go, it has its limitations," Barclay conceded. "But she's done enough damage, hasn't she?"

Janeway nodded. "Yes. But I'm not willing to risk more than I have to in order to destroy Lsia."

"I am," Barclay admitted.

"Focus on taking care of the Doctor, and leave the rest to me," Janeway ordered.

Barclay nodded and followed her out. They parted ways at the turbolift as he hurried to join the Doctor in sickbay and prepare for the worst.

The moment Admiral Janeway entered the brig, Lsia knew that the end had come. She had seen the admiral angry, disappointed, and defiant. This was the first time she had seen Kathryn Janeway pushed beyond the possibility of mercy.

The admiral came right to the point.

"You've lied to me," she said simply.

Behind her, Emem had risen to his feet in his cell. Lsia suspected that Tirrit and Adaeze had already done the same.

"I have done what I thought best to secure my people's future," Lsia replied. "Surely you cannot fault me for that."

"I agreed to help you. We've discovered an interesting energy field out here in the wastes, along with the wreckage of the first ships you sent out here to try and locate Seriar. Our people assure me that we can safely traverse the field. We might be only hours away from finding the answers you are seeking. But that wasn't enough for you."

"Admiral, your courage is undeniable, and your crew's ingenuity does you credit. But you have yet to live a single full life. I've lived dozens, as have my companions. Don't take it too hard. There are limits to what you can conceive. In time, we will show you the truths that lay beyond your limits. You need not fear us. But you *will* follow us."

Janeway smiled mirthlessly. "I've been told by my superior officers that I sometimes have difficulty following orders I don't agree with. I don't see that changing under new management."

"For your sake and that of your crew, you should reconsider," Lsia said.

"My crew," Janeway said calmly. "There's a great deal I might be willing to come to terms with, but an attack on my people is not one of them. You promised me that the slaughter of innocents that you refer to as a 'consciousness transfer' had come to an end. But that wasn't true. You have compromised one of my officers. I can't allow that to stand. Our former agreement is hereby rescinded. You presided over the transfer of Xolani's consciousness into the bioneural systems of the shuttle you stole. That means that the *word* you would use to sever the connection between him and any host is known only to you."

Lsia remained silent, stilling her anticipation.

"You will tell me that word so that we may attempt to safely separate Xolani from his current host."

"And if I do?"

"That will depend entirely on the success of our efforts to save the life of the individual you have taken."

"Very well," Lsia said. "*Tryshanthal.*"

The force field separating Lsia from the admiral suddenly blinked out of existence. As soon as it did, Lsia *felt* as if an unbearable, constant pressure had been lifted from her mind. The anti-psionic field Janeway had trusted to safeguard her people had fallen along with the cell's energy barrier.

Lsia smiled, not in victory, but in acknowledgment that this holographic body she had chosen was becoming much more than a malleable form. Finally, the sensations she had desperately missed were returning, and with them came a rush of fierce joy.

Janeway immediately stepped back. "Lieutenant," she said sharply to the brig officer. "Restore the force field."

Emem had already stepped out of his cell and placed his hands on Janeway's upper arms, securing her. "It's too late for that, Admiral," he said softly, relishing this moment as surely as Lsia did. "Your ship is now ours to command."

Janeway attempted to shake him off, but his grip was too strong.

The lieutenant raised his phaser and aimed it at Emem. Janeway felt Emem's grip tighten and feared he was about to use her as a human shield. A heartbeat later, the brig officer fired.

Nothing happened.

Almost simultaneously, Janeway bent her elbow and tapped her combadge, saying, "Janeway to Captain Chakotay."

No response.

Lsia stepped out of her cell, her head held high. "Naturally, I have taken certain precautions. Your weapons are now inhibited by a dampening field. Your internal communications have been restricted to me and my companions. Your primary and auxiliary systems will no longer accept commands without my authorization, including navigation."

"How thorough of you," Janeway noted.

"I have had a great deal of time to think," Lsia reminded her.

"You once said that your greatest wish was for our people to resolve their differences without further bloodshed. Is that still true, or does it only apply when you possess the upper hand in a negotiation?"

"As I said before, our earlier understanding no longer applies. However, we will resolve our differences with a minimum of bloodshed, if possible."

Lsia smiled condescendingly. "Admiral, you understand that any aggressive action taken against me or my people will only result in further loss of life."

"I do."

"Then would you be so kind as to accompany us to the bridge?"

20

PALAIS DE LA CONCORDE

Growing up, Commander Tom Paris had attended plenty of First Contact Day events. He had stood in his father's shadow, conscious of the silent expectations that followed him like a spectre everywhere he went. That demon had grown to mammoth proportions by the time he'd entered the Academy and first tasted the exquisite discomfort of a full-dress uniform.

Today he moved among a thousand other officers, ambassadors, and high-ranking members of the Federation Council. The uniform was as uncomfortable as ever, but the ghost of presumptions past no longer dogged his steps. The path he had forged for himself had been circuitous, treacherous, and uncertain, but it had brought him to a place where he could finally stand unapologetic among his peers.

Whether that would still be true in a few hours was another matter.

His mother maneuvered through the press of people milling casually about with practiced ease. She carried herself like approachable royalty, warm in her greetings. She had a staggering knowledge of guests' names, along with their spouses' and children's in many cases. Any notable event in their lives was commented upon with appropriate grace—*a well-earned promotion, Commander . . . you have my deepest sympathies on your loss, Captain . . . your sixth grandchild, Madam Ambassador? How proud you must be*—and was received with matching cordiality. Many took a few moments to say kind things about Owen Paris and to note how proud he would be to see his son following in his footsteps.

Paris and his mother had done this complicated dance without misstep for more than an hour when Julia directed him toward a set of doors near the rear of the hall. They were guarded by a pair of security officers detailed to President Bacco. Everyone in the room was anticipating the president's entrance. As soon as the president's party arrived—Bacco, Admiral Akaar, and T'Saen, the Vulcan ambassador to the Federation—they would formally receive all of their guests before the ceremony began in the adjacent dining hall.

It seemed that many of the experienced guests had the same inclination. Their hope was to secure a spot as close to the front of the receiving line as possible, thereby accessing the dining room in short order and availing themselves of the refreshments within.

As Paris stared at those doors, he began to sweat. The course of his career, if not his life, was now dependent upon his ability to convince a woman he had never met and a Starfleet Admiral whom he knew only in passing that their priorities for the next hour should include ignoring a thousand people who were much more important to the Federation than he was.

"Mom, this might have been a bad idea," Paris whispered. In response, Julia's knees buckled beneath her, and he automatically wrapped an arm around her waist to hold her up. "Mom?" he asked, his concern genuine.

Julia appeared to rally, fanning her face conspicuously with her hand. "I'm sorry, darling, it's just so warm in here," she said faintly.

One of the security officers at the door immediately tapped his combadge. Another security officer appeared at Julia's side, as if she had arrived via site-to-site transport, and asked, "Are you all right, ma'am?"

Julia looked plaintively toward the young woman. "Marshianna?" she asked.

The lieutenant's lips broke into a smile. "Mrs. Paris?"

"How good to see you, dear," Julia said. "I'm fine. I just felt a little faint for a moment."

"This way," Marshianna said, leading Paris and his mother toward the closed dining room doors and slipping inside with them. Hundreds of tables had been set and dozens of uniformed servers moved about preparing for the assault of hungry guests that was about to begin.

The lieutenant led Julia toward a chair at the nearest table and poured her a glass of water from a carafe. Julia accepted it gratefully, admonishing her kindly for making too much fuss over an old admiral's wife.

"Admiral Paris was my mentor, ma'am," Marshianna insisted. "No one finer has ever worn the uniform."

Julia drank again, then asked, "Do you think the president would mind if I skipped the receiving line this year?"

"Of course not," Marshianna said. "You rest here. The doors will be opening any minute now."

"You are so kind."

"My pleasure, Mrs. Paris."

"Return to your post before someone misses you," Julia insisted.

Marshianna smiled, adding to Paris, "If you need anything else, come to me." She then hurried from the room, closing the doors behind her.

The moment she was gone, Julia shot to her feet.

"Mom?" Paris asked.

"This way," she said assuredly.

They moved quickly to a side door that blended so well with the wall that it was practically invisible. It accessed a short hallway. Through the doors to their left, the clattering of pots and pans and the sound of raised voices suggested that the kitchen was on red alert. There were three other doors along the hallway to the right. Before Paris could properly orient himself, another security officer exited through one of them, followed by President Nanietta Bacco, Admiral Leonard James Akaar, and Ambassador T'Saen. Bacco was midconversation with the ambassador. Admiral Akaar immediately noted Paris's and Julia's presence in the hall, but his concern shifted quickly to surprise.

"Julia?" he asked, stepping out of their small assembly and moving toward her.

Tom Paris had always respected his mother. Now he was also in awe of her. Senior covert operatives with years of experience couldn't have done better than Julia Paris just had.

"Leonard," Julia said warmly, extending her hand.

Akaar easily stood almost a meter taller than Julia. He bent at the waist and opened his arms to her. Behind them, Bacco and T'Saen turned to see what had caught Akaar's attention.

"What a pleasure to see you, Julia," Akaar said as he held her briefly. "It's been too long."

By this time, Bacco had stepped toward them. "What have we here?" she asked.

Akaar released Julia, saying, "Madam President, you remember Julia Paris, Owen's widow."

"Of course," Bacco said, extending her hand. Paris could not tell if she did, or didn't, but that was part of the president's well-known charisma. Nanietta Bacco had led the Federation through some of its darkest hours, including the Borg Invasion, and had done so without ever losing the common touch. She was genuinely beloved, even by her political opponents.

"Madam President," Julia greeted her warmly. "The letter you sent after Owen's death was so thoughtful and touching. I cannot thank you enough."

"Your husband was an extraordinary officer who served the Federation with dignity and honor. He is deeply missed," Bacco replied. This time, Paris was certain she knew whom she was talking about.

That should have been the end of it. An awkward accidental meeting could not be expected to derail the president's schedule. Julia had other ideas.

"Madam President, may I trespass on your kindness? I know you have a busy day ahead of you, but it would mean so much to this old Starfleet widow if you would take a moment to speak to my son, to *Owen's* son. He has come with troubling news about his crewmate Seven."

Bacco's gaze shifted past Julia, and her eyes locked with Paris's. The veil of politeness shifted without falling as her eyes hardened visibly.

"Commander Paris," Akaar said, breaking the spell and stepping past Julia.

"Admiral," Paris said, snapping to attention.

"This is Owen's son?" Bacco asked.

"Commander Thomas Eugene Paris, Madam President," Akaar said. "He is currently assigned to the Full Circle Fleet as the *Starship Voyager's* first officer."

Bacco smiled in apparent recognition. "You're a long way from your post, Commander Paris," she said, then added, "Leonard?"

"At ease, Mister Paris," Akaar ordered.

Paris separated his feet and accepted the hand that President Bacco extended toward him. "An honor to meet you, Madam President."

"Where's Seven?" Bacco asked, cutting right to the chase.

Paris responded by tapping his combadge three times. Three chirps responded, and Paris said, "She is about to exit the Tamarian Embassy. The moment her signal is detected on Federation soil she will be transported directly to Starfleet Medical and brought to the head of a classified project there, a Commander Jefferson Briggs."

"Is she ill?" Bacco demanded.

"No, ma'am," Paris responded. "Although my superior officer, Admiral Kenneth Montgomery, has certainly reported in error to Admiral Akaar that she is. Seven has been classified by Starfleet Medical and the Federation Institute of Health as a public safety hazard."

"Is this true?" Bacco asked of Akaar.

"Commander Briggs has spent the last year studying the illness that struck Coridan, Aldebaran, and Ardana," Akaar said softly.

Bacco nodded in understanding. "I don't blame him for wanting Seven's help. She's the first person I would have called."

"Madam President, Admiral," Paris continued, "Seven has uncovered many troubling facts regarding Commander Briggs's research. She is returning to his lab to confirm the data she and several of my officers gathered over the last few weeks."

"Why was she at the Tamarian Embassy?" Bacco interjected. "Does this have anything to do with the refugees the Tamarians have taken in, or the fact that Ambassador Jarral has apparently forgotten the few words of Federation Standard he once knew and is refusing to reply to my office's requests for information? Ambassador Garak is having a field day with the press at my expense, and while that just means it's probably Tuesday again, it never does much for my mood."

"Commander Paris was ordered to locate Seven and return her to Starfleet Medical," Akaar said. "It's taken you a long time to act on that order, Commander."

Paris swallowed hard and lifted his chin. "I had my reasons, sir. If we could speak for a few minutes in private, I can make them clear to you. If Seven could be here now, she would. She sent me, hoping I could convince you to listen."

"Were we just ambushed by Owen Paris's wife?" Bacco asked of Akaar.

"We were, Madam President," Akaar said coldly.

Bacco nodded thoughtfully, then called to one of her security officers, "Cancel the receiving line. Open the dining room doors and begin the appetizer and beverage service."

"Madam," Akaar began.

"No," Bacco cut him off. "For Seven, I'll make the time. When we finally join our guests, they're going to be disappointed. I'd just as soon they not be starving as well." Turning to T'Saen, she added, "Madam Ambassador, I'm going to have to beg your indulgence for a little while. I apologize for the inconvenience."

T'Saen nodded.

Bacco then gestured to her lead security officer, and he led her, Akaar, and Paris back through the doorway she had just come through.

Paris chanced a glance at his mother's face in passing. The pride beaming from her eyes reinforced his confidence. The knowledge that Seven would soon be at Briggs's mercy steeled his resolve.

TAMARIAN EMBASSY

Seven stood with Doctor Sharak in the embassy's small sitting room. She had spent the last day and a half with the refugees. More had been targeted by Briggs. All had learned to control their catomic response by briefly joining the small gestalt created by Seven, Axum, and Riley. Once the threat had been contained, none were inclined to pursue a deeper connection with the gestalt. Seven had expected Axum to attempt to cajole them more forcefully, but perhaps Riley was making headway with him, at least as far as her people were concerned. He allowed all of them to disentangle themselves from the whole without resistance.

Axum and Riley were aware that Seven was about to return to Starfleet Medical. They could not hide their fear from her or their gratitude.

The silence between Seven and Sharak was comfortable. Their discussions had focused on the ultimate fate of the refugees, should Seven's and Paris's efforts fail. Sharak had assured her that the Children of Tama would care for their new friends as long as was required. Ambassador Jarral had promised they would be welcome and safe.

Finally, Seven's combadge trilled three times. The sound set her heart racing, but she took a deep inhalation to calm it as she returned the signal to Paris, tapping her badge three times. Turning to Sharak, she saw his stoic resolve waver. Taking both of his hands in hers, she said, "Doctor, had I followed your advice, it is likely we would not be here now."

"What advice?"

"You cautioned me not to enter the Commander's lab without you."

Sharak bowed his head.

Seven gently lifted his chin to look again into his eyes. "Commander Briggs is an anomaly. The Starfleet officers I have known understand the difference between right and wrong. They do not waver in their commitments, nor do they allow their fears to dictate their actions. They have much in common with the Children of Tama. No matter what happens, do not allow this incident to sour you or your people on continuing to nurture and strengthen relationships with the Federation. Do not allow yourself to become another casualty of Commander Briggs. He is not worth it."

"I will not," Sharak assured her.

They embraced briefly. Sharak moved past the officers guarding the embassy's front hall and unlocked the door, opening it for Seven.

She left the embassy without a backward glance, ignoring the shouts that arose at the sight of her from the handful of reporters stationed at the embassy gates.

Ambassador Garak had enjoyed the last few days. The silence of the Tamarian Ambassador following Garak's leak to the press had confirmed his suspicion that the embassy's guests were more than met the eye. Try as he might, however, he could not discover their origin. Every contact he had utilized to help him unravel this mystery had failed.

This had only increased his determination to uncover whatever it was that the Tamarians were hiding.

Several times a day, he made a point of walking the embassy's perimeter. When it suited him, he did so in full view of the press and continued to offer them calculated tidbits certain to whet their appetites. Their numbers had dwindled today, as was expected. Most were busy covering the First Contact Day events. There were hundreds of official receptions and parties happening all over the planet.

He was due at the Palais, but had no interest in suffering through the receiving line. Within the hour, the doors to the banquet hall would be open and he would slip inside and do his duty for Cardassia. Until then, he sat across the street from the embassy on a low bench beneath a large shade tree.

The moment he saw the embassy's front gates open, he rose in surprise and anticipation. When the striking figure of Seven of Nine was escorted through the gate, he hurried to intercept her, along with the few die-hard reporters whose diligence was apparently about to be rewarded.

How marvelous, he thought.

"Seven of Nine," he called to her.

Her head turned sharply in response, but before Garak had come within ten meters of her, she disappeared in a cascade of light.

Garak stood stunned, pondering this development. Filing it away for future reference, he turned his steps toward the Palais.

21

VOYAGER

It didn't take Admiral Janeway long to consider Lsia's request. As she did so, Emem released his viselike grip on her arms and stepped toward the brig's duty officer.

"Your weapon, please," Emem said, extending his hand to accept it.

The young man looked to Janeway, who nodded. Once Emem had taken the phaser, he took a moment to adjust its settings, turned to Tirrit's cell, took aim, and fired into it.

To Janeway's surprise, it functioned perfectly. To Lsia, she said, "Our weapons are useless unless one of *your people* activates them?"

"Should you ever offer me your allegiance, I will explain the modification. It is for our security, nothing more."

Janeway chaffed at Lsia's presumption. She understood exactly how their weapons had been disabled, but until she regained control of the ship or chose to damage several critical systems, Lsia's *modification* would stand. The admiral watched as Emem repeated this procedure with each cell. When he was done, each of the canisters that Commander Glenn had created to house the Seriareen's consciousnesses had been reduced to a steaming, warped chunk of useless metal.

He then turned and placed the weapon at the base of Janeway's neck.

"We will not have this conversation again, Emem," Lsia chastised him.

"Even you cannot give me a reason to spare her now. She is of no further use to us."

"These people are not our enemies, Emem," Lsia countered.

Janeway disagreed, but held her peace.

"Your rash actions have already cost us all of our former allies," Lsia continued. "We will require new ones in short order. Should the time come when they prove to be more trouble than they are worth, we will execute all of them. Until then, we will operate under the assumption that in time, they will see the wisdom of our actions, the benefits we may offer them, and the futility in attempting to resist us." Gesturing toward the brig's door, Lsia said, "Admiral."

The group made their way into the hall. As they crowded into the turbolift that would take them to the bridge, Janeway made sure she was standing just inside the entrance. At the last moment, she jumped out and watched the turbolift doors close on their four shocked faces. She then locked the doors manually. Ducking down the hall, she sprinted toward the nearest Jefferies tube, opened the door and stepped inside, sliding down the ladder with the energy of a first-year cadet. The sound of phaser fire pinged through the hall she had just cleared. When footsteps did not follow it, she redoubled her efforts.

Lsia had let her go. That was a mistake she would soon come to regret.

Finally free of the fear that he had been harboring a traitor within his matrix, the Doctor turned to the problem he had recently dismissed as unsolvable. Commander Glenn had been right. It was not possible to separate a Seriareen from their host by force while the host lived. According to Lsia they would naturally depart the host at the moment of death. This was not the most daunting obstacle. Depending upon *how* the host died, and especially under controlled circumstances, revival of a Seriareen-free individual could begin immediately. The greatest obstacle by far was the unknown. There was no way to know what a mind and body that had housed a Seriareen consciousness would look like once the essence departed. Bringing the mind back to what it had once been would likely be significantly more difficult than restoring his program and its memory files.

The Doctor had begun to run several simulations of revival techniques that could shield the neurological system from further trauma and was considering a number of new drug combinations that might accelerate the healing process when his computer refused to accept further input.

"Reg," the Doctor called.

Barclay and Counselor Cambridge had left him undisturbed once they returned to sickbay but stood together near the door to the office studying him with the care a munitions expert gave to a device that might explode at any moment.

"Yes, Doctor?"

"Something's wrong with my control panel."

Barclay immediately crossed to the Doctor's side and after a few frustrating attempts to restore its functions, shook his head.

"Excuse me, please, Doctor," Barclay said. "I'll return as soon as I can."

Commander B'Elanna Torres had led Decan and the security officers to main engineering by way of an arms locker on deck sixteen. There, she had retrieved a phaser for herself and offered Decan his choice of weapons. He had selected a type-2 phaser like hers.

"Surely you do not intend to kill any officer we might find who has been taken by this Xolani. He would simply move on to another host."

"I know," Torres said, her jaw tightening. "But he'll need his host's command codes to access our primary systems. He might not be willing to give her up right away."

"Her?"

Torres nodded.

As they turned the corner and moved double-time toward the doors to main engineering, Torres saw Admiral Janeway extricating herself from a Jefferies tube.

Torres motioned for the team to stay put as she rushed toward Janeway. Heedless, Decan followed after her.

"Something wrong with the turbolifts, Admiral?" Torres asked.

"One just took Lsia, Emem, Tirrit, and Adaeze to the bridge," Janeway replied. "Lsia spoke a single word and, I believe, activated a program similar to the one you thought you disabled. The brig's force fields dropped. We've lost internal communications and have been locked out of all primary and auxiliary systems. Our weapons have been blocked by a dampening field. The range may be fairly narrow, however. Emem was able to override it with a minor adjustment."

"Admiral?" a voice called from the opposite end of the hall. Torres turned to see Lieutenant Barclay running toward them and breathing heavily. When he finally reached them, he started to speak, thought better of it and placed his hands on his knees to facilitate a few deeper breaths. Finally he said, "Something is wrong with sickbay's control systems."

"They've ceased to function?" Janeway guessed.

Barclay nodded vehemently.

"Lsia has control of the ship," Torres realized as they hurried back toward the security team.

"Have you found Xolani?" Janeway asked.

"No, but I have a pretty good idea where he is."

Janeway nodded. "If it's the same program, how quickly can you override it and restore control of our systems to us?"

"It won't be the same program," Torres replied bitterly. "That was a feint, meant to lull us into complacency."

Janeway nodded, then considered the security team. "Cover all of the exits," she ordered. "No one leaves engineering without my authorization. Lieutenant Barclay, wait here," she added.

"If I'm right, and he's in there, how do we take him down?" Torres asked. "Can we risk stunning him?"

Janeway looked to Decan. He nodded. "I don't think that will be necessary," the admiral replied.

"Hand to hand?" Torres asked.

"Something like that."

Barclay stepped aside as Janeway and Torres led the security team into main engineering.

There was a tangible sense of tension in the air. Several officers reported simultaneous system failures. Lieutenant Conlon stood at the main control panel that faced the combined warp/slipstream core. Her back was to them.

A few officers took note of their arrival and paused in their efforts. Lieutenant Decan stepped forward and briefly studied each face. After pausing for a few extra seconds on Lieutenant Conlon, he turned to Torres and nodded. The Vulcan then stepped silently closer to *Voyager*'s chief engineer.

A wave of nausea similar to the ones that had crippled her in the first months of her pregnancy washed through Torres. She had allowed herself to hope, even though she had known better as soon as the Doctor recounted Xolani's memories. Conlon's unusual insensitivity had been easy to dismiss, given her stress levels. The obvious errors in her report on the power surges, however, Torres should have taken more seriously. She didn't believe that Conlon had been compromised for long. As she thought back over the last few weeks, it seemed likely that Conlon had been taken either just before or immediately after she had begun repairs on the holodecks. Still, Torres doubted that there was anything the Doctor would be able to do to save her friend now. That reality not only sickened her, it enraged her.

As a rule, Torres did everything with the entirety of her being. Her love was as fierce as her grudges. Every loss she had ever suffered hit her with the same intensity as the one that had defined her: her father's rejection and departure when she was still a young girl.

She hadn't known Conlon very long, but given the number of their interactions and her easy companionship, Nancy had become part of Torres's inner circle.

Now she was gone.

Clearly sensing a shift in the room, Conlon lifted her head from the panel and turned. Her eyes widened in alarm as she noted the new arrivals.

"Commander, I'm so glad you're here," she said. "We have a problem. A few minutes ago, I was locked out of our primary systems. I'm trying to override it, but my command codes aren't working."

Janeway shot a questioning gaze toward Decan. He shook his head in response.

"We do have a problem," Janeway agreed, "but my guess is you won't be interested in helping us solve it, will you, Xolani?"

Conlon's hands dropped to her sides. She straightened her shoulders and lifted her chin defiantly. "If you harm this body, I will simply take another."

"We know," Decan said, taking the initiative. With his hands raised before him to demonstrate that he meant no harm, he closed the distance between them, saying, "Your species is unlike any we have ever encountered, and having spent so much time among us, you must realize by now that it is not in our nature to simply destroy what we do not understand."

Xolani considered him warily.

"It may not be in their natures, but it still runs awfully strong in half of mine," Torres said, moving closer. "Step away from that panel."

Xolani turned and raised an arm to counter Torres's movement. Decan used the momentary distraction to place his right hand to Conlon's shoulder, his thumb resting on her trapezius nerve bundle. A quick pinch and Conlon's body fell to the deck like a bag of rocks.

Captain Chakotay knew this place: the calm before the storm. His nerves stretched taut with each minute that passed without word from Kathryn. They were near to breaking. He reminded himself that control was an illusion. To attempt to assert it now would lead to rash, ill-conceived actions. He must surrender to reality as it unfolded and wait to act until he was certain of his advantage.

After confirming that the bridge crew retained sole custody of their bodies, Lieutenant Lasren had been dispatched to join a security crew and begin his deck-by-deck search for Xolani. Waters had taken his station at ops.

Lieutenant Aubrey manned the tactical post. Devi Patel had no end of unusual readings to keep her busy at her science station. Gwyn sat ready at the helm, making slight adjustments as the wastes buffeted them about, even at station-keeping. Lieutenant Kim sat at his left hand, General Mattings at his right.

The storm was about to break. He considered the myriad possible permutations of the threat he was about to face. When Ensign Gwyn reported that the helm had grown sluggish and Patel advised moments later that her panel was no longer responding, he rose to his feet.

"This is Captain Chakotay to all hands. Red alert."

The lights above did not dim, nor did alarm klaxons sound. Chakotay tapped his combadge again and realized that it did not bleep to alert him that a channel had been opened.

"Waters, is the comm system down?" Chakotay asked.

"Aye, sir," she replied.

"What does that mean?" Mattings asked, rising to stand beside the captain.

"It means someone is interfering with our operations. I'd be amazed if the next report doesn't confirm that we've lost access to all of our primary systems."

"Does this happen a lot around here?" Mattings inquired.

"More often than I'd like," Chakotay admitted. "Secure the bridge," he ordered.

All bridge officers retrieved their personal sidearms and readied themselves to meet an attack. Aubrey and Kim covered the turbolift entrance while Waters and Patel moved to do the same for the deck entrance.

"My weapon was not transported aboard with me, Captain," Mattings noted.

"That's standard procedure," Chakotay said. "Our transporter buffers remove them."

"Without it, I'm not much use to you in a fight."

"We'll protect you with our lives if need be, General."

"I know that. I'd just like to return the favor."

"You already did when you rescued our admiral," Chakotay reminded him.

Silent anticipation gnawed at Chakotay's innards. Finally, the turbolift doors slid open and Lsia stepped out. Aubry's and Kim's phasers were immediately trained on her.

"Welcome to the bridge," Chakotay said. "Lieutenant Kim?"

"Don't move," Kim advised Lsia.

She turned to him and smiled benevolently. "Lower your weapon," she said.

"I don't think so," Kim replied.

At this, Emem stepped forward.

"Remain where you are," Kim ordered.

Emem replied by lifting his phaser toward the lieutenant. Kim immediately fired. The phaser clicked in his hand, useless.

"Mine doesn't have that problem," Emem advised him.

Kim stepped back as every officer on the bridge pointed their phasers at the intruders and verified that theirs were as useless as their first officer's.

"I understand from Admiral Janeway that you have detected a large energy field," Lsia said as her companions moved calmly onto the bridge.

"We have," Chakotay said. "Where is Admiral Janeway?"

"Probably in main engineering by now," Lsia replied. "She chose at the last minute not to join us and is certainly working to restore control of your ship to your crew. She will find that a daunting task."

"I'm willing to wait," Chakotay said.

"I am not," Lsia said. "Stations, gentlemen," she ordered. Emem moved to the tactical panel above the bridge's chairs. Tirrit moved to operations. Adaeze hurried to Patel's science station as Lsia stepped down into the command well and approached the conn. As they did so, they relieved all of the bridge officers of their weapons.

"Everybody step aside," Chakotay ordered.

Confused faces met his as Lsia said, "A wise choice, Captain."

"I don't know about that," Mattings observed. "I realize your weapons are useless, Captain, but we do have them outnumbered."

"We do. We might even successfully subdue most of them. Of course we can't risk killing them. That would just add to the body count when they choose their new hosts from among my bridge crew. And Lsia is a hologram. She can assume any form she wishes and would be pretty hard to beat in a stand-up fight."

"You're just going to allow her to take your ship from you?"

"I didn't say that. Admiral Janeway and at least two of the best engineers in Starfleet are working right now to reverse whatever Lsia did to seize control of the ship. I don't think we should make their job any harder by forcing Lsia's hand. In my experience, raw power grabs of Starfleet vessels rarely end well for the grabbers. This ship has thousands of moving parts. It takes a minimum of forty-seven people to run all critical stations. She's got five at the most."

Mattings smiled uncertainly. "You're taking an awful lot on faith here."

"That's because I've invested it in extraordinary people."

"Captain?" Ensign Gwyn called from the conn. She stood over Lsia, studying the readings on the navigation panel.

"Report," Chakotay ordered.

"You might want to sit down. Everybody else should hang on to something," Gwyn advised.

Chakotay sensed forward motion beneath his feet as the image on the main viewscreen began to rotate.

"She's taking us toward the energy field, isn't she?" Chakotay asked.

"Aye, sir," Gwyn replied.

Chakotay sat. Mattings did not.

"General."

"I'm accustomed to standing at times like this," he said.

Chakotay shrugged. "Suit yourself."

"Corridor six-nine-one-seven-two-eight is showing sixty-two percent viability," Tirrit reported from ops.

"The containment-field diameter is eight times greater than anticipated," Adaeze added.

"Eight?" Lsia asked, alarmed.

"He must be hungry," Emem noted.

He? Chakotay thought. *Hungry?*

"Executing corridor transversion in five, four, three," Lsia counted down.

Chakotay grabbed his armrests as the ship began to buck under the strain of the wastes' instabilities. As before, he experienced a brief sensation of freefall before the corridor Lsia had targeted—for what he assumed was a maneuver similar to Gwyn's bounce—pulled *Voyager* forward.

The sudden acceleration that followed pressed him firmly back into his seat.

"You might want to adjust the inertial dampeners," Waters advised Tirrit. "It's that one, there," she added, pointing to her control panel.

"Do as she says," Lsia ordered.

Chakotay expected Lsia to slow the ship when they reached the end of the corridor seam's stability. Instead, she only made a light course correction as they returned to normal space.

She then repeated the same maneuver flawlessly two more times, using the next two nearest corridors.

In less than four minutes, a journey that should have taken them more than a day was over, and *Voyager* slowed as it approached the massive energy field that supposedly surrounded Seriar.

Without turning, Lsia said, "You have a fine ship, Captain. She has performed exceptionally well."

"I expect you to return her to us in the same shape you found her," Chakotay noted.

"Why would I do otherwise?" Lsia asked. "We have a great deal of work ahead of us."

"*You* do," Chakotay corrected her. "Apart from saving us from your inexperience with our systems, my people will not lift a hand to assist you."

Lsia shook her head sadly. "We shall see," she replied. "Tirrit?"

"Requesting ingress," he replied.

Chakotay watched in amazement as the visible energies of the field, a small fraction of the entirety of exotic radiant particles that created it, began to swirl and move before him.

"How in the world?" Lieutenant Kim marveled beside him.

"What is it?" Chakotay asked.

"They're using the protectors to carve out a clear space through the energy field," Kim reported.

"We should probably do the same on our way out," Chakotay whispered.

"You really think we'll be able to retake the ship by then?" Kim asked.

"Absolutely."

"How?"

Chakotay did not answer. *Voyager* was moving again, slipping inside a tunnel of empty space while around them raged an energy field unlike anything he'd ever seen before.

Their motion was steady at full impulse. They were moving through normal space. Soon enough, the terminus came within visual range. A distant bright-white mass lay several thousand kilometers beyond the energy field.

It wasn't a planet.

Voyager cleared the energy field, and Lsia slowed the ship.

As every individual on the bridge struggled to make sense of what they were seeing, General Mattings fell to his knees.

Commander Torres and Admiral Janeway stood beside Lieutenant Barclay, who had joined them as soon as Conlon had been removed from engineering. Several of the junior engineering officers had abandoned their inoperative posts and collected themselves behind the admiral and fleet chief engineer, observing their efforts to regain control of the ship.

Neither Janeway nor B'Elanna seemed to mind that this had become a teachable moment.

Lieutenant Neol had taken it upon himself to monitor the feed from the bridge's main viewscreen. From time to time he reported on *Voyager*'s progress under Lsia's command. It was clear to Barclay that whatever Lsia was doing, she had planned it for months and was now executing it as quickly as possible. It obviously included taking *Voyager* within range of the presumed coordinates of Seriar.

Torres had begun her work exactly as Barclay would have. Rather than immediately attempt to break into the new control sequence, which could theoretically damage many systems simultaneously, she was searching for a way to view the program Lsia had initiated. Analysis would hopefully show a weakness.

The first problem was accessing it, and that was proving incredibly difficult. Conlon, *Xolani*, Barclay reminded himself, had constructed his own command pathways separate from Conlon's command codes. Everyone's codes were now useless, and Xolani had locked the system down before he had confronted Torres and Janeway. Nothing Torres attempted could convince the main computer to display anything beyond current status reports, all of which were nominal.

Slight stresses on hull integrity and inertial dampeners were detected as *Voyager* began to utilize several subspace corridors to cut the distance between the ship and the energy field surrounding Seriar. Even Torres was surprised at how quickly the new control program responded to these potential threats, rerouting power in the same way she would have done had she had access right now.

When Torres stood back from the control panel and crossed her arms at her chest, Barclay's anxiety intensified.

"We don't have a lot of good choices here," Torres advised Janeway.

"Couldn't we manually override propulsion?" an eager ensign asked from the back of the assembled pack.

"How so?" Torres asked.

"The first time Admiral Batiste took control of the deflector array, we intentionally broke the dish," the ensign replied.

"We were in open space, Quinn," Torres reminded him. "These wastes are treacherous. We need all systems operating at peak efficiency to survive."

"So we don't destroy anything. A few magnetic constrictors out of alignment and a dozen well-placed conduit leaks could slow her down and buy us some time."

"We'll consider that plan S," Torres replied.

"S?" Janeway asked.

"We're going to try everything else within our power first, and if that fails and we're totally *screwed* . . ."

Janeway chuckled grimly.

"But I like the way you're thinking, Quinn," Janeway noted. "We're open to any reasonable suggestion at this point."

"How about an unreasonable one?" Torres asked.

"Go ahead," Janeway urged.

"After Admiral Batiste pulled that stunt, I decided this was a vulnerability Starfleet had never adequately addressed," Torres began.

"Alien possession of a senior officer?" Janeway guessed.

Torres nodded. "It occurred to me that our basic command code structure could be slightly modified, but it was risky if, for instance, *I* was the officer compromised."

"What did you do?" Janeway asked, equal parts alarmed and intrigued.

"I created my own access key," Torres said. "It is designed to override all security protocols and allow me to directly access our central processors, even if my command codes have been disabled. It targets our root files, bypasses the fail-safes, and allows me to alter our most basic programming."

"What are you waiting for?" Janeway asked.

"I've never tested it," Torres admitted. "After I'd finished it, I decided it was a bad idea. Even now, I don't know if it will work. If it does, it shouldn't take me long to override whatever Lsia has done and restore our proper command paths. If it doesn't . . ."

". . . we're screwed?" Janeway finished.

Torres nodded again.

Janeway sighed. "When all of this is over, you, Lieutenant Kim, and I are going to have a lengthy discussion about Starfleet protocols. The days of any officer—"

"Wait a minute," Torres interjected. "We didn't survive for seven years out here by blindly adhering to the rules. We did it by following the spirit of them and making accommodations as the need arose, some of which have now become standard aboard Starfleet vessels."

"Improvisation in an emergency is one thing. *Planning* to break the rules is a little different," Janeway countered.

"If I'd actually followed through and tested that program, we might already have control of the ship," Torres argued.

Janeway shook her head, frustrated. "Where is it?"

"In my quarters."

"Ensign Quinn, take three security officers to the commander's quarters and retrieve the program file," Janeway ordered.

Torres provided Quinn with the location of the file at her workstation, and the ensign quickly departed.

The ship's motion seemed to cease abruptly. Lieutenant Neol said, "Admiral, *Voyager* has reached the edge of the energy field we detected."

"So soon?" Janeway asked.

"Yes, Admiral."

"I wonder if there's another option," Barclay said suddenly as inspiration, or desperation, struck.

"I hope so," Torres said.

Stepping up, Barclay moved to the interface and called up the holodeck control systems. To his surprise, and everyone else's, he was granted access.

"That's interesting," Torres noted. "She's taken control of every primary system, and auxiliary one, *except* the holodecks."

"It's a discrete entity," Barclay reminded Torres. "It has its own power systems and controls. It interfaces with the main computer for data retrieval but is otherwise autonomous. It's also the one system Xolani was never able to compromise."

"But that doesn't help us," Torres said. "All you can do from here is run any holodeck program you'd like."

"*All I can do*," Barclay said with emphasis, "is *manage* any holographic program currently running on this ship."

Torres considered this. Janeway seemed to understand the implication sooner. "Wasn't Meegan's program designed to integrate with the *Galen*'s systems?"

Barclay shook his head. "As soon as the fleet's complement was finalized, I added integration protocols for her mobile emitter and the Doctor's to all nine of the original fleet ships, in the event they transported to one of them and their mobile emitters were damaged. That way, they could retain their functionality by routing their program automatically through the ship's own holographic systems."

"How thoughtful of you, Reg," Janeway said, beaming at him.

"Which reminds me," Barclay added. "I need to add that protocol to the *Vesta.*"

"We're moving again," Neol reported.

"Where?" Janeway asked.

"Some sort of tunnel has been created through the energy field. We're entering it now," he replied.

"Is the only way to activate this protocol and slave Lsia's holographic matrix to *Voyager*'s system by damaging her mobile emitter?" Janeway asked.

"Let's find out. May I?"

Torres nodded. "By all means."

Janeway then turned to Decan, saying, "Get to the bridge. Make sure Chakotay knows we will have options for him shortly."

"What are your orders for him in the meantime?" Decan asked.

Janeway shrugged. "Captain's discretion," she replied.

Barclay set to work, modifying his program to detect "Meegan's" mobile emitter and override its autonomy. His focus became singular. All ambient sounds, including the murmured conversations of the rest of engineering, faded into so much white noise until Neol's voice sliced through.

"What is that?" he asked.

Torres and Janeway stepped away from the main console and moved to Neol's display panel.

After a moment, Janeway said softly, "The Source."

Captain Chakotay had no idea what he was looking at but he did understand General Mattings's reaction. An area several million kilometers in diameter, void of any stars, planets, or debris, was surrounded by the energy field. At its center was a bright white ring that seemed to spin on an unseen axis. Its constant motion was throwing off massive amounts of exotic radiation. A steady stream of protectors collected the highly charged particles and carried them to the surrounding field, where they were contained.

Chakotay had seen several artistic renderings of the Confederacy's "Source" in the last few months. None of them had captured the magnificent power of whatever this thing was or the awe it truly inspired.

"You were never looking for Seriar, were you?" Chakotay asked.

Lsia's eyes remained glued to the viewscreen as she replied, "Seriar was destroyed in the conflict that led up to our incarceration. This *was* its location, but I could not be certain he had returned here until now."

"That's a life-form?" Chakotay demanded in disbelief.

"The Obihhax," Lsia replied. "A living god."

"Would you mind giving us a better look?" Chakotay requested of Tirrit.

"It's that one there," Waters advised Tirrit.

Tirrit followed her direction, and the magnification was increased until the Obihhax filled the main viewscreen. From Chakotay's left, Lieutenant Kim let out an audible gasp.

It wasn't just a perfect torus. It was an ouroboros: a massive white serpentlike creature that had caught its tail in its mouth, absolute stillness in constant motion.

"Let me guess," Chakotay ventured, "this Obihhax is one of the creatures that your people used to carve the subspace corridors."

"The *hax*, yes," Lsia replied, nodding. "At the height of our glory, there were dozens. They are subspace-born and must be trained to remain in normal space. They prefer to live and feed in their natural home. We taught them to carve our corridors with great precision. All but this one were destroyed in the last battle."

"Then what's an *Obihhax*?" Kim asked.

"In the end, nine Seriareen remained. Our ship was the *Solitas*. We served under Obih. We were on the run, attempting to protect the last living hax. We were confronted by a large armada of Nayseriareen. They were about to destroy the hax. There was only one way to save it. Obih was released from his body, and his consciousness entered the hax. We were captured shortly after he fled. But when I saw the vast quantity of new corridors the Confederacy claims, as well as many beyond their territory, I knew the Obihhax had survived. He must have searched for us, carving new corridors as he went. Those not sustained by new wave forms or *protectors* have begun to collapse. The Confederacy's remain in use because they learned how to create new wave forms for themselves."

"Are the protectors naturally created by the hax?"

"They are a by-product of its motion through subspace. They are drawn to its energy. Even now, they are tending to its needs. They are *of the hax* and serving it is their highest purpose," Lsia replied. "Countless wave forms have abandoned their corridors to come here and wait on its pleasure."

General Mattings pulled himself to his feet. His face glistened with tears that continued to fall.

"I don't believe it," he said simply.

Lsia shrugged. "You would deny the evidence of your own eyes?"

"Whatever use you people made of this creature thousands of years ago is no longer relevant," the general replied. "It has a new purpose now, a sacred purpose. Do *your eyes* not see that?"

"The circumference of the hax is more than a hundred kilometers," Kim noted. "We've never encountered a corridor that wide."

"It has grown," Lsia admitted.

"Do you intend to use it to carve new corridors?" Chakotay guessed.

"We must awaken it first. Obih must know that we have returned. Once that is done, he will follow us to a safer place from which to begin to rebuild our civilization. In time, all inhabitants of this quadrant and, eventually, this galaxy, will understand their proper place in the order of things. They will revere the hax, they will worship it, just as your people have come to revere and worship the Source, General," Lsia insisted.

"It seems to me that the people of this quadrant decided a long time ago that your idea of order was not to their liking. What makes you think now will be any different?" Chakotay asked.

"It will take time," Lsia conceded, "but what is time to those who live forever?"

Lsia entered a series of new commands. *Voyager*'s course was altered and the ship began to move on a direct line toward the center of the Obihhax.

"Wait," Chakotay said. "Just how close do you intend to take us to that thing?"

"There is only one way to rouse him," Lsia replied.

"Ensign Gwyn, how long until we reach the hax?"

"Nine and a half minutes," Gwyn replied.

Chakotay had waited patiently until now for some sign that Kathryn, B'Elanna, or Conlon would restore control of *Voyager*'s systems. Time was about to be up.

22

PALAIS DE LA CONCORDE

The room into which Commander Paris was led was filled with antique benches, sofas, and settees spaced artfully over dark wood floors and ornate rugs to create several intimate sitting areas, though it could easily hold a hundred people. The light-yellow walls were lined with ancient maps of several Federation worlds.

President Bacco moved to the nearest corner, where a small oval table rested. Crossing her arms at her chest, she said, "Let's have it, Commander Paris." Akaar stood at her side. The security detail was ordered to keep watch out of earshot.

Paris nodded, then tapped his combadge again. This time, two short trills were followed by a longer signal. After a few moments of silence, during which Paris dared not breathe, the signal was repeated back to him. He placed a hand on the table to steady himself as he exhaled his relief.

"Seven is in," he advised them.

"Are we in the middle of a report or a covert operation?" Akaar asked.

"A little bit of both, sir," Paris replied. "This combadge has been modified to allow me to retain a constant open channel with Seven."

"Can she hear us?" Bacco asked.

"No, Madam President. But as soon as she is in position, we will be able to hear everything she does."

"Why don't you grab us some chairs, Leonard?" Bacco asked. "*Carefully*; that pair over there is about seven hundred and fifty years old."

Tossing Paris a glance of restrained contempt, Akaar did as she had asked.

"How much do you know about Commander Briggs?" Paris asked President Bacco.

"I'd never heard of him until a few minutes ago," Bacco replied.

Akaar returned with a single chair for the president, and as she seated herself, he said, "Briggs is a senior medical research specialist. He has done groundbreaking work in genetics and epidemiology. He was the only candidate Starfleet Medical seriously considered assigning when the catomic plague was discovered."

"His work in genetics included extrapolating the Planarian genome," Paris interjected. "They were an extinct race that possessed unique and powerful regenerative capabilities."

"*Were?*" Akaar asked pointedly.

Paris nodded, but before he could continue, a female voice came clearly through his combadge. "*This way*," it said simply.

"Seven has activated her combadge," Paris whispered.

"I thought you said she couldn't hear us," Bacco whispered back.

"She can't."

"Then why are we whispering?" Bacco asked.

"*Hello, Seven,*" said a male voice Paris immediately recognized.

Paris raised a hand to forestall further conversation as Bacco and Akaar leaned forward to listen.

STARFLEET MEDICAL, CLASSIFIED DIVISION

"I hoped you had received my message," Briggs said. He was seated in his private office behind a workstation. Seven stood opposite him.

"If by *message* you are referring to the pain and suffering of nineteen former residents of Arehaz whose catomic molecules you attempted to modify and then injected into your test subjects, then *yes*, Commander Briggs, I did," Seven replied.

"You left me no choice, Seven," Briggs insisted. "Your samples as well as Patient C-1's and Doctor Frazier's no longer accept modification. In fact, they disappear completely from any test subject into whom they are injected after only a day." Briggs rose and circled his desk. Leaning against it and facing Seven directly, he asked, "How did you do that?"

"What makes you think I did anything?" Seven asked.

"You are the only random factor in this equation. My previous experiments failed, but they were instructive failures. There is no other explanation beyond your involvement for what I'm seeing now. You somehow still control the catoms that were once yours, don't you? Even after they have been extracted, they are still connected to you."

"It is my belief that all catomic particles exhibit collective properties," Seven advised him.

His eyes widened at this.

"Upon what do you base this belief?"

Seven smiled mirthlessly. "Experience."

Briggs stood upright. "Excellent," he said. "We've wasted too much time already. I've held up my end of our agreement. It's time for you to honor yours. You will begin by giving me a full report on all of your catomic research."

"You have reneged on several key points of our agreement," Seven corrected him. "I will, however, provide you with the data you require insofar as it is instrumental in curing the catomic plague."

Briggs sighed. "Fine. We'll start there."

"There is one piece of data I require in order to properly direct your efforts."

"What?"

"Did you intentionally create the catomic plague?"

Briggs was clearly taken aback at the inference. "Of course not," he retorted.

"Allow me to rephrase," Seven said. "Did you *accidentally* create the catomic plague?"

Briggs closed his mouth in a tight line and his eyes hardened. Finally he began, "I don't see the relevance . . ."

"If I can determine the precise point of origin, it will enable me to track down every mutation, variation, and replication. In order to completely eradicate the plague, every affected particle must be neutralized."

"That will never be possible," Briggs said. "We don't even know how many people might have been affected who were never brought in for treatment. The plague's viability so many months after it first appeared suggests—"

"Your infection rates have been artificially inflated, Commander," Seven cut him off.

Briggs shook his head sadly. "Surely you have not given credence to the unfounded speculations of Doctor Sharak and Lieutenant . . . what was her name?"

"Wildman."

"Yes, Wildman."

"Long before I was briefed on the discoveries of Doctor Sharak and Lieutenant Wildman, I saw you perform multiple experiments on the same alien female. This was troubling, apart from the fact that she was clearly not suffering from the plague. More than once, I saw you kill that female and irradiate her remains. It made no sense until Doctor Sharak exposed Ria, the Planarian you had planted on Coridan. They then discovered the exact same woman hiding within the evacuated area on Aldebaran. There were several additional versions of her developing in maturation chambers."

"You have no proof," Briggs began.

"I know. No proof of your Planarians' existence will ever be found. Your control over them is absolute. Not only were they willing to infect countless innocent individuals with the plague at your request, their work is equally thorough when it comes to destroying themselves and all evidence of their lives. I imagine there is a great deal about Planarians that you have learned since you re-created them, just as I assume there is a lab somewhere off-world where a steady stream of replacement test subjects are being grown as we speak. How many times have you regenerated this female to further your research?"

Briggs smiled warily. The look in his eyes suggested that she had just gone from a source of help to an imminent threat. But there was pride in it as well. Part of him *wanted* Seven to know the depth and breadth of his genius.

Finally he said softly, "One thousand, nine hundred and sixty-one."

PALAIS DE LA CONCORDE

President Bacco had listened with growing consternation to the conversation transmitted through Paris's combadge. Akaar had placed both of his meaty fists on the table and was leaning over it, completely absorbed by Briggs's words.

When Briggs admitted to re-creating almost two thousand copies of a single life-form in order to conduct his experiments, Bacco rose from her seat. She looked ready to crawl through the combadge and throttle Briggs with her bare hands.

"Correct me if I'm wrong, Admiral," she said softly, "but didn't the Federation outlaw genetic engineering of sentient life-forms a few hundred years back?"

"Yes, Madam President."

Bacco waved over a security officer and said, "Get me Esperanza immediately."

The officer nodded and departed. As Seven questioned Briggs further about the regenerative properties of the Planarians, the president's chief of staff, Esperanze Piñero, entered and hurried toward her.

"Do you have any idea how many people you've just—" Piñero began.

"Shhh," Bacco hissed, then added softly, "I want the head of Starfleet Medical and the Federation Institute of Health in my office within the next five minutes."

"Is this really . . . ?"

"Asses in my office," Bacco said, carefully enunciating each word.

Piñero stiffened, taken aback. "Right away, Madam President."

STARFLEET MEDICAL, CLASSIFIED DIVISION

"It was not my intention to re-create her species," Briggs insisted. "But the potential inherent in Planarian genes for regeneration of diseased tissue was too significant to simply ignore."

"Of course," Seven encouraged him.

"The first Planarian cells were created from several humanoid species and a few lower life-forms. Once the DNA sequence was complete, the cells began to multiply at rates I had never imagined. I had an embryo within days. She shouldn't have lived more than a few hours. *But she did.* And as she continued to develop, I found the thought of destroying her unconscionable."

"It must have been very difficult for you," Seven said with as much sympathy as she could feign.

"Naria and I worked together for more than two years before Coridan. After, she *wanted to help.* She *demanded* that I use her and her sisters as test subjects. She knew how critical my work was and only wanted to see me succeed. I have never imposed my will upon her or any of them. If anything, they've pushed me."

"Coridan?" Seven asked.

Briggs became more animated as he spoke, beginning to pace the small room and gesture broadly as if to conjure the images he was creating from thin air.

"I was on Coridan, attending a medical conference, when the Borg attacked. Naria was with me. She was my *assistant.* We always listed her species as Kyppran, given the deep pink color of her flesh when her emotional state was unstressed. No one ever questioned it.

"As soon as the attack began, all officers with medical training were ordered to triage facilities. It was grisly work. There was little we could do for most of our patients. Our supplies were extremely limited, and there was no way for Starfleet to get aid to the planet's surface with so many cubes in orbit.

"At the end of the second day, I was called away from surgery for a special mission. Part of a cube had crashed on the surface and several drones were aboard. I was instructed to study those we recovered, in hopes that I could figure out why they were no longer attempting to assimilate us.

"I'd never seen a Borg before. I'd studied them in the abstract, but the genuine article was something that defied belief. The fusion of organic and technological components, the brilliance of the nanoprobes . . ." Briggs trailed off as if overwhelmed by the remembered ecstasy. "I'd only been at it a few hours when the transformation began. I knew something unusual was happening, but I had no idea at the time that the Caeliar existed, let alone what they intended to do. I thought perhaps I had activated some sort of self-immolation program within the drone. I *had to stop it* for my analysis to continue. I fired a phaser at point-blank range into his head, hoping it would slow the destruction of his nanoprobes. He died instantly. The transformation ceased. The particles I detected that had flooded his body during the transformation, his *newborn catoms*, however, did not give up the fight so easily."

"You extracted them?"

"I began to extract as many samples as I possibly could. To this day, I have no idea what airborne virus joined with the catoms I had damaged at the moment of their birth, but within hours everyone who had been anywhere near the drone, including three dozen medical staff members, began to show signs of the plague."

"Why weren't you infected?" Seven asked.

"I was working in a biohazard suit," Briggs replied. "I followed all procedures for storing potentially hazardous samples before taking them back to my lab. I was asked to head up this division a few weeks later, when it became clear that the virus had spread. No one ever connected its existence to my work, other than me, of course."

"Do you still have those samples?" Seven asked.

Briggs nodded.

Seven smiled in relief. "You chose to lead this project in order to correct your own error," she said.

Briggs shook his head. "I didn't realize for some time that it was my actions that had created the plague. That became clear about the same time I realized that there was no way to cure it. Only by unlocking the programming of catomic molecules would it be possible to neutralize the particles that had joined with the virus. Quarantine was our only option."

"If you knew this to be true, why continue?" Seven asked. "Why not simply institute the strictest quarantine procedures possible and allow the plague to die a natural death by denying it further hosts?"

"How can you of all people even ask that question?" Briggs demanded, clearly incensed. "The Borg killed sixty-three billion people in a matter of days. The Caeliar ended them in minutes. Did they ask your permission before they stripped you of your Borg components? No," he answered for her. "They simply decided that *they knew best*. Is this the action of a benevolent, peace-loving species? If individual rights are irrelevant to them because they do not exist as individuals, how can our way of life ever mean as much to them as it does to us?

"The Caeliar are now the greatest potential threat the Federation faces. They will return and when they do, we must be ready. We must unlock the secrets of catomic matter. We must master catoms and we must learn how to turn them against their creators, or like the Borg, when the Caeliar do return, we will be every bit as vulnerable to their will as the Collective was."

There were a number of flaws with this premise, but Seven did not bother to enlighten him. It was clear that there was no point in wasting her breath. Briggs was a man defined by fear. It was understandable, given the magnitude of the horrors he had witnessed. But he would never accept that adding to the horror, even with the best of intentions, was not an appropriate response.

"Did you make this argument to your superiors when you realized that curing the plague was not an immediate option?" Seven asked.

Briggs shrugged. "When I floated the possibility to the head of Starfleet Medical, I was advised that further study of catomic matter was ongoing but that *aggressive* experiments were years away from approval."

"You knew that your work would only continue as long as the plague did," Seven realized.

"It's difficult to be the lone voice in the wilderness, particularly when you know you are right," Briggs admitted. "Without Naria, I could never have continued. But *she* encouraged me. *She* understood. A handful of cells are all that is required to re-create her, and her genetic memory is astonishing. Each new iteration is born with accumulated knowledge of her predecessors. Each one is born with the same determination to assist me. I could spend the rest of my days studying Naria and her sisters and barely scratch the surface of the wonder that is the Planarian species. I've set aside that work, *my true calling*, because my oath to Starfleet demands that above all, I protect the people of the Federation, even from their own ignorance.

"One day, the Caeliar will return. With Naria's help *and yours*," he said with emphasis, "they will find our people ready to meet them as equals and to fight them, if need be. My peers might think me foolish, but history will judge me as wise."

Seven bowed her head.

"There is so much to be done," he said, smiling. "I should have told you sooner. I see that now. I apologize, Seven."

PALAIS DE LA CONCORDE

As soon as Briggs had begun to elaborate on Naria's creation, Bacco had shot Akaar a meaningful glance. He had stepped away briefly from the table to order a security detachment assembled to transport into the classified lab and take the Commander into custody.

By the time Briggs had begun to wax rhapsodic about the threat the Caeliar posed to the Federation, Bacco moved closer to Paris, saying, "You have my thanks, Commander Paris. It appears the debt of gratitude I and the Federation owe to Seven keeps growing. You'll leave this to us for now. I swear to you, we will make this right. The admiral and I are going to need a full briefing from both you and Seven, along with Doctor Sharak and Lieutenant Wildman, before this day ends."

"Of course, and thank you, Madam President," Paris replied.

Akaar joined them again at the table. "Commander Paris?"

Paris immediately shot to attention.

"At ease," Akaar ordered. Then he extended his hand and Paris shook it firmly. "Job well done, Commander. Your father," he began, then shook his head. "*You* should be very proud of yourself."

"If you'll excuse me," President Bacco interjected, "I need to go fire a few people."

"I'll join you shortly, Madam President," Akaar advised her.

STARFLEET MEDICAL, CLASSIFIED DIVISION

"Your apology is irrelevant," Seven said as the whine of transporter signals filled the room.

Six security officers armed with phaser rifles appeared to the shock and dismay of Commander Briggs.

"What is the meaning of this?" Briggs demanded.

"By order of Admiral Leonard Akaar, you are under arrest, Commander Briggs," one of the officers replied as a second moved to secure Briggs's hands behind his back with restraints.

"You?" Briggs asked of Seven.

"Me," Seven replied.

"This is a mistake," Briggs warned. "You need me. You need men and women willing to do whatever is necessary to defend the Federation."

"The Federation *you* would create is indefensible," Seven said simply. "The Federation is, above all, an idea, a belief, a moral and ethical framework you have abandoned. How have your choices differed significantly from those you ascribe to the Caeliar and judged horrific? You have seen darkness, you have witnessed atrocity, and your response was to become what you beheld."

"The plague—" Briggs began.

"You've told me all I need to know," Seven cut him off. "I no longer require your assistance to complete the task you were originally assigned."

"But . . ."

"He is yours," Seven said to the lead security officer. With a nod, he tapped his combadge and two of the men flanking Briggs were transported away with their prisoner. The others followed Seven from the office. Together they began to search for the chamber where Axum and Riley were still being held in stasis.

The hard part was over, but Briggs had been right about one thing. There was still much to be done.

23

VOYAGER

Chakotay tensed as the doors to the turbolift were forced open. When Lieutenant Decan slipped through them, his face slightly flushed, the captain relaxed. Decan had clearly climbed up the shaft leading to the bridge from several decks down.

"Don't move," Emem ordered Decan, raising a phaser at him.

"I have no intention of moving," Decan said.

"Did the admiral send you?" Chakotay asked.

"Yes."

"Silence!" Emem shouted, crossing to the Vulcan and placing the business end of his phaser at Decan's temple.

"Lower your weapon," Chakotay ordered forcefully. "We will proceed calmly as long as you refrain from injuring my people. If you'd rather turn this into a free-for-all, we can do that too."

"Do as he says," Lsia ordered Emem, who complied. Decan moved quickly to stand by Chakotay's side.

"I don't know about you, Captain," Mattings said, "but I don't take kindly to anyone who presumes to give orders in my control center. In fact, I can't understand why you haven't lifted a finger yet to end this fiasco. Hostile aliens have taken control of your ship, and you act like we're on a routine mission. That one says she wants to rouse the Source, but have any of you considered the possibility that she could harm it?"

Chakotay turned to face Mattings. Decan hadn't spoken another word, but he didn't have to. That Kathryn had sent him meant that help was on the way. His job was to keep everyone alive long enough for it to arrive.

"I think there's a great deal our Seriareen friends are missing here," he replied evenly.

"Captain?" Mattings asked, clearly disgusted that Chakotay hadn't met this situation with force sufficient to put an end to Lsia and her people by now.

Turning back to Lsia, Chakotay said, "Your goal, unless I've missed something, is to take the hax to some distant, secluded area of space and, from there, use my ship to begin forcing other species into alliances like the one you formed with the *Kinara*. The hax will take you anywhere you like at speeds that surpass even our slipstream capabilities, and you will attack or coerce other civilizations as necessary. Over time, you will begin to build a base of power from which you will expand your influence over all sentient species you encounter in this quadrant."

"Yes," Lsia said.

"Lsia," Emem said, his tone of warning clear.

"But the Obihhax has already achieved this goal more simply and elegantly than your proposed course of action ever will," Chakotay said.

Lsia turned to face him, clearly puzzled.

Chakotay continued quickly, "You want power to direct the actions of others. You want them to acknowledge your will and your choices for them as superior to their own sense of self-determination. You will impose your own sense of order, your own code of conduct upon them and, in return, demand obedience, respect, and faith in your abilities to lead them through the challenges all sentient beings face as they move through their lives."

"We are the superior life-forms, Captain Chakotay," Lsia said.

"Then prove it by following the path the Obihhax has already prepared for you," Chakotay suggested.

"The Obihhax has reverted to a dormant state in anticipation of our return," Lsia insisted. "Once he understands that he is no longer alone, he will aid us in our efforts to expand the reach of our power."

"I don't know about that," Chakotay mused. "He's already achieved what you say you desire. I'm not sure why he would give that up now."

Mattings snorted. Chakotay met his eyes briefly and received a faint nod of respect from the general.

"Your Obihhax has become the central focus of reverence of a Confederacy of planets larger than any I have yet encountered in the Delta Quadrant. Species that never heard of the Source before joining the Confederacy have set aside their old forms of religious observation in deference to the faith of the Leodts and Djinari in the omnipotent being that led them through the darkness and brought them to a world where they could build a new way of life, far more peaceful and prosperous than the one they left behind.

"Their methods were brutal," Chakotay said with a nod to Mattings, who clearly did not take offense. "I doubt even Mister Emem would be disappointed in their willingness to use whatever means necessary to create the order they believed their Source demanded of them. In its name, they have destroyed planets, billions of life-forms, and artificially created and enslaved countless wave forms. They have relegated their females to second-class citizenship until they have proven their worth through procreation, and stripped of their rights any who failed to live up to their ideal work ethic or maintain material success.

"I have no idea how many Confederacy citizens have ever had a direct sense of the Source or can claim to have experienced first-hand any connection to it. My operations officer attended a Confederacy religious service and told me that, for most, their faith is hollow, a habit they persist in despite their inability to confirm by any means the reality—let alone the power or intentions—of the Source. They sense nothing when they lift their voices in prayer.

"But still, *they believe.* The Source has captured their spirits and imagination. Its purpose fills their souls. The general here is the first Confederacy citizen to ever lay eyes on the hax. He has learned its history from you, and even he still believes it is his god made manifest.

"And somehow, the Obihhax achieved all this, without firing a single shot. Clearly it has discovered something you have not. Think about that, before you presume to know the mind or will of this *living god* of yours."

Lsia shifted her gaze to Emem. A strange look had come over the face of the man Chakotay could still only think of as "Kashyk."

"Our course is set," Emem said defiantly.

"If the will of the Obihhax proves to be other than we believe," Lsia noted, "we will know soon enough."

These words had barely left her lips when she vanished from her seat at the conn.

One minute, Lsia had been seated at *Voyager's* flight controls. The next, she found herself standing in a black room crisscrossed by an orange grid. Admiral Janeway stood before her. Just behind her, Lieutenant Barclay was operating a control panel.

Focusing her will, Lsia tried to return to the bridge.

Nothing happened.

"Oh, Lsia," Janeway said, shaking her head almost compassionately.

She tried to speak, but no voice escaped her lips.

She searched her memories for a more intimidating species and tried to alter her form.

Her current form held.

The admiral observed her dispassionately.

"Despite everything you apparently believed to be true, I wanted to help you. I *would have* helped you," Janeway said. "Instead you forced my hand and left me no choice."

Lsia struggled to form a response and was suddenly conscious of how unseemly her efforts must appear.

"Don't bother," Janeway suggested. "Control of your program has been transferred to *Voyager*'s holographic system. We've disabled your vocal subroutines. Nothing you can say now will make a difference."

A bright gold field snapped into existence around her. It formed a column only a few feet wider than the reach of her arms, had she been able to extend them. At her feet, a new canister, similar to the ones Emem had destroyed, sat open, ready to receive her. She tried to hide the terror in her eyes as she lifted them again to meet Janeway's.

"The anti-psionic field is stable," Lieutenant Barclay confirmed.

"I know you have questions," Janeway said quickly. "I'm sorry there isn't time to answer them. You're going to return to containment now, and I sincerely hope you use the next several thousand years better than you did the last."

Lsia tried to lift her arms to touch the blazing field.

They betrayed her, remaining motionless at her sides.

Janeway turned to Barclay. "Lieutenant?"

"Computer," Barclay said without stammer or hesitation. "End program."

Lsia felt the pull of the darkness. She no longer had eyes to see or a form to sense her surroundings. The only safety she could find was cold and lonely.

She remembered the sensation. She cried out soundlessly at the injustice of it.

It turned out that form was not insignificant at all.

Its absence became the sum total of her reality.

Again.

*   *   *   *   *

"Stop that," Counselor Cambridge ordered.

The Doctor ceased pacing momentarily.

"It's not as if the motion releases any neurochemicals that will ease tension. Can you even *feel* tension?" Cambridge asked.

"Reg has been gone too long," the Doctor said.

"I know that."

"You should go after him," the Doctor suggested.

"Bloody hell," Cambridge said. "I'm not leaving you alone right now."

"Why not?"

"Because I was ordered to see to your well-being while you attempt to save our compromised crewman," Cambridge replied.

"Coward."

"Sometimes," Cambridge agreed.

They paused at the sound of hands attempting to force open the door to sickbay. They had sealed it behind Barclay when he departed.

"Reg?" the Doctor called out, moving closer to the door.

"Lazio," a female voice shouted through the door. "We have Lieutenant Conlon. She needs medical attention."

The Doctor and Cambridge rushed to assist her in manually forcing the doors open from the inside.

A pair of security officers carried Conlon's limp form into sickbay. Three others, clearly exhausted by the exertion of carrying her up eleven decks, sat in the hall outside attempting to calm their ragged breathing.

"Over here," the Doctor said, directing them to deposit Conlon on the main biobed at the rear of sickbay.

"What is our status?" Cambridge asked of Lazio.

"The Seriareen have taken control of the ship. We're locked out of all systems. Admiral Janeway and Commander Torres are working on it. Lieutenant Decan identified Conlon as Xolani and then neutralized him."

The Doctor was studying Conlon's still form for signs of injury.

"Vulcan nerve pinch," Lazio added. "I really have to learn that one of these days."

"Your team should remain here," Cambridge ordered.

"Aye, sir," Lazio replied, joining the others in the hall.

Cambridge then moved to stand opposite the Doctor over Conlon's body.

"Will she wake up any time soon?"

The Doctor retrieved a hypospray and placed it against her neck. It hissed as it released its contents.

"No," the Doctor replied. "But I can't do anything else for her until sickbay is once again operative."

Commander Torres monitored the holodeck controls, her hands poised over her console. Her heart skipped a few beats when Barclay successfully transferred Lsia to the holodeck. It paused altogether when he ordered her program shut down and resumed its rhythm when the computer indicated that the program was no longer running.

One down.

Turning her attention back to her panel, Torres watched for any sign that Lsia's absence would trigger modifications to the control sequence that was currently running.

Seconds passed.

Nothing changed. Lsia's last commands to navigation were locked in, and no further orders would be accepted that were not entered by a Seriareen.

"Damn, damn, damn," Torres said.

Quinn and his team had returned with her program. The isolinear chip was at her fingertips, and the interface port on her console was already open and ready to receive it.

"Time to intercept the Source?" Torres asked.

"Seven minutes, fifteen seconds," Neol replied, still monitoring the bridge's feed.

"Damn it," Torres said again.

The only thing that might make this situation worse was corrupting the ship's central files. They weren't under her control, but they were functioning properly. If *Voyager* lost shields, propulsion, or any of a dozen other critical systems right now because of her access key, they would not survive.

Of course, without Lsia present to make any last-minute adjustments to their course or speed, they might not survive anyway. It did not appear as if any of her companions had taken control of the conn in her absence.

Torres thought back over her program's parameters. It had been designed with this exact eventuality in mind, minus the massive alien life-form the ship was approaching and the toxic radiation it was generating.

It should work.

In the past, she would not have hesitated. But in the last few months, hesitation had become her default position. She trusted nothing: not her body, her mind, or her instincts. Plans carefully made and well-executed had left her alone and frightened. As losses and failures piled up around her, the confidence with which she had once carried herself had become another casualty. The visceral need to protect her daughter and her unborn son was primal but it only heightened the fear that stayed her hand over the isolinear chip.

Suddenly, Tom's voice drifted into her mind. *"You take it for granted, B'Elanna, how good you are."*

Did she?

"It's going to be okay."

Was it?

"I wouldn't want to be aligned with the forces of darkness and destruction, because their track record against us stinks."

Torres smiled.

She might not believe in herself, but nothing the universe had yet devised could shake Tom's faith in her. That had been true in darker moments than this.

"Six minutes, thirty-seconds," Neol advised.

If Tom were here now, there was no doubt whatsoever in her mind what choice he would have her make.

Torres inserted the chip into the interface.

• • • • •

"What have you done with Lsia?" Emem barked as soon as she dematerialized. He punctuated the gesture by again raising his phaser. This time it was pointed at Chakotay.

The captain sensed the immediate change on the bridge. All of his officers were probably feeling the same surge of adrenaline at Lsia's unexpected departure. You didn't have to be an empath to feel the tables turning.

"Ensign Gwyn," Chakotay said, ignoring the phaser momentarily. Turning his head slightly, he noted with satisfaction that she had already slid back into her chair and was attempting to resume her duties as flight controller.

"She locked in our current course. I still can't override it," Gwyn reported.

"Keep trying," Chakotay ordered.

"Captain!" Emem shouted.

Chakotay noted that Tirrit and Adaeze had also stepped away from their stations and were aiming their phasers at him.

"In answer to your question, Mister Emem," Chakotay replied, "I have no idea what happened to Lsia. You ordered Lieutenant Decan not to speak the moment he arrived."

Emem's face was clenched with rage, and the hand holding his phaser had begun to tremble. Chakotay remembered the real Kashyk taking disappointment much better.

Emem's aim shifted to Decan. "I am afraid I cannot satisfy your curiosity either," Decan said with typical Vulcan reserve. "Anything I would report at this time would be pure conjecture."

Throughout this brief exchange, Chakotay had noted Kim moving incrementally closer to Emem to gain a better tactical position, but slowly enough not to attract his attention. Waters and Patel were assuming similar positions behind Tirrit and Adaeze. Mattings stood with his arms crossed, his eyes shifting between the three armed aliens.

"If I had to guess," Chakotay said, "I would assume that Admiral Janeway, Commander Torres, and Lieutenant Conlon have had more success than Lsia anticipated in countering her efforts."

"Lieutenant Conlon was compromised by the other Seriareen, sir," Decan advised.

"What?" Lieutenant Kim shouted from behind Emem.

Emem turned immediately at both the sound and the fury of Kim's voice.

Kim did not stop to think. He simply coldcocked Emem and sent him over the tactical station and rolling to the deck in front of the command chairs.

With dexterity Chakotay would not have guessed the general possessed, Mattings moved briskly to aid Kim, retrieving the phaser Emem had dropped as he fell and issuing a swift kick to his midsection to keep him down. Kim moved swiftly to leap atop Emem and began pounding him furiously with his fists.

"Lieutenant Kim, stand down!" Chakotay ordered.

The sound of phaser fire erupted behind him.

Turning, Chakotay saw that both Tirrit and Adaeze had hit the deck with massive phaser wounds to their chests.

Relieved and confused, Chakotay moved behind Kim and lifted him off Emem. "I told you to stand down, Lieutenant," he shouted, more to reach Kim than to chastise him.

Emem had curled into a blood- and sweat-slicked ball on the deck, but was still breathing.

"What happened to them?" Chakotay asked of the room at large.

Patel was the first to report. "They fired upon each other." She was already kneeling over Adaeze, checking him for a pulse. "He's dead, sir."

"So is this one," Waters advised from ops.

"Harry?" Chakotay said softly to Kim.

He turned to lift his face to his captain. The devastation he was struggling to contain was winning the war. He had apparently skipped from shock at Decan's report straight into anger and despair.

"She . . ." Kim struggled to say, then returned his ravaged gaze to Emem, who had the good sense to stay down.

"I know," Chakotay said softly. "But this isn't going to help. The Doctor will—"

With another guttural growl of rage, Kim kicked Emem again.

"Lieutenant Kim, you are relieved," Chakotay said.

At this, Kim deflated and stumbled into his chair beside Chakotay's, burying his face in his hands.

"Decan?" Chakotay asked next. He was not surprised to see the Vulcan standing calmly beside him, his eyes closed. Clearly he had already anticipated Chakotay's primary concern.

Decan's eyes flew open. "They are gone."

"You're sure?" Chakotay asked in disbelief. His luck had never been that good.

"I sensed both of them leave their hosts and depart the ship."

"Where did they go?"

"Captain," Gwyn said suddenly.

Chakotay looked back to the main viewscreen. The motion of the hax had begun to slow perceptibly. Its massive jaws began to widen and its tail slipped free. It still retained a circular shape, but the circle was now broken.

"Please," Emem coughed.

Chakotay looked down to see him struggling to lift his head. His face was lit with an emotion the captain had never seen from either Emem or Kashyk: reverence.

Emem looked to Chakotay, pleading. "Release me."

"You know I can't do that," Chakotay said.

Emem shuddered as another deep, wet cough sent blood and phlegm flying from his lips.

"Perhaps . . . Mister Kim . . . would like to finish . . . what he started?" Emem suggested. "Xolani chose well . . ."

Chakotay felt Kim tense beside him. As he moved to place a restraining hand on Kim's shoulder, General Mattings lifted the phaser he had retrieved during the fight, aimed it directly at Emem, and fired.

The weapon did not disintegrate Emem, but left a huge black hole in his midsection.

And a smile on his face.

Chakotay moved immediately to stand in front of Mattings and placed a firm hand on the arm that held the phaser. The general released it to him without a struggle. "You understand that if my transporters were working right now, you'd already be in our brig," Chakotay said softly.

"I couldn't stomach another word from that bastard. Someone had to do right by your Mister Kim. I'm surprised at you, Chakotay."

"And nothing you do surprises me anymore," Chakotay replied, shaking his head in disgust.

Mattings lifted his chin, then crossed to Kim's side and bent low to speak softly to him.

A number of warring impulses rose within Chakotay but he quickly prioritized them. "Decan?"

"Emem followed the others, sir. He is gone as well."

The ship, which had maintained a fairly steady course up until now, began to rumble and buck. Chakotay looked back to the main viewscreen. The hax was reorienting itself, its tail unfurling behind it.

"Gwyn, what's our time to intercept?"

"Less than four minutes."

"And our heading?"

"When the hax was unbroken, we were headed directly for the center of its circumference. Our course has shifted a little with the hax's motion."

"Torres to Chakotay."

"Please have good news for me, B'Elanna," Chakotay said.

"Lsia's overrides have been deleted. You should have control of all systems now."

"Captain Chakotay to all hands. Red alert," Chakotay ordered. He had never been so relieved to hear the alarm klaxons begin to wail.

"Conn responding," Gwyn reported.

"Reverse course, Ensign," Chakotay ordered.

Just as the words left his lips, Admiral Janeway stepped onto the bridge. At the same time, the mouth of the hax began to snap open and closed in a fierce biting motion. A high-pitched screech pierced Chakotay's mind. The sensation was similar to the telepathic contact of the protectors. As the bone-chilling sound grew louder, the hax's head turned toward *Voyager*.

The moment Captain Chakotay's voice sounded over the comm, the Doctor moved into action. He had already attached a neural monitor to Conlon's forehead. Finally its data began streaming over the console in front of him. He had also prepped hypos of netinaline, lectrazine, and acetylcholine to revive the lieutenant when the time came.

Nurse Bens had been on duty when the Doctor first called Cambridge to sickbay and stood ready now to assist the Doctor. He ordered Bens to activate a surgical arch over Conlon and bring a level-ten force field and an anti-psionic field online around the biobed.

"Hang on," Cambridge said, stepping close to the field as it sprang into existence. "What exactly is your plan, Doctor?"

"I'm going to stop her heart," the Doctor said calmly. "Shortly thereafter, this monitor will confirm the absence of all neurological activity, at which point we will assume that Xolani has left her body. Then—"

"Where is Xolani supposed to go?" Cambridge demanded. "We need one of those containment canisters Glenn sent over, don't we?"

"Do you happen to have an extra one in your pocket?" the Doctor asked.

"No, but we should take a few minutes, now that we are able, and find one."

The Doctor tapped his combadge, saying, "Sickbay to Lieutenant Barclay, please respond."

"Go ahead, Doctor."

"Do we have any of the containment canisters for the Seriareen at hand?"

"Four were destroyed. We just used the spare one Commander Glenn sent over to capture Lsia."

"Thank you, Reg. Sickbay out."

"Keep the lieutenant sedated," Cambridge suggested. "We can be back in range of the *Galen* in a day, maybe less."

"She doesn't have a day. It may be too late already," the Doctor insisted.

"But Xolani," Cambridge argued.

"You let me worry about that," the Doctor said.

"I can't," Cambridge retorted. "I understand the urgency of the lieutenant's condition, but I hardly think exposing your program to possible alien possession is your best choice here."

The Doctor continued to work as if he had not heard.

"Doctor, don't force me to relieve you of duty," Cambridge shouted.

"Feel free," the Doctor said. "But know this: We've already lost one crew member to the Seriareen. I refuse to lose another."

"Doctor, I . . ." Cambridge began, but stopped midthought. "*Merde alors*, you want this fight, don't you?"

"You did say you had no philosophical objection to revenge, Counselor," the Doctor noted. His preparations complete, the Doctor verified his readings one last time and activated an electromagnetic pulse strong enough to shut down Nancy Conlon's heart. He waited patiently for it to work, approximately ten seconds, and muted the faint alarms that sounded as his patient began to crash.

"Doctor, you have no idea if you will even be capable of acting once Xolani attacks your program," Cambridge said.

"He already tried once and failed. There was a reason for that."

"What was it?"

"I don't remember," the Doctor replied with feigned cheer. "Let's find out together."

The Doctor's eyes were glued to his patient's neural readings. It seemed to take several lifetimes for all traces of brain activity to cease. In fact, it was only two minutes.

The assault that followed was immediate.

It was also familiar. The Doctor hadn't been prepared for the first invasion. The immediate sense of a new set of operating instructions attempting to overwrite his program felt oddly commonplace the second time around.

Rather than allow Xolani's consciousness access to his primary matrix, the Doctor immediately restricted all of the new data to a short-term memory buffer he had cleared for this express purpose prior to killing Nancy Conlon. Once the data had been gathered there, it immediately began to search for new pathways through which to inject itself into the Doctor's main files.

The Doctor simultaneously activated his self-diagnostic subroutine, which instantly recognized the data within the buffer as foreign. The data was quarantined, temporarily unable to affect any of his primary systems, and the Doctor received an internal request from the diagnostic.

Allow interface?

As all of this was occurring at the speed of his holographic processors, fractions of fractions of seconds, the Doctor agreed.

"Hello Xolani."

"Emergency Medical Hologram Mark One?"

"Yes. You may call me Doctor."

"This form is not sufficient."

"I know. Tragic, really, as it's the only one you can possibly access now."

"Release me!"

"Hmmm . . . no."

"Please, Doctor."

"I'm not refusing because you failed to ask nicely the first time. I'm refusing because you and your kind are a pestilence, undeserving of compassion or mercy."

"I could assist you. You intend to restore my host's former neurosynaptic pathways. I can provide you with a complete map of them as I found them when I entered her body."

Against his better judgment the Doctor was intrigued. The "map" Xolani referenced was, indeed, critical data, and information that was not present in any officer's baseline medical files.

The best scans Federation medicine could provide of the referenced pathways were only taken in the event of neurological damage, which Conlon had never suffered until now.

"You'd do that?"

"Despite what you may believe, Doctor, we are not monsters. We are enlightened life-forms. There is so much you could learn from us."

"For the small price of ceasing to exist."

"The choice is simple. Your life, for hers."

"But you already said my form was insufficient."

"In time, and with several modifications, I could make it sufficient."

"Am I blushing? You really know how to compliment a fellow."

"This form's data transmission and transfer routines mimic the brain but is significantly less complex. It is, however, capable of creating new pathways as new stimuli are introduced and incorporated into existing data. It does so automatically. Much of the data is inessential to your program's designated functions. Purge that data and allow me to insert myself into its current paths. From there, I will be able to direct your program's actions."

"The data you refer to are the personal experiences I have accumulated over the last eleven years of my existence. They permit me to better understand and interact with my fellow life-forms. They make me who I am."

"Large blocks of data once routed from these pathways into your long-term memory have been permanently segregated. Clearly not all of your personal experiences are essential to your definition of self."

"Can you access that data?"

"Yes."

"Can you give me access to it?"

"I could transfer all of your existing memories into a single file, including those you can no longer access. You would essentially continue to exist there, while I assumed control of all other operations."

The Doctor paused again. It was a tempting offer. To be whole again. To spend the rest of his program's existence as the man he once knew himself to be. Could that possibly be enough?

Probably not.

Imperfect as he now felt himself to be, suicide, even if heaven was guaranteed in the bargain, was still suicide.

That did not, however, make it an entirely unworkable suggestion.

"No."

"Please, reconsider."

"No. You had your chance to demonstrate how enlightened you and your people were. You claim superiority but your actions are those of common thieves. I am not perfect. I never was. I am a work in progress. You, on the other hand, are about to be nothing more than a bad memory."

The Doctor terminated the interface and accessed the autonomous protocol Admiral Janeway, in her infinite wisdom, had thought to grant him. He had assumed, until now, that any choice to utilize this new function would be agonizing. As it turned out, only one realization gave him pause.

Transferring Xolani from the quarantined buffer where he currently resided into his segregated buffer would not be sufficient to eliminate him. He must be deleted. The Doctor briefly reviewed the commands now available to him and understood in a tragic moment of irony that Reg had not thought to allow the Doctor to only delete certain memories that were currently segregated. The entire file would be lost when he destroyed the Seriareen and with it even the muted memories of Seven he had managed to retain.

Reg might be able to fix this oversight. But that would give Xolani time to fight back. The longer he existed inside the Doctor's program, the more likely it was that he would find a way around or through his security protocols.

More important, Nancy Conlon was already dead and only the Doctor could bring her back.

Without further hesitation or remorse, the Doctor transferred Xolani into the segregated buffer Lewis Zimmerman had designed and Reg Barclay had modified. He then deleted the entire segregated file and was immediately granted an overwhelming rush of solace through the "dopamine effect" Zimmerman had included in the subroutine.

It had taken the Doctor less than one second to secure his matrix and sacrifice forever a small piece of his soul. Once done, he ordered Nurse Bens to lower the force fields and enter the surgical area. He then set about reviving Nancy Conlon.

Admiral Kathryn Janeway stepped down into the command well and moved to Chakotay's side. She immediately noted the body of Kashyk lying on the deck, his face mangled and bloody, his torso charred. Before she could ask, a familiar shrill whine sounded and his body vanished in the cascading brilliance of transporter beams. Seconds later, the bodies of Tirrit and Adaeze were taken.

"Dead?" she asked of Chakotay.

"Tirrit and Adaeze turned their weapons on each other. General Mattings executed Emem," he replied.

Janeway immediately looked to the general, her eyes blazing.

"In my defense, Admiral, he was asking for it," Mattings noted.

Janeway's jaw clenched. She felt Chakotay's hand come to rest on her arm. The look in his eyes clearly communicated that he shared her disgust at the general's actions, but the situation was more complicated than they had time to discuss at the moment. "He literally was," Chakotay said softly. "Decan says they've all left the ship."

"To go where?"

"We don't know. Ensign Gwyn, I thought we were trying to move away from the hax," Chakotay said as the creature grew larger on the viewscreen, now clearly approaching the ship's position.

"That's a hax?" Janeway asked.

"Technically, the Obihhax," Chakotay corrected her. "It's a subspace-born life-form the Seriareen used to carve their corridors. This one was combined with an ancient Seriareen essence named Obih several thousand years ago."

"This is why Lsia brought us here," Janeway realized.

"She intended to rouse it, which she did, and then tame it in some way. She would have had us guide it away from here," Chakotay advised.

"How?"

"We didn't get that far."

The view of the creature from the bridge was more alarming than it had been in engineering. Its massive head came to a diamond-shaped point. At its widest, the head was ringed by spherical gray protrusions. They might be eyes and would give the creature three-hundred-and-sixty-degree sightlines. Behind the protrusions, several sheaths of long, spiked tendrils flowed outward in all directions, a headdress of sorts. From there, its body extended for kilometers, its girth the size of several *Vesta*-class starships.

Its motion suddenly became incoherent. Ceasing its forward motion, it thrashed about as if attempting to elude capture. But its head and most of those eyes remained focused on *Voyager*.

Its cries still reverberated through Chakotay's mind. Several other bridge officers also appeared to "hear" it, including Gwyn. The helmsman was clearly doing her best to comply with Chakotay's orders, but *Voyager*'s motion was as sluggish as the creature's. The only two people on the bridge seemingly unaffected by the psionic communication of the hax were Admiral Janeway and General Mattings. Chakotay wondered if this had anything to do with the fact that neither of them had experienced direct telepathic contact with the protectors.

"Every time it moves, the creature is throwing off new energy waves," Gwyn reported. "It creates new subspace instabilities with every shift."

"Can you navigate around them?" Chakotay asked.

"Not quickly," Gwyn replied.

"Best effort," Chakotay ordered.

"Aye, sir."

"This is nothing compared to the size of the new instabilities it would create should it decide to start making new subspace tunnels," Janeway noted.

"Do you think it would agree not to if we asked it nicely?" Chakotay asked semiseriously.

Suddenly, the Obihhax surged decisively toward *Voyager*. If its intention was to appear menacing, it succeeded.

"Back off," Gwyn said, clearly shocked. "And pipe down," she added, briefly massaging her temple.

Captain Chakotay watched as the creature's head lifted, and it cried out again.

"Captain," Waters called from ops. "Three new energy readings have been detected. They're emerging from the hax."

Chakotay inhaled sharply. Three of the spiked tentacles near the hax's head had begun to elongate. Once they had reached a length of a thousand meters, they separated from the main body.

"Are those . . . ?" Chakotay began.

"Offspring," Janeway suggested. "I guess we know where the Seriareen went."

The three new, smaller versions of the creature began flitting about the head. Whether they were communicating with it or simply trying to get its attention was hard to discern.

"Lieutenant Aubrey, I assume our weapons are once again online and functional?"

"Aye, sir," Aubrey replied.

The Obihhax again brought its head down and looked ready to cross the few thousand kilometers that separated them and take a bite out of the ship.

"Fire a warning shot," Chakotay ordered. "Don't hit it, but let it know we can defend ourselves if it forces us to do so."

"Captain, no," Mattings said quickly, but too late to stay Aubrey's hand.

A short series of phaser bursts flew forth, and for a moment, it looked like an explosion had detonated all around the hax. *Voyager* shuddered under the impact of its own phasers.

"Report!" Chakotay demanded.

"The shots were refracted by the various instabilities," Aubrey said. "I don't think we should do that again," he added.

"That's a problem throughout the wastes," Mattings noted.

334 • KIRSTEN BEYER

"You picked a hell of a time to share that information," Chakotay said, clearly furious.

"We came out here as friends. I wasn't anticipating a fire-fight," Mattings said.

The shots did have the effect of disorienting the Obihhax. It arched its body downward, and the head momentarily disappeared from the viewscreen. Waters automatically adjusted the magnification on the display, and the hax could be seen writhing strenuously.

"We can't let the hax leave this area," Chakotay noted.

"But how can we force it to stay?" Janeway asked. "Or better yet . . ."

"Eliminate all of them," Chakotay agreed.

Harry Kim's head shot up. "Friends," he said softly.

"Harry?" Chakotay asked.

Kim rose, staring at the viewscreen.

"We have friends here," Kim said.

"Who?"

"The protectors."

"These wave forms were created by the hax," Chakotay reminded him. "They have no idea who we are."

"The ruptures allow any wave form existing anywhere in subspace to access this area," Kim said. "We don't need to worry about the ones that are already here. We need to call the ancient ones."

"They'll hear us?"

Kim nodded.

"Harry, are you sure you can do this right now?"

Kim's eyes locked with his captain's. "I apologize for my outburst, sir."

Janeway had no idea what "outburst" Kim was referring to, but figured the explanation would figure prominently in Chakotay's report, should they all live that long.

Chakotay studied Kim. "Apology accepted. Do it."

Kim moved quickly to the ops station, and Waters stepped aside to allow him access. As he began to work, Janeway said, "We might be able to create a firing solution using photon torpedoes targeted to avoid any of the subspace instabilities."

"Aubrey," Chakotay ordered, "see if it's possible."

"Aye, sir."

"Any detonation large enough to destroy the Source would take us with it," Mattings advised.

"If the choice is sacrificing ourselves to keep this creature from carving its way through inhabited systems, I can accept that," Janeway replied coldly.

"The Source would never hurt us, Admiral," Mattings argued.

"You can't know that."

"Yes, I can."

Finally, several familiar shapes emerged from a nearby instability and moved toward *Voyager*. The ancient protectors had arrived.

"Good work, Harry. What are you telling them?" Chakotay asked.

"I'm trying to make them understand the danger the hax poses to us. I'm asking them to contain it."

"You mean destroy it?" Mattings asked.

"If that's the only way," Kim replied.

"No, son," Mattings said, stepping toward the ops station and looking up at Kim. "You can't."

"General," Chakotay said, "do not give orders to my crew."

"It's not an order, Captain. It's a request. The Source is ours. You have no right to destroy it."

"It's a fascinating life-form, but it's also an immediate threat to this ship and the galaxy," Chakotay said.

The protectors Kim had summoned began to merge and expand in size. As they did so, they began to move toward the hax, clearly ready to act against it.

"There has to be another way," Mattings exclaimed. "With all you people have learned in your travels, you expect me to believe that the best you can do is just kill it?"

"No, no, no," Kim said suddenly.

The forward motion of the protectors had ceased, and they were beginning to separate.

"What's the problem, Lieutenant?" Chakotay demanded.

Before Kim could answer, the hax let out another shriek and moved toward the ancient protectors, weaving in and out through them.

Kim was clearly struggling to interpret the data he was receiving. "They won't harm the hax," Kim finally replied.

"Make them understand what will happen to us if they don't," Chakotay ordered.

Kim transmitted another message. This time, in response, one of the ancient ones broke off from the group and began to move swiftly back toward *Voyager*.

"Aubrey, prepare countermeasures," Chakotay ordered. "Disperse it."

"Wait," Kim said. "It's transmitting a response."

"Well?"

"They believe we have been corrupted by our exposure to their creators," Kim reported, aghast. "Otherwise, we would never ask this of them."

"The Confederacy did what they did for material gain," Chakotay said. "We're trying to survive."

"I'm afraid they don't see the distinction, Captain," Kim said.

"Can they at least protect us from the creature?" Janeway asked.

"I'll ask," Kim replied.

Moments later, the nearest protector again altered course and rejoined the others. Gwyn was slowly but surely putting more distance between the ship and the hax, but not enough to make anyone on the bridge feel safe.

"I guess we'll take that as a 'no,' " Chakotay said.

"They didn't say 'no,' Captain," Kim reported. "They said we did not require their protection."

Suddenly, the three smaller creatures that had been moving erratically near the head of the Obihhax broke off and began to move decisively toward *Voyager*.

"I think they were wrong," Janeway noted.

"Aubrey, do you have a firing solution for our torpedoes?" Chakotay asked.

"Can I ask them something?" General Mattings requested. "Can I ask the Source something *through the ancient ones?*"

Chakotay turned to Janeway. "At this point, can it hurt?" she said.

"Go ahead, General," Chakotay replied.

Mattings was momentarily overcome with embarrassment. "I'm sorry. I'm not used to praying, let alone in public."

"Whatever you plan to say, General, make it quick," Janeway insisted.

Stepping closer to Kim and leaning over his console to speak softly, Mattings began, "I know what you are. I know what you've done for my people. I know that your plans for us are greater than any one moment in time can contain. Not for myself, but for those who have come to know and trust in you, I ask your mercy. I ask you to continue to guide us, to watch over us, and, as you see fit, to reveal yourself to us. Please, do not abandon us. We are a better people, thanks to you."

Silence fell heavy over the bridge. Given the fact that the protectors did not speak in words, but in images, Janeway wondered how Kim had translated the general's message.

As the hax began to move, she stopped wondering.

Its writhing stilled. Turning its head again toward the ship, it lurched forward, covering more space in a single motion than it had until now. As it surged, its mouth opened wider.

"Source, no," Mattings said softly.

"Gwyn, evasive maneuvers," Chakotay ordered.

The Obihhax continued forward until it reached the three small hax it had just released. Their forward momentum ebbed, and they were suddenly sucked back toward the open mouth of the Obihhax. With a violent screech, the Obihhax brought its mouth closed around them, swallowing them whole in one bite.

It then lifted its head gracefully and reversed its direction, heading toward roughly the same point it had occupied when it had first been discovered.

The ancient protectors Kim had called had begun to expand

again, this time joining with many of the other wave forms native to the area.

Finally, the hax's motion took a new shape.

Or rather, an old one.

Its body turned back on itself, the head moving with heretofore unseen speed. It took hold of its own tail, sucking it into its mouth, and once again began to spin in a perfect circle.

Mattings lifted his head. Tears streamed down his face.

"It seems your prayer was answered," Janeway said.

"Or maybe he didn't like the other Seriareen," Mattings offered.

"Now that you know what it is, an ancient alien consciousness combined with an unusual life-form, are you still content to follow it?" Janeway asked.

"Thanks to your willingness to prevent the Seriareen from taking it from us, my people will have all the time we need to make that choice."

"You have our gratitude as well, General," Janeway said.

Mattings shook his head. "The Source chose to spare us. Our philosophers and clerics will argue for years to come about why and what it meant."

"Or you could just ask it," Kim suggested. "I don't think the ancient protectors are going anywhere."

Mattings lowered his head. "I wouldn't presume."

24

STARFLEET MEDICAL, CLASSIFIED DIVISION

As Seven moved through the halls Commander Briggs had sullied, she tried not to meet the curious eyes of the officers who were now in the process of being rounded up by the security team Admiral Akaar had dispatched. All of them would surely argue, when the time came, that they had no knowledge of the Commander's activities or true intentions. In most cases, it would likely be the truth.

Seven could not pity them. History was filled with examples of charismatic leaders who led multitudes down the wrong path by the force of their will and repeated reminders of the justness of their cause. Starfleet officers were trained to follow orders and to trust the judgment of their superiors. But they were not required to check their consciences at the door when they left their quarters. The worst of the offenses Briggs had perpetrated here were his unethical experiments, and those he had performed secretly, with the help of his Planarians. But it shouldn't have taken Seven or Sharak or Commander Paris to uncover the truth. Anyone could have asked the questions they did and followed them to their logical conclusion.

That these people hadn't was troubling. Was it human nature to follow where the strongest personalities led? Were *Voyager*'s officers unique, given that their duty had required them to blaze trails rather than walk well-worn paths?

Seven did not know. But it was a question she intended to put to Admiral Akaar, and she fervently hoped he would invest the necessary time and resources required to find the answer.

As soon as she reached the stasis chambers, Seven set these thoughts aside and focused her efforts on reviving Riley and Axum. Riley came to first and embraced Seven warmly as soon as she was roused.

It took Axum a long time to open his eyes. Seven had refrained from reaching out to him through their catoms. She knew part of him would resist leaving the safety and power of his gestalt behind. But she also knew that what they had shared while unconscious could easily be re-created when he woke.

She was counting on it.

Waiting beside his chamber, Seven studied his face. The violence of Axum's past was carved in deep ruts that ran across it. Fine white hair grew in spurts from his scalp, but did not conceal the scar tissue where his left ear should have been. Seven noted that his left hand was missing every finger but the thumb. Still, these surface traumas were nothing compared to those that had mangled his mind and spirit.

When his eyes finally opened, Seven forced a smile. The moment their eyes met, tears began to glisten in Axum's, and he turned away, clearly self-conscious.

Seven lifted her right hand to touch his face. He flinched, pulling away, then turned back to look at her, ashamed.

"Resistance is futile," she teased softly.

He rose up on his elbows and brought his legs down over the lowered side of the stasis chamber. He dared not risk standing so soon, but at least this way, they could meet each other on a more or less equal plane.

Finally, Axum lifted his hands and extended them toward her, palms up. Seven mirrored the gesture. Their fingers touched, the heels of their palms met, and their fingers intertwined.

Releasing one hand, Seven lifted hers to his left cheek, brushing her thumb over it in a gentle caress. Axum placed his over hers in response. They remained like that in silence for several moments, content to slowly take in the feeling of each other's touch.

For the first time.

TAMARIAN EMBASSY

Three days later, Axum and Riley arrived at the Tamarian Embassy. They had been transported from the lab directly to Starfleet's main hospital facility to recuperate from their time in stasis and begin to restore their muscle strength. Both responded more quickly to therapy than anticipated. Both were attended during their stay by President Bacco's personal physician.

Seven used that time to work with the rest of the former residents of Arehaz. They heard from her lips the entire story of the catomic plague; its accidental birth and the path of devastation it had left in its wake. Most had given their permission to allow Seven to link with them through their shared catoms and through that link they had come to know more about the catoms that were unique to them. They had agreed that the plague, while not their doing, was their responsibility to eliminate.

Those who resisted were reminded—not by Seven, but by their peers—of the debt they all owed *Voyager*'s crew. Three times the former Borg had been close to annihilation, and three times the crew of the intrepid vessel had come to their aid.

Finally, all chose to answer Seven's call to perform a duty for which they were uniquely qualified.

When Riley and Axum arrived, they assembled in the large embassy ballroom. The children had spent most of their days outside, running wild over the embassy grounds under the watchful eyes of Julia Paris, Ratham, and the Tamarian staff who had grown quite fond of them. As they played, all of the former Borg who had chosen not to join the Caeliar gestalt seated themselves in a large circle and willingly entered their own.

As Seven had suspected, the power of the joined state mirrored that she had shared with Axum and Riley but was expanded by several orders of magnitude.

Together, the small gestalt focused its attention on the catoms of the original samples Briggs had removed from the drone he had killed midtransformation. The errors and mutations were obvious and were immediately corrected. From there, the gestalt expanded its consciousness to the wider galaxy, searching for particles that matched the mutated viral catoms. As they were discovered, they were repaired. The virus was destroyed, and the catoms reverted to a neutral, harmless state.

Once all had been found and neutralized, they were collected, drawn forth from planets thousands of light-years distant and sample containers that had been removed and secured from Briggs's lab. Through the will of the gestalt, these catomic particles were redistributed among the existing members and absorbed. They were added to those already present and upon acceptance were seamlessly integrated into their bodies.

Despite their relative lack of experience, Riley's people adapted quickly to working again as one. They naturally looked to Riley for guidance, but did not require much. Axum and Seven focused their efforts on maintaining the stability of the gestalt as the others explored and reveled in a new kind of collective existence.

It seemed like moments, but had been more than twelve hours when the work of the gestalt was complete. Silence reigned among them briefly, then threatened to expand into eternity. All now understood both the scope and limits of their joined state, and while momentary curiosity flamed briefly here and there—along with gratitude, wonder, and an overwhelming sense of peace—the next step was painfully obvious.

Nocks was the first to separate himself from the others. The moment he began to reassert his individuality, Axum spoke.

"Wait."

"No."

"It is not necessary . . ."

But Nocks was already gone.

Jilliant followed, and with each departure, Axum poured more of himself into the gestalt, filling it with wonders untasted and realms unexplored.

Had Seven not prepared all assembled for this moment, it might have gone differently.

Each departure felt like a gaping wound being ripped open in the fabric of their communion. When politeness and temptation failed, Axum attempted to hold those that remained by force.

Seven and Riley countered Axum's will, releasing the others with gratitude until only *Axum/Seven/Riley* remained.

"Why did you let them go?" Axum cried out, agonized.

"You know why," Riley responded.

"How can one know this power and willingly refuse it?"

"It comes with a price, Axum," Seven reminded him. *"Those of us who have begun to understand the value of our individuality are as unwilling to part with it as we were when the Caeliar first asked."*

"But we are one," Axum countered. *"Our individuality is an illusion. Our catoms were designed to exist in a joined state. What*

we have accomplished here is but a fraction of what we could learn together through our new gestalt."

"You are right," Riley agreed. *"But we choose to learn in a different way now. This state, while familiar and even comforting, is also an illusion. We are not Caeliar. That is the gift they gave us, the choice we made. I am Riley Frazier."*

With that, Riley departed, leaving *Axum/Seven* alone.

"You knew," Axum accused.

"I did more than that. I taught them how to resist you before we began."

"You did not trust me to honor their wishes?"

"I did not believe you would be able to overcome your fear of solitude once our work was complete."

"You used me, *just as the Borg used us."*

"I never agreed to maintain the gestalt indefinitely. None of us did. You assumed that once the others joined, they would have no desire to depart. You were wrong."

"Only because you frightened them."

"No, Axum. You did. You cannot hide your need from us. We understand it, but we do not share it."

"They will return," Axum said. *"As individuals they are small and weak. Together, we are so much more."*

"Now who sounds like the Borg?" Seven asked.

"You will see."

"No, I will not."

"You cannot deny the truth of what we are."

"What we are is ours to decide. The greatest gift you gave me, Axum, was not the experience of conjoined power. It was the ability to control my own catoms, to determine my own destiny, and to choose for myself how best to use that which the Caeliar left me."

Seven tasted the fear born of Axum's sudden comprehension.

"This is the last time you and I will ever meet anywhere but as individuals in the real world," she assured him.

"No. Wait," he pleaded. *"How do you know that other threats, greater than this plague, are not out there? What if our gestalt is needed again?"*

Seven did not respond. Instead, she ordered her catoms to revise their programming and eliminate their ability to access other catoms directly; just as Riley, Nocks, Jilliant, and all of the former Borg had done when they departed the gestalt.

When she opened her eyes, most of the others had risen from the circle. Riley waited. Extending a hand to Seven, she helped her stand. Then both turned to see Axum gazing up at them with unconcealed anger.

He came to his feet unassisted.

"Axum," Riley began.

"Answer my question," he demanded of Seven. "Do you understand the value of the gift you have just tossed aside?"

"I do," Seven replied. "And it is possible that there are other threats out there that might best be answered through catomic interference. But I have not abdicated my right to live my life on my own terms. Not every crisis the universe faces is mine alone to solve."

"I should never have refused the Caeliar," Axum said bitterly.

"Perhaps not," Seven agreed. "But you did."

"For *you*," he insisted.

"In time, I hope you will come to see that choice as one you made for yourself, Axum," Seven said. "I have been where you are now. I know what it is to find oneself suddenly alone. I survived because I allowed others to help me remember how to live in a community but not solely *for* the community."

"We will help you, Axum," Riley interjected. "Starfleet has agreed to take us anywhere we want to go. We have not yet decided where that might be, or if all of us will make the journey. But you are welcome to come with us. We will never abandon you."

"You have gained much more than you have lost, Axum," Seven said. "One day, you will see. One day you will remember. Until then, I wish you peace."

"Annika," Axum said, reaching for her hand.

She stepped closer to him as Riley moved away to allow them a little privacy.

"I have done everything you asked of me. I showed you the true potential of your catoms. I let you go, I helped you save the children of Arehaz, together we cured the plague threatening your beloved Federation. But still, I am not worthy of your affection?"

"You lied to me. You used my feelings for you to confuse and blind me. I will not do the same to you. We both deserve better than that.

"Until you know who you are, you will never be capable of accepting my love, or anyone's." Seven continued, "You seek comfort, an escape from the pain of building a new life as an individual. Were I to agree to stay with you now, you would come to despise me. My presence would not give you the strength you need. It would only remind you daily of all you believe you have lost."

"You would make it bearable."

"It would be a lie."

"I see."

"If you need me," Seven began.

"You will be on the far side of the galaxy, in the arms of another man," Axum finished for her.

Seven recoiled, as if struck. "The anger you feel right now will pass."

"I hope not."

25

VOYAGER

Commander Liam O'Donnell had no difficulty locating *Voyager*'s briefing room, where Admiral Janeway awaited him. *Demeter* had arrived in orbit of the First World several hours before *Voyager* and *Galen* were due. He might have spent that time framing an argument in support of his command

choices in the best light possible. Instead, he spent it with Brill
and his staff, reviewing the new planting schedule and finalizing
the hybrid seed selections he had made for New Talax. Captain
Farkas had been headed in that direction, and he assumed
the rest of the fleet would regroup with *Vesta* there when they
departed the Confederacy.

As he made his way through *Voyager*'s halls, he turned his
thoughts to the immediate future. Should Admiral Janeway take
issue with his choice to take Bralt to the Ark Planet, he might be
facing serious disciplinary action. She could return him to the
Alpha Quadrant. It would pain him to be separated from his
crew, especially now, as he had begun to understand how important they were becoming to him. O'Donnell found himself preparing to fight for the position he had grudgingly accepted a
year earlier. That was unexpected, like so much of his life lately.

Admiral Janeway was seated at the head of the room's only
table when he entered. As she nodded for him to sit, her face
held none of the warm congeniality with which she had greeted
him aboard the *Vesta* at their first real meeting. Instead, appraising eyes met his. He suddenly gained a visceral appreciation for
how his specimens must feel when he placed them under his
microscope.

"Welcome back, Commander."

"Admiral."

"I have reviewed your report on *Demeter*'s tour of the Confederacy and your detour first to the Ark Planet and then back to
Vitrum. I have also received a rather lengthy letter from Overseer
Bralt thanking me profusely for allowing you to 'devote yourself
entirely to lifting the veil of ignorance under which he labored
prior to your display of the protector's capabilities.'"

O'Donnell smirked. That sounded like Bralt. "Is that . . . ?"

"A direct quote, yes," Janeway replied.

While part of O'Donnell hated the thought of owing a debt
of gratitude to Rascha Bralt, he had to admit that the officious
bureaucrat had grown slightly less repugnant over the last few
weeks. It was painful to think that his career's continuation

might be credited to a man whose existence was defined by political expediency untethered to moral principles. But then, life was pain.

"At what point in your travels did you decide that your duty to the people of the Confederacy superseded your duty to this fleet?" Janeway asked.

"I never saw the two as incompatible," O'Donnell replied. "You ordered me to review the Confederacy's agricultural capabilities with an eye toward improving them."

"Should a formal alliance be created," Janeway noted.

"In my opinion, it was impossible to determine how best to help the Confederacy without knowing how receptive Overseer Bralt would be to the myriad possible improvements I could suggest to him. He embraced the potential the protectors provide his people, but had he not done so, I would have been forced to find other means to alleviate the suffering the current policies created."

"So you were just being thorough?"

"It's one of my worst faults."

"Is there a reason that once you settled upon your preferred course of action, you did not choose to send word to the fleet before returning to the Ark Planet?"

"I never intended for our little educational sabbatical to delay our return to the fleet as long as it did. I made no secret of our intended destination or length of absence to the CIF vessel that had taken us to Vitrum. I apologize if I worried you."

"I might be willing to accept that apology if I thought it was genuine, Commander."

"Admiral, I understand that our mission is currently subject to an unusual level of scrutiny by Starfleet Command. But I'm not capable of allowing fear of reprisals or micromanaging administrators to dictate the demands of my conscience. I didn't give Bralt the command codes to our vessels or access to our classified databases, nor did I offer aid to the thousands of starving residents of Vitrum, even when their misery offended me to my core. I asked the representative I had been assigned to advise to step outside his comfort zone, and I showed him the use we had made of a tool that was already at his disposal. I am guilty of forcing a small mind to think bigger, and if that is not the definition of my duty as a Starfleet officer, then perhaps I misunderstood what I was signing up for."

"You put yourself and your ship in great danger in the process."

"I'm pretty sure risk to life and limb was somewhere in the fine print, Admiral."

Janeway shook her head. "There is nothing you would have done differently?"

"No, Admiral."

"Good."

"Admiral?"

"I can count on one hand the number of senior officers I have served with who would take that kind of initiative. You have done a great deal to effect meaningful, positive change here, and you earned the regard of the aliens with whom we were making first contact. While your methods are unconventional, they get results. You stepped right up to every line Starfleet has drawn to limit our actions but you never crossed them. I would have preferred to be advised of your intentions directly, but I'm guessing you were unwilling to risk the possibility that I would refuse you."

"The thought did cross my mind," O'Donnell admitted.

"That's because you and I don't know each other all that well," Janeway said, smiling faintly. "I could never fault you for taking the same action I would have in your place. Although I have to admit, you have just given me a great deal of insight into the challenges *my* commanding officers have faced over the years. I understand their pain. I'm also not going to allow my feelings or my needs to limit the potential of the officers I command. The fact that you are still assigned to this fleet as *Demeter*'s captain means I trust you until you give me reason to do otherwise."

"Thank you, Admiral."

"I'm on my way now to meet with Presider Cin for the last

time. She's asked that you join us so she can express her gratitude in person."

"I'm honored, Admiral, but is that really necessary?"

"I'm afraid so, Commander."

O'Donnell sighed. "Admiral, may I speak freely?"

"I'm fairly certain that ship has sailed."

"I don't think we should kid ourselves about accomplishing meaningful change here. Bralt's choices were dictated by greed and a perverted sense of individual responsibility that exists to sustain the Confederacy's power structure. I did not alter his basic beliefs. I merely pointed out an incredibly efficient means for him to dramatically increase productivity on planets that are in transition."

"And managed to feed thousands of hungry people in the process," Janeway noted.

"Does it matter that he's feeding them for the wrong reasons?"

"Not to them or to me. That's the most frustrating part of our work, Commander. Often, we only get to see the beginning of a story for the planets we encounter. Neither of us have any idea what the Confederacy will make of the insights gained from our time here. It has to be enough that we remained true to *our* values when confronted with a belief system that is radically different from our own." After a moment she added, "When we began this mission, you had already decided it would end with disappointment. Is that still your assessment?"

O'Donnell shook his head. "I don't know. There's so much more we could do here, if they could just see . . ."

"That our way is better?"

"It is."

"I agree. But *our way* is the result of thousands of years of individual beings grappling with their ignorance and clawing and scraping their way toward a more inclusive, harmonious future. We fall short of our own aspirations all the time. What matters is that we keep trying. And that we show compassion and respect for those we encounter. We've moved beyond the ideas that limit the potential of the Confederacy. They will do the same eventually. The universality of many of our beliefs among advanced civilizations we have encountered suggests to me an inevitable forward motion among all sentient life-forms, even if we don't live long enough to see it come to fruition."

"So we're out here planting seeds?"

Janeway smiled. "In a way."

O'Donnell returned her smile. "That, I can do."

THE FIRST WORLD

Presider Cin's official residence was a palatial edifice on a hill at the northern edge of the capital city. It was surrounded by park-like grounds. Rolling hills of green were interspersed with creeks that flowed down toward the heart of the business district. The tall tower where the ceremony of welcoming had been held could be seen kissing the sky in the distance.

Captain Chakotay had accompanied Admiral Janeway, Commander Glenn, and Commander O'Donnell to their final conference with the presider. As with most diplomatic events, the major points of discussion had been agreed upon by both sides prior to the meeting.

Chakotay stood silently by as Presider Cin thanked them all profusely for ridding the Confederacy of the threat of the Seriareen. Their discovery of the Obihhax was a well-guarded secret, for now, and no further exploration of the wastes was under contemplation. Continued study was warranted, but it would have to wait for a more politically favorable climate.

Cin had barely survived the vote of no confidence called by First Consul Dreeg. The presider enjoyed considerable support from the CIF, and their votes had helped her carry the day. Dreeg was licking his wounds but determined to continue to press his agendas. He had finally accepted there would be no transfer of technology from the Federation.

Praise was heaped on Commanders O'Donnell and Glenn. Chakotay was pleased to learn that Glenn had been busy while the *Galen* held position at the border of the wastes waiting for *Voyager* and the *Third Calvert's* return. She had devoted herself to studying the bureaucracy and laws that applied to the clinics that served the Confederacy's *nonszit*, or nonproductive members of society who had lost their rights as citizens. She had discovered, much to her surprise, that the central government had allocated resources for grants to other kinds of public service organizations when private donations ebbed. No medical clinic had ever applied for a grant. Most of the doctors were too busy saving lives to think about jumping through administrative hoops. Glenn had prepared a report that would assist Kwer, and others like her, in navigating the arcane bureaucracy to secure these grants. The commander had transmitted it to Kwer as soon as the fleet had regrouped in orbit of the First World. Cin was pleased to report that funds, which had gone unclaimed for years, were finally being allocated.

The presider had also advised them that she was closely monitoring the developments on Grysyen. Dreeg and the Consortium had dictated the government's previous policy. It would take time to turn public opinion. The Unmarked had become a rallying point for Confederacy fears. They had been the name and face of the worst to which the *nonszit* might descend without appropriate motivation. To her credit, Cin understood the nuances of the situation and had quietly made overtures to the leaders of the rebellion on Grysyen. Her intention was to end the strife between the Unmarked and their government. Chakotay did not believe any solution would be easy to implement, but he was comforted by the presider's willingness to try.

While no formal alliance could be contemplated at this time between the Federation and the Confederacy, Cin assured them that they would be departing as friends and that future contact would be anticipated with pleasure.

Given all they'd endured during the months the fleet had spent with the Confederacy, Chakotay was both relieved and frustrated. That it had ended well was testament to his people's fortitude and the trust of a few crucial Confederacy individuals.

He couldn't help but think that the fleet's greatest accomplishment had been the restoration of the Ark Planet and the subsequent introduction of the ancient protectors to the Obihhax. Their continued development would be worth monitoring, had the resources existed to do so. He only hoped the Confederacy would not retreat from all they had learned, but somehow he doubted their willingness to embrace it in all of its complexity at this time.

The meeting was winding down when they were interrupted by one of Cin's assistants. The ranking general had arrived. Cin had indicated that General Mattings wished to speak privately with Captain Chakotay. It would have been unspeakably rude for Chakotay to refuse, which was likely why the general had asked Cin to facilitate the meeting.

On a bright summer afternoon, Chakotay found himself touring the grounds of the presider's palace with a man he had come to respect and despise in equal measures.

"I appreciate you speaking with me, Captain," Mattings began once they had entered an area lined with tall hedges surrounding a large fountain.

"What do you want, General?"

Mattings did not seem at all taken aback by Chakotay's tone. "A favor."

"I might not be the best person to ask."

"No, I think you are exactly the right person."

"What favor?"

"I'd like you turn over the bodies that were taken by Emem, Tirrit, and Adaeze to us."

Chakotay was both stunned and intrigued. "Why?"

"In the next few weeks, I'm going to lead a small fleet out of Confederacy space. We're going to seek out the Devore, the Vaadwaur, and the Turei. I'd like to be able to return the bodies of their dead to them."

"Seriously?" Chakotay asked.

"Yes. Once that's done, we're going to attempt to find whatever is left of the *Kinara*. We could wait for them to return, but I think it's important for us to demonstrate our willingness to make the effort. I've been asked by the presider to advise them that we are still open to negotiating for passage through our territory."

This had always been the problem with Mattings. Once Chakotay was certain the man's odious qualities far outweighed his redeeming ones, he did something completely unexpected.

"It's a good idea," Chakotay agreed. "But I'm surprised you're willing to risk it."

"The risks don't concern me."

"They should. The Devore, Vaadwaur and Turei aren't going to welcome you with open arms."

"Maybe not. It'll take time for us to get to know one another. Hopefully, we'll find some common ground. If not, I know how to deal with them."

"This is a big step for the Confederacy," Chakotay noted. "Most of your exploratory missions in the past were intended to annex new territory."

"More isn't necessarily better. Sometimes it's just more. Mister Kim pointed that out to me once. We don't need more territory. We need to secure what we have. Fighting to the death everyone who shows up is not the most effective way to accomplish that. I'm starting to think there might just be something to this notion of going in peace to seek out new worlds and new civilizations."

"It's not for the faint of heart."

"I never thought it was."

Chakotay stopped and turned to face Mattings. "I'll pass along your request to Admiral Janeway. I'm sure she'll agree."

Mattings began to study the top of his boots. "I decided the first time we met that you were a man whose respect was worth earning. I know there are issues on which you and I are going to have to agree to disagree. But I don't believe we are as different as you think."

Chakotay paused. It bothered him to think that this might be true. But he couldn't deny it either.

"Had I been born here and inherited your cultural legacy, I

might have found myself on a path similar to yours. Early in my career, I left Starfleet. In exchange for cessation of hostilities, the Federation abandoned my people to an alien species, the Cardassians. I killed a lot of them and never lost a moment's sleep over it. Today, the Cardassians are on better terms with the Federation. I wouldn't be surprised if one day, I found myself serving beside them. It's easy to decide that everyone out there whose interests come into conflict with yours deserves death. It's far too easy to achieve this with the tools at our disposal. But no one will ever be able to kill their way to peace. Even the Borg couldn't do that."

"Why didn't you kill Emem the moment you had the chance?"

"There were other options. His death didn't make Lieutenant Kim's life easier. All you did was give Emem exactly what he wanted."

"He was a threat."

"We don't act in the heat of the moment except in times of war or self-defense. We allow those trained to uphold our laws to mete out justice, and we accept their choices, even when they wound us deeply. It's not a perfect system. It's just the best one we've come up with so far."

"We were in a state of war against the Seriareen the moment they took over *Voyager*."

"Even then, General, the use of force must be a last resort."

"You prefer to talk a man to death."

"Never underestimate the power of words. Look what yours did when you spoke honestly to the Obihhax."

"The Source."

Chakotay smiled, shaking his head. "*Your* Source. My subspace-born hybrid life-form."

Mattings chuckled and extended his hand to Chakotay. "Safe travels, Captain. I do hope our paths cross again one day."

Chakotay accepted the general's hand, touched that Mattings had chosen to bid him farewell with a human gesture rather than a formal Leodt bow. "As do I."

.   .   .   .

GALEN

Lieutenant Nancy Conlon remained in a coma five days after her resuscitation. She had been transferred to the *Galen*, where there were private rooms for long-term patients.

Lieutenant Kim had spent much of his off-duty hours by her bedside. Until she awoke, there was no way to determine the extent of the damage Xolani had done to her mind. That she was alive and stable was a good sign.

Each evening when he entered, Kim brought a bouquet of flowers. The first four days he had settled for replicated roses. Once *Demeter* had rejoined the fleet, Kim had asked Lieutenant Url if there were any fresh flowers on board and he had sent over a huge bunch of white, pink, lavender, and yellow blooms that resembled wildflowers.

Kim began his vigil by changing the water in the vase that sat by Conlon's bed and arranging his new botanical offering. The Doctor had suggested that as long as Kim was content to keep Conlon company he should speak or read aloud to her. The sound of his voice would stimulate neural activity and could help with her recovery. Kim had brought an assortment of novels on a padd, but tonight, as it had every night, it lay untouched on the table by her bed.

"So where were we?" Kim asked as he settled himself into a chair. When Kim had tried to select a book Conlon might want to hear, he'd been confronted by the reality that as deeply as he cared for Nancy, he didn't know what she'd enjoy. Kim had decided to tell her his story instead: *Harry Kim, the Early Years*.

"I think I'd just applied to the Academy," Kim began, but trailed off as the pallor of Nancy's face struck his heart anew. "If I'd actually passed the entrance exam the first time, we would have been in the same class. I wonder if we would have become friends."

He felt his throat tightening at the thought of roads not traveled and opted to change the subject.

"We'll be departing for New Talax first thing in the morning.

I won't be able to see you tomorrow night because we'll be in transit. But as soon as we arrive and get settled, I'll come over and check in. I hope Tom and Seven have sent word. The custody hearing must have ended by now. I can't imagine what's been keeping them.

"I don't know about you, but I'm ready to have Tom back on duty. I'm kind of surprised Chakotay let me resume my post after I attacked . . . I mean . . . the captain said he understood, that I was in shock. I wasn't myself.

"I didn't know how to tell him that I *was.* I knew exactly what I was doing, and if they hadn't pulled me off Emem, I would have killed him with my bare hands."

Kim's voice was cold, calm, and flat. "The Seriareen didn't have to do this to get what they wanted. Even if they'd told us about the hax, we would have taken them there. Admiral Janeway would have helped them. We were stupid to trust them. We should have just shoved them all back into containment the minute Admiral Janeway was rescued. I'm starting to think that not every question needs an answer.

"And maybe if we had, Xolani wouldn't have . . . *you wouldn't have* . . . I'm sorry, Nancy. This is all my fault."

"No, it isn't," a soft voice came over Kim's shoulder.

Kim turned, startled, and found Commander Torres standing in the doorway.

"Hi, B'Elanna."

"I'm sorry to interrupt. I promised Miral I'd bring this over tonight."

Kim watched as Torres added a new drawing to those that lined the wall at eye level. The newest was an abstraction: large beige and brown spheres interspersed with small, bright red ones.

"Every morning she asks me if she can see Nancy, and when I tell her no, she makes another 'well' drawing," Torres said.

Kim smiled faintly as he saw the large capital letters running along the bottom of the drawing: HOT FUDGE SINDAY. "Her printing is coming along," Kim noted, "but her spelling needs some work."

Torres smiled bleakly as she turned to face Kim over Conlon's still body.

"This isn't your fault," she said again, crossing her arms over her chest.

Kim sighed. "If I'd never suggested to Chakotay that we try and answer that old distress call, we'd never have found the protectors or the Confederacy. Lsia might have found the hax on her own and we'd never—"

"It's mine," Torres interrupted.

"Huh?"

"I've spent the last few days scrutinizing our reports and logs."

"Why?"

"I was looking for the first indication we missed that Xolani had entered *Voyager*'s systems."

"We've already been over this, B'Elanna. The first power surges that indicated the transfer of Xolani from the shuttle were all within tolerable limits. There were too many systems damaged on that shuttle to pinpoint anything in our diagnostics, and the surges were too random to set off any red flags."

"You're right. We couldn't have reasonably been expected to find him then."

"And the same is true about his movements. Until he attacked the Doctor's program and the other holograms, there was no reason to suspect anything. Granted, we might have dug a little deeper into the holographic malfunctions when we found them, but there was the admiral's capture and the destruction of our deflector dish. It was only after we backtracked the progression of the surges that we discovered Xolani."

"I've been distracted a lot longer than that," Torres admitted.

"Come on, B'Elanna. You didn't miss anything."

"Yes, I did."

"What?"

"Stardate 58672.2."

"That was months ago," Kim said, "right around the time of the memorial service at New Talax."

"The last few weeks of my first trimester I came down with the worst morning sickness. I lived in my 'fresher. About the same time, I started to obsess about our quarters. I couldn't figure out how we would find room for the new baby."

"I didn't know that."

"I didn't want anyone to know I wasn't at my best. I didn't want anyone to think I was somehow less capable because I was having a rough pregnancy. I drove Tom crazy, but he kept it quiet."

"That's understandable."

"It's unforgivable," Torres said. "I'm the chief engineer of this fleet. It's my responsibility to catch the problems less experienced officers miss, to make sure everyone is doing their job properly. I wasn't capable of that at the time but my pride and my fears about the new baby prevented me from telling anyone."

"So what happened on Stardate 586 . . . what was it?

"58672.2. You logged an error in your personal archive. The system was retrieving data randomly rather than in order by stardate. It was a minor corruption. You fixed it yourself, but you still reported it."

Kim thought back. "I remember that. Tom came to me early that morning and told me Chakotay wanted to find a mission for us with the potential for significant discovery. I pulled up my logs and saw the anomaly. The logs were out of order. I figured it was just a glitch."

"It wasn't."

"When I began my search, my personal log about Kes's birthday was displayed at the top of the list, which was weird. I got a little nostalgic. After I reread the entry, I remembered the wave form communication. I hadn't thought of it in ages. Almost every search I did after that included references to our first contact with that wave form. That's what prompted me to pull the original data file out of my archive."

"And to suggest to Chakotay that we investigate the wave form's distress call."

"After the captain approved the mission, I thought maybe it was a sign," Kim said.

"Xolani spent an inordinate amount of time in your personal database. He had accessed several others by then, but yours was the only one he corrupted because it was the only one he came across that referenced our contact with the first wave form. *He* reordered the display. *He* reminded you of that contact. *He* wanted us out here and did everything short of taking possession of your body to get us here," Torres said.

Kim's stomach lurched and his mouth was suddenly filled with a sour, metallic taste.

"I saw your error report later that day. Protocol demanded that I follow up on it, even though you had already made the appropriate repair. I didn't because I was too tired to think straight. It was all I could do to keep my head up and what little I could eat down. If I had done my job properly, I would have found the power surge that accompanied the corruption Xolani created when he reordered your logs. Force of habit would have sent me searching for other similar corruptions, and I would have tracked it back to the shuttle. I'm not saying I would have connected all of the dots, but I would have known what to look for going forward. I would have found him long before he attacked the Doctor and Nancy."

"If he had realized you were tracking him, he might have taken you instead of Nancy," Kim realized.

"Maybe," Torres agreed. "But he would have risked exposing himself long before we discovered the rest of the Seriareen. It only took us a couple of days to realize what he'd done to Nancy. Crazy as I was at the time, he could never have hidden in my body or anyone else's long enough for us to reach the Confederacy. We would have known what Lsia was up to before the *Kinara* ever showed up."

"B'Elanna," Kim said, "it was a minor error. Anybody would have chalked it up to a random system anomaly. They happen all the time."

"When you were having a tough time balancing duty and your personal life, you erred on the side of duty. I didn't."

"The mistake you made wasn't overlooking the error," Kim

insisted. "The mistake was not asking for help when you knew you needed it."

"Could you two keep it down, please?" a soft voice requested.

Both turned in surprise to see Nancy looking groggily back and forth between them.

"Nancy?" Kim said immediately, taking her hand in his.

"Hi, Harry," she murmured.

VOYAGER

Admiral Kathryn Janeway stood in cargo bay one, where the bodies she had just ordered released to the *Third Calvert* were stored in stasis. The Doctor had chosen to preserve them in the event an autopsy might aid him with Lieutenant Conlon. Her progress had made that unnecessary. Janeway had agreed with Chakotay that General Mattings's gesture of returning the bodies would aid him with diplomatic overtures on behalf of the Confederacy.

She hadn't given much thought to Kashyk's ultimate dispensation until Chakotay had presented her with the general's request. Janeway hadn't had time for personal concerns since *Voyager* had set course through the wastes.

Something undone had brought her to the cargo bay. When she had first seen Kashyk's face on the *Vesta*'s viewscreen, she had been too shocked to untangle the complicated emotions that arose. As soon as she'd realized that he was under the influence of an alien consciousness, Janeway had made an internal vow to free him.

That he would probably never have done the same for her didn't matter. They had parted enemies, and any accord between them would likely have been too much to hope for, even had she been able to separate Emem from Kashyk's body.

But the torment he had endured prior to his death, so similar to what she had experienced at the hands of the Borg, troubled her deeply. She knew better than to torture herself with "what-ifs." Some things were beyond her power to command.

But not to wish . . .

Placing a hand over the transparent aluminum that showed Kashyk's face at rest, she forced herself to bring to mind the man she had known before Emem had taken him. Most of the memories were unpleasant. His condescending manner was grating, as was his delight in finding small ways to irritate her. His ultimate betrayal still stung.

But for the few days they had worked together toward a single goal, she had seen more than the Devore Inspector. She had seen the man. She knew he had been lying to her. On some level, she had always known it. But there had been brief moments, including their parting kiss, when she knew that in another lifetime, when their respective duties had not dictated their choices, they might have been kindred spirits.

She hated knowing this, especially now. Had both of them been free when they met to follow their hearts rather than their orders, might they have been able to find enough in common to make the rest irrelevant? Could differences that ran as deep as theirs ever truly be bridged? She had spent her entire career working to build such bridges. In Kashyk's case, and the Confederacy's, the beliefs that divided them had proven impossible to overcome. That failure of imagination, on both their parts, left them weak and vulnerable to forces like the Borg and the Seriareen.

Like it or not, as sentient beings concurrently inhabiting the same space/time continuum, they were one. Only together could they stand against the forces of nature that always seemed ready to toss them on the rocks. Was it their need to be right that made them retreat to the safety of their beliefs? Or was this how it was meant to be? Was this constant struggle the crucible that led to individual enlightenment, and was that, ultimately, the most one could ask of this existence?

"I wish you . . ." she whispered, but could not find a word that encompassed all she truly wished for Kashyk and for herself. She settled for, ". . . peace."

26

MONTECITO, NORTH AMERICA

On the night before Commander Paris, Doctor Sharak, and Seven were scheduled to return to the Delta Quadrant aboard the *Home Free*, Julia Paris outdid herself.

The guest list consisted of her son, his fellow officers, and friends. This included the newly minted *Lieutenant Commander* Wildman, her husband and daughter, who had just returned to Earth, Doctor Riley Frazier and forty-six troubled souls, the Tamarian woman, Ratham, Gretchen and Phoebe Janeway, John Torres, and Tom's sisters, Kathleen and Moira. The Paris family home was the setting for a lavish dinner, live music, and dancing. Axum was the only invited guest who had chosen not to attend.

The house Julia Paris had built was finally filled with the sounds of love and laughter she had always envisioned. She had hoped gatherings such as this would include her husband and grandchildren.

But Julia would take what she could get.

Commander Tom Paris moved through the night as if in a dream he wished might never end. His sisters were incredibly relieved that, despite the custody hearing, he and Julia had made their peace. Moira apologized privately for her testimony. Given the few facts Julia had shared with her prior to the hearing, she had believed it to be the right choice. All she had learned since then had caused her to reconsider. Kathleen was considerably more reserved and watched both Tom and Julia throughout the night searching for some sign of a crack in their jovial façades. Paris and his mother had already spoken at length several times since their successful joint mission to assault the First Contact Day reception. Julia had found new purpose in her work with Riley's people. She would continue to act as an unofficial envoy between them and the civilian services established to aid Federation refugees. Julia now intended to expand that work and had already volunteered to assist other displaced families still struggling in the aftermath of the Invasion. Paris shuddered to think of the force of nature he had just unleashed on the Federation Refugee Division. They had no idea what was about to hit them.

He knew it would take time for B'Elanna to come to grips with all that had transpired, but Paris pledged that when the Full Circle Fleet's mission was done, their first priority on returning to Earth would be introducing Julia Paris to her new grandson.

Paris enjoyed a lengthy discussion that night with John Torres. He thanked him again for his appearance at the hearing and shared the happy news of his son's imminent arrival. Torres was deeply moved, but did not make any demands. Paris assured him that he'd pass along John's words to his wife. Ultimately B'Elanna would have to decide how much time and attention she wished to give her father. But it was not lost on Tom that John was his children's only living grandfather, and that was a relationship he did not intend to see squandered.

Doctor Sharak was in rare form, regaling Julia, Seven, Sam, and Gres with the tale of his visit the previous day with President Bacco. Paris joined them midway through the doctor's tale.

"She is truly a great leader," Sharak observed. "Her apologies could not have been more sincere. For any person who bears her responsibilities, it would be impractical to take the suffering of individuals personally, but she holds them in her heart."

"She is a leader of great intellect and compassion," Seven agreed.

"Ambassador Jarral could scarcely believe his good fortune," Sharak continued. "He feared she would ask for his recall when she learned that he accepted the refugees from Arehaz."

"*Cthulia. The flames burning,*" Ratham interjected.

"*Liaka of Penthal. The river rising,*" Sharak retorted. "Instead, President Bacco marveled at his courage and refused to accept an apology. She insisted that all of the blame for what Riley's people have suffered was her responsibility and reminded Jarral that true friends must always demand the best of one another, especially when they fail to live up to their expectations."

"Her words were more colorful than that," Ratham insisted.

"Have I misunderstood the meaning of the term 'horse's ass'?" Sharak asked.

Sam Wildman laughed so hard, she looked ready to burst into tears. "No, I don't think so," she replied through her mirth.

Wildman sat blissfully beside her husband, whose arm was draped over her shoulder. Paris, Wildman, and Doctor Sharak had met privately with the president as well to accept her thanks on behalf of the Federation. Following that meeting, they had been briefed by Admiral Akaar.

The court-martial of Commander Briggs was still pending but would be a swift affair. Paris knew that even the Federation had deep, dark holes down which those who shared Briggs's moral failings tended to fall. The Commander wasn't going to be spending his days at the New Zealand penal colony to which Tom had once been dispatched. When that court-martial ended, no one was ever going to hear of Briggs again.

Both the head of Starfleet Medical and the Federation Institute of Health were in the process of being replaced. All of the officers who had served with Briggs, including Doctors Frist and Everett, were under investigation. Paris knew that even if they were ultimately cleared of any knowledge of Briggs's actions or complicity, their next posts would be considerably less high-profile than their last. Starfleet officers and presidential appointees were expected to follow orders, but not mindlessly. The cult of personality Briggs had established should have set off numerous red flags. The entire situation clearly troubled Admiral Akaar deeply. Paris didn't doubt that Akaar would diligently follow the investigations of these officers with an eye toward preventing any similar fiascos in the future.

Paris and Sharak would be returning to the fleet with commendations for bravery and initiative in their files. Wildman had received a promotion along with her choice of billets. To

Paris's surprise, she had requested a transfer to Ktaria. Apparently the Wildman family was moving to Gres's homeworld and were thrilled at the prospect. Gres and Naomi's detour to the planet had lasted more than a week, and during that time, Naomi had made an important decision. Paris watched as Seven extricated herself from the group and moved toward Naomi, who was seated beside Gretchen Janeway near the dessert buffet.

To his surprise, Phoebe Janeway moved to take the spot Seven had left next to Paris.

"It's good to see you again, Miss Janeway," Paris greeted her.

"Phoebe, please, Commander Paris."

"Tom."

Phoebe smiled hesitantly. "I wonder if you could do me a favor, Tom?"

"Name it."

"I grew up idolizing Kathryn, even though I never shared her passions. Before she was lost in the Delta Quadrant, I would have argued with anyone who said they knew her better than I did."

Paris nodded for her to continue.

"I don't think that's true anymore."

"It's not unusual. I grew up in the same house with my dad but I don't think I *really* got to know him until after we got back from the Delta Quadrant."

"Who is she?" Phoebe asked. "What I meant to ask is, *who is she now?* What's it like to serve under her?"

Paris smiled. "It's challenging. It's never dull. But she's not cold and distant like a lot of people in her position. When she sees you struggling, she rolls up her sleeves, get right down in the ditch with you, and starts shoveling."

"You're fond of her?"

"I owe her my career and my life, several times over, Phoebe. *Fond* doesn't begin to cover it."

Their conversation continued well into the wee hours of the night. When it ended, Phoebe made one last personal request of Tom Paris.

. . . .

"When Kathryn was your age," Gretchen Janeway was saying as Seven settled herself beside Naomi, "she lived and breathed tennis."

"Not parrises squares or velocity?" Naomi asked.

"They weren't played at her school. She went to a traditional secondary school rather than Academy prep. Her father and I always assumed she'd end up at the Academy, but we wanted to make sure she had as much experience outside of Starfleet as possible."

"Why? If all she wanted was to serve in Starfleet . . ." Naomi began.

Gretchen smiled benevolently. "Children like Kathryn, so focused and so driven, could easily end up with a very narrow view of the universe. I was content to have her follow her passion into the service, but she needed to know about the world she was signing up to protect. There's more to life than Starfleet, even for her most dedicated officers. Not that she understood it at the time. She rebelled in every way she could imagine."

"Admiral Janeway, a *rebel*?" Naomi asked in disbelief.

"One day, ask her to tell you the story of her most memorable diving experience with Mark Johnson," Gretchen suggested conspiratorially. "She was about your age at the time."

"I will," Naomi said, her eyes widening.

"Excuse me, ladies," Gretchen said, rising. "I need to find our hostess and see if I can get the recipe for that amazing vegetable pie."

"See you later, Mrs. Janeway," Naomi said cheerfully.

"Count on it, Miss Wildman," Gretchen replied with a wink.

Once she was out of earshot, Naomi turned to Seven. "I don't think Admiral Janeway has much in common with her mom. Mrs. Janeway is so . . ."

"What?" Seven asked, truly intrigued.

"Easygoing?" Naomi suggested.

"You have not had sufficient opportunity to observe Admiral Janeway off-duty," Seven said. "You might be surprised by her occasional lapses in decorum."

Naomi shrugged, suddenly thoughtful. "I wonder if I'll ever see her again."

"She will return to Earth when the fleet's mission is done. It may be a few years," Seven allowed.

"But I won't be here. I don't know where I'll be by then."

"She will always find you," Seven insisted. "Never doubt that."

Naomi smiled. "You think I made the right decision?"

"I think you are much happier now than I have seen you in some time," Seven replied. "Wrong choices seldom bring one the sense of peace I see in you."

"Ktaria was like nothing I've ever seen," Naomi said. "It was so beautiful, the jungles, the wildlife. It's part of me too. I want to *know* it, not just study it in a classroom at the Academy."

"I think you are very brave, Naomi," Seven said.

"Brave?"

"The Academy, for all of its challenges, was a known quantity. Your life, once you graduated, would progress along a familiar course. Instead, you are choosing to embrace another path."

"I still might go back to the Academy one day," Naomi said.

"And if you do, you will likely be better prepared than you were this time to endure the rigors of that life."

"Speaking of endurance, have you spoken to Icheb?" Naomi asked. "I sent him a message when I got back, telling him I was withdrawing from the Academy, but I haven't received a response. Do you think he's mad at me?"

"I would not assign any meaning to his silence at this time," Seven cautioned her. "As long as you are pleased with your choice, he will accept it and continue to support you. You are very dear to him, as I'm sure you know."

"I'd like to see him before we go back to Ktaria."

"I'm not sure if that will be possible," Seven said. "But I will give him any message you wish."

"How? You're going back in the morning, aren't you?"

Seven's face clouded over. Both she and Paris had spoken at length with Admiral Akaar about Icheb and the critical role he had played in their mission to uncover Commander Briggs's designs. Neither had been allowed to speak to Icheb since they learned of the termination of his internship and both feared the worst. Akaar had agreed to take their words into consideration and to speak with Icheb's academic advisor. They were unaware of any disciplinary actions to be taken against Icheb, but given the nature of his many transgressions over the last several months, such actions seemed inevitable.

Seven had already decided that should Icheb lose his place at the Academy, she would ask Admiral Janeway to accept him as her personal aide, the same way she had asked Captain Eden to accept Chakotay when they first rejoined the fleet. Seven simply could not bear the thought of Icheb alone on Earth, denied the only life of which he had ever dreamed. Seven had asked Admiral Akaar to keep her advised of Icheb's status.

"I intend to remain in touch with both you and Icheb," Seven said simply. "I will not allow the physical distance between us to become an obstacle to our friendship."

Noami smiled brightly. Seven listened attentively as she began to speak of the cousins she had met on Ktaria and the home she and her parents would share there. It was nice to think that Seven would be leaving at least one of those dearest to her in such a joyful place.

STARFLEET HEADQUARTERS

It had been a long day for Starfleet's commander in chief. His first meeting of the morning had been with Admiral Kenneth Montgomery. Akaar had formally advised Montgomery of his intention to assume operational command of the Full Circle Fleet. He had given Montgomery the choice of resigning immediately or facing disciplinary action that would result in a demotion at best, or a court-martial at worst.

Leonard James Akaar had no doubt which course Montgomery would choose: the same course he always chose, that of least resistance.

Initially, Montgomery had protested. Both knew that several medical and science research facilities within Starfleet were now dedicated to unlocking the secrets of programmable matter. While Akaar was content to allow line officers, like Tom Paris, and civilians, like Seven of Nine, to enjoy the illusion of claiming the moral high ground, those at Starfleet Command knew better.

Akaar had proceeded to lay out the full extent of Briggs's atrocities, many of which surprised Montgomery, but wouldn't have if he'd bothered to read Paris's report. Even Ken Montgomery had the good sense not to argue that Briggs deserved what was coming to him. But where had Montgomery erred? He had strictly followed the chain of command.

Akaar had replied that no one occupying a sensitive position within the upper echelons could ever use plausible deniability as an excuse for poor judgment. It was Montgomery's first responsibility to provide the officers under his command with the latitude and support they required to face the challenges presented to them. He had failed to do that on numerous occasions. All of his decisions were designed to keep his ass well covered. Now, more than ever, Akaar needed people determined to act in the Federation's best interests, especially when it was inconvenient. Moreover, they must have a firm grasp of their respective moral compasses.

Ken Montgomery was not Starfleet.

The rest of Akaar's day had been occupied with the latest reports of the Typhon Pact's movements. He had been called to the Palais for an emergency briefing regarding the Romulans. No one really knew yet what to make of the new praetor, Gell Kamemor, so every scrap of intelligence received was gnawed to the bone.

By the time he returned to San Francisco, Cadet Icheb had been waiting outside his office, as requested, for more than three hours.

The last several weeks of Icheb's life had been agonizing. When his latest internship was rescinded, his advisor had indicated that he was being placed on academic restriction, pending suspension. Lieutenant Commander Blayk had not reported anything untoward when he had requested a transfer for Icheb. But Icheb was the first cadet in recent memory to lose placement in two separate internships within days of reporting to each.

No questions had been asked. No disciplinary hearings had been convened. But Icheb felt the scrutiny of each of his instructors and was under orders to limit his movements to his classes and his quarters until further notice.

It was only a matter of time.

When he had been summoned to Admiral Akaar's office, Icheb was relieved. The waiting was over. He did not regret any of his choices. He could not have done less for Seven. But when he tried to imagine a future that did not include Starfleet, the knots in his stomach pulled tighter, and he found it impossible to focus his mind.

He entered the admiral's office and stood at attention. The admiral sat behind his desk, considering Icheb in silence for an unnerving period of time. They had never been formally introduced. Unless the admiral was telepathic, Icheb wasn't sure what intelligence might be gained from this extended pensive observation. It might only be intended to test Icheb's ability to endure excessive anxiety. Of course, it was not his place to ask, or speak, or breathe deeply until given leave by Akaar.

"You've been a busy young man these last few months, Cadet Icheb," Akaar finally began without preamble. "Illegally accessing a classified lab at Starfleet Medical, intentionally sabotaging their sensors to hide your movements, executing unauthorized transports from Earth Orbital Control, deleting transporter logs, and tampering with their software to temporarily mask Seven's comm signal."

Icheb swallowed his terror. Akaar could separate him from the Academy, but he couldn't kill him.

He didn't think.

Akaar rose from his desk following the list of grievous acts and moved to stand directly in front of Icheb. The admiral was impossibly tall. As he crossed his arms over his chest, Icheb had a spectacular view of the lower half of the admiral's uniform sleeves.

Of course, he couldn't see the admiral's face, so the odd tenderness in Akaar's voice when he spoke again was completely unexpected.

"Do I have another Jim Kirk on my hands here?"

It took every ounce of discipline Icheb possessed to refrain from looking up. Akaar came to his aid by sitting back against his desk. With only a slight elevation of his chin, Icheb was finally able to meet Akaar's eyes. The admiral's gaze was hard, but not cold. Icheb was tempted to take the question as a compliment, but dared not believe it possible.

"It is clear to me that you no longer possess the ability to conduct yourself appropriately as a cadet. You have given me no choice but to order that you be separated from the Academy."

Icheb felt his face falling but otherwise remained still.

He had expected no less.

"You're not being drummed out of the service, Icheb," Akaar continued. "You're graduating early. Effective immediately, I am assigning you to the Full Circle Fleet, which is now under my direct supervision. It is my fervent hope that Admiral Janeway and Captain Chakotay will have more success than your Academy instructors did in taming your renegade impulses.

"You are, in my estimation, a rare breed of Starfleet officer. Your career will go one of two ways. Your determination to follow your instincts and the dictates of your own judgment, even when they go against your given orders, will either lead to catastrophe, in which case Starfleet will be well rid of you, or you will rise up the chain of command.

"I hope it will be the latter, but I won't be surprised either way."

With that, Akaar rose again to his full height. He turned and took a padd from his desk, offering it to Icheb.

"Here are your new orders, Ensign. Take them, and get out."

Icheb did as he had been instructed.

27

NEW TALAX

Vesta's journey from the Kinara's rendezvous point back to New Talax had gone off without incident. Captain Regina Farkas had used the time—before their safe arrival and receiving notice that the fleet was en route—conducting a level-1 diagnostic of the restored communications relays. There was no sign of further tampering or cloaked vessels in the area.

Farkas's instincts told her that Thulan was a decent fellow. He also appeared to be a man of his word.

Ambassador Neelix had not hesitated to offer the captain New Talax's hospitality. Vesta's crew was too large to visit the colony en masse, but regular visits of small groups were scheduled as appropriate, and each day a variety of fresh Talaxian dishes appeared in the mess hall for the crew to sample. Neelix had also shared all the intelligence his people had gathered over the last few months, and descriptions of several previously unknown Delta Quadrant species were added to Vesta's database.

Farkas's patience had been tried waiting for word from Admiral Janeway, and when it finally came, her relief had been palpable. Before Voyager, Demeter, and Galen arrived at New Talax, the Home Free had returned with Commander Paris, Seven, Doctor Sharak, and Ensign Icheb. Their briefing had chilled Farkas to her core, but she had congratulated all of them on a job well done, certain that Admiral Janeway would echo that sentiment.

Doctor Sal requested admittance to the captain's ready room shortly before Voyager, Galen, and Demeter were due. Farkas remained seated at her desk, but set aside the reports she'd been reviewing as Sal took the seat opposite her and put her feet up on the captain's desk.

"New boots?"

"Just replicated. Like 'em?"

"Black has always been a great color on you. It matches your soul."

"I've completed the routine physical evaluation of our new ensign. He'll be assigned to *Voyager*?"

"That will be up to Admiral Janeway."

"He seems like a good kid. His sense of humor could use a little work. He takes himself a bit too seriously."

"After all he's seen in the last few months, I don't know how he could do otherwise."

El'nor nodded, placing her hands behind her head and leaning back. "It's a fine line, Regina."

"Perhaps, but I've never had much trouble figuring out which side of it was the right one to stand on. I'm not surprised that men like this Commander Briggs exist. What defies belief are the actions of his superior and subordinate officers. And what scares the hell out of me is the thought that if Tom Paris doesn't piss off his mother and end up in a position to help Seven and Sharak, the whole story probably ends very differently."

"I'll admit I was tempted to tender my resignation to Starfleet Medical when you told me about that classified lab. If they knew what was going on and condoned it, that's evil. If they didn't, they're criminally obtuse. But then I realized they have the same problem we do, only on a larger scale. We lost too many seasoned officers during the Invasion. Those left behind lack experience and judgment and are living with varying degrees of PTSD. We face existential threats on a fairly regular basis out here. The folks back home are not accustomed to seeing devastation on that scale and getting right back on the horse."

"I'm not willing to chalk Briggs's actions up to a neurosis, El'nor."

"No, he was a special kind of sick. But the fears that allowed him to justify his megalomania are common."

"You think it's widespread?"

Sal nodded. "Yes. And I think it's going to make the next

several years, if not decades, very hard for the Federation. Balancing security against the values we hold dear requires commitment."

"Do you think the Caeliar are still out there?"

"Somewhere. Along with the gods only know how many other strange new life-forms. But if history is any guide, most of them will be friendly enough; jackasses in their own special ways, but worth meeting, nonetheless."

"The Confederacy was not that bad."

"Yes, they were. But it's good to be reminded from time to time what it looks like when the scales tip too far toward self-preservation."

"Don't start. Commander O'Donnell will be back shortly. You can trade self-righteous judgments with him."

"Is he single?"

"Get out of my ready room, El'nor."

VOYAGER

"Daddy!"

Miral had either grown or started lifting weights during Tom Paris's absence. She almost knocked him off the transporter pad when she rushed him and jumped into his arms the moment he materialized.

"Baby," he said, pulling her close and reveling briefly in the smell of her fine black hair and the feel of her little arms and legs wrapped around him.

B'Elanna waited as he carried Miral down from the pad and didn't bother trying to disentangle her as she pulled her mother into the embrace, holding to both of her parents for dear life.

"I missed you both so much," Paris said as he held all that was best in the universe in his arms.

B'Elanna stepped back and studied his face. Catching his infectious grin, she said, "I take it it all went well?"

"You doubted me?" Paris teased.

"Never," his wife assured him.

In the solitude of their bedroom, once Miral had finally fallen asleep in hers, Tom told B'Elanna the story of the last few months. She listened patiently, holding him close. He knew better than to expect her to join him on the same page as far as his mother was concerned. It was enough that she refrained from insisting that no matter what happened, Julia would never see her grandchildren again. Two years from now, they might have to face a difficult conversation. For now, there was no reason to push it.

"Did you do anything interesting while I was gone?" Tom finally asked.

B'Elanna pulled back, propping her head up on her elbow. "Not really. We left without securing an alliance with the Confederacy. Oh, and we found Meegan."

"Really?" Tom asked, sitting up. "How did that go?"

"We're still here. She's not. We almost lost Nancy Conlon."

"Is she going to be all right?"

"The Doctor thinks she will, but for now, we just have to wait and see."

"This is not a great time for *Voyager* to lose her chief engineer. You've got enough to worry about," Tom noted.

"I know." After a moment, B'Elanna said, "The women of the Confederacy are expected to do nothing but bear and raise children from the time their bodies are capable of procreation. It's a societal norm held over from the early years when replenishing their dwindling population was a problem. I met a few of them, and they thought *I* was the one whose priorities were out of line."

"Did you . . . ?" he began hesitantly.

"You think I got into a physical altercation with another pregnant woman?" B'Elanna asked, semiseriously.

"No . . . never . . . of course not."

"At first I wanted to. Beating some sense into them and the men who flourish under that system was tempting. But now I don't know."

"Okay, you are officially scaring the hell out of me."

"We made a choice to have a family. I owe Miral and our

son the best I can give them. They need my time, my energy, and my undivided attention. When they're older, things will be different. But right now, I think I need to look again at my choices. There's only so much of me to go around. I've done both jobs as well as I could, but I don't think I'm doing either of them well."

"Miral is fine."

"She is. She's a trooper. And I keep her busy. But pretty soon, she'll have to share me with more than you and my duties."

"The fleet is still in one piece."

"I've made more than a few critical errors over the last several months: potentially fatal errors."

"Are you saying you want to resign your position?"

"I don't *want* to. But I'm starting to think I should."

Tom lay down again and pulled B'Elanna close to him. "Whatever you decide, I will support you. You know that. But I don't know if letting go of being an engineer, the thing that has defined you, will help as much as you think it might. There will be regrets."

"I'll just have to live with them."

"Or . . ."

"Or what?"

"Is it possible that the problem is the amount of work you've been doing alone?"

"Maybe."

"What if we got you some help?"

"What kind of help?"

"We already have Kula, and now that I'm back, you'll have an extra pair of parenting hands. It's your position as fleet chief engineer that's overwhelming."

"The engineering staff of all four vessels is stretched as far as it should be. I won't have people working extra shifts to pick up my slack."

Tom smiled. "How about a new ensign assigned as your personal aide, someone who could review all requests, prioritize your reports, and help you create a realistic schedule? You know, *help*."

"An *ensign*? It would take me longer to train them . . ."

"What if the ensign was Icheb?"

B'Elanna sat up. "Icheb?"

"Yep. And it just so happens, you're sleeping with the officer in charge of personnel for the starship to which he has been assigned."

"That's right, I am," B'Elanna said, nestling closer to her husband. "Of course, Harry won't be acting first officer after tomorrow morning, so I should probably ask him to put in a good word with you before he steps down."

"Aw, come on," Tom pleaded. "How am I supposed to get that image out of my head? Don't do that."

"Never leave me again, and I won't."

The Doctor had been right.

Hugh Cambridge had been wrong.

From the moment Cambridge received word that Seven had returned to the Delta Quadrant aboard the *Home Free* and would be at liberty to see him within hours, he had turned that disquieting, impossible truth over in his mind.

Just because she was back, all would not necessarily be as it had once been. He would not know until he saw her. His dread of that moment intensified with each second that passed. He tried to keep busy. He refrained from contacting her directly. She was required to attend several briefings. Duty first.

By the time his door chime sounded, Cambridge had convinced himself that whatever her intentions, both would be best served by sacrificing the pleasure of their intimacy in favor of a safe professional relationship. He had already grieved her loss once. There was no reason to do so again.

Then Seven stepped into his quarters.

I am an idiot, Cambridge remembered immediately.

She did not throw herself into his arms. She did not smile warmly. She stood before him, her lithe, intoxicating body clad in a deep-plum pantsuit, a knit shawl wrapped around her shoulders. She had aged in the last few months, though it was not evidenced by deep lines or dark circles in any of the telltale places. Her eyes spoke of revelations she would rather have been spared. They were tinged with defiance.

Conscious of the dangers posed in allowing this bewitching creature to again take his heart in her hands, Cambridge stepped toward her until they stood less than half a meter apart.

Why does it feel as if she might still be in the Alpha Quadrant? he wondered. It was entirely possible, he realized, that she might have returned, but not for him.

"I have been unfaithful to you," she said without preamble.

Accept whatever wretched apology she may offer and allow her to leave while your dignity remains intact.

"I don't recall either of us taking any vows before you departed," he uttered to his disbelief.

Her head tipped slightly to the right.

"You deserve to know the truth," she said.

"Had you come to me with any other story, I would have known you were lying."

"You expected me to betray you?"

"Yes."

"I should go."

Yes.

"No."

"Do you require details?"

Yes.

"No. There is only one question I would appreciate you answering."

"Ask."

"Why did you come back?"

Neither of them moved for a very long time.

Finally, Seven took a single step forward, closing the distance between them to millimeters. Bowing her head slightly, she rested it on his left shoulder, her forehead gently touching the rough flesh he had refused to shave in anticipation of her arrival.

Her warm, real, sweet presence, along with the scent of spiced honey, banished all thought beyond the truth that, apparently, he could forgive this woman anything.

This was a problem.

Hugh Cambridge didn't give a damn.

Lifting his arms, he wrapped them around her.

Lieutenant Harry Kim entered Captain Chakotay's ready room with his final report as acting first officer in hand.

"Lieutenant," Chakotay greeted him.

Kim offered him the padd and turned to go.

"Have you given any thought to how we should proceed now that Commander Paris is back?" Chakotay asked.

Kim paused. "I assume he will resume his duties as first officer, and I will return to my previous post."

Chakotay lifted his eyes to meet Kim's. "You hated the job that much?"

"No," Kim said immediately. His captain waited silently for him to continue. Finally he said, "I think we both know I'm not quite ready for it."

"We do?"

"I almost killed a man on the bridge during a crisis situation because his people had harmed someone I care deeply about. If it happened again tomorrow, I think I would do the same."

"And you believe that means you're unfit for command?"

"It was conduct unbecoming an officer."

"Harry."

"It means I'm weak."

"It means you lost control in a moment of passion," Chakotay corrected him. "Lacking sufficient experience to respond in the best way possible to every situation is not the same as weakness."

"It feels the same."

"I know," Chakotay said. "Were you able to play a perfect sonata the first time you picked up your clarinet?" he asked.

"Of course not."

"No. You *practiced*, for how many hours?"

"Thousands. Tens of thousands, maybe."

"You were acting first officer for a little more than a hundred days. You think that's enough time to decide once and for all what you're capable of?"

Kim said nothing.

"I'm going to add two gamma shifts per week to your duty roster going forward. You'll have the bridge," Chakotay said. "Go another two years without almost killing anyone, and we might just make a command officer of you."

"I . . . I don't know what to say, Captain."

" 'Yes,' followed by 'sir.' "

"Yes, sir," Kim said.

GALEN

Gamma shift was well under way when a soft knock sounded on the partition separating the Doctor's private office from his sickbay.

"Lieutenant Conlon," he began without looking up, "I will not approve your transfer back to *Voyager* until—"

"Hello, Doctor," Seven interrupted.

"Seven?"

As she stepped into his office, a genuine smile played over her lips. "Are you busy?"

"I am. But I am also pleased to see you." He rose from his chair. "Is something wrong?"

"I missed you," she replied. "A great deal has happened and I wanted to, that is, I *hoped* we could talk."

"Of course," the Doctor said, gesturing for her to sit. Once she had settled herself, he did the same. "I trust you saw Axum again."

"Yes. He was not the man I remembered or expected to find."

"A great deal of time had passed, Seven. And he had suffered in the interim."

"I know."

"And the plague?"

"Cured."

"How?" the Doctor demanded. "Did you find a way to reprogram damaged catoms?"

"I did. *We* did."

"You and Axum?"

"And the others the Caeliar left behind."

The Doctor leaned forward. "Tell me how."

"I will," Seven replied. "I've learned a great deal about my catoms since last we spoke. And I will share all I have discovered with you. But not tonight."

"Then . . . why?" the Doctor began.

"Before I transported over, I spent some time with Counselor Cambridge."

"Of course you did. I'm sure he was relieved to see you."

Seven gazed at him warily.

"I know how important he is to you."

"Doctor, what's wrong?"

"Nothing."

"Doctor," Seven said simply, "I have known you for many years. You have been one of my closest friends. You are every bit as important to me as anyone I assign that designation. Something has changed. I sensed it before I departed, and I apologize for not taking the time to address it then. I should have. *You* have changed. I do not understand the differences I perceive in you now. If I have injured you personally, please tell me how and allow me to make amends."

"Did the counselor suggest you speak to me?"

"No. Why would he . . ."

"I'm sorry, that was unfair," the Doctor said quickly.

A brief silence followed during which the Doctor calculated the odds that anything short of the truth would result in Seven departing his office in the next several hours.

Once those calculations were done, he began to speak. He told her what Lewis Zimmerman had done when confronted with his concerns regarding Seven's relationship with the counselor. He explained the initial modifications his creator had made to his program and the enhancements Lieutenant Barclay had added after he had been damaged by Xolani's first attempt to hijack his program. He confirmed that in banishing Xolani, he had lost many essential memories of their past relationship forever. He admitted that while he understood that this course of events had been predicated upon his deep affection for her, it was no longer possible for him to *feel* as he once had, given the fact that those feelings could not be supported in the absence of the contextual data he had lost. He expressed regret but assured her that he had made peace with his choice.

Seven listened in silence, asking only a few pertinent questions. When she seemed confident that she had grasped the magnitude of what had transpired, she asked, "If you could somehow restore those lost memories, would you do it?"

"I can't," the Doctor said flatly.

"Then you do not wish to remember?"

"I do, but . . ."

"The first real memory I have of you after you had removed as many of my Borg implants as possible, I was standing in the cargo bay. I had just completed a lengthy regeneration cycle. You stood before me, describing the modifications you had made to my hair and eyes."

The Doctor smiled. He didn't remember.

"You were so pleased with yourself," Seven said. "I immediately respected your sense of self-assurance. You were not plagued with the same fears and doubts as the others I had met. It was refreshing."

The Doctor allowed this moment, this new memory in the process of being created, this experience he would relive in the future in perfect clarity, to settle into his permanent long-term memory files.

Epilogue

VESTA

In honor of the full fleet's return, Neelix had invited the senior officers of all four fleet vessels to join his family for dinner on the second night of their stay.

Admiral Janeway planned to attend, but found it impossible to leave her quarters. Less than an hour ago, Tom Paris had brought her a gift from home. It leaned against her desk, enclosed in a large, hard rectangular case. She had been unable to tear her eyes away from it since Paris had departed.

Her concentration was broken when the chime to her quarters sounded. "Enter," she called.

Captain Chakotay did as she had commanded.

"You're already late for dinner," he chided her gently.

"I know," she sighed. "Go ahead without me."

Chakotay moved to sit beside her on the sofa situated perpendicular to her desk and followed her gaze until his came to rest on the unusual black case.

"What is that?" he asked.

"A gift," she replied, "from my sister."

"Are you going to open it?"

"Someday."

"Did your conversation with Admiral Akaar and President Bacco go well?" Chakotay asked, clearly searching for a more understandable explanation for her present detachment.

"It did," she said, tearing her eyes from the case and resettling herself beside him to look up into his eyes. "I was commended by both of them for our work with the Confederacy as well as the deportment of our officers in the Alpha Quadrant. I know I probably shouldn't take all the credit for their ingenuity, but I did anyway," she teased.

"You can take the credit. I don't need it," he assured her, smiling broadly.

"Ken Montgomery resigned."

"Not of his own accord, I hope," Chakotay said, his smile fading. "He didn't deserve an escape hatch."

"Akaar would never say, but I don't believe it was Ken's choice."

"Either way, Starfleet is well rid of him."

"He wasn't a bad man, Chakotay."

"No, he just did bad things. You're not sorry?"

Janeway shook her head. "No. But we are now under Admiral Akaar's direct supervision."

"Good."

"You think so?"

"Yes. This mission is vital to Starfleet's interests. I'm glad they finally realized it." When she nodded thoughtfully, he asked, "What were their orders regarding Lsia and the other Seriareen we've retrieved from the asteroid field?"

"I advised them that several of my officers had suggested that we destroy the canisters, but I did not concur with the recommendation."

"Why not?"

"They're a menace, but they're also a unique sentient life-form."

"They're also a threat to our safety."

"We'll keep the containment canisters in storage behind an anti-psionic field. The next ship in our fleet that has cause to return to the Alpha Quadrant will transport them back and Starfleet will take custody of them."

"And do what?"

"Put them someplace where they can't threaten anyone until such time as we have the ability to safely study them further."

"Works for me," Chakotay said.

Janeway returned her gaze to the case.

"Come to dinner," he suggested.

"I'm not all that hungry."

"Neelix would be devastated if you missed it, Kathryn."

"I know," she agreed, "but even if I go, I won't *be* there."

"Then open it. How bad could it possibly be?"

"You don't know my sister."

"I've seen her angry."

"Yes, but have you ever seen what she does with her anger? She can do more damage with a paintbrush than I've ever done with a phaser."

"You argued before you left. She never said goodbye. Maybe this is her way of doing that."

"That's what I'm afraid of."

"Since when are you afraid of anything?"

"You're not going to let this go, are you?"

"Nope."

Resigned, Janeway crossed back to her desk and lifted the case onto its surface. Steeling herself, she carefully unhooked the clasps on the side of the case and opened it. Her breath caught in her throat at the image her sister had captured in heavy, textured brush strokes and vivid, rich colors.

The night sky was alive with moving stars. The trunk and branches of the tree were lit by a bright, full moon. The tiny willow leaves glistened like diamonds. Two figures, caught near the end of their childhood, sat atop a low-hanging, sturdy branch. The larger of the two was ephemeral, indistinct, and held the smaller in a protective embrace. The smaller one was more vivid, an almost photo-realistic image of Phoebe. Her face was etched with wonder as she gazed up at the night sky.

"That's gorgeous," Chakotay observed softly.

Janeway nodded, unwilling to risk speaking. Finally, she removed the canvas from its case and, holding it before her, moved to the wall across from her desk. A short utility shelf rested there, and Janeway placed the painting atop it, leaning against the wall. She then crossed back to sit on the front of her desk and continued to stare at it.

Chakotay moved closer to examine it. In the lower left corner he could barely make out the initials "PRJ." In the lower right hand corner two words were inscribed.

"Is that the title?" Chakotay asked, puzzling over it.

Janeway nodded. "*At Onement.*"

"Where is *Onement*?" Chakotay asked.

"It's not a place," Janeway clarified. "It's a state of being." After a few more minutes of silent contemplation, she said, "We should go."

Chakotay extended an arm for her to take. She moved toward him, then hesitated. "We're late. If we arrive together, arm-in-arm, people will talk."

Chakotay turned slightly, lowering his face to hers, and kissed her tenderly. As their lips parted he whispered, "Let them."

Kathryn's eyes locked with his. She nodded faintly with a mischievous smile. Threading her arm through his, they departed her quarters as one.

ACKNOWLEDGMENTS

Were such things possible, I would have this novel arrested for attempted murder. When I began this process, the story I had in mind seemed too big for one book. Turns out, it was probably too big for three. It began with a question. I hoped in the writing of it to find the answers I need to make my life a little more bearable. With the help of these characters who have made their home in my brain for many years now, I found a few. Not as many as I'd hoped for, but it was a big question, and I remain a work in progress.

It wouldn't have happened without my editors, Margaret Clark and Ed Schlesinger; my agent, Maura; my friends, who know who they are by now; my family, whose patience apparently knows no bounds; my fellow authors, particularly Una McCormack; and as always, my David and my Anorah, who make my life worth living.

This book is dedicated with awe, humility, and deep respect to Colonel Catherine "Cady" Coleman (retired), astronaut, scientist, and inspiration.

I hope she remembers why, because I'll never forget.